Designing Hearts

Designing Hearts

ROBIN STRACHAN

CAVEL PRESS

Seattle, WA

Camel Press
PO Box 70515
Seattle, WA 98127

For more information go to: www.camelpress.com
www.robinstrachanauthor.com

Cover design by Sabrina Sun

Designing Hearts
Copyright © 2015 by Robin Strachan

ISBN: 978-1-60381-260-3 (Trade Paper)
ISBN: 978-1-60381-261-0 (eBook)

Library of Congress Control Number: 2015933250

Printed in the United States of America

Acknowledgments

The art of *feng shui* has fascinated me for over twenty years. The idea of promoting well-being through order and beauty in the very place where life has essential meaning, the home, is such a simple concept. Intentions (thoughts, which have creative power) bring about actions that lead to the results we seek.

Over the years, I've developed quite a few rather inventive ways to use the creative and destructive cycle of *feng shui* for enhancements to several of my homes, and I'm happy to say, they've worked to my satisfaction. Maybe those "fixes" were a bit unorthodox, but who says humor and imagination can't play a role in *feng shui*?

There is always a point in the process of writing a novel when an author faces the reality of personal limitation. Clearly, writers need lots of assistance and hand-holding. At least one skilled editor is essential, preferably more than one. Test-readers are needed to make sure the book makes sense, flows, and is an enjoyable read. But even more essential is an army of family and friends who stand by you through thick and thin, read drafts, provide endless amounts of encouragement, and provide meals and snacks so you have the strength to carry on.

I would like to begin my acknowledgments by thanking my daughters, Lauren Fritts and Elizabeth Gretz, for believing in my talents. I'd also like to thank my son-in-law, Tim Fritts, who treats me as though I'm the best mother-in-law in the world; my parents, Bill and Shirley Strachan, who have always been there for me; and my grandbabies, Caroline and Will, for the happiness you bring to my life.

In addition, I want to acknowledge several spiritual mentors and wise friends who have taught me so much—not only about *feng shui*, but also about the power of faith, how to tap into my intuitive gifts more strongly, and the amazing ability of positive thoughts to create the world of my dreams. A big thank you goes out to Karen Schultz, who taught me yoga and *feng shui*, helping create sanctuary wherever I lived or worked; Lyn Williams, who taught a very enjoyable *feng shui* class and offered tips; and Patt Jones, who provided instruction in *feng shui* that helped me sell a house in a down market.

To Catherine Treadgold, publisher, and Jennifer McCord, associate publisher, of Coffeetown Enterprises/Camel Press in Seattle, I can only say that I consider it a lucky day indeed when you invited me to join your troupe of authors. Thank you for believing in my work. Thank you for brilliant suggestions, insightful questions, and encouragement. Thanks for being fun to work with!

A special thank you goes to a friend and colleague, Marian Barlage, for her patient work in showing me the finer points of social media.

And last but certainly not least, to my Angels, thank you for always being there to support, protect, and guide me. It is really you who make it all happen. But thanks for letting me think that it's me.

Chapter One

T HE MUSICAL ALARM ON HER laptop calendar jingled its three-tone reminder as Jill Hennessy looked up from an enormous stack of wallpaper catalogs. She was ready for a break. She'd just spent two hours hunched over her work table, reviewing hundreds of samples for a client. Rising from her chair, she arched her back in a catlike yoga move to ease the stiffness in her neck and shoulders. If she left now, she wouldn't be noticeably late. She had scheduled a lunch meeting with Tom Becker, managing partner of the architectural and design firm where she worked. Despite her best intentions, the morning had gotten away from her.

Checking her cellphone, she noticed that her husband David had phoned mid-morning. He almost never called during the day, and she was disappointed to have missed him. She quickly punched in the code to her voicemail, but found no messages. He probably just wanted to remind her to pick up his dry cleaning. Grabbing her purse, she closed the office door, careful not to interrupt Monica, her assistant, who was calculating a column of numbers.

"I'm heading over to have lunch with Tom now," Jill said

when Monica's fingers finally paused, suspended over the keys. "If David calls, would you tell him I'll call him back after lunch?"

"Sure thing." Monica's fingers resumed their rapid movements. "Before I forget, will you tell Tom that the new painter, Denny MacBride, filled out his HR paperwork?"

"Tom finally hired a new painter?" Jill's face broke into a grin. "He just told me last week that he didn't think we needed another one. It's all about the budget, you know." She rolled her eyes.

"You must have been persuasive. Oh, and Jill? Wait until you see this guy." Monica leaned back in her chair and batted her eyelashes. "He can color my world anytime."

"Always nice to have painters that go well with the décor." Jill winked. "Be back in an hour or so."

Before leaving the building, she ducked into the restroom and gave herself a quick inspection in the large mirror over the sinks. She drew a comb through chestnut hair cut in a sleek, chin-length style that emphasized high cheekbones and a peaches-and-cream complexion. She wet a finger and rubbed away a speck of soot beneath large, cobalt-blue eyes, fringed with naturally thick eyelashes that required only a touch of mascara. Despite a healthy appetite, she was blessed with an hourglass figure that was still a trim size eight. *Not bad for late forties*, she thought, glad that she was secure in her marriage, with no need to obsess over the small signs of aging—the faint lines at the corners of her eyes and across her forehead. Satisfied with her appearance, Jill refreshed her rosy matte lipstick, blotted it with a tissue, and headed out the door and down the backstairs.

She took the grassy shortcut from her building to the nearby shopping plaza that included her favorite lunchtime deli. When she pushed open the front door, Tom Becker was sitting at a corner table, staring off into space. He looked distracted and tired—a mood she had observed more and more lately.

She also noticed that he had thoughtfully ordered her favorite lunch: a turkey sandwich with sprouts on whole grain with guacamole and a chai tea latte.

She cleared her throat to get his attention and arranged her purse strap over the back of the chair. "Hey, thanks for ordering for me. Did I just interrupt a heavy thought?"

His eyes met hers in a way that confirmed her impression. "I was thinking about something I'd like you to do. I haven't mentioned it yet because I'm almost afraid to ask."

Jill eased into her chair and removed the lid from her latte. "No, Tom, I won't help you paint your foyer this weekend. You need a professional for those vaulted walls over the stairs. Or is *that* why you finally hired another painter?"

For a moment, Tom's expression went blank. Then he offered his shy, crooked smile. "Okay, you were right. We did need another painter. We can't afford to get behind on projects, especially with revenue down this quarter." He paused. "Actually, I wanted to ask you to do something for us in the way of marketing and public relations. I know you're going to give me a dozen reasons why it's not a good idea, even though it is."

"If I do, I'm sure they'll be good reasons," Jill said mildly. "Go on."

"Just listen. The community college has a continuing non-credit education program for adults called 'Communiversity.' I thought maybe you could offer a class on *feng shui*. It'd be a new way of marketing our services."

While Jill's eyes widened in dismay at the thought of teaching a class, Tom continued as if his idea was a fait accompli. After taking a huge bite of his Reuben sandwich, he stabbed two battered French fries into a pool of ketchup, crammed them into his mouth, and said, still chewing, "You'll be great." He took another few seconds to swallow the mouthful of food before adding, "After you get the hang of what works, we could try a class onsite in the new conference room. I'm thinking it could help bring in new customers."

"But I've never taught *feng shui.*" Jill's brow furrowed as she stirred her latte.

"It'll be good for you," he said. "I know you hate public speaking, but you're actually better at it than you think."

"I doubt that. Do you suppose there's even enough interest in *feng shui* to fill a class?" Jill gingerly bit into her sandwich, half hoping the idea would flop. But she knew that in Tom's mind, the class was already a done deal.

For as long as she could remember, she had avoided public speaking. Although she loved visiting with clients one-on-one or in small groups, whenever she was required to make a presentation, she carefully prepared her remarks and either memorized or read them verbatim. That way, there was less chance of flubbing up and embarrassing herself. Unlike David, her husband of twenty-five years, Jill suffered from stage fright. David was used to performing for an adoring public and seemed to relish his role as a celebrity news commentator and talk show host for a major television network. As she picked at her lunch, she couldn't shake the feeling of anxiety that Tom's suggestion produced. Nevertheless, she knew her partner was right: it was important to broaden her comfort zone for the sake of the business. Clearly, revenue was down enough to cause concern.

The lunch hour passed quickly as they discussed current design projects and ways to keep them on schedule. There were some new projects in the pipeline, but Tom needed to finalize details, and nothing was certain. He glanced at his watch and frowned. Then, picking up his lunch tray, he said, "Sorry, I've got to run. HR needs to meet with me about our benefits package. We're probably going to switch healthcare providers again this year." He chewed the inside of his cheek. "The economy is pinching us hard—right in our collective bottom line."

"Ouch. Sorry you have to deal with all that." Jill winced in sympathy. "Okay, I'll teach the class. I'll start putting together a syllabus and call somebody over at the community college to find out when the next session starts."

"They already have 'Introduction to *Feng Shui*' listed on their website. Classes start in two weeks." Tom grinned and ducked as Jill playfully threw a wadded-up sandwich wrapper at his face. "I figured I could talk you into it, eventually."

Jill stayed behind to finish her latte as Tom headed back to the office. She had to admit that his idea for her to teach a *feng shui* class was brilliant, one she might have suggested herself—if there had been someone else to teach it, that is. Throughout her marriage, she had always admired David for his ability to host nightly news and talk shows without breaking a sweat. He made it look easy.

There he is, she thought, and her heart skipped a beat as David's handsome face suddenly appeared on the television screen above the lunch counter. She turned sideways in her chair to get a better look at her husband, dressed impeccably in a charcoal-colored suit. She noticed it was not the light gray suit he had worn at home that morning as he left for the network's offices in New York City. He was surrounded by a crowd of what appeared to be security officers, reporters, and camera-wielding crews. But there was something different about this press conference. The crowds did not look friendly; instead they lined his path like a gauntlet.

In the background, the well-known voice of Hollywood entertainment host Mary Fox could be heard saying, "It's the latest scandal to rock television news. Did conservative political commentator David Hennessy, a voice for family values, have an affair with a young female colleague?"

Jill froze in her seat, her breath coming shallow and rapid, as video footage of David continued, showing him being ushered into a waiting limousine. The teaser ended with, "Get the whole story tonight at five o'clock and again at six on *Entertainment Tuesday*."

Leaving the remains of her sandwich, Jill snatched her purse from the chair and rose on wobbling legs. As she stumbled out of the deli, beads of sweat formed on her upper lip. She felt on the verge of throwing up. It was fortunate, at least, that no one else in the deli knew her identity. Yanking her square compact mirror from her bag, she stopped for a moment to study her reflection. The attractive, carefully made-up face she had seen in the restroom mirror less than an hour earlier now appeared different to her. In its place she saw a woman nearing fifty, crow's feet clearly etched at the corner of her eyes, a jawline that was no longer firm and youthful, with hair that needed frequent touch-ups to keep its shiny chestnut color.

She had always taken considerable pains to look her best. Until this moment, she had believed herself to be lovely and youthful in every way. David had always told her so, and she had believed him. Had he been lying to her all these years? She smoothed her hands across the front of her navy skirt and back to her waist with shaking hands, and felt the rise above her waistline—barely noticeable most days. Today, however, her tummy definitely felt bigger. She leaned over to stop the second wave of nausea that engulfed her and touched her knees, noticing with dismay that they, too, had more flesh on them than in years past. *I'm not the young woman I used to be.* Standing up straight, she took a few deep breaths to steady herself, wondering what else she might not have noticed before today. *Have I let myself go?* Surely there was a reason David had strayed. *Why didn't I allow the dermatologist to do the filler around my cheekbones and mouth? I should have tried harder to get to the gym.*

She was grateful, at least, that Tom hadn't been there to hear the television promo. In college, Tom and David had been fraternity brothers, but not particularly good friends. Rather, Tom and Jill gravitated together as friends and study partners, and had remained close. Years later, after Tom started his own architectural firm, Jill joined him as an interior designer, eventually becoming a full partner. She and Tom were still the best of friends, but Jill knew that he often held his tongue regarding David. As thoughts paraded through her mind—mental film clips of years gone by—Jill wondered whether Tom's coolness toward David over the years had anything to do with playboy behavior she hadn't known about in college.

She felt shaky and light-headed as she made her way back to the office—taking the longer route this time. Tears welled up in her eyes at the thought of David's betrayal, but she blinked them away. By this time, the story had to be on the Internet. That meant her coworkers might already know what had happened. It was more important than ever that she appear poised and unruffled—show them the face of a celebrity wife.

As she walked along the path to the office, she ransacked her mind for signs from the night before or early that morning that something was amiss with David. He had gotten home around eleven o'clock the night before. He'd been attending a cocktail party, or so he said. This, in itself, wasn't unusual. David often drove home later at night in an effort to miss heavy evening traffic from New York City to the Connecticut suburbs. Jill was barely asleep when he silently raised the covers and crawled into bed, spooning against her. She felt his mouth graze her bare shoulder and then, feeling grateful that he was home, she turned to face him and raised the silky nightgown over her head, initiating lovemaking. Afterward, she nestled her head against his shoulder and strummed her fingers against his chest as his heartbeat slowed. He whispered his usual, "Love you, babe," and fell asleep. She wondered how it was possible for an unfaithful man to make love to his wife, as David had done last night.

Just hours ago, earlier this morning, she had handed him a mug of coffee while he shaved. As he stood before the bathroom mirror in his white boxers, naked from the waist up, he looked so gorgeous that Jill leaned in for another kiss. Flashing a grin, he wiped shaving cream off her cheek with his towel, kissed the tip of her nose, and finished dressing. Then he grabbed a homemade muffin and a banana and left for the city—his usual routine. Nothing about his actions suggested that anything out of the ordinary was about to happen.

"Are you okay?" Monica asked in alarm, rushing around her desk to meet Jill.

Up and down the hallway, there were no signs of life. In fact, the entire second floor was suspiciously deserted for this time of day. Feeling numb, Jill realized her coworkers knew what had happened. Monica rounded the corner and circled an arm around Jill for support as she unlocked Jill's office door. A moment later, Tom appeared and gathered Jill against him as the first tears flowed. He patted her back as she sobbed.

"I don't understand how he could do something like this!" Jill cried, finally pulling away from Tom's embrace. "I've worked so hard to be the best wife I could possibly be, to support his career, raise his sons, to be there for him. What more could I do?"

"There is nothing, *nothing* more you could have done. You don't deserve this," Monica muttered, her strong features strained in anger. Monica was tall and heavyset, but she wore her size well, projecting a larger than life confidence. She usually wore slacks and cashmere sweaters and would have made an excellent TV cop. Anger visible on her face, she added, "Did you suspect anything at all?"

Jill shook her head and collapsed in her desk chair. "I had no idea. He acted so …. We were together last night and …." She shook her head again—*too much information.* "How could something like this happen? He's everything to me—always has been. I thought he felt the same way."

Tom dropped into a chair and leaned forward. "Jill, if you haven't talked with David yet, it would be good to hear what he has to say first." The suggestion was gentle and balanced, typical of Tom. "I know he loves you. Sometimes men do stupid things. And it's possible he's been wrongly accused."

"Yes, it's possible," Jill said, blowing her nose. "But please,

Tom, I need to know. Did he cheat on me when we were in college?"

"If he did, I wasn't aware of it," Tom said. "It was mostly his ego that bugged me. I'm just saying you'd be better off if you gave him the benefit of the doubt until you know the truth. Whoever is accusing him might've made the whole thing up to get publicity."

"You're right. It could be a publicity thing." But Jill's voice trailed off as an ugly certainty took root. David had been away from home more often than not the past year. He often stayed overnight in the city, complaining that he was too tired to commute home to Connecticut. He also was missing in action most weekends. Although Jill realized now that his frequent absences the past year were suspicious, it had never occurred to her that he could be unfaithful.

"He's always been my Prince Charming," she said, shaking her head. "Stupid of me, I know. Or maybe I just wanted to believe in fairytales." Deep down, somehow she knew the story on *Entertainment Tuesday* was true.

Tom and Monica exchanged worried looks. "Do you want one of us to take you home?" Tom took her hand and warmed it between his. "You shouldn't drive, as upset as you are."

"I'll be fine. But thank you." The vertigo had passed and Jill was clear-headed again. "The drive home will give me time to pull myself together before I talk to David."

"I certainly hope he has something to say in his defense," Tom said, his mouth set in a thin line.

Chapter Two

During the twenty-minute drive home to Stamford, Connecticut, Jill fought waves of dread and anxiety. She was traveling the same route as always, returning to the spacious home where she and David had raised their twin sons, but she felt strangely disoriented. It all looked different somehow, as if she were seeing it through new eyes.

Although the boys were fraternal twins, both had inherited their father's good looks: glossy, dark hair, chocolate-brown eyes with dark lashes so long, they curled, and expressive faces that could be intensely serious or charmingly mischievous. Like David, the boys were nearly six feet tall with the same moderate build that looked great in any cut of clothing.

Jill, with her fair complexion and nut-brown hair that tended toward cowlicks, couldn't have looked more different from her sons. Deep down, she knew she was attractive, but she had never believed that her looks measured up to David's. She often joked that she knew the identity of the twins' father but wondered who the mother might be.

The boys, Liam and Finn, were twenty-four and living on their own now, so it was just David and Jill in the big house.

Finn was newly married to his high school sweetheart, Missy, and lived a short distance away. Liam shared a Greenwich Village apartment with his partner, Brian. Of the two boys, Liam was the one who most resembled his father—ironic, considering that their relationship had become so strained.

It had always been a point of pride for Jill that simply by looking at Liam or Finn, she was able to conjure up a distinct image of David in her mind. She feared that from now on, the mere sight of her sons might bring pain instead of pleasure. This possibility brought new tears to her eyes.

As she drove, a stream of memories rushed through her head, making David's affair even more surreal. How could she have missed the signs when something so awful, so destructive to their marriage was happening right under her nose? Why, of all people, had David acted so recklessly, heedless of the risk of damage to his public persona? What could have caused such a change in his character? Even worse, did he love this other woman? If the answer was yes, Jill was certain it would tear her apart.

David Hennessy was a familiar face in millions of American homes as host of a syndicated, popular evening talk show. It didn't hurt his popularity that he'd been voted year after year as one of the sexiest men alive by *Celebrity* magazine. In his early years with the network, David had been a field reporter. As his star rose, he was tapped to become first a morning talk show host and then the host of an award-winning evening program focused on changing times in America.

As the network became more extreme in its corporate point of view, David's own beliefs became increasingly intransigent. His disposition at home was just as inflexible. Jill knew that David clearly understood on which side his bread was buttered, and his impressive ratings were proof of that understanding. As a young man, he had been more objective in his approach to most topics—a beacon of journalistic, objective integrity. However, as the years went by, he began to adopt the network's more extreme mindset, publicly and personally. Jill recognized with a pang of disappointment that while her husband's popularity and ratings depended on maintaining a more extreme viewpoint, his public and private lives were now one and the same.

Unfortunately, this way of thinking was spilling over into his family life with hurtful consequences for Liam, their gay son. David had made it clear that he disapproved of Liam's "lifestyle choice." He insisted that Liam was just going through a phase.

"He's confused by all the moral ambiguity in the world today."

"It isn't a choice, David. It's who he is," Jill said in frustration after Liam slammed out of the house, hurt and angry over his father's unwillingness to meet Brian. "Support who he is or risk losing your son."

David waved away her comment. "I can't accept this. Remember those girls who hung all over him in high school?"

"Yes, I do remember. They were his good friends. And if you recall, he took your second cousin to prom. Liam knows who he is, even if you don't."

Jill often worried how deeply Liam could be hurt if the media ever picked up the story that David Hennessy had a gay son. Far from being ashamed of Liam, Jill was proud of him for living an authentic life. At the same time, she suspected that Liam kept his sexuality private—except from supportive family members and close friends—because he loved his father and didn't want to do anything to hurt his career. Not surprisingly, this caused even more stress for family members, but most especially for Brian, Liam's partner.

Jill acknowledged that she could have been more insistent that David stop ignoring Liam and fully embrace the reality of his son's life, accepting Brian as a member of the family as she did. Other members of their family accepted Brian. Jill's mother had reassured her that David was a big enough person that he would come around, eventually.

"Don't be afraid to speak your mind to your husband," her mother said several times.

Jill wondered now at her own reluctance to confront David on the subject of Liam's well-being. Had she feared all along that standing up to him would irreparably harm her marriage? But now, knowing that David's alleged affair indicated a huge rift between them anyway, she wished she had spoken up to help Liam. It might not have changed the course of events, but she would know that she had done everything possible to support her son.

Jill had to admit that it had been a long time since she and David had discussed anything serious. It was all superficial between them. Although he told her often enough that he loved her, she now saw that he'd been detaching more and more. Discussions usually resulted in David waving his hand dismissively at Jill or mocking her opinions.

"Okay, honey," he'd say with a smile, but the tone was condescending. "You go ahead and think that."

Remembering the attentive young man who had captured her heart in college, Jill found it difficult to reconcile her feelings for the primetime, larger-than-life character David had become. But having been a celebrity wife for so long, she also understood that ratings equaled reality in the minds of many. Forced to live on the public stage, they'd been giving a theatrical performance of sorts, and Jill played her part well.

Jill and David had been introduced at a sorority party when she was an interior design student and he was a political science and broadcast major. David's fraternity was located directly across the street from Jill's sorority house. During the first month of their sophomore year, she secretly admired the handsome, dark-haired boy with the arresting brown eyes and charismatic grin who parked his aging Triumph Spitfire with impunity in the no parking zone. Campus security officers, especially females, turned a blind eye to any infractions where David Hennessy was concerned.

Jill had her own circle of friends, but was quiet and introspective by nature while David was popular and always surrounded by people. She was surprised when he broke away from the crowd at a Friday night mixer and introduced himself to her. They spent the entire evening talking about anything and everything, and for the first time, she felt comfortable letting down her guard with such a popular guy. David seemed to know how to draw Jill out of her shell with sincere questions and the gentle yet protective stance that made her feel safe with him. She had never experienced that kind of instant, comfortable rapport with a guy while also being so attracted to him. When he invited her to an outdoor concert and brought along a picnic basket with crusty French bread, cheese, and a thermos of red wine, she was a goner. They began dating steadily, and for the next three years were undeniably the couple in the campus Greek system most likely to wed. Jill fell hard for David's quick sense of humor and easy way with people. Wherever David went, he was the center of attention.

"That kid will be a star someday," her mother predicted. "There's something about him you just have to watch."

Jill, with her quiet, more reserved personality, basked in the glow of being David's Girl and then David's Wife. Everything about her world seemed brighter because he was in it. After graduation, when he was hired as a field reporter for a small television station in southwestern Pennsylvania, David quickly became a celebrity in every household within a six-county area. The station was flooded with calls asking to see more of him on the air. Wherever he did a live broadcast, crowds (mostly female) gathered. Within six months, he was named to an evening anchor role, and advertising revenues shot through the roof during the nightly broadcasts. It wasn't surprising when a much larger network affiliate in southern Connecticut invited him to join their news team. David jumped at the chance to move from Pennsylvania to Connecticut, close enough to New York City that he could envision his next big career move. He fully intended to end up at the network's main studio, and no one who knew him doubted that he was well on his way.

Meanwhile, Jill took a job as an interior designer for a Eurasian furniture company, and at the insistence of the owner, began taking classes in *feng shui*, a Chinese art form that used natural elements such as wood, fire, water, and earth to help people enhance their spaces. From her own life, she knew that *feng shui* could create balance and harmony, bringing about positive change.

Madly in love and having the time of their lives, Jill and David married that summer in Stamford and moved into a two-bedroom starter home near her parents, where they lived in honeymoon bliss. After their twin boys were born, Jill and David set up housekeeping in a stately colonial in Rosewood Estates, an up-and-coming neighborhood near the best schools. David insisted that Connecticut was where he wanted to raise a family. With her parents nearby to help with the twins, Jill couldn't have agreed more.

"This is a house that can grow with us," David said as they nestled one night in their new Early American four-poster bed.

Jill had never been happier. As she learned more about the fundamentals of *feng shui* and put them into practice, she knew that her own home reflected her sense of contentment and fulfillment. But over the years, as David's career skyrocketed and he moved quickly into a national reporting job, Jill and the twins saw less and less of him. His handsome face and irresistible smile appeared regularly on the cover of newspapers and magazines, and he was often a guest on late night talk shows. Jill was thrilled when he landed a job co-hosting a news magazine filmed during the day. It allowed him to be home most evenings in time for a late supper, just the two of them. He was even able to spend time with the family on the weekends. Life seemed ideal, even with his daily commute back and forth from Manhattan.

David wasn't content as a co-host and eventually ended up

with his own show. Gone were the days when he was home for dinner, except on Saturdays and Sundays. He rarely made it to the twins' peewee soccer games, and missed their high school graduation when it conflicted with the announcement of a presidential hopeful. Jill, who was enormously proud of David's career, excused him from the usual responsibilities of marriage and parenthood, and eventually adjusted to life as a married woman living mostly alone.

"Do you ever wish you'd married someone other than David?" Monica asked one day in her typical blunt fashion as they took a coffee break in the office kitchen.

Jill had just learned that David was planning to stay overnight in the city again, and could hardly contain her disappointment. She missed seeing him and longed for time alone together. He hadn't been home more than one weekend night in several weeks and had missed two family gatherings. Even Finn, ever his father's champion, was thoughtfully silent when David missed his new daughter-in-law Missy's birthday dinner. Of course Jill made the usual excuses, but he wasn't buying.

"I don't want to judge, but I wouldn't be happy living like that." Monica looked intently at her.

Jill took a thoughtful sip of coffee. "I'm very happy with David, and I'm happy *for* him. Look at who he is and what he's accomplished." Then, seeing the skepticism on Monica's face, she added, "I still feel the same way I did the first time I saw him."

Monica raised one eyebrow. "But what do you get from marriage other than the honor of being Mrs. David Hennessy? He's never there for you. For all intents and purposes, you're a single woman without the benefits of being single."

"He's a very busy man with a lot of demands on his time," Jill said, jumping to David's defense. She did, however, recognize the truth in what Monica said. "Everyone wants a piece of him. Celebrities have different demands on their lives than other people, and spouses and children learn to deal with it."

Monica looked unconvinced. "I couldn't live like that. But I guess you're used to it by now."

Jill tried to dismiss Monica's comments in the same way she ignored other critical remarks about David so often lobbed her way by friends and neighbors. It was easier to defend him than to acknowledge the doubts that began creeping into her thoughts, eroding the sense of stability she worked so hard to maintain. Rather than absorb the thoughtless comments and careless slights David levied on her and the boys, she tucked them away at the back of her mind, occasionally reviewing them so that, like old photos, they became dog-eared and achingly familiar. She glossed over her hurt feelings by remembering how special she'd felt to be singled out by David as the woman in his life.

"Whatever time David and I have together is precious to both of us," she insisted, averting her eyes as Monica flashed another doubtful look. "Besides, I knew it would be this way when I married him."

Jill longed for more attention from David, and she had briefly considered demanding that he make it a point to be home on weekends. But then she wondered if making such a demand would put more stress on him and push him away. Either way, the request would be pointless. David was her husband, but he was also the property of the network and his viewers. As his wife, Jill was expected to be supportive, flexible, and independent—a role she performed naturally as the years went by.

The drive from the office to their home that day was the longest Jill could remember as she agonized over what she would say to David. It would be a painful discussion, possibly marking the end of her marriage. She was anxious to hear directly from him what had really happened, but afraid that the truth might be more than she could handle. She had no idea when he might arrive home but wanted to be prepared for whatever happened. As she left the main road and rounded the corner onto her normally quiet, tree-lined street, her stomach lurched. "Oh, no," she said under her breath, clutching the steering wheel in a death grip, her knuckles white as bone.

A group of onlookers were gathered outside the Hennessy home, including at least two reporters and two cameramen. A man with a large digital camera crouched beneath a tree on the wide, grassy median, readying himself for a shot. A television van was parked haphazardly in front of the house, its portable tower stretching into the sky. Private security officers directed traffic, attempting to stop anyone who didn't live in the neighborhood. Jill was forced to stop as well and let them know it was her home that was the center of all the attention.

One officer said, "If I were you, I'd get as close to the front door as possible and run like hell inside. Sorry, ma'am," he added when he saw her stricken face.

Jill noticed many of her neighbors standing outside their homes, craning their heads for a better view. When they saw her car enter the circular driveway, their stares turned grim and their jaws started to flap. Jill knew that from now on, nothing would be the same. She decided not to enter the house through the garage, fearing that she might be followed inside. More than anything, she wanted to protect their home from such a violation of privacy. She could see David's black Range Rover parked in the garage and quickly hit the button on her visor to close the automatic door.

She held her head high, unwilling to let anyone see the fear or devastation she felt to her core. She parked as close to the house as possible, intent on sprinting to the front door. Before she could get the car door fully open, a female reporter who looked vaguely familiar thrust a microphone in her face.

"Mrs. Hennessy, would you care to comment on the statement made by Amber James that she and your husband have been having an affair?"

"I haven't yet spoken with my husband," she said, wanting

to give David the benefit of the doubt, but realizing that she sounded naïve.

Amber James. It was a name she recognized, although it took her a moment to bring the image of the other woman to mind. *Young. Pretty, with long blonde hair. One of his assistants.*

Jill steeled herself. No matter what, she still had her pride. She was an intelligent, successful woman who cared deeply about her family. She would hold her head high, learn the truth straight from David's mouth, and then decide how to handle the situation. Whatever happened, she would remember that it was important to be dignified and strong. She was her mother's daughter, and it was time to stand tall.

"Mrs. Hennessy, can you confirm that your husband and Miss James have been romantically involved since last year?"

"I can't confirm anything right now."

"What are you planning to do next?" one of the reporters asked.

"I'm planning to go into my house, if you'll excuse me," she said, shock turning to indignation as she ducked under the microphone and pressed through the photographers and reporters blocking her path.

Turning to glance again left and right as she moved toward the front steps, she saw more neighbors standing on their porches and in their front yards. There was curiosity and yes, sympathy, visible on some faces, shock and anger on others. Despite David's long-time celebrity status, the Hennessy family had always lived private lives. Nothing like this had ever happened on Briar Lane.

"Please stay off our property," she stated as loudly as her tremulous voice would allow, hands fumbling frantically for her house key. As she reached the entry, David flung open the door and pulled her inside.

He embraced her, then stepped back to look at her ashen complexion. "Jill, it's not what you think."

Jill stared at him in amazement and the beginning of

outrage. "I think we have a mess on our hands," she said, putting her purse on the table in the foyer. "I think you owe me an explanation. I think I've been made to look like a fool, for starters. That's what I think. Or are you trying to tell me you're innocent?"

She walked away from him and began closing all the plantation shutters at the front of the house. David went into the kitchen. When he returned, he handed her a vodka martini with three olives—his specialty. "Here, drink this."

Jill accepted the martini without tasting it and plunked it down on the coffee table. "This isn't exactly cocktail time, David. I hope you don't think a martini is the best way to greet me when there are paparazzi, reporters, and our neighbors watching us like we're on a reality show. For God's sake, you know how much I hate living in a fishbowl! The public, my parents, and probably even our sons know what's going on, but I'm just learning about it now from a television announcement? How could you?" Tears blinded her and streamed down her face.

"First of all, she means nothing to me. You're my wife and I love you."

"Is this the way you admit the truth—that something was going on?" Jill asked indignantly, her eyes flashing. "Apparently, she means *something* to you!"

"What happened means nothing. It's regrettable. You have to believe me."

Jill was so outraged, she was shaking. "It's 'regrettable?' I can't believe you just said that. After all the years we've been married, I've never, until this moment, realized that I have absolutely no idea who you are."

"Don't be ridiculous. I'm the same man I've always been." David's expression darkened and his mouth settled into a hard, thin line.

Yet a hint of something deeper, less certain, fleetingly crossed his face. Was it despair? She thought for a moment he might crumple to the floor before he regained his composure. The sight of an expression that wasn't his usual arrogant self-confidence was oddly comforting to Jill and caused her to soften for a moment.

"David, I've never even worried about anything like this. I've always trusted you. I'm hurt and I'm shocked, but I'm mostly disappointed … in you."

Running his fingers through his immaculately styled hair, David blew out a long breath. "I don't know what to do, Jill." He looked at her plaintively. "We've been through so much together." He squeezed his eyes shut. "We can get through this. We need to think of our sons. I've called Finn and Liam to tell them to stay out of the spotlight as much as possible and that everything will be okay. We'll all be okay. Honey, this will blow over and we can rebuild our marriage. You'll see." David gulped his drink, looking up at her in desperation. "The public's memory is very short."

"Unfortunately, mine is not." Picking up her martini glass, Jill flung the contents in his face and left the room.

Chapter Three

THE NEXT MORNING, DAVID, WHO had slept in the downstairs guest room, waited to be picked up by the network limousine. He managed to look calm and unruffled as he adjusted his silk tie in the hallway mirror. "I made coffee," he announced, handing her a cup. "You take cream and one sugar, right?"

She gave him a withering glance. "I haven't put sugar in my coffee for years. You must be thinking of someone else."

He didn't flinch, although a look of wariness crossed his face as he put her cup down on the hallway table in front of her. His manner was so calm that Jill was caught off guard. In fact, there was nothing at all in his demeanor to indicate that he was about to spend the day defending his honor to the American public.

Jill's eyes were like boiled onions, her nose swollen and raw from a sleepless night of soul-twisting pain. She knew she looked terrible. Her favorite pink plush robe had seen better days. Her feet were bare, her hair was mussed, and she wore no makeup. But for once, she didn't care how David saw her. As he prepared to embrace her, she stood stiff and straight, arms folded tight across her chest.

"I understand how upset you are, sweetheart." He lifted her chin and looked into her eyes. "It's the worst thing we've ever endured, but we'll get through it together. I promise it will never happen again. And I want you to know that you won't have to go through this alone. Someone from the network will be in touch to provide counsel and some directions. I'll be home as soon as I can. Then we can talk about what to do next."

"Directions for what? Is that how we're handling this, David?" Her eyes bore into his as pain seared her chest, a feeling suspiciously like a glowing piece of charcoal wedged next to her heart.

"Jill, we need help. This kind of thing has to be managed by experts. We'll get counseling and whatever else we need to get through this." He touched her cheek. "Whatever you need will be provided." Something about the polished, patient tone of his voice reminded Jill of all the times she had listened to him encourage and coax a news source to provide a more thorough answer to a difficult question.

"Whatever I need," she repeated in a monotone. "Of course, the network thinks it can manage me in this situation. I'm just collateral damage. Our marriage has become part of who and what you are—a valuable network commodity. Okay, I get it, but I don't have to like it or accept it."

He sighed. "I'm in the public eye, Jill, and that means you are, too. I know how hard this is, believe me. I'm already dealing with more hell than you could ever imagine. We'll be guided through this until it's over." He kissed her on the cheek. "I promise everything will be okay."

It took a few moments after the front door shut behind him for Jill to realize that not once had David said, "I'm sorry." Although he had called the affair "regrettable," she wondered whether it was too much to expect a heartfelt apology from one's spouse for such a gross infraction of their marital vows. Flipping the lock on the oak door, she fastened the heavy deadbolt, peering through one of the cut-glass side windows at his retreating figure. She wondered how she would get through the coming days, or if she even wanted to. As she watched David walk confidently to the limo, stopping to speak briefly to a raven-haired female field reporter from a competing network, Jill saw that the media gaggle was getting stirred up again on the street.

She wasn't surprised a few moments later to see her mother's champagne-colored Buick Regal appear in the driveway. As she exited the car, Nancy Brenneman took a quick backward glance over one shoulder and hot-footed it to the front porch steps. Two reporters, one laboring under a huge video camera, emerged from a van and hurried to catch up with her. But Nancy, who carried a basket with a red-checked cloth napkin covering its contents, was too quick for them.

"Just making a delivery!" she told them with a cheery smile and disappeared into the house. "I thought you might need sustenance," she said, as she handed the basket to Jill. "I've brought fresh muffins and scones—lemon curd and your favorite, cinnamon-honey butter. I figured you're not up to eating much right now, but maybe this would taste good to you."

"Thanks, Mom, but this isn't exactly like having a bad cold, and I'm not seven."

"You're still my daughter, and I say you need to keep up your strength."

Nancy Brenneman was a celebrity in her own right, although most people wouldn't know it from looking at her. She wrote a popular syndicated household hints column, *Nancy Knows,* which provided advice on a wealth of topics from housework to gardening, lawn care to car care, and money-saving green tips for every household. Well past the normal age for retirement, she still showed no signs of slowing down. Her most recent book, a compilation of readers' favorite columns, was titled *Nancy Knows: Keeping it Clean and Green.*

"Thanks, Mom," Jill said as she was swept into her mother's arms and her face peppered with concerned kisses. "You're lucky they didn't catch up with you outside. That would give them a whole new bunch of headlines: 'Nancy knows everything, except son-in-law's infidelity.' "

Nancy chimed in, "'Nancy knows, but how much?' Or what about this one—'What advice does Nancy have for cleaning up her own family's mess?' "

They managed a weak laugh together before falling silent. Jill's eyes were downcast now, tears beading on her lashes. Her mother's hand gently touched her cheek and lingered there. Jill raised her eyes, noticing that Nancy's face suddenly appeared years older. Her lips trembled, revealing the depth of her concern. In her mother's eyes Jill saw a reflection of her own pain.

"Sorry I didn't call you and Dad last night, Mom, but I couldn't talk. David kept trying to assure me that everything will be okay, but how can it be? This all feels so unreal, as if I'll wake up at any moment and find out it was just a nightmare."

"You look feverish." Nancy placed her cool palm across Jill's forehead.

"I don't think I'm sick ... heartsick, yes," Jill answered in a nasal voice as she tried to inhale the aroma of the basket's contents. "Actually, now I'm moving right along from devastated to pissed off." She offered her mother a wan smile and wiped her nose with a tissue, wincing at the soreness.

"Well, anger is a rung above depression on the ladder of emotions. I see you're helping David organize his belongings," her mother said, biting her lower lip. She'd noticed the pile of suitcases Jill had removed from the hall closet.

"I think it's best if he lives someplace else for a while. I can't bear to look at him right now, and as long as he's here, we'll have *that* going on outside." She opened one side of the plantation shutters and indicated several members of the media sitting on the grassy knoll, drinking Starbucks, their cameras ready for the next big photo opportunity. "They'll be here," she paused, frowning, "until David isn't."

"I assume you've seen some of the coverage," her mother said as she headed for the kitchen.

"Actually, I haven't," Jill said with a heavy sigh. "I started to log on to my laptop this morning, but just couldn't deal with reading something I knew would make me feel even worse. I'm sure the morning shows are having a heyday with this. How big of a loser do I appear to be?"

Nancy shrugged. "You're not the one who deserves to be judged. I'm sure there are people who will be curious whether you're going to play the role of the jilted wife who stands by her man. People who are quick to judge a situation that is none of their business are not the ones who count. Just for the record, Dad and I don't have an opinion about what you should do. This is your life, your choice. But you know, with the public's appetite for drama, this could go on for a while. I must say, that little trollop, Amber, has some nerve. She probably wanted to advance her career in television the easy way. But then again, it takes two to tangle. Obviously, David was thinking more with his little head than his big one."

Jill let out a guffaw. She never knew what kind of outlandish statement might come out of her mother's mouth. "Mom, you and your expressions …. I have to admit, though, there was plenty of drama." She remembered David's shocked face as he mopped the martini from his hair, face, and designer shirt.

"I'm much more worried about Finn and Liam than about myself right now," she continued, moving quickly toward the phone. "David said he called both of them yesterday, but I haven't heard a peep out of either one of the boys yet." She experienced a new wave of fury. "David didn't say he actually talked with them. What if they found out what's going on the same way the rest of America did?" Feeling suddenly murderous toward David, Jill picked up the remote phone from its cradle and punched the speed dial for Liam's cellphone.

He answered on the first ring. "Mom, are you okay?"

"I've been better," she admitted. "What about you? How did you find out?"

"Google alert. I'm really pissed at Dad. He called again this morning, but I'm ignoring him. What an asshole!" Liam was never one to mince words. "I talked with Finn last night right after the story aired at five o'clock. Missy was pretty upset, so Finn decided to stay home with her. We thought it was probably best to leave you and Dad alone to talk. Mom, did you even know this *Amber*?" Liam uttered the name with distaste.

"I knew she was a production assistant on the show. I met her at the holiday party last year. I thought she was cute, although she reminded me of a Barbie doll—you know, too big up top for the tiny waistline. I expected her to tip over." Jill shook off the thought. "She's young for your father, but he's not the first man to fall for a younger woman with, um, impressive features. Then again, he's always been irresistible to women." She felt a heaviness descend on her. "I should know."

As she continued stealing surreptitious glances through the plantation shutters, she saw Liam's twin, Finn, bounding across the front lawn. She quickly opened the door and greeted him with a one-armed hug. "I'm on the phone with your brother."

"Tell him to get his butt over here fast. We need a united front." Finn waited by the door while his mother finished talking with Liam.

"Tell Finn I heard that. I'm crossing over into Connecticut now," Liam said. "Will I need a stick to beat my way to the door?"

"Now there's an idea," Jill replied. "Bring a big one." She hung up as Finn gently pulled her into his arms, his cheek resting atop her head. Jill relaxed into her son's strong, loving embrace.

The phone rang again, and Finn reluctantly released her. Jill noticed the number on caller ID. "It's the network," she said, taking a ragged breath.

Nancy rolled her eyes and pursed her lips. "Spin time."

"Yes?" Jill answered crisply after the second ring. She didn't think that the solicitous tone she generally reserved for contact with her husband's producer was required of her on this occasion.

"Jill, this is Bob. I thought I might catch David at home. How are you holding up?" Bob wasn't a bad guy, but the word 'insincere' always came to Jill's mind whenever she talked with him.

She was incensed. "To be perfectly honest, I'm not holding up that well. Oh, and David just left. I'm sure you can reach him on his cellphone."

There was a long pause before Bob spoke. "Of course, this is a terrible shock for you, Jill. I just want you to know that we're hurting right along with you and that we're here to defend David and support you, along with your family, throughout the coming months. We know this type of situation can be devastating. We'll do whatever it takes to help you and David support each other."

Now Jill understood. "David tells me that you'll provide counseling and whatever other services I need."

"Of course. Anything you request. Just name it."

"I might need a good divorce lawyer."

Her biting comment had the desired effect. Bob was silent for a moment. "Of course, we're talking about therapy or communications assistance. You're very upset, of course, but we know you'll get through this just fine. You're a strong woman, Jill, and you and David have been married a long time. Think about your sons. Take heart that David is a precious commodity, and we'll protect his interests. Caring for him means caring for his family." He stressed the word 'family.'

"I get it," Jill answered. "Don't worry about me, Bob. I'll be fine." She hung up and leaned her head wearily against the kitchen wall. Nancy enveloped her daughter in her arms, smoothed her hair, and whispered encouragement when fresh tears flowed.

Finn handed his mother a tissue. "Blow," he said.

Jill let out a hollow laugh as Finn, a new physician's assistant, led her to sit down at the kitchen table and patted her back. Within twenty minutes, Liam arrived, followed by Missy, Finn's bride of just four months. Jill absently fingered the teaspoon resting on her saucer while Nancy poured a bracing cup of tea for her, adding just the right amount of milk and sugar. Jill glanced around the table and suddenly realized that no one had gone to work. In fact, she hadn't even remembered to call her own office to let them know she wouldn't be in today.

"Shouldn't you all be at work?" she asked.

Liam, a commodities trader in the financial district, shrugged. "I can be gone for a day. We can only assume that Dad's fall from greatness won't affect the world marketplace too much." It was a family tradition to use sarcastic humor to diffuse difficulties, and Liam was a master at it. He took a gulp of tea before adding, "The timing of this is bad, of course. The U.S. economy is still recovering."

Finn exchanged worried glances with Missy, a registered nurse. "Actually, we both need to get to work soon, but we can be a little late, given the situation."

Jill rubbed her eyes. "How long can this drama possibly last?"

"Three and a half weeks is standard," Nancy said matter-of-factly. "The public's attention span wanes after that."

Missy flashed a worried look at Finn and sputtered, "Are you serious, Gran?"

"Actually, she's probably right, honey. You have to remember that your father-in-law is one of *Celebrity* magazine's sexiest men alive," Jill said dryly. "Every female in America who still has a pulse will want constant updates for a while."

"Not to mention a percentage of gay men." Liam grinned wickedly at his twin.

Finn reacted to Liam's comment with a snort before saying in a subdued tone, "Sorry, Mom."

Jill offered her sons a smile, even as she raised one eyebrow in mock reprimand. She was glad the somber mood had begun to lift, but there was still an important unanswered question in her mind. "Did either of you guys suspect anything was going on with your father?" She tried to phrase the question as if the answer didn't matter one way or another. The reality was very different. If David had sworn their sons to secrecy, forcing them to remain silent in order to protect her, she would show him no mercy.

Liam stared off into space and let out a long breath. "I saw Dad and a young woman together at a sidewalk café about four months ago. Brian convinced me not to go over and talk to them. He thought it would be awkward … because Dad said he didn't want to meet Brian."

"And you never told Dad what you saw?" Finn asked, shaking his head. "You never told me, either. Why not?"

"You know I don't talk to Dad." Liam frowned at his brother and then turned to Jill. "I didn't think it was in anyone's best interest, especially yours, Mom. Once I said something like that, I wouldn't have been able to take it back. And what if it was nothing? Brian said it might be a business dinner."

"Do you think Dad is going through a midlife crisis or something?" Finn asked.

"That 'midlife crisis' excuse is crap," Liam snapped, fixing an impatient look on Finn, who shrugged. "I'm sure Dad is just flexing his celebrity muscles. There might've been other affairs, too, for all we know."

"We don't know that." Nancy, who had remained uncharacteristically quiet as her grandsons spoke, met Jill's eyes.

Jill yanked a used tissue out of the sleeve of her robe and gingerly swabbed at her sore nostrils. "It doesn't matter whether he's had one affair or more than that," she said. "He's broken my trust. I don't think things can ever be the same between us."

"Give it some time. Perhaps with counseling, the two of you

can repair your marriage," Nancy said in a soothing voice.

"But what's love without trust?" Jill asked, her blue eyes pooling again.

She took a sip of tea to clear the lump in her throat that threatened to take away her breath. She watched Finn take Missy's hand as if to say, *I will never do this to you.* Jill leaned over and put her arm around her daughter-in-law's thin shoulders. Missy's cornflower-blue eyes were red-rimmed. She twirled her finger around a blonde ringlet, and at that moment she looked ten years younger than her twenty-four years.

"We'll all get through this. You'll see," Jill assured her.

IT WASN'T UNTIL JILL WAS left alone to shower and take a nap that she remembered she still hadn't checked in with her office. It was odd that Tom Becker hadn't been in touch yet this morning. She called the company's main phone number and punched in Tom's extension.

"Tom, I'm taking a few days off," she said without preamble.

"I guessed that. How are you?"

"Okay until the next wave of shock hits and I fall apart again," she admitted. "The business doesn't need this kind of publicity. I'm really sorry."

"Hey, any publicity is good publicity," Tom said in his usual bland tone. "I'm sorry, Jill. Forgive that remark. I feel bad about what you're going through. Don't worry about a thing. Just take whatever time you need."

"If anyone calls me in the next couple of days, tell them to leave a message on my cellphone." She swore she could hear the words that hung unspoken on the other end of the line.

Tom let out a long breath. "Jill, don't forget I was your friend before we became business partners. Whatever you need, I'm here."

Hot new tears formed, and she blinked them back. "I appreciate that. Friends and family are what I need most right now."

"I don't want to see you until Monday at the earliest, unless you need something. Do you hear me?"

"I'm listening. Thanks," she said and replaced the phone in the handset.

Jill and Tom had met freshman year in college and had taken many of the same classes, often studying together in the library. In fact, if it hadn't been for David's appearance in her life sophomore year, she and Tom might have drifted together as a couple. He was a widower now. Tom's wife, Janice, had died suddenly from a brain aneurysm just four years ago.

Jill stared off into space, contemplating whether to check in with Monica, too, but she knew (even if Monica didn't say it) that her assistant was probably thinking, *I told you so*, and rejected the idea of calling her in favor of taking a hot bubble bath. Then she got busy. When David returned home late that afternoon, she greeted him at the front door with five suitcases.

"What's this?" he asked, sounding stricken.

But Jill could see the restrained, fully prepared look in his eyes. She kept in mind that she was the one betrayed and that there had been a string of lies for a year or more that had gotten them to this moment. She steeled herself before speaking, amazed that she could sound so strong when her insides were like jelly.

"It's better if you go someplace else. I need space to think," she said and couldn't resist adding, "I'm sure Amber would love for you to stay with her."

"I told you, I'm not in a relationship with Amber. It was just sex, Jill. Stupid of me, but that's the truth. How can I make you believe that?"

She froze in her tracks, shocked at the callousness in his voice and his uncharacteristically devil-may-care attitude toward infidelity. "Well, then go have sex," she said with a dismissive wave of her hand.

"Jill!" He moved toward her, but the fierce look on her face stopped him in his tracks.

"Don't touch me." She fixed him with a hard stare. "I've always been the kind of woman who believes in fixing whatever is broken, rather than simply giving up. But the damage you've done to us may be beyond repair. I'll have to think about it." She turned on her heel and left him standing alone by the front door.

JILL REALIZED, AS SHE MOVED woodenly through the next few days, that even if neither of them had ever acknowledged it before, their marriage was as much a part of David's public persona as his ability to touch hearts with a memorable interview, celebrity or not. David was the epitome of American manhood: handsome, successful, moral—and married with two sons. His fall from grace threw an entirely unwholesome cast upon what had been heretofore an unsullied icon. David was now officially a cheating husband with a wife who had thrown him out of his own home.

Chapter Four

AFTER DAVID WAS GONE, THE blitzkrieg of media interest outside fizzled after about three days. Jill was vastly relieved. There were still dozens of messages on the home answering machine from friends and relatives, but she generally chose to ignore them. She had no idea how to answer their questions, and the prospect of returning so many calls was exhausting. Instead, she sent quick text messages. She nibbled at meals brought over by neighbors, finished several of David's most valuable bottles of wine, and cocooned inside the house, alternating between watching home design shows and wandering from room to room. She had no desire to do anything other than sleep.

She tried to avoid watching entertainment talk shows and reading popular news stories because of the coverage of David's affair and his move from their home, but sometimes they just jumped out at her. Even worse were the speculative stories about what might happen next—reconciliation or divorce. In the one tabloid story, the photo of Jill was as unbecoming as the photo on her driver's license. It was a not-so-subtle implication that she wasn't attractive enough for David. In another story, a photo of David was arranged between photos of Jill and Amber. The headline read, "Love Triangle Jilts Jill." Jill had a firm policy of not talking with the media regarding David, but knew that any news reports or publicity would be one-sided as a result.

All she wished now was to return to a point early in their marriage, when everything was as she believed it to be. Should she have taken whatever measures were necessary to protect and preserve her marriage? Yet she had to acknowledge that this kind of oversight necessitated suspicion and jealousy, resulting in fear that any attractive female could be a potential threat. That had never been her style. No, what she really wanted now was to feel secure in a man's love—to know that he could be trusted with her heart.

It took several days for the neighborhood to return to normal. Cars still made their way slowly down the street, drivers and passengers craning their necks for a look at the Hennessy house. It was easy to keep the shutters closed and stay safely indoors, but Jill felt embarrassed by her public marital troubles in her neighborhood. Rosewood Estates was a stable neighborhood where most residents had lived for decades, a place where families shared the bounties of their gardens and kept an eye on one another's children. But while Jill enjoyed a close relationship with their neighbors on Briar Lane, she realized that David had remained a virtual neighbor, existing mostly on their television screens. Now it occurred to her that perhaps he had also been her virtual husband. She wondered if others thought the same.

On Sunday, Finn and Missy arrived for dinner, as usual, bearing one of Missy's lattice-topped golden cherry pies. Liam appeared later with Brian, unwrapping an enormous loaf of crusty sourdough bread and a bottle of Jill's favorite cabernet sauvignon. Jill had a pan of lasagna in the oven and was tossing a salad when she heard the cheery voices of her offspring.

As she accepted the offerings of food and wine, Jill couldn't help thinking of David: the way he often stood at the kitchen island filching slices of fresh bread and dipping them in olive oil, a goblet of red wine in his hand, as he talked expansively on a topic that was of current interest to him.

"Good bread plus good wine equals a good time," was his favorite saying.

Even though he had missed most meals at home over the past year, Jill was aware that he was notably absent tonight. She was determined to have family time regardless. And now that David was gone from their home, Liam was willing to come to dinner because Brian was welcome. They had not felt welcome together whenever David was present.

Brian sat down at the baby grand piano and entertained everyone with snippets of songs he had written for a new Broadway musical, *Elephants in the Room*. Brian was a gifted pianist, songwriter, and fanatic Mets season ticket holder. He was also twelve years older than Liam—and clearly sensitive on the subject. He had been headlining at a popular restaurant and suffering the throes of unrequited love from a recent breakup when Liam Hennessy appeared. Liam was attracted to Brian's quick wit as he entertained customers, as well as his tall, sandy-haired good looks. Brian's first impulse was to reject Liam solely on the basis of their obvious age difference, but Liam's persistence paid off. After dating exclusively for two years, they were now living together in Brian's Greenwich Village apartment.

"What kind of foo-ool ignores elephants in the room," Brian sang in his rich baritone while Finn and Missy draped themselves over the baby grand. Liam remained in the kitchen to help Jill with the meal.

"Have you spoken with your dad yet?" she asked as Liam slathered the cut sides of the loaf of bread with herbed butter generously laced with roasted garlic.

"What for? Dad called this afternoon, but I was busy. I did

call him back, though, and left a message. I told him how hard it's been for all of us and that I hope she was worth it."

Jill raised her eyebrows. "And have you heard back from him since then?"

"Of course not. Dad talked to Finn yesterday. He said, and I'm not paraphrasing, 'Your mother is making this more difficult than it needs to be.' "

Jill stood rooted in place, bracing herself against the wall as Liam's words sunk in. Was it possible that David truly did not comprehend the unspeakable cruelty in his comment? How could he be so thoughtless, so completely self-centered? His actions had caused pain and suffering to someone he claimed to love, and yet, he didn't think she needed—or deserved—time to recover? Although she was accustomed to David's selfishness, this was beyond anything Jill could fathom coming from him. Was it possible Liam had misunderstood?

Jill shook her head in disbelief. "Those were his exact words?"

"It's all about what Dad wants. Has he apologized to you yet?"

"He's still having difficulty saying those exact words. I think it's because he doesn't fully realize that his actions have had consequences, or how much he's hurt all of us."

Liam waved the long, serrated breadknife in the air. "You always give him a pass, Mom. No matter what he does, you find an excuse for it." His jaw worked furiously. "What you've never been able to see is that Dad thinks of you as an extension of him. Your feelings don't matter as long as you accommodate whatever it is he wants."

Jill bit the inside of her mouth, drawing blood, as his words hit a raw nerve. Liam stabbed the knife through the crusty bread, making a loud noise as it hit the wood cutting board. "It goes to show how little attention he pays to you or your interests or accomplishments. It used to piss me off that you held everything together at home while he was free to come and go as he pleased. Finn and I grew up with a father who was MIA."

Jill leaned against the counter as she considered Liam's words. "I realize it must seem like I always make excuses for him. To be honest, I thought I was doing the right thing by holding him up in the best possible light, for the sake of you and Finn. I wanted you to have good growing-up memories with your dad." She chose her words carefully. "But maybe standing up for him as I did was also what I needed in order to feel better about him, about *us*." She paused, drawing a deep breath. "I was wrong."

She carefully removed Liam's fingers from the knife and set it aside before wrapping her arms around her son's waist. She laid her head on his broad chest and heard the powerful beating of his heart. "Someday, I hope your dad will realize how much he missed. But I need to say this: if I have failed, in any way, to do or say or be what you or your brother needed where your father is concerned, I'm deeply sorry."

"I don't hold you responsible at all for Dad's mistakes. I certainly won't hold my breath for Dad to suddenly get a clue about how he failed at fatherhood," Liam said. "I hate that this is happening to you, but to tell you the truth, I'll be really mad—at you, Mom—if you allow him to come home." Liam gave his mother a fierce hug and stepped back.

Out of habit, she reached up to smooth the dark brown hair from his forehead and watched as he impulsively shook it out of place again. As an infant and toddler, Liam had resisted being held. He was a child always on the move, while Finn, the quieter of the twins, had been content to observe Liam's antics from the safety of Jill's hip. From the time the twins were old enough to display distinct personalities, Liam had always been a mini version of David. In fact, looking at her handsome son now, as he stood so tall before her, Jill thought Liam had never looked more like a younger version of David. It suddenly occurred to her that the very fact that Liam looked so much like his father might be part of David's negativity toward Liam. Was it possible that David was threatened by the fact that his gay son was nearly a mirror image of his younger self? Did David think this reflected something about his own manhood?

Jill took a sip of her wine. "It's too soon to know what I'll do, but I have to believe that he's truly sorry. At the same time, I don't want this to permanently affect yours or Finn's relationship with your dad."

"Don't make this about Finn and me, Mom—especially me. Since he found out I'm gay, he could care less whether I'm here or not. I think you need to understand that as far as Dad is concerned, the world revolves around him. I don't think he's capable of that kind of depth. Frankly, I doubt he'll ever understand what he's done to you."

He jerked away from her touch and leaned against the kitchen island. "When I told him about Brian, Dad asked whether I realized the effect my news might have on others. He meant himself, of course. You were dealing with it in a way that told me you cared more about me than what anyone else thought. You've always been great to Brian. Then Dad said it could just be a phase and I might grow out of it, and that I shouldn't talk about it, just in case. He still refuses to meet Brian." An angry look crossed Liam's face. "Imagine what his public would think if they knew David Hennessy has a gay son. Maybe I should offer to give an interview: 'My Life as David Hennessy's Secret Gay Son.'"

"Liam, our actions should never be prompted by vengeance," Jill insisted, shaking her head. "That kind of thing wouldn't necessarily have the effect you intend, either. If your private life somehow becomes public, it won't even touch your father. Look what's happened in the past week. He's still on the air, and people are buying up those tabloids. *People* magazine can't get enough of the story, and he's trending as a top newsmaker on every Internet home page."

Liam frowned. "So truth really is stranger than fiction. His fans probably think it's some kind of smear campaign. David Hennessy, all around nice guy, would never cheat on his wife!"

"People believe what they want to believe," Jill said and winced as the truth of that statement hit home. "The fact is, he's been a big star for too long, and people always seem willing to forgive someone they admire, no matter what that person does. Anyway, the network will spin the news so that it makes your dad look good. That's their job." Jill smoothed her fingers through her hair. "If a story airs about your personal life, I'll be sorry for your loss of privacy. But I'll also be relieved, in a way—yes, I will," she insisted as Liam opened his mouth to interrupt. "I'll be relieved because you can stop worrying how your dad might react. You can live your life freely, Liam."

"What about you, Mom? Why don't you take your own advice? Live your own life?"

"I deserve that," she said. "I'm trying. I'm just not sure what my own life looks like, but I'll find out. I guess what I'm really trying to say is that I wish with all my heart that you and your father could have a good relationship. Surely you still love him, even if he has disappointed and hurt you?"

Liam was silent, thinking. "You're a good person to say that. I don't know if I can be so forgiving."

"He loves you, Liam," Jill said, moving toward him again and looking directly into his eyes. "It has always seemed to me that your dad struggles to make sense of the world, to find answers to issues that aren't easily resolved. He hasn't yet realized that you're a grown man with your own life. He wasn't always like this, believe me. When he was younger, I rarely heard an unkind or judgmental comment cross his lips about anyone. This David is not the man I married or the proud daddy who was so happy when you and Finn were born." She let out a long breath.

"I wish you could just say it, Mom. Maybe he was an okay guy when you met him, but he's turned out to be a lousy husband and father." Liam turned his face to hide the angry tears that sprang to his eyes, but he wasn't quick enough.

Jill saw the tears and recognized that until he met Brian, Liam hadn't been able to express sadness without resorting to rage, or by retreating. In years past, he'd disappeared—often for days at a time. This new ability to feel and express hurt was a side of Liam she was relieved to see. Yet it had come about because of David's bad behavior, which had been so costly to her and the family. She wasn't sure how she felt about her husband anymore. Yet she had to acknowledge that anger, betrayal, distrust, and sadness were all present and accounted for.

At David's suggestion, Jill agreed to marriage counseling. Perhaps in the safety of a professional's office, where David could feel sure of confidentiality, he might open up and tell her why he had been unfaithful. Feeling anxious, she listened to David tell her on the phone about a psychologist he already knew, someone who could schedule them right away.

"I was referred to Dr. Barry by someone here at the network," David told her the evening before the appointment. "I'll meet you there at two o'clock."

Feeling more than a little wary, she drove into Manhattan to meet David at the office of Dr. Benjamin Barry, whose paunch and salt-and-pepper hair and beard gave him the appearance of a slightly younger, better-fed Sigmund Freud, although it was clearly a studied effect. He invited them to sit down together on the leather sofa. That created tension when Jill sat on one end, David sat at the other, and then they moved by degrees closer together. He took her hand.

"I'd like to begin by hearing from David what has happened and where things stand," Dr. Barry said with a kind smile. "Then we'll ask you for your thoughts, Jill. Is that okay? It's helpful if we can hear each other speak without interruptions."

She sat stiffly beside David on the roomy leather sofa and listened quietly as he talked. Despite her attempts to listen without judgment, she experienced repeated stings of disbelief and something that felt suspiciously like indignation as he recounted to Dr. Barry how difficult this entire experience had been and how many times he'd been forced to answer deeply personal questions.

"On top of the nightmare of being in the public eye, I feel helpless that I can't even show my wife how I feel about her because I'm not living with her now. All I want is to fix what needs to be fixed in our marriage. It's been frustrating to be in this limbo." He squeezed Jill's hand meaningfully. "I feel bad about what has happened, and I want the chance to show her how much I want things to be the way they used to be between us years ago."

Jill remained silent as anger roiled inside her. Again, she was struck by David's implication that his infidelity had been the result of a fissure in their marriage without explaining exactly what he meant. Beyond being offensive, this seemed to be a thoughtfully designed tactic to divert attention and blame from his choices and actions.

"Jill, was the affair a surprise to you, then?" Dr. Barry asked. "Did you suspect anything at all?"

She blinked. "The word 'surprise' is an understatement," she said, removing her hand from David's. "Perhaps it was trusting of me, but no, I didn't suspect anything. Looking back, I can see that he was home a lot less often than usual, but he always had a plausible excuse. The afternoon that I found out about the affair, I could hardly believe what I was hearing. It was even worse that I learned the news on national television. Oh, and then, of course, there was the swarm of media people and paparazzi on our front lawn when I arrived home. Yes, I'd say it was a surprise."

She realized that her response sounded sarcastic, although she hadn't intended for it to come out that way. It was the truth. At least, she thought, David had the good grace to look ashamed. He took a deep breath, furrowed his brow, and turned toward her on the sofa, looking meaningfully into her eyes.

"Jill, I would have told you, but you weren't answering your cellphone."

"You called my cellphone once but didn't leave a message. You could have called the office number, but you didn't. Then you texted me, but didn't say we had a problem; you just asked me to call you."

"What kind of message could I have left you or texted? 'Jill, our world is about to explode?' "

She fixed him with a stare. "How about, 'Jill, it's really important that we talk as soon as possible. Something terrible has happened, and I want you to hear about it from me first.'"

Dr. Barry's bushy gray eyebrows lifted noticeably. "It is highly unusual for a spouse to hear the news the way you did, Jill," he said. "I can tell how hard this has been for you."

Halfway through the hour-long session, as David continued talking about the pressures he endured at always being in the public eye, the lack of privacy in his life, and the constant strain of being "an authority figure to millions," Jill began to feel strangely detached. He had been her husband for twenty-five years, but right now, he seemed more like a stranger.

"Jill, do you have any questions to ask of David before we end this first session?" Dr. Barry repositioned the silver readers he wore perched low on his nose as he balanced an expensive silver pen between two long, slender fingers.

"I'd just like for him to tell me why this happened. I'm trying to understand. And I'd like to hear it from him."

David stiffened on the couch next to her. Jill looked down at her hands, noticed the slight tremor, and anxiously smoothed her skirt, aware that they were now at a crucial moment in the counseling session. Either David was willing to answer the direct question or there was no point in continuing the discussion.

Again, Dr. Barry's eyebrows waggled. "David?" He leaned

back in his leather wingback chair, crossing one knee over the other, listening intently.

David heaved a long sigh and slumped back against the sofa. "At some point, I think we need to get past that question," he said. "I don't know why it happened. I may never know why it happened."

Jill rose to her feet, picking up her handbag. "It didn't just 'happen,' David. You make it sound as though the affair happened *to* you—as if you were an innocent bystander. I've always been there for you, no matter what you wanted in life, but you chose to have an affair, anyway. Was it just the inconvenience of the commute home to Connecticut, when Amber was so handy?"

"Jill!" David cried out, struggling to his feet.

"No, really, David. Perhaps you should spend some time here with Dr. Barry by yourself so you can figure out a reason for what you did. Otherwise, how do I know infidelity won't just 'happen' again?" She narrowed her eyes at him, surprised at the depth of rage she felt, but more shocked that she could express it.

He nervously adjusted his tie, fingers fumbling with the knot. "Why can't you just take my word for it? I've been your husband for twenty-five years. Doesn't that count for anything?"

The psychologist leaned forward in his chair. "Trust really is at the heart of what we need to resolve," he said, offering a thin-lipped smile. "Jill, I hear your husband asking for your trust. We can work on rebuilding trust, if you're willing."

"Actually, Doctor, he's not asking for my trust. You are. He's letting me know what he expects from me, and he assumes I'll do it. That's how we communicate. That feels really unfair to me right now, and I don't think I can continue doing what's expected of me like I did before. Right now I need answers to help me understand."

David was silent, his jaw working back and forth. She could read in his body language that he was on the verge of losing control as his hands balled up into fists at his sides. He took a step toward her, but she fixed him with a furious look that stopped him. Jill couldn't contain herself now as words too long unexpressed bubbled up from the depths of her core.

"Why is it, David, that you cheated on me in the most public, humiliating way possible—hurting not only me, but our sons and our families—and yet I'm the one who will have to put forth most of the effort to fix the situation? A situation, by the way, I can't comprehend, and that you can't even explain. How is it that you betrayed the faith I placed in you, and then you want me to work even harder to save this marriage?"

David frowned. "You know the pressures that come with my career, Jill. You've known that all along. And I haven't ever heard you complain about the good life I've provided for you."

"No, you're right; you've never heard me complain," she said. "But I think you've forgotten that I've been a major contributor to that good life as well. I've worked hard, too, at a career. I've done it while also trying to nurture a happy, stable home life for us and our sons. Yes, you've been a good provider, and I certainly understand the pressures on you. I've had them, too. The reason you've never heard me complain is because I knew it was part of our marriage. Now I'm not sure I want to live with those pressures anymore."

She noted the shocked, disbelieving look on David's face when he realized that progress toward a quick resolution wasn't assured. As she left the psychologist's office, she felt relief that she had spoken up and expressed her true feelings. She had no idea what would happen next in her life, whether she and David would return to being a couple again or whether a new life beckoned.

ON HER FIRST DAY BACK in the office the following Monday, Jill was grateful that none of her colleagues pressed for details or expressed opinions about David. Instead, they offered encouraging words and supportive hugs, and then everybody got back to work. She spent the day in her office reviewing architectural drawings, color choices, and samples of cabinets and countertops.

"Hey, I don't think I ever gave you information about the new painter," Tom said, poking his head in her office doorway. "I put his résumé and some before-and-after shots from his portfolio in your inbox. I think you'll love this guy's work."

Jill, who was comparing samples of floor tiles, didn't look up. "Thanks. I'm glad you hired him. Our other painters are either perpetually late or grouchy."

Before going home that afternoon, she picked up the heavy yellow envelope containing the résumé and photos of Denny MacBride, the new interior painter, and stuffed it in her briefcase. There would be time later that evening to review his information. On the way home, she stopped at ShopRite for a few groceries, nodding and offering quick greetings to people she knew as she made a pass through the produce, deli, and wine sections. Hearing whispered comments and sensing the outright curious stares in her direction, she decided to forego picking up more than one bottle of wine lest people think she'd taken up heavy drinking. Her face was hot with embarrassment, and sweat trickled down her back as she anxiously counted up the items in her basket. Fifteen was too many to go through express checkout. She quickly put back three items and made it through the express line before dashing to her car and the blessed isolation of her house.

That night, following the late news, when her thoughts were too loud to permit relaxation and certainly not sleep, she wandered through the house plumping cushions, tossing junk mail, and replacing items on shelves to relieve the week's clutter. She knew from experience that the *feng shui* principle of keeping a home in good order promoted feelings of calm and ordered thinking. Now more than ever, she needed to keep her thoughts clear and moving in a positive direction. As she worked, she carried a cup of chamomile-lavender tea with her, but kept forgetting where she put it until it grew cold.

She wearily climbed the stairs to the second floor, intending to continue de-cluttering. Instead, her efforts derailed as she found herself surrounded by decades of memories. The walls and hall table on the second floor landing were filled with framed family photos, many from the earliest years of her marriage. Her eyes fell on one picture taken of her and David on their June wedding day so long ago. She hardly recognized the wide-eyed girl in the photograph, linking fingers with her handsome new husband. Her lips were open in a near laugh, and her face wore an expression of innocent newlywed expectation.

Glancing at the mirror above the table, she lightly touched both ring fingers to the slightly bluish circles under her eyes. Although she observed no visible wrinkles, she noticed the slight parentheses around her mouth and the looseness around the jaw line that age and gravity inevitably brought on. Still, she looked good for her age.

On the other hand, with the exception of the distinguished gray at his temples and the crinkled laugh lines that merely lent character to his face, David appeared much as he had on their wedding day. He was still gorgeous, still able to capture her breath whenever she laid eyes on him. A sob erupted, making her throat ache as she took the photo from the wall and held it to her chest.

"You're a bastard!" she told him, tears welling up and trickling down her cheeks. Angry at herself for succumbing once more to emotion, she scrubbed at her cheeks with one fist and realized that Liam was right. Throughout her life with David, she had defined herself first as David's girlfriend, then his fiancée, and then his wife. Even the twins were David's sons, and she was the mother of David's sons. If she and David actually divorced, would she define herself as his ex-wife? Although she'd maintained a successful career and had enjoyable work she loved, she still thought of herself entirely in terms of who she was with David. Without David, who was Jill Brenneman Hennessy? The network, too, had made money off the package.

Anyone without the inside scoop on the Hennessy household would be surprised at this insight. They assumed she had the perfect life. Truth be told, she had believed that fantasy, too. But now her perfect life seemed little more than a sham, a cosmic joke played on her for believing in forever-after love. Even worse, the thought of starting over on her own, minus a spouse, left her feeling overwhelmed and adrift. And yet, what was the difference between being married to David and being alone? Not much, she had to admit now.

Another serious consideration was the large, comfortable home she loved and intended to keep, no matter what happened between David and her. The house was all she had of their life together, and she wasn't about to give it up, at least not yet. She had lovingly remodeled and redecorated it from attic to basement, applying *feng shui* fixes to every square inch. She didn't need David's salary to pay the mortgage or household expenses. In fact, she didn't need anything from him … other than an explanation to help her understand why he had thrown away their past, present, and future on a woman whose relationship, he admitted, meant nothing to him. She wondered now if that was how he viewed women in general.

The affair couldn't have been just about sex; there had never been a shortage of that in their marriage. For this reason, if for no other, she had never suspected him of infidelity. Given David's insistence that his affair with Amber was "just sex," Jill wondered whether this was how he viewed sex, even with her. Or perhaps he had craved sex with a new woman, a younger one.

Jill knew that if they divorced, there would be a financial settlement that would provide security in a misguided attempt to compensate her. But how did one put a price on a quarter century-long marriage, the end of a lifetime of dreams? After days of acute stress and the growing awareness that her life would never be the same—and that there was nothing she could do about it—she fell across their bed, still clutching the wedding photo to her heart. When the pain finally became too great, she permitted herself the release of healing tears until she fell into an exhausted, dreamless sleep.

Chapter Five

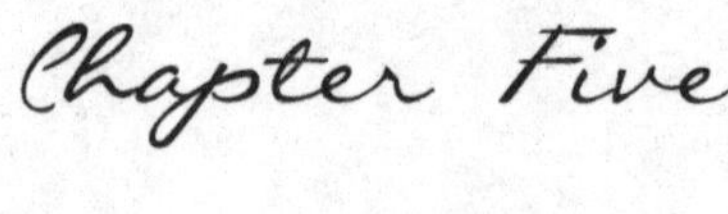

AS THE NEXT FIVE DAYS went by, Jill focused exclusively on her work and family, avoiding any tendency to wallow in self-pity. Meanwhile, David took a month-long leave of absence from the network. She heard from him occasionally, mostly when he left cryptic messages instructing her on what to say if his mother, sister, or brother called the house. She began to feel like a message service and told him so.

"I'm sure your family would love to hear from you directly. No one has called the house in days. If they did, I wouldn't be able to say anything other than what I know, which isn't much."

David had not responded for two days after that, and Jill was grateful for the reprieve. These days, whenever she thought about him, or when he called or emailed, the feelings of embarrassment and gut-wrenching hurt still reared up. Yet she could already tell that those moments were decreasing in number, intensity, and duration, and that she was feeling better and stronger each day. It also helped to realize that she had no regrets about her own actions in her marriage. *What doesn't kill us makes us stronger,* she thought, already realizing the truth in the adage.

Meanwhile, Jill received an email from the Communiversity program director at the community college, letting her know that nine students had enrolled in the Introduction to *Feng Shui* class. Jill's stomach flopped and her throat became dry when she heard the news. *Too late to chicken out*, she thought. Now it seemed the only thing to do was show up to teach the class. The rest of that week passed in a flurry of activity as Jill handled her design work while preparing feverishly for the class. Like it or not, this was a period of out with the old, in with the new. There was no way to undo what had transpired in her personal life. At least she still had her career—doing work she loved and that she knew could help people. She intended to be well-prepared for her students, whatever their reasons might be for taking a class on *feng shui*.

On Tuesday of the next week, the start of her first class, Jill was too agitated to concentrate on her work. She left the office early that afternoon, determined to put her nervous energy to good use. The second week of September arrived with a barrage of high heat and extra humidity that kept most people indoors in air-conditioning. Barefoot and holding a glass of iced tea against her forehead for relief, Jill decided it was time to tackle cleaning the patio furniture before cooler weather arrived. She donned a light-blue sleeveless top and a pair of faded denim shorts that she would not have been caught dead wearing in public. Since she was alone, the desire for comfort had won out over modesty. She reached inside her shirt, unhooked her bra and wriggled out of it, then flung it onto the table in the foyer so she'd remember to take it upstairs later. Then she pulled on a pair of long, blue-rubber gloves up to the elbows and headed to the patio with a bucket and a soft-bristled brush.

As she dragged the garden hose onto the patio and connected it to the spigot, she thought about the chain of recent events and was even more grateful for closeness with family, coworkers, and friends. Sometimes, however, the jagged cracks that remained of her former life still threatened to swallow her whole, especially at home in the quietness of the late evening. But overall, she took comfort in the routines of work and home care, and frequent conversations with the boys, Missy, and her parents.

She turned on the outdoor faucet and aimed the hose into a bucket. Then she added the tea tree oil cleaner her mother recommended in her household tips column, and began scrubbing each of the redwood chairs. Taking a long drink of her iced tea, she stopped to wipe the cold glass over her steaming cheeks and started in on the chaise lounge with a vengeance. She was sweaty and miserable as she baked in the sun, sweat trickling down her face and neck and between her breasts.

"I must be crazy starting this project today," she muttered, "but at least the cushions will dry fast in this heat."

Twenty minutes passed before she took a break. Sliding open the glass patio doors, she stepped inside the air-conditioned kitchen and basked in the coolness that enveloped her. She poured another glass of iced tea and gratefully sank into a kitchen chair. Soon she would need to take a shower and get ready for class. Feeling a bit more refreshed, she pulled on the blue rubber gloves and was about to go outside again when the doorbell rang. *Must be a neighbor*, she thought as she went to investigate. But when she opened the front door, she saw a man wearing a striped blue-and-white golf shirt and pressed khakis.

"I hope I have the right place. Are ye Jill Hennessy?" the man asked with a noticeable Scottish lilt to his voice. He was very good-looking in a wholesome boy-next-door kind of way, dark hair highlighted by strands of silver, and a smile that, no doubt, melted female hearts. Even hers wasn't immune today.

"I am." Her voice sounded weak, even to her own ears. Yanking off the hideous blue rubber gloves, she wished desperately that she were dressed in something a little less

Daisy Duke. She crossed her arms across her breasts and noticed the bra slung over the table in the foyer. She grabbed it and threw it into the hall closet, her face flaming.

The man was clearly amused, but too well-mannered to react. "I'm Denny MacBride," he said with a slight roll of the 'r' in his name. "I'm your new painter. Monica said you have the drawings and design plans for the Colver house, and that I should pick them up on my way over there. She said she'd let you know I was on my way."

Jill glanced at her cellphone and noticed there were two text messages. Monica had texted to warn her of Denny's arrival while she was out scrubbing the patio furniture. "Oh, gosh, I'm sorry!" She was mortified at her appearance. "Monica did try to let me know. It's so nice to meet you," she said, forgetting her discomfort for a moment as she pumped his hand. "I took a look at your résumé and some photos from your portfolio. I'm very impressed with your work." She glanced down at her outfit. "Sorry for my appearance. I …I've been cleaning patio furniture. I look awful."

"I think you look just fine, Jill." His engaging grin told her he was entirely serious. "Sorry to show up without prior warning. If those drawings are available, I'll not trouble you any longer."

"Please come in. It's too hot to stand outside, and it'll take me a few minutes to find those drawings and plans." She began darting around looking for her briefcase, which inexplicably had disappeared from its usual place beside the back door. She left Denny in the living room as she searched through all the downstairs rooms.

"Oh, no," she said, catching sight of her bedraggled appearance in the downstairs bathroom mirror, hair sticking up in weird cowlicks from the humidity. Why, oh why, did she have to meet this handsome Scotsman for the first time looking like a molting chicken? After several minutes, she located her briefcase on a kitchen chair, removed the designs, and returned to Denny, who was studying a painting on a wall above the Queen Anne chair.

"It's a nice paintin'," he said, rubbing his chin with his fingers. "I don't recognize this artist's name, but I like the simplicity of the subject. The green of those three pears, with one rolled on its side beside that blue-and-white china tea cup …. The composition is fine."

Jill handed him the design drawings rolled up inside a cardboard tube. "I'm not normally into still life paintings, but this one had so much *life* in it, I couldn't resist. Do you like art?"

"I do." His expression didn't change.

"Denny MacBride," Jill said slowly as it dawned on her why his name seemed so familiar. "You're an artist! I've seen your paintings; they're wonderful. In fact, I recently recommended two of them for a client's home." She was struck speechless for a moment.

"Thanks." He looked embarrassed. "I've been fortunate that my work has been well received." He smiled and cleared his throat. "Before I go, I wanted to mention that I agree wholeheartedly with the color palette ye've selected for the Colvers' house. But I'm concerned that the color in the library is a wee bit on the light side. I'd like ye to consider going two shades darker to this more velvet shade, and really make the color pop with those golden oak floor-to-ceiling bookshelves. Here, look at this shade and see what ye think."

He handed her a sample palette featuring a range of rich, nature-inspired greens. In all of her years of professional experience as a designer, Jill had never had a contract painter second-guess her color choices. In this case, she thought he was right.

"I think it's a wonderful suggestion. We'll need to clear the color change with the homeowners, but I'm sure they'll like it as much as I do. Why don't we meet at the house a few minutes early, before you start painting?"

"That'd be ideal. I'll brush a little color on the wall, and you can make sure it's okay." His eyes met hers and lingered for a few seconds, causing Jill to blush. "I plan to be there by eight thirty tomorrow."

"I'll see you then."

After Denny left, Jill slapped herself lightly on both cheeks. She was shocked to find herself thinking of Denny, his twinkling eyes and handsome smile. She cringed, remembering how she looked when he met her.

"Nice going, Jill," she mumbled, wishing she could rewind the entire day and start over. She would make sure the woman he saw the next morning looked her professional best.

DENNY MACBRIDE HAD NO SOONER driven away before the phone rang. Startled by the sudden noise, Jill took a deep breath and looked at caller ID, hoping that it wasn't David. But the number on the screen was her parents'.

"Jill, I hope you aren't in the middle of anything," Nancy said in greeting. "I haven't talked to you since the weekend. Dad and I wondered how things are going."

"Fine, I think. I'll have to start getting ready soon for my first *feng shui* class tonight, but I can talk for a few minutes."

"Still as nervous?" Nancy asked.

"Yes, but I've got hand-outs and notes. Hopefully, that'll keep me from disaster."

"You'll do fine." Nancy's voice was reassuring. "Are you getting any relief from all the attention?"

"Everyone at work is still being careful not to say the wrong thing or pressure me for info, although I know they'd love to hear all the sordid details. Strangers are staring at me and whispering in the grocery store. There are still looky-loos cruising down the street, and I may never finish eating all the food."

"Funeral food?"

"All the favorites. My freezer is jammed with casseroles, soups, bread, brownies, and coffee cakes. The neighbors have all been so nice, but it really does feel like there's been a death:

the demise of my marriage. Oh, and David emailed last night to tell me that he really wants to come home and start working things out. I told him I wasn't ready for that yet."

"Life in a hotel room just isn't the same, eh?"

"Actually, I have no idea where he's staying now. Knowing David, he isn't suffering, though."

"Ten bucks says he's at the Waldorf."

"Could be," Jill said, grimacing. "We keep our own credit cards, but for all I know, the network might be putting him up somewhere. I hope so. I don't need to face debt I didn't expect on top of everything else."

"So, where do things stand now? Have you spoken with an attorney?"

"I have. I didn't really want to take any action yet, but there were some tricky things, like what David's rights might be as far as our house is concerned. I was advised to file for legal separation, if I wasn't going to allow him to live here, and to make sure certain financial agreements are in place. I hired a very good attorney who I met a few years ago. Tom and I designed her house, and I like and trust her. She's got a good reputation for being tough but fair, and she encourages mediation; that is, if I actually decide to go through with the divorce."

"Information is always good to have," Nancy replied. "Have you considered that saving your marriage might be an option?"

"I can't say, Mom." Jill nibbled on a ragged cuticle. "This happened for a reason, even if I don't understand what it might be. I don't know why David cheated, and he didn't respond when I asked. But how will I ever be able to trust him again? I need legal advice because if things get ugly between us, I could end up losing a lot more than my self-respect."

Nancy was silent for a moment. "You have not lost your self-respect, Jill, because you did nothing wrong. That's a normal reaction, I'm sure, but you need to keep things in perspective. It's certainly telling that David wants so much to come home.

As for his lack of an explanation or apology, do you suppose he's been instructed not to admit fault? He's been the one carrying the banner for family values."

"I'm sure that's part of it. A public apology would mean admitting to the very behavior he claims to despise. However, I'm not the public. I'm his wife. Even when we went to a counselor, I got the feeling that David had no intention of apologizing."

"An apology would be the best place to start," Nancy agreed. "There will be tough days to come, but I believe everything will turn out for the best, and you'll come through this just fine. By the way, Dad and I are proud of how you've handled yourself throughout this entire ordeal."

Jill felt a lump forming again in her throat. "Thanks, Mom," she said, her voice barely audible. "I've always had great role models."

"True."

Chapter Six

AS SHE DROVE TO SOUTHERN Connecticut Community College, Jill thought about the unexpected visit from Denny MacBride earlier that afternoon. He was surprisingly humble and down to earth for such a talented, successful artist. His paintings certainly commanded an impressive price, and he was the featured artist at a respected Manhattan gallery. She remembered the twinkle in his eyes as he took in her bedraggled appearance and felt her cheeks redden again involuntarily. True to Monica's word, Denny was, indeed, a very attractive man. In many ways, Jill thought he was every bit as handsome as David, but in a more approachable, less professionally styled way. She looked forward to seeing Denny the next morning at their clients' home.

The scent of summer rain and overripe vegetation hung lush and heavy in the air as Jill stepped out of her Subaru in the community college parking lot. She stopped to take in a fragrant breath and gave her outfit a last-minute once-over, wishing she had worn slacks instead of a skirt. Warily glancing up at the sky, she noted a promising sliver of blue peering through the roiling gray and optimistically tossed her umbrella onto the passenger seat.

College students, many weighed down with backpacks and carrying fast food bags, hurried past her into the 1970s-style, sprawling redbrick complex of the community college. Butterflies fluttered in Jill's stomach as she made her way along the concrete sidewalk from the faculty and visitors parking lot to the college's main entrance. As she walked through the main entrance, her self-doubts resurfaced. She still wondered whether she could keep a class of adult students engaged for ninety minutes each Tuesday evening for an entire semester. Juggling an armload of folders containing handouts and reference books, she walked through the main doors and down the long, acrid-smelling, carpeted hallway to room C103. As she stepped inside, nine sets of eyes met hers.

"Good evening," she said, swallowing hard. She flashed a nervous smile as butterflies swarmed alarmingly in her stomach. Glancing around the room, she noticed with relief that a big screen television was available on the back wall. If worst came to worst and she ran out of things to say or they looked bored, she could let the students watch a design show on the Home and Hearth Television network while providing a running *feng shui* commentary. She deposited a stack of hand-outs on the desk, wrote her name on the chalkboard, and turned to get a better look at her students, who appeared to range in age from late twenties to mid fifties, mostly women. There were two men who looked to be in their early thirties. That was two more than she expected to see.

She pulled out her notes and began to read them. To her dismay, her left hand shook so hard, the pages fluttered. She kept her eyes focused on the page. "I'm glad so many people are interested in *feng shui*," she began, pronouncing the term '*fung shway*' in case there was any confusion. "My name is Jill Hennessy, and I'm an interior designer with the architectural firm of Becker, Hennessy and Johnson." She looked up in an attempt to make eye contact and offered a weak smile before returning to the page. "First, let's define what we'll be learning about this semester. My definition of *feng shui* is pretty simple. It's an ancient Chinese art form that helps us design and organize our work and living spaces in attractive and meaningful ways to create balance and harmony in our lives. Sounds pretty harmless, right?"

She looked up from her papers. Nine sets of eyes stared at her. A few students smiled in a stiff, polite way. *Great, I'm already losing them.* Jill swallowed again and continued, "Our firm, which was founded twenty-one years ago, is strongly committed to *feng shui* when designing homes and commercial spaces. I'm sure you'll agree that it isn't at all weird or unusual for people to give great thought to the arrangement of rooms, their décor, or the placement of their furniture. *Feng shui* is about making deliberate choices with the intent of enhancing health, wealth, and happiness. The premise is that the thought or intent of what we want precedes the physical change, which ultimately brings about what we desire."

She took a quick swallow of water and surveyed the class. One of the students was doodling in her notebook, and a young man glanced at the clock. Jill felt heat rise in her cheeks and realized that she had just lost her place in the notes. Scanning the page, she went to the next bullet point and began again. "The way our homes are designed and where we place our belongings can mean the difference between feelings of well-being and the exact opposite: a sense that our lives are somehow out of sync. We want energy, the *chi*, to flow freely."

Jill desperately wanted to put down her notes and just talk to the class, realizing that she needed to connect personally with her students. But what if they were already wishing they hadn't taken the class? She flipped a page on her notes. Perspiration dotted her upper lip, and she wiped it away with her finger.

"Is that the same *chi* that can be helped by acupuncture?"

Jill looked up from her notes in surprise. The student who

spoke was an attractive woman in her early thirties with sleek, dark brown hair that fell long and loose about her shoulders. She wore studious horn-rimmed glasses that she casually pushed up to hold back her hair. Her beige suit and cream-colored silk blouse looked expensive, and at the end of her long, slender legs were matching beige pumps with sensible yet stylish three-inch heels. She looked to be a woman who knew where she was going in life and could have any man she wanted.

The answer to this question wasn't part of Jill's prepared remarks, but the woman looked like she really wanted to know. "That's a great question." Jill smiled and tried to look as though she was taking the interruption in stride. The reality was very different. "Please tell me your name."

"I'm Kristen."

"Thanks for that question, Kristen. I'll try to answer as best I can." Jill paused to gather her thoughts. "*Chi* is a universal flow of energy. It flows through our bodies, um, but it's actually found everywhere and in everything." She tucked her notes under her arm to keep from dropping them and picked up a piece of chalk, drawing a quick square on the chalkboard. With her back to the class, she took a deep breath and continued diagramming.

"From a *feng shui* perspective of *chi*, let's say that this is your living room and the front door is here." She drew short parallel lines to signify the front entrance. "We start looking at *feng shui* from the main entrance of the home."

Drawing a large circle in the center of the living room, she continued, "If you were to put a big table in the middle of this room, it would block the *chi*—the energy flow—not to mention your own movement in and out of the room. It would be sort of annoying to walk around that table, and the room wouldn't feel comfortable or inviting. Sooner or later, you'd probably bang into the table and hurt yourself. If you didn't have the ability to move the table to a better spot, you'd avoid that room rather than remain in it. That's lost space in a home."

Jill wasn't sure where to go next in her prepared notes, so she picked up a design book that contained an example of a room she thought displayed poor design choices. She held up the photo for everyone to see. "The flow in a home or work space is very important, and it's why so many architecture and interior design students study and pay attention to *feng shui*. As we peer from the foyer into this large room, take a look at the lowered ceiling at the entrance to the room. It obviously accommodates ductwork, but a *feng shui*-conscious architect would avoid overhangs like this. Why?"

A plump, pleasant-looking young man in the back row spoke up. "It interferes with my view of the room, almost as if I was standing at the entrance to a cave. I'm Chris, by the way."

"I completely agree with you, Chris," Jill said. She took another breath and kept going, feeling as if she was having an out-of-body experience. "This overhanging ceiling limits a full view of the space, and that creates the perception of limitation in that room. This is something that you would want the architect or contractor to correct, if you're building or remodeling. Yet most times, appearance and ease of movement can be enhanced through simple and inexpensive corrections. Sometimes it's just about changing colors or repositioning furniture or belongings."

A young woman with pale skin and short, curly blonde hair touched the gold cross at her throat, opened and shut her mouth as if she wanted to say something, and then remained silent. Jill took note of the gesture and guessed what the student wanted to ask. *Uh oh, I didn't think to include anything about this, either,* she thought, and decided to address the issue.

"Oh, and by the way, *feng shui* shouldn't threaten the belief system of any religion, either. Create a space where you can live and work happily while being thankful for all the blessings in your life, and ultimate good will flow into your life experience. When we feel good, we attract more good."

She glanced over at the second male student, who eyed her with a mixture of interest and amusement. He was in his mid thirties, she guessed; decidedly handsome with a distinguished cleft chin and wavy, dark-brown hair that curled slightly over the collar of his golf shirt. But it was his eyes that captured Jill's attention and caused her to pause for just a moment. They were an arresting blue-green, a reflection of the teal color of his shirt. She was uneasy as she finished her thought, sensing there was strong emotion behind those eyes. By now, she was feeling more comfortable. She returned to her notes, but only as a guide.

"This semester, we're going to learn how to avoid blocking positive energy flow in a room through the placement of furniture and objects as well as choice of colors," she said. "We're also going to learn how to adapt or apply *feng shui* 'fixes' or 'cures,' as we often refer to them, to problems in our homes that may prevent us from feeling our most happy, healthy, creative, prosperous, successful, even romantic selves. I hope that each of us can make strides toward what we want most in our lives."

While the other students' faces registered enthusiasm, the teal-eyed man's expression changed to a look Jill couldn't quite decipher. He leaned back in his seat and averted his eyes, raking his teeth over his lower lip. He seemed to be struggling. Jill wondered why he had enrolled in the class, since he was clearly skeptical. She hoped that at some point, he would volunteer information about himself.

"If anyone wants to comment or ask a question, please jump right in." She swallowed hard and nodded encouragement to the woman wearing the cross, who had tentatively raised her hand.

"My name is Shelly. I've heard that a person struggling with an issue such as infertility can be helped by *feng shui*."

Jill nodded. "In my experience, that's certainly true. In fact, several of my clients who have made enhancements to their homes are now parents—in some cases several times over."

Shelly's expression brightened. "But how does *feng shui* work?"

"It's quantum physics." It was the handsome, teal-eyed man who spoke up now.

"Excuse me?" Jill couldn't contain the surprised laugh that escaped.

"Quantum physics," he repeated. "It's what you said before. The basic premise is that everything is made up of energy particles, including the energy of our thoughts, and those thoughts have the power to create. What we think about becomes real. That's physics." He shrugged.

"I don't think I've ever heard *feng shui* described quite that way before, but I completely agree with what you just said, and I'm glad you believe there's a scientific basis for why it works. By the way, what's your name?"

"It's Joel Foster."

"Thanks, Joel. Now that we've talked about what *feng shui* is and why it works, this seems like the perfect segue to the next important point of information about *feng shui*: the *bagua*." She pronounced it *bog-wa*.

Jill handed out copies of a rectangular grid with nine squares. "The *bagua* is a nine-square diagram that we superimpose over our homes. Each square of the *bagua* called a *gua* corresponds to a particular space in the home that's affected by natural elements such as fire, water, wood, metal, or earth." She drew a circle on the chalkboard to include each of the elements and then turned to the class.

"If you've ever played the game Rock, Paper, Scissors, you'll see that it works kind of the same way." She made the sign of a rock with one fist and wrapped her open hand over it to symbolize a sheet of paper. "Paper wraps around rock, but scissors cuts paper, and rock breaks scissors." She pantomimed with her hands, first laying her palm flat for paper, then creating a fist for the rock, and cutting the air with two scissor-fingers.

"You get the concept, I'm sure. It's a lot like that in *feng shui*."

As she considered the simplest way to describe the *feng shui* elements, she began to feel more confident. "The term *feng shui* means 'wind and water.' We're utilizing natural earth elements to enhance our living spaces. In *feng shui*, fire burns trees, but that same destructive fire also produces ashes which nourish and create earth. There is a destructive and a creative side with all the elements. Water douses fire, but feeds trees. Metal chops trees, but creates and can even carry water in a metal bucket or through pipes. Earth uproots trees, yet the minerals in the earth also create metal. It all makes sense, if you think about it, and it's helpful in remembering how to add or subtract from a space to solve a problem. One element has power over another, depending on the area you are trying to correct or enhance."

With everyone's attention now focused on this concept, she perched at the edge of the desk, beginning to enjoy herself. "We start looking at the *bagua* at the front entrance of the house, wherever the main door is located."

"What if the door I use most often isn't the front door?" Kristen asked. "Most of the time, I go in and out of the house through my garage."

"Good question. If the primary entrance to your home is through the back door or even a side door or the garage, you could start at either place as you consider how the *bagua* works in your home. I prefer the front door, though. It's entirely your choice which door to use as your entrance, Kristen."

She moved back to the chalkboard and located the square she wanted to highlight. "This part of the *bagua*," she said, pointing to the upper left hand square, "corresponds to the prosperity area of the home. Whenever you perceive yourself lacking in prosperity, you want to enhance this area to create openness for abundance. But it isn't only money you want to draw. Remember that true prosperity is the flow of good we experience in all aspects of our lives—relationships, health, knowledge, skills, family, and so on. If you are without an income, of course you want more money in your life. Who wouldn't? You can set forth your intention to attract more money and then make some physical and symbolic changes to that area of your home or workspace."

Jill grinned as several hands shot up. Clearly money was of interest to this group. "Don't worry," she said. "We'll study the prosperity corner in much greater detail."

A pretty middle-aged woman raised her hand. "The prosperity corner of my house is a bathroom. That can't be good," she said in a light-hearted way. She had honey-colored hair pulled back in a barrette and a sweet expression. "My name is Trish, by the way."

"Water flows, so water is a good element in the prosperity corner." Jill said. "Unfortunately, you're correct in thinking that the toilet isn't such a great feature."

There was general laughter at the remark. Jill felt on top of the world at this response as she provided reassurance. "It's not hopeless, Trish, honest. You'd want to make sure you applied a symbolic fix so that all of your resources don't get flushed down the toilet." Jill tapped her chalk on the desk. "In *feng shui*, we often deal symbolically to correct issues. So if it were my house, I might simply tie a piece of red yarn or red ribbon around the outgoing pipes—same with the pipe under the sink. Red is a power color to overcome the problem. It's my intention to protect my resources. Remember, it's all about your thoughts."

"I'll try that," Trish said mildly. "Perhaps I could accessorize with something that represents prosperity."

"How about a basket of lottery tickets on the toilet tank instead of a box of tissues," quipped Pam, the woman sitting next to Trish. "Or maybe you could get one of those gold paper crowns for the top of the tank and consider it a royal flush," she finished helpfully.

Members of the class exchanged amused glances, but several of them began taking copious notes. Jill grinned at Pam's suggestions and passed around a hand-out on basic *feng shui* tips. She realized with surprise that class time was passing quickly.

"Trish, I'll be glad to take a look at your bathroom sometime and make suggestions," Jill said. "I'm sure it's not a big deal." Desperate to continue building rapport, she had an idea and blurted it out before thinking it through. "By the way, I consider one home consultation visit part of everyone's tuition." Instantly, she realized this would take more time than she had anticipated investing in the class. But the words were out of her mouth now.

"Can we get to that sooner than later? No telling how much money I've already flushed down the commode," Trish answered with a grin.

Each member of the class began to participate in the lively discussion as Jill continued explaining that the other eight blocks of the *bagua* corresponded to fame and reputation, relationships and love, family, health, creativity and children, knowledge and skills, career and life purpose, and even benefactors and travel. After a ten-minute break, the students continued asking Jill questions as they shared challenges they perceived in their own living and work spaces. The class was over before she knew it. Jill was pleased with her students' willingness to consider what she presented, minus the sarcasm she occasionally endured when she mentioned *feng shui*.

At eight o'clock, she said with some relief, "It looks as if our time is up. You have my office phone number, cellphone number, and work email address on the syllabus, in case you think of any burning questions. Each week, we'll examine a different area of the *bagua*. Next week, our topic will be the health square."

As she made her way back to the parking lot and opened her car door, she noticed Joel unlocking his car, which was parked near hers. With a slight smile, he lifted his hand in a friendly farewell gesture. She waved back.

"I loved your comment about quantum physics," she called out. "Thanks for helping me out tonight. I was a little nervous."

"You're welcome. I thought you did just fine. You didn't even need your notes," he said with an understanding smile and disappeared inside his vehicle.

Chapter Seven

WHEN JILL ARRIVED HOME THAT evening, she found a message on the answering machine from David, along with several calls from him without corresponding messages. Knowing David, she guessed that he had called repeatedly, hanging up in frustration when she didn't answer, before finally leaving a message. She pressed play and listened intently.

"Jill, we have to talk," he said. "I know you're angry, but living apart isn't allowing us to take care of this problem. If you don't call, I'm coming over."

Jill immediately dialed his cellphone number and wandered into the den. The last thing she needed tonight was a confrontation with David, who was quoted in an entertainment weekly as saying, "I love my wife and intend to stay married to her until death do us part. I want the two of us to strengthen our marriage and overcome what has happened. It's never too late to save something as important as a marriage."

As she read the article, Jill had frowned, sensing that David again was distancing himself from the affair. It bothered her that, rather than taking responsibility for his actions, he preferred to imply publicly that there were problems in their relationship. Besides being embarrassed, she felt hurt and confusion. She wondered why he had never said anything directly to her about his concerns regarding their marriage.

When he answered his cellphone, she could hear that he was in a restaurant. There were the unmistakable background noises of silver clinking, low voices, and soft music. She suggested that he call her back, but David clearly wanted to talk with her now.

"Excuse me," she heard him say in an authoritative manner. "Is there somewhere private I could take this call?"

Jill wondered fleetingly where he was dining and whether he was alone. David was not the type of man who liked to dine alone, preferring room service, take-out, or delivery over a table for one. She took a sip of diet Pepsi, wrinkling her nose at the bubbles, and sat down in David's enormous leather chair to wait.

"Jill, I don't like what's happening to us." His tone was abrupt.

"I don't like it, either," Jill said quietly. "I especially don't like the reason it happened."

"I wish I could turn back the clock. I wish I'd known then what I know now." His voice sounded weary now.

"What is it that you know now, David?" she asked softly, not sure of what she hoped the answer might be.

There was an extended pause. While she awaited his answer, she focused on the floor-to-ceiling bookcases in front of her that were filled with David's books—mostly non-fiction by politicians and columnists—and a collection of broadcasting awards and plaques. Here and there, framed photos depicted David with a kindly looking, crinkle-eyed Ronald Reagan; two generations of smiling Bush presidents; and a timeless Walter Cronkite with his arm around David's shoulder. This room, she realized, was a living museum to David Hennessy. The essence of him was still palpable here. Feeling a choking sensation, she bolted out of the den to the living room, where she curled up on her favorite overstuffed floral sofa, tucking her feet underneath her.

"I know I should have been more careful and made a different choice," he said finally. "I know that I value our marriage. I meant what I said earlier. It's important that I come home."

Jill softened for a moment, but then remembered the calculated coolness of his demeanor on the night she had learned of his betrayal. The memory bolstered her resolve to be firm and to say what she was thinking without holding anything back. "David, I can't help but wonder if the only reason you wish you'd been more careful is so you wouldn't have been caught," she said. "And, yes, I know you want to be here because I created a wonderful home for us and our sons. Of course you would miss that."

"Jill," he said with a touch of impatience, "it isn't like you to be so stubborn and unforgiving, so unwilling to listen to me."

"I am listening, David," she said with a sad shrug of her shoulders. "The more important issue is that now I'm also listening to what *I* think, what *I* want. You're right. It isn't like me not to concede to your wishes, not to give you whatever you want, whenever, wherever, however you want it. But things are different now. I wish I'd insisted that you come home every night, instead of blindly thinking I could trust you. Then you wouldn't have had so many opportunities to cheat on me. And if I'd been less willing to give you so much of myself, I wouldn't be wondering who in the hell I am without you ...." Her voice trailed off.

"You don't have to be without me, honey. Let me come home so we can go back to the way things used to be."

"How far back would we need to go?" she asked, feeling the need for clarity, wondering how many years he might have been dissatisfied with their relationship. "David, I just wish I understood." She heard the long exhalation, but there was no response. "Whatever it is that caused you to turn your back on us can't be fixed without me understanding what I want and need now in a relationship," she told him. "Frankly, it's high time I learned who I am on my own before I decide if we can be together again. I also don't want you to pressure me or use our sons to gain a foothold over me. I'll make this decision on my own and in my own time."

She heard another sigh before he said, "I guess I have no choice. But will you return to counseling with me?"

Jill hesitated. "David, I think you need to continue seeing the counselor on your own so that you can better understand your actions and what motivates you. I'm in a process of looking very carefully at my own choices and actions. At this point, I'd rather not set an appointment for us to talk together with the counselor until I know why you behaved the way you did."

David was silent. "Very well," he said crisply. "The ball is clearly in your court. Dr. Barry says I need to be patient with you. I guess I can try."

After the call, she continued to sit quietly on the sofa, reflecting on what was happening in her life. She now experienced the first gentle nudges of forward motion—a sense that even the *feng shui* class was happening for a reason. She realized that, in just the past few weeks, she had grown into a stronger person. Teaching a class, when she had always been so afraid of public speaking, was a giant leap forward. She was definitely becoming more assertive when it came to communication with David, and it seemed not only right, but easier than she might have thought. Whatever happened, communication in a relationship was crucial, and if she couldn't communicate with David, how could she begin to rebuild trust?

Fate may have dealt her a hard blow in the form of David's betrayal. Yet she hoped she would be a good teacher for the nine students who wanted to learn about *feng shui* and how it could aid them in achieving their innermost desires. But Jill knew— even more than wanting to help these nine strangers resolve their challenges—that it was time to begin envisioning her own future, setting intentions for what she wanted most in life. Her desires had never wavered: a strong, loving relationship with a man, a happy family life, good health for herself and her loved ones, success in her life's work, a good reputation, personally and professionally, and prosperity enough to feel secure and to allow her to be generous with those she loved. Now she planned to apply all the principles of *feng shui* that she had come to understand so well through her work to create the life she wanted, the life she now understood was entirely about her own needs, her own choices.

"Let it begin," she whispered, placing one hand over her heart.

Chapter Eight

PREPARING TO MEET DENNY MACBRIDE on the job site the next morning, Jill selected a periwinkle-blue sheath dress with a hand-painted silk scarf and beige patent leather peep-toe pumps. Peering into the bathroom mirror, she carefully applied rosy matte lipstick and blotted it with a tissue. Then she donned pearl drop earrings and a slender silver bracelet with dark-blue sapphire stones that the twins had given her on her last birthday. The morning light caught the fire of the square-cut diamond wedding set on her left hand, and for a moment, her breath caught. She started to take off the rings but couldn't bring herself to remove them yet.

When Jill arrived at her clients' sprawling home in Westport, she saw that Denny was already parked in the circular driveway, his truck windows open to let in the cool morning air. She heard the unmistakable sounds of a popular morning show on National Public Radio. He was busy dunking a teabag in a large steaming travel cup, but as she approached the car, he looked up.

"Good mornin," he said with a smile that enhanced the laugh lines around his eyes.

As she watched him step out of the truck, she took note of his gray dress slacks and blue pinstriped button-down shirt. He pulled an enormous leather briefcase from the passenger side. She wondered whether he had brought a change of work clothes.

"I thought you said you were painting today," Jill said, admiring his appearance.

"I am."

"Aren't you going to change clothes?"

"No need to," he said as he walked with her to the front porch. "These are walls, not ceilings. For ceilings, I dress down." He grinned.

Jill shrugged. If the man wanted to ruin his good clothing, that was his business. After visiting with the homeowners about the wall color, Denny returned to his truck and brought in a new can of paint. He opened his briefcase to select one of the expensive brushes lined up inside, pried off the lid of the paint can, and stirred the velvety contents. Then he dipped in his brush until it was saturated with paint and laid a fine, matte coat across one of the library walls. Jill was mesmerized at the fluid motion of his hand, which seemed to be one with the brush. Even with the smell of wet paint, she noticed the masculine scent of soap and spicy aftershave emanating from him as he moved near her. She watched as he finished the section with a flourish.

"Thank you for suggesting this color. It's perfect," she said. Already, the wheels in her head were turning at the thought of using Denny as a color consultant.

Having received the go-ahead on the color selection, Denny began painting in earnest with a roller. He had a large area of the wall covered within a few minutes. At this rate, he'd be finished with the library by early afternoon. Plastic sheeting covered the oak floors, but other than this standard precaution, Denny showed no concern about spills or drips. He apparently had no need for taping, either, as evidenced by his sure hand as he cut in around the woodwork. No wonder Tom had moved so quickly to hire him.

But it was Denny's confidence without arrogance that appealed to Jill. He had an effortless way with clients and had been able to gain the homeowners' confidence in a matter of minutes. The man knew his business; there was little doubt about that. She also recognized that it was Denny's competent manner and dry Scottish wit, coupled with his professionalism and remarkable skills that would turn clients into repeat customers. She preferred Denny's manner over the firm's other contract painters, who tended to bristle, particularly with more demanding clients.

"I'm heading out now," she told him. "I'll check back with you later." But her feet seemed to be glued to the floor as she watched him work.

Her words caused him to pause in mid-brushstroke. As he turned to face her, something ancient and familiar inside Jill broke free. She stood silent before him, still not moving, until he broke the spell. "I'll call when I'm finished with this room," he said, tilting his head to study her expression.

"Okay, thanks," Jill answered and walked quickly to her car, breathing deeply to clear her head. What was it about this man that unsettled her so? For the rest of the day, she was shaken, unable to concentrate. She kept to herself as much as possible and barely spoke to anyone.

"Earth to Jill. Come in, Jill," Tom said, waving a hand in front of her face as she stood at the copier. "Hey, are you okay?" he asked.

"Just a little preoccupied. Nothing major," she answered and drifted back to her office before he could ask for more details. She was beginning to feel that events of the past three weeks were somehow related—that David's affair, their subsequent separation, and the meeting with Denny were inextricably linked. It was as if destiny had taken a strong hand in her life, catapulting her forward. In some unconscious way had she desired and compelled such radical change?'

By the second week of class, Jill was more confident as she drove to campus. In fact, she almost looked forward to teaching. But when she entered the classroom at six thirty, the tension among her students was nearly palpable. At first no one spoke or made eye contact with her. After a few agonizing moments of silence, as she noticed the carefully averted eyes, Jill perched on the edge of the desk. "Is anything the matter?" she asked.

Meredith was the first to speak up. "I think we're all just realizing who you are, Jill. I didn't make the connection last week that you're married to David Hennessy. I hope this isn't embarrassing or painful for you, but we can't pretend forever that we don't know who you are."

Jill's face reddened. "It's always better to get things out in the open," she answered. "Difficult or not, it's the truth. Better to clear the air."

"Are things okay for you?" Meredith continued gently. "I can't imagine what you've been through the past several weeks."

"Everyone asks, but I'm not sure how to define 'okay.' I'm fine … today, at least. As for the day I learned what was going on and the past few weeks, well, that's a whole other story. It's one of the unfortunate realities of living with celebrities that when they stumble or fall, the whole world has front row seats. I used to think there was a veil of privacy over me, but I learned the hard way that isn't the case."

She shrugged. "But enough about my unfortunate selection as heartbreak movie of the week; it's good to be here with all of you. Tonight, I'd like to tell you about one of my favorite squares of the *bagua*, the one corresponding to health." She rubbed her hands together eagerly and stood up. She was confident she could maintain a good flow of communication tonight. "All of us look great and appear to be in good health—aside from the occasional aches and pains of adulthood. Is that mostly true? Are all of the family members who live in our homes enjoying good health, I hope?"

Joel cleared his throat. "My wife has breast cancer and is going through chemotherapy. Things have really been rough for her lately."

Jill's heart sank. Joel looked dreadful tonight, his face a study in misery. Even his striking teal eyes were a less vibrant color. There was silence for a few moments before others turned to Joel, offering supportive comments.

"I'm sorry to hear that," Jill said, swallowing hard. "Now I understand why you're interested in *feng shui*. Of course, you want your home to be conducive to your wife's recovery. When someone is recovering, they deserve as much joy and as little stress as possible. That's why it's so important that whatever she sees each day is pleasant and brings her serenity and joy."

Joel nodded grimly. "We have a fifteen-month-old daughter. It's tough enough on a baby to have her mom so sick, but she doesn't understand why my wife is gone so much or why she doesn't have the energy to play with her or pick her up."

Jill bit her lower lip as she considered how to respond. Then she had an idea. "Would it help if I provided you with an in-home consultation this week? Everyone gets one, but I think you need to be first."

"I'd really appreciate that," Joel answered, raking his hands through his hair. "Even if I don't completely understand *feng shui*, I'll try anything if it helps Diana."

During their break at seven fifteen, Jill made arrangements with Joel to visit his home the next morning. There was little time to waste with Diana's health situation, and she really wanted to help them. More than that, she wanted to do something concrete, and she had ultimate confidence in *feng shui*. By setting the intention to help Diana and using *feng shui* fixes, she believed that Joel would feel more hopeful, too.

"Diana will be at the hospital getting her chemo, and she

always feels lousy afterward," Joel said. "It would be great to have something positive to tell her. Do I need to do anything to prepare for your visit?" He shifted from one foot to another, looking embarrassed. "I probably ought to clean the place, at least."

For the first time in a week, Jill felt strong and purposeful. "For now, just have faith in the process. We'll create an environment of good health and serenity that will provide a strong foundation for Diana and support her journey toward good health."

"Thanks," Joel said. He looked away, but Jill caught the anxiety that remained in his eyes.

As the class returned to their seats, Jill went to the chalkboard. "Remember how I told you last week about the game Rock, Paper, Scissors? Scissors cuts paper, paper covers rock, and rock pounds scissors. Let's review the five elements again: wood, metal, fire, earth, and water. When these elements are balanced in your home, all is well. We use the same elements either to prevent something from happening, to improve a situation, or to remedy something that isn't so good." She held up a pack of matches.

"When there is a forest fire, trees burn. That's destructive. However, the result is earth—dirt and ashes. That's creative. Metals are mined from the earth—again, creative. A metal bucket or pipes hold and carry water. Water nourishes trees, and wood is a fuel used to light a fire. Those are the creative uses for these elements. More destructive examples are when fire melts metal, metal chops wood, wood uproots earth, earth blocks the flow of water, and water extinguishes fire." She drew this cycle on the chalkboard. "All the elements are good; yet, they also can be destructive, depending on how we use them."

She held up a drawing of the nine-square *bagua*. "It's important to understand this concept as you apply fixes in *feng shui* to areas of your home. Now let's talk about the health area, which is found in the middle section of the *bagua*. This square is in the center of your home, balancing and touching all other areas. I think that's because health is so central to our overall well-being. Now I want you to picture in your mind which area of your home corresponds to health."

Trish spoke up. "I bet the health area isn't a good place for a toilet, either." Everyone laughed.

"We can work around this little toilet challenge, Trish," Jill reassured her, joining in the laughter. "Let go of all your worries about toilets. You've got to have them somewhere. In fact, you may be relieved to learn that a bathroom is in the first floor health area of my home."

She drew a square on the chalkboard. "In my downstairs bathroom, I've created a sort of Santa Fe retreat for myself. Earthen materials are great in this area, so I thought it would be an ideal place to showcase my love of the Southwest. I have terra cotta tile floors, and the walls are painted a light adobe color. There is a yellow Native American sun symbol on the wall, and my accent colors for towels and rugs are in earthy colors—turquoise and greens. Since fire creates earth, I needed something red in that room, so I have a small pebble garden with a large red candle. It's a bathroom, though, so there is definitely water in there from the sink, toilet, and shower. That's a problem because we know that water douses fire."

"So how did you fix it?" Trish asked.

"Very easily," Jill said with a wink. "Metal comes from the earth, and metal creates and holds water. But in this case, the flow of good, represented by water, is being diminished. So just to be safe, I tied a fire symbol—a small strand of red yarn, which is a power color—around each outgoing pipe because, through my intention, that fixes the problem. Now the two elements are balanced with my intention. The most important thing is that the earthy elements are strategically and intentionally put there by me to enhance good health in my home. The only element I would want to actively avoid in the health area is wood, which uproots earth."

Joel had a quizzical look on his face. "We have a huge wooden staircase curving from the first floor to the second in our health area. That's a problem, right?"

"We'll take care of that tomorrow," she said. "Short of removing it, there are other options."

"I appreciate hearing that," he said, and for the first time that evening Jill noticed a glimmer of hope and humor on his face.

When class ended, Joel walked Jill to her car while they made final arrangements for the next day's visit. "I don't mean to seem negative, but I'm struggling to balance the science that I understand with what seems like play-acting," he said as he held open the car door for her.

"*Feng shui* tends to bring out interesting reactions from people until they figure out the fundamental concepts and how they work," Jill agreed. "There's no reason not to enjoy the creative process, and creativity *is* child-like, Joel. So, yes, *feng shui* can feel like play, and that's a good thing."

"But I don't want to be naïve about what could happen, when Diana's doctor tells us to expect the best but prepare for the worst," he said. "She's still very ill, and the chemo hasn't gotten the job done yet."

"Joel, do what the doctor says: expect the best. Believe that ancient Chinese wisdom has merit as you work with western medicine."

"Well, when you put it like that," he said, "I guess there's room for some hope."

"Look, I wouldn't be teaching this class if I didn't believe one hundred percent in *feng shui*. One of my most pessimistic design clients had large oak beams across her master bedroom ceiling. I took one look at the room and noticed immediately that one of those beams lined up over the bed, hitting her and her husband right about hip level. Not surprisingly, they were having difficulties conceiving. As part of redecorating for them, I suggested they simply reposition the bed to avoid that beam over their reproductive organs, and she was pregnant within a month. They now have two children, and she's a believer."

Joel chuckled. "Whatever you do to our house, please don't enhance fertility."

Chapter Nine

AT NINE O'CLOCK THE NEXT morning, Jill rang the doorbell of Joel and Diana Foster's home, an older two-story fieldstone house situated about a mile off a winding, wooded road. A dog's rumbling bark announced Jill's arrival. Joel appeared at the door, carrying a blonde, wispy-haired cherub, thumb planted firmly in her mouth. She was wearing pink footie pajamas with a grape juice stain on the front.

"Jill, please come in. This is Zoe."

Jill smiled at Zoe, who had her father's remarkable teal eyes. The sober, mature expression on her baby face didn't change as Jill touched her soft, dimpled fingers. But then Zoe hid her face in Joel's shirt, glanced back at Jill, and smiled playfully. "Peek-a-boo," Jill said, laughing.

"And this is Jack, our dog." Jack was a smelly chocolate Labrador with matted fur.

"Animals are a wonderful part of a healthy home," Jill said, avoiding Jack's drooling mouth as she followed Joel inside. "They keep energy moving throughout the house." She resisted the temptation to make another comment about the importance of keeping an animal well-groomed, since it was obvious that Zoe was enough of a challenge.

Joel put Zoe down, and she took off, toddling into another room. "Look, if you just tell me what to do, I'll do it. I don't know much about *feng shui*. I'm a physicist—materials science, actually—but I've started to read about research going on in the science of mind."

"What have you been reading?"

"Well, this stuff isn't new, I guess, but there are actually experiments going on around the world. Scientists are trying to explain things that people have been trying to figure out for centuries—why prayer seems to work, for one thing. It all seems to point in the same direction—that thoughts have the power to create through energy. What we believe actually can become real through focus and the power of our emotions. Diana believes she's getting well. After what you and I talked about last night, I'm thinking that maybe I'm the one who needs *feng shui*. I need to change my thoughts so they can be stronger on her behalf."

"That's certainly the right attitude," Jill agreed. "The success of *feng shui* depends on the intention of the person making the changes. I think it's important that you try as hard as you can to believe that the love you feel for Diana and how much you want her healthy again can, in fact, make a positive difference. Believe for Diana and for Zoe."

Jill turned and her eyes widened as Zoe returned, carrying a round, clear sack in her arm and a security blanket over her shoulder. "Is that what I think it is?"

Joel sprang forward in an attempt to dislodge the object from Zoe's hand. "It's her mother's prosthesis. Diana was nursing Zoe one evening, right after she was born, when she found the first lump. Her doctor ordered an immediate biopsy, and we learned it was stage four cancer. Obviously, breastfeeding had to be stopped, and Diana lost her right breast. One night, Zoe reached for the prosthesis while Diana was reading to her, and Diana just gave it to her to hold. Now, Zoe is fascinated by her mom's fake boob." He wrestled it away from Zoe and placed it on top of a bookshelf, handing her another toy as a diversionary tactic.

He shrugged and offered a half smile, but only succeeded in looking young, vulnerable, and scared. "I don't know whether it's a good idea or not to let her hold that thing all the time, but since there aren't any rules for how to help a baby when she can't have her mother, I try to let go of judgment about what's good or bad."

Jill had never experienced tragedy on this scale. Her heart ached for the frightened father who was helpless to protect his wife, the sick young mother who might not live to see her baby daughter grow up, and the confused toddler who had literally lost her place at her mother's breast. Jill's eyes fell on a photo on the bookshelf of Diana, a stunning young woman with blonde hair the color of corn silk, a smile worthy of a toothpaste ad, and deep dimples. She looked carefree—a woman in the peak of good health, her entire future ahead of her.

"See that photo?" She pointed to it. "That's the Diana we're working for."

She pulled out a chart with some ideas for the health area of the *bagua*. "This curving staircase is a problem, so let's concentrate on fixing that."

"What's so bad about a curving staircase? I thought it was the fact that it's made of wood that we needed to fix."

"Do you remember when we talked about *chi* in class? *Chi* is energy, and energy needs to move freely. *Chi* doesn't move as well in a spiral situation. This staircase isn't exactly a spiral, but the energy could lose its force as it turns up and around. The first thing we can do is hang a mirror on the wall near where the staircase turns to redirect *chi*. The other problem is that there is so much wood in this area, and wood uproots earth. The earth element is what we want to enhance, along with fire."

Jill slowly turned around as she surveyed the entire area,

frowning slightly. "Let's get that big snake plant out of this area by the stairs. A few small leafy plants won't hurt anything, but we don't want a lot of green in this area, since they represent trees and wood, and certainly not a spiky green plant this large. The clay pot is beautiful, but I'd put that snake plant with its sword-like leaves in the reputation area of the house instead. If anyone messes with you, that warrior plant will take care of them!"

"I like that." Joel grinned.

Jill walked around assessing the health area and taking notes. She thought about ways to keep the energy in the circular wooden stairway from interfering with the energy balance. "Fire warms up the health area. We need to introduce some red in here, but I want it to be beautiful and enhance the décor, not stick out like a fire hydrant."

Joel stood nearby, biting his lower lip. "Maybe you can suggest something we can buy when Diana is feeling better. I don't trust myself to pick things without her."

Jill paused. "The color on the walls is 'sand dunes,' am I right? It's nice and earthy, and it looks great in an area like this. It's a nice color choice because there are so many other colors you can coordinate with it."

Joel nodded. "You know your paint colors."

Jill walked around the room, her finger resting against her chin. "It would be nice to have the fireplace in this area, but it's not really close enough to help, so let's think of another way to introduce more red into the health area. As a designer, I prefer not to fix problems using symbols if I can enhance the area with a feature that actually adds value to the home."

She went to her briefcase and pulled out a fan of carpet samples. "We're obviously not going to paint the stairway red. But I have something you could add to the stairs that not only would be a strong fire element, but also aesthetically pleasing. Would you consider an oriental runner for these stairs in a rich burgundy?"

Joel shrugged. "I guess so. I'm not very good at visualizing stuff. Diana is the creative one."

"The pattern I have in mind also hides dirt well and cleans up easily with a vacuum. That's a big deal when you have small children." She showed Joel a sample of what she had in mind. "I'm going to leave this for you to share with Diana. If she doesn't like the idea or you'd rather not make a decision now, we'll figure out something else."

Joel dropped a pair of Zoe's shoes and some books on steps already littered with Fisher Price toys, a laundry basket, and a pile of athletic shoes. "Sorry about the mess," he said. "I can't seem to keep things straightened up."

"Just do the best you can to keep this area in good order," Jill advised. "It's important to keep these stairs clean and free of clutter. Oh, and avoid decorating with anything green in this area. Green is wood, and wood uproots earth. If you want another decorative item, select a painting for the wall in the stairwell—something with mountains, I think. Peaks or points are important in the health area. Mountains are an earth symbol."

Joel wearily rubbed a day's growth of stubble on his chin. He looked confused and overwhelmed. "I doubt I could pick anything suitable. I might need you to point me in the right direction."

Jill smiled. "I think we've got you covered on anything you need," she said, pulling out her tape measure. "For now, let me measure the area on these stairs and see how much runner is needed." She measured carefully, tapping numbers into her phone.

"Actually, there is enough of this pattern left over from another project that I'm sure I'll have what you'll need," she said. "And I know someone who can do the installation for free." She winked. "If you help me, that is."

"Helping out is the least I can do. Thank you, Jill. The Oriental runner is a nice idea," Joel said. "I'll pick up Diana in a little while and tell her what you said. Frankly, I don't think she'll care one way or another. She feels terrible after chemo. She'll probably say, 'Just do it.' "

"It's very important that she's happy with whatever you decide, so please wait until she feels better so she can be clear-headed about the decision. I'll leave this sample for you to show her."

Joel picked up Zoe, who was beginning to fuss. "I wish I had as much faith as you do in something as simple as moving things around to change a bad situation," he said. "I've always put my entire faith in science. We thought the surgery would get all the cancer, but it showed up in her other breast. None of the treatments have worked so far, and she got depressed when she lost her hair. That's when I got really scared for her; I thought she'd give up. No matter what happens, everything just seems to get worse, and yet, she still believes she'll recover."

Jill placed her hand on his arm and squeezed it. "It means so much that you support her, and that you're here with Zoe when Diana can't be."

Joel's face darkened. "Every time she starts another round of chemo, I get angry at what she has to go through. I'm not sure I'd have her courage if the situation were reversed." He shook his head. "This *feng shui* … well, Diana is a big believer in the power of her mind to heal her body. I guess I'm not as comfortable with what I can't explain."

He shifted Zoe to the other side and kissed her rosy cheek. "I'm willing to try anything, believe anything, if it helps Diana. Zoe needs her, and so do I."

"I'll hold all of you close in my thoughts. Zoe, be a good girl for your daddy," she said stroking the baby's chubby cheek. Zoe flashed another mischievous, toothy grin and hid her face against Joel's chest.

"Thank you," Joel said wearily. "I'm glad I decided to take your class. I appreciate everything you're doing for us." The tension in his jaw had lessened somewhat, but Jill could still see the despair in his face—the deepening lines of tension and the striking eyes dulled by exhaustion and shaded by dark circles.

"I'm happy to help. Give me a call or let me know next week in class what you want to do about the carpet runner. This will be an easy fix; I promise."

She got into her car and backed out of the driveway. As she looked into her rearview mirror, she saw Joel standing with Zoe, cradling her head against his chest. She thought of Zoe carrying around the soft plastic prosthesis next to her heart and swallowed hard.

"This just has to work," she said as she drove back to the office, forgetting for the first time in ages about her own problems.

AFTER WORKING LATE THAT DAY, Jill parked her car in the garage and entered the house through the kitchen. The house was silent, except for the tick-tock of the grandfather clock in the hallway. The kitchen still smelled faintly of stale breakfast coffee and toast. She rummaged through the refrigerator and found a wedge of sharp white-cheddar cheese that she paired with Triscuits and a bunch of red grapes.

Then she poured a glass of chardonnay and took her snack to the den, where she turned on an episode of *House Calls*, a show that helped homeowners improve the look and value of their homes. She wondered if the producers of Home and Hearth Television would ever consider a show that taught people the principles of *feng shui*. As the idea took root, she resolved to give it more thought. Now that she no longer feared public speaking as much, she thought it might even be fun.

The phone rang and Jill leaned over to pick it up. "Hello?" she asked absently.

"Jill, it's me," David said impatiently. "I've been calling for hours. Check the machine."

"Oh, hi," she said and popped a grape into her mouth. "I just got home. Things have been extra busy since I started teaching this class."

"Well, I guess that's good," David said in an offhand way. "You asked where to send mail. I'm staying at an apartment in Manhattan near the studio. Can you take down the address?"

Jill pulled out a pencil and pad of paper. "Go ahead." She wrote down the address David gave her, wondering whether he was staying with someone else, and if that someone was a woman.

"I'll probably be there for a while, until we decide on the next step. I mean, whether I come home or … you know."

Jill swallowed. There was an awkward moment of silence. "David, now that we're legally separated, I know the house is an issue. We can work out the details. I'm not planning to do anything with it until I get used to all the changes in my life."

"So you're still just as angry." David let out a long sigh.

"I don't feel *as* angry anymore, no, but the past couple of weeks have convinced me that I want to look toward the future."

"And when you look there, you don't see a future with me."

"I can't imagine that right now, no."

"It hasn't been but a few weeks since this all happened, Jill. Of course you have a right to lick your wounds."

Jill sat up straighter, instantly incensed. " 'Lick my wounds'? I'm not a cat, David. And, actually, it was an entire year that you were involved with someone else, not just a few weeks. You hurt me, and I'll probably never understand why. Was it just sex? Because you know, David, you've never told me why. If it was just about sex, I'm really confused because in my memory, there was never a shortage of that between us."

"I wish I could change what happened. You have no idea how much." There was a long silence. "Let me know what you decide," he said and hung up.

She stared at the receiver, shaking her head. He still could not tell her what happened or why. Reaching into the drawer in the coffee table, she pulled out a stack of old photos. She shuffled through them until she found one of David and the boys taken on vacation fifteen years ago at Block Island off the coast of Rhode Island, one of her favorite places. As she remembered the good times they'd had together as a couple and with their sons, she was nostalgic, but not quite as sad. There was peace in the certainty that she had loved David and given him the best she had to offer. It was important to remember now that without David, she wouldn't have Liam and Finn.

After all the tears she had shed over the past few weeks, she was beginning to realize that she had arrived at a place that felt suspiciously like acceptance. She also had come to the conclusion that she couldn't go back to life with David knowing, as she did now, that he could so easily break her trust. Even worse, their entire life over the past year had been built on a deception. David's inability to apologize spoke to a deeper truth about his character. Was he sorry for what he had done? She believed that if he was, it was only because he had been caught.

Although she had never pictured herself as a divorced woman, she began to feel hopeful that in time, she'd come to fully embrace this new beginning. The next several months wouldn't be easy—of that she was quite sure. But it was possible, she was sure, to create a new life with family, friends, the design work she loved, and her new vocation teaching *feng shui*. Maybe she'd even fall in love and marry again. Did a middle-aged bride take her vows with the same starry-eyed enthusiasm to love, honor, and cherish?

With a sigh, she had to admit she was grateful that she could still think of a man in a romantic way. Not surprisingly, her thoughts turned to Denny MacBride. She had never known a true Scotsman before, and this one was definitely intriguing. Nevertheless, the idea of dating anyone at this age seemed daunting. Although she'd had other boyfriends, David had been her only lover, and she wasn't even sure what to expect with another man. She thought of Denny's warm smile and those laughing brown eyes and looked forward to seeing him.

"Life goes on," she said, and raised both eyebrows in surprise at the sheer novelty of the idea. For the first night in weeks, she wiggled her toes over to David's side of the bed, resolving to begin looking for new furniture to replace the bedroom furniture she had kept all these years for reasons of sentimentality rather than style.

Ordering new furniture tomorrow would be the first step in her new life.

Chapter Ten

BEFORE SHE LEFT FOR CLASS the following week, Jill was delighted when Joel called to say that Diana loved the idea of the carpet runner for the stairway in their home. "She thinks it's worth doing. She said she's glad the western world is starting to embrace things like acupuncture and *feng shui* that the Chinese have practiced for thousands of years."

"I totally agree. How's she doing?" Jill leaned against the kitchen counter, listening intently.

"Not good," he admitted. "She's struggling to keep anything down, even chicken broth, and she's attached to an IV. The visiting nurse stops in twice a day, and her mother is here helping out with Zoe. Obviously, given the situation, I won't be in class tonight. You probably won't see me again until Diana feels better."

"Please give her my best wishes, and take good care of yourself, too. Let me know if there is anything else I can do to help. Is it okay if I give the rest of the class an update?"

"I'd appreciate that. I don't know how to thank everyone for what they've done for us. Pam and Trish brought meals by over the weekend. Meredith dropped off an incredible dinner from her catering business, and Kristen gave us a gift certificate for maid service. Chris sent over a CD of healing guitar music. I had no idea when I took this class that I'd meet such great people."

"They are great people," Jill agreed.

"We're at a critical point now in her treatment. If this round of chemo goes well, we might actually be looking at a positive outcome." Joel paused and let out a heavy breath. "That is, if the treatment itself doesn't kill her."

That night, Jill shared the conversation with her other students, who expressed their desire to continue helping Joel and Diana. The women decided to organize another round of meals for the next week. As Jill looked around the room at the students who had known each other for just three weeks, she felt certain they would remain friendly long after the class was over.

She went to the chalkboard and illustrated the *bagua*, circling the square in the lower left-hand area that corresponded to the subject of tonight's class. "Tonight we're going to talk about the knowledge and skills area of the *bagua*, which is found in the square directly to the left of the front door as you enter the home. Who needs special help with this area?"

"I do," Amy said. Springy auburn curls framed a heart-shaped face with skin the color of fine porcelain. Amy had gorgeous, bottle-green eyes and a figure as lithe and slender as that of a ballet dancer. "I'm learning to be a yoga and meditation instructor."

"The knowledge and skills part of the house is the best of all possible areas for meditation, I think," Jill said. "That's because we concentrate on this area of the *bagua* when we want to learn something or when we'd like to sharpen our skills in a particular subject." She held up a photo with symbols used in this area. "The knowledge and skills area is a place where we can combine several elements together in a creative way—specifically water, wood, and metal. The primary color we want to use is blue, but we can also use black because it signifies water."

"I have a huge reference manual called *The Gigantic Black Book About Everything* that has information about ... well, everything," Pam said. "No matter what else is wrong with that area in my house, if I put that book on my coffee table, am I covered?"

"Just make sure the information is up to date," Jill said, smiling. "Symbolically, that type of reference book isn't a bad idea. This area is also a nice place for a small fountain and a big green plant—as long as you keep the water clean and the plant healthy. Pick off dead leaves. If you have any metal statues or a bust of a famous, smart person, this is a good area for it. I keep all my *feng shui* books in this area of my home."

Chris frowned. "My knowledge and skills area is in my garage. It's actually part of the house, not a separate structure, so I guess I have to consider that space as part of the *bagua*, right? It's not that bad out there, but I don't think I'll be doing any serious reading in my garage."

"Attached garages, where the space 'invades' the *bagua*, are actually quite common. I wouldn't worry about it at all. Store some reading materials out there, even if it's just the instruction booklet to your weed trimmer. You could also put a plant in the window, as long as it gets lots of light and you clean the glass. If you're keeping the garage clean and orderly, from a *feng shui* perspective, your mind will also be clean and orderly." Jill paused and waited for the inevitable.

"So, watching porn should never be done in the knowledge and skills area of the *bagua*?" Pam quipped, her cat's eye glasses perched low on her nose.

There were snickers. Shelly looked at Pam with a mixture of shock and disapproval. By now, it had become apparent that Pam considered herself to be the class clown, although her attempts at humor were often crude. Yet Pam clearly had a heart of gold. Jill was sure that her off-color humor masked deep feelings of insecurity.

"I knew that one was coming." Jill chuckled and shook her head at Pam. "Actually, you bring up a great point. Like it or not, it's important for us to remember that whatever it is we desire in life—whether it's a lasting relationship, stronger family ties, health, prosperity, or even fame—requires us to take care in all other areas of our lives. It doesn't do much good to accentuate the family area of your home if you're going to cheat on your spouse." She blushed, realizing what she had just said. "Heavy drinking, drug use, smoking, cheating on your taxes … whatever you do that falls short of the ideal isn't good for your overall well-being. Remember that squares in a *bagua* flow into one another. You can't fix a problem in one area of your life if another area is not in good order."

It was a lively discussion as everyone talked about the knowledge and skills areas of their homes and the challenges they perceived. Jill realized from their questions and the suggestions they made to one another that they were beginning to have a much deeper understanding of *feng shui* principles and were starting to apply them to their living spaces. Over the past few weeks, as Jill had gotten better acquainted with her students, she learned that their reasons for taking the class were as varied as the individuals themselves. She hoped that not all of her students were in as dire a situation as Joel.

Amy—the beautiful woman in her twenties with auburn curls and the graceful body of a dancer who wanted to start her own yoga studio—had taught English as a Second Language in Tokyo and returned to the United States determined to live a life more in keeping with the spirituality she adopted in Japan.

Trish wanted to enhance her prosperity corner after a divorce left her with a low-paying secretarial job and a shabby apartment. Her husband of twenty-two years had lost his business and then decided he didn't want to be married, either. Trish, who had just turned forty-five, had been a stay-at-home wife and hospital volunteer, unaware that her husband's business was in trouble until just before it went under. After the divorce, she was forced to move out of her beloved home into a cheap, one-bedroom apartment. Jill empathized with the trauma of Trish's situation and felt fortunate that she had maintained her own stable income all the years of her marriage.

"I just need to start generating more income," Trish confided that evening on break. "I want to be able to feel pride in myself and my home again. I don't want to be afraid of the future."

"Concentrate on what you want, and feel happy emotions when you think about it," Jill advised her. "Believe in the power of your intentions."

Chris, a talented singer/songwriter, wanted to enhance his reputation and broaden his chances for fame. He'd been selected for the hit show, *Stars*, but after just two weeks had been cut by the judges. As soon as his classmates heard he'd been on *Stars*, they treated him like a celebrity.

"They said I didn't have that ineffable star quality," Chris said with a sigh.

"What the eff!" Pam said, shaking her head, which brought a laugh even from conservative Shelly.

Painfully shy by nature, Chris was in his element only when performing onstage, he claimed. Off stage his sweet sincerity was infinitely appealing, yet he'd been told that he lacked the charisma that spelled star power. To make matters worse, his mother, who had been his biggest fan, died suddenly of a heart attack shortly after his appearance on *Stars*.

"With the right song and the right break, I can get the attention of a music label," he said with what Jill recognized as forced confidence.

Meredith, a single mother with three teenage sons, owned a catering business that she intended to expand. "I need to sell my house so that I can buy a place with a bigger kitchen," she said. "Plus, I'm Italian on both sides of my family, but I've never been to the actual place that inspires all my recipes. So in addition, I'd love to have enough money left over to travel to Italy."

Kristen, an attorney, desired true love after her engagement ended, but three years worth of bad dates followed. "I've been on every online dating site you can imagine and have met mostly two kinds of men. Either they want you to be their 'beck and call' girl, or they're looking for a mom and a meal ticket. I'd like to truly enjoy a man's company without all the games. I don't want to settle for 'Mr. Right Now' just to say that I'm in a relationship."

Joni, a quiet, elegant woman in her forties, struggled with "family-of-origin difficulties," as she put it. "In my family, there is only one way to survive, and that's to be absent as much as possible," she said with a sigh.

After twenty-eight years as a paralegal, Pam wanted a career as a romance novelist. "For years, I've been reading romance novels and thinking, 'I can do this.'" She looked wistful. "I have a good income as a paralegal, but it's not enough anymore. I want to enjoy my work. I want to write books that take people away from their troubles to a place where there are always happy endings."

Shelly was experiencing infertility in an extended religious family where every woman of childbearing age was either pregnant or already a mother several times over. Even worse, her husband was reluctant to undergo fertility testing, and Shelly believed he was afraid of discovering he was the one with the problem. Shelly was frustrated and becoming angrier as her biological clock ticked its way into her thirties.

Jill knew from experience that the practice of *feng shui* could result in remarkable life changes for people. Time and again, as she worked with clients to fix challenges in their homes and offices, she had witnessed miraculous events. Now that she had gotten to know her students better, she hoped that these classes and the time she was investing in their consultations could help them achieve their strongest desires. She also knew that as she worked with each of them, she was likely to experience positive effects in her own life. Feeling an unexpected sense of exuberance, she drove home, resolving to take a fresh look at her home and make some fixes.

LATER THAT WEEK, JILL DROVE to a nearby suburb to visit with Amy, the student from her class who taught yoga and meditation. Amy lived in a newer complex of townhomes with a man-made lake. She answered the door wearing a silk, cream-colored kimono-style dress adorned with green leaves, yellow chrysanthemums, and a wide yellow sash. Her fiery red hair was swept up in a stylish topknot and fastened with black lacquered chopsticks. It was clearly a studied look, but Jill thought the overall effect was striking.

"What a gorgeous outfit. It really suits you." Jill lightly touched her cheek to Amy's. "I hope I can help with your knowledge and skills area, although from the appearance of your apartment and your outfit, I think you already have a good grasp of *feng shui* and what else might be needed."

"I've gotten a lot of useful information from your class, and I've spent time considering furnishings and what colors I want. But I'm still not sure that I've placed my furniture quite right or what else I might need," Amy said, indicating the sparsely furnished apartment. "I like a lot of open space, but the knowledge and skills area has hardly anything in it. I usually meditate on a cushion on the floor."

"You have a chair over there in the benefactors and travel area that I'd love to see relocated into the knowledge and skills area. That would be good placement for that piece, since blue and white are ideal colors in this area," Jill said. "From a purely design standpoint, I'd recommend a deep-blue Oriental rug, if you can find one. You don't need to spend a lot of money. Most discount home stores have them. That kind of rug would look terrific with the hardwood floors and that sofa. Toss some blue-and-white throw pillows in various designs onto the sofa to tie it all together."

"I remember you said something about statues in this area. I have a gold Buddha in another room," Amy said.

"Buddha would love to be in this area." Jill looked around. "I think I saw him over there in your fame and reputation area."

Amy stood in the center of the room, running her finger lightly over pursed lips. "What about plants in here?"

"A tall green plant would work well. Keep the bamboo plant in your prosperity corner." Jill leaned against the windowsill and glanced outside at the lake, which featured a fountain in the center. "You have such an obvious love and appreciation for the Japanese culture. How long did you live in Tokyo?"

"I majored in Japanese in college and taught English for three years there," Amy explained. "Then I had a bad breakup with a man—a Japanese man I met while teaching—and I just couldn't bear to live there anymore. It was hard for me there, even though the majority of people were very kind to me. That was a true testament to their gracious culture, since this red hair is a dead giveaway that I'm not Japanese."

"I bet you turned a lot of heads."

Amy smiled. "After I came back to the U.S., I decided to stop teaching English, except as a volunteer for an English as a Second Language class at the community college. The idea to teach yoga and meditation came gradually to me, but now I know it's really what I want to do."

"I had a yoga teacher I liked a lot, but she moved to Soho," Jill said with a rueful look. "That was just too far to go for classes after work. Will you be teaching your class anywhere nearby?"

"The community college has a room I can use, and it seems like a pretty central location. Would you like me to refer you to another yoga teacher closer to where you live?" Amy was already rifling through a drawer in her coffee table for a business card.

"Actually, I'd like to use the teacher I already know."

"But I thought you said you didn't want to commute into the city."

"I meant you."

Chapter Eleven

JILL SAW DENNY MACBRIDE THREE times that week at the homes of two clients. They were becoming friendly enough now that he texted and emailed her several times to touch base between visits. She looked forward to seeing him, although she felt conflicted. Was it possible to remain friends when there clearly was chemistry between them? Denny also stopped by the office one afternoon to pick up his check—something that didn't escape Monica's notice.

"Something tells me that our new painter has designs on you," she said to Jill, who blushed to the roots of her hair.

"We've got a great working relationship," Jill corrected her. "He's good at what he does, and he's friendly and nice, period. That makes working with him more fun for me."

"Mm-hmm," Monica said. "We have direct deposit, you know."

Jill rolled her eyes. "Don't let your imagination run away with you. I'm still married."

"You're legally separated and planning to divorce a cheating spouse. Surely it couldn't hurt for you to consider going out with him," Monica insisted. "You deserve some fun after what you've been through, and I have a feeling he'd be a lot of fun."

"Just for the record, Denny hasn't asked me out. And, anyway, I don't think it's a good idea," Jill said. "For one thing, I'm really busy with projects and teaching my class. Plus, Denny and I work together. I'm guessing that somewhere in the personnel policies, it says, 'Don't date the subcontractors.' "

"It doesn't. I checked," Monica said.

When Jill arrived at the home of new clients that week to do an initial consultation, she was told by the wealthy couple that the reason they had chosen to work with her firm was due in large part to Denny MacBride's recommendation. After many years of using Denny's services for interior painting, the couple had been informed that he was working exclusively with Becker, Hennessy & Johnson.

Jill was elated and immediately drove over after the consultation to the work site where Denny was painting. She intended to thank him for the referral, but knew that there was more to her motives than appreciation. When she saw him, her heart predictably skipped a few beats.

"Well, this is a nice surprise," he said, eyes twinkling. "Are you here to check up on me?"

"Actually, I'm here to thank you for referring a new client to us. That old millhouse is spectacular, and I'll enjoy redecorating that master suite. Denny, Tom and I really appreciate that you're referring your regular painting clients to us. Thank you. Is it true what they said, that you're only working with us now?"

"That's right," Denny said. "I'm working on a new exhibit and need time to finish up a few large pieces. Besides, you're keeping me busy enough. I hope you know how much I enjoy working with you, Jill." He gazed into her eyes.

Jill felt a blush creeping up her neck. "I enjoy working with you, too," she said honestly. "It's wonderful to know that I don't have to worry about clients being satisfied with how the painting process is coming along … or the painter's work habits or manners. I hear nothing but compliments."

Standing so close to Denny, she was conscious of the subtle scent of soap emanating from him. He shifted his weight to his other foot, his eyes never leaving hers. They stood together without speaking for a few moments as deeply unsettling feelings coursed through Jill. She had a strong urge to move closer and realized with embarrassment that, unconsciously, she had just done so. Denny's eyes widened, but he didn't move.

"Jill," he started to say as her face flamed, "are you …?"

"I'd better be going," she said quickly, stepping back. "I just wanted to say thanks again."

"You're welcome." He smiled gently at her. "I hope you do decide to check up on my work."

Jill hurried to her car, started the engine, and drove off. She regretted stopping to see Denny, for surely he had read in her eyes the growing attraction she had for him. It wasn't right to feel this way, not so soon after separating from her husband. It would be a rebound relationship—never a good thing. What would people say, especially after David's behavior?

She also knew that, at least in part, her feelings for Denny came from being alone without David when, for so many years, she had been part of a couple. She missed intimacy and the affectionate behavior of being held and kissed by a man. Far from feeling repelled by the idea of lovemaking after her husband's betrayal, she longed for it, missed what she had enjoyed during her many years with David. Whenever Denny was near, she had a yearning to be held by him. Jill knew that she was growing ever more attracted to him, and that she thought about him more and more. She just hoped that her desire for Denny wouldn't end in disappointment for either of them.

The fame and reputation square of the *bagua* was the subject of the next *feng shui* class, a subject that Jill expected to result in a lively discussion. This area was located in the center of the top three squares of the *bagua* between prosperity and love and relationships. She planned to highlight Chris and his desire for a career as a singer/songwriter. She had asked him to bring a video of his performance on *Stars* so that the class could help him envision his next big move. His classmates were so enthused, in fact, that they were already planning a group outing on Saturday to hear him perform at a club.

"This is the area of the home you want to improve if you want to build your business, gain self-confidence before embarking on a new career, and protect or enhance your career and reputation," she told her students, who sat in a semicircle around the television.

Jill popped Chris's DVD into the machine and hit play. "If you want to become well-known for what you do, like Chris, the fame and reputation square is an easy way to get respect."

They watched in fascination as the host introduced Chris, and he stepped forward to sing his own arrangement of an Elton John song, "Harmony." Chris's tenor-baritone voice and singing style evoked a different kind of soulful feeling to the rock and roll classic. Jill felt her chest swell with pride as she watched Chris sing.

"This is where I blow it," he warned them with a grimace. "Watch how I turn and run like a deer in the headlights. I should've stepped forward, bowed to the audience, and then stood in front of the judges to get my scores. Instead, I turned to get the heck off stage before realizing I hadn't yet heard what the judges had to say." His face reddened at the memory.

They watched as Chris finished the song, bowed, and took off stage right. The host called him back for the judges' comments, which were mostly positive regarding his choice of music and performance. It was an awkward moment, but completely understandable and not nearly as bad as he described it.

"I think you're being too hard on yourself. You were great, and anyone would be nervous being judged by anyone as harsh as that one woman," Jill said. "She's way too tough on people."

"I knew the song well, and it was perfect for my range. I

think I clutched because I was afraid she'd pick apart my performance," Chris said.

"Jill's right. That woman slams everyone," Pam said. "That's just what she does. It's only natural that you'd worry. But her comments weren't that bad, and everyone else thought your song was great."

"A little self-confidence can go a long way," Jill said reassuringly. "We need to be able to see ourselves as others see us. So now, let's look at the elements and important shapes and colors for fame and reputation. They include fire, wood, lights of any kind, the color red, triangles and rectangles, plants of any kind, and photos or symbols representing what you want to become or how you want to be viewed."

"Did you say triangles and rectangles?" Kristen looked confused. "Is one shape more powerful than another?"

"I think triangles are the more powerful shape in this area because triangles are the shape of a flame, and fire is the most powerful element in this area. Rectangles are easy to introduce, too, through framed pictures or even a piece of rectangular furniture like a coffee table."

"What happens if your reputation has already suffered by something that you can't go back and fix, like losing on *Stars*?" Chris asked anxiously.

"Chris, I don't believe your reputation has been hurt by not winning *Stars*. Only one person can win," Jill pointed out. "The very fact that you made it onto the show is evidence of your ability. But if you're worried about what people are saying, I recommend getting a cactus."

Chris looked amused. "A cactus?"

"If you've got a cactus, it shouldn't be placed anywhere in a home other than this area. Imagine that anyone who says anything negative about you is getting jagged by that cactus."

Pam laughed. "So that's the problem. I guess it's time to move the cactus out of my bedroom."

Kristen snorted. "I'm the one with all the bad dates. I'd

better check to make sure I don't have a cactus or any other dangerous object in my relationship corner. Maybe I should move my cuticle scissors, too, just to be safe."

Jill sat on the edge of the desk, dangling her feet as she waited to regain their attention. "It's really important in the fame and reputation square to be careful of unintentional hazards. Obviously in an area where fire is important, you don't want water or even pictures of water. Keep the fame and reputation area as clean as possible, for obvious reasons. You don't want your reputation trashed."

As Jill and her students trooped out to their cars that night, they finalized plans to see Chris perform at a nearby club. Jill smiled her encouragement at him. "I'm really looking forward to hearing you sing. I'm bringing my son and daughter-in-law, too."

She had already made plans to spend that Saturday evening with Missy and Finn. Liam and Brian were going to Brian's parents' home in Vermont for a family reunion. Jill looked forward to an evening out with her students and a chance to get to know them better.

"Thanks, everybody, for coming out Saturday night. With my mom gone, I never have any real fans in the audience," Chris said.

"I bet she's still watching over you," Pam said, reaching over to pat his hand. "Anyway, I feel just as proud as if you were my own son."

ON SATURDAY EVENING, JILL PICKED up Finn and Missy from their apartment in Norwalk. The young couple's two-bedroom apartment was small yet uncluttered, arranged carefully, and furnished with modern, colorful pieces, mostly from IKEA. Jill noted with pleasure that her *feng shui* suggestions to Missy had been heeded. As they walked out to Jill's car, she also noticed that Finn put a protective arm around Missy as they made their way across the uneven sidewalk.

"You sit in front, Missy," Finn said, and opened the door for her, making sure she was belted in before getting in the back seat.

Jill smiled, watching the gentlemanly way her son cared for his wife. Finn and Missy had been sweethearts throughout high school and college, and had married earlier that year. Having watched Missy grow up right along with Finn, Jill loved her like a daughter.

On the drive over, Finn told Jill that David had invited him to play golf the following weekend. "I think he really wants to make it up to Liam and me," he said. "Liam is ignoring him until he invites Brian, too. I don't think that will happen anytime soon."

"Does that hurt Brian's feelings, do you think?" Jill frowned.

"Nah, Brian says he's lived long enough as a gay man that he's used to it. He thinks Liam needs to 'man up' and see Dad on his own."

"Liam has a lot to overcome where your dad is concerned. I just hope for Liam's sake that it's not too late for them to reestablish a relationship."

Finn was quiet for a few moments before saying, "I know this is none of my business, but where do things stand with you and Dad?"

"It definitely is your business," Jill said. "I won't bore you with all the details, but your dad and I are legally separated at this point. The legal part was necessary because I asked him to leave our home. He isn't fighting me on anything, which I appreciate, and he says he wants to do right by me. The house is an issue, of course, but we'll work that out."

"He's sorry for what happened, Mom, even if he can't admit it."

"I'm sure he is." Jill was silent for a moment. "But trust is important in a marriage. It's a value that I uphold for myself. I don't know how I'll ever trust him again—not the way I once did. But I'm also realizing that I want more from marriage now.

I'm different after finding out about his affair. I don't know whether your dad is willing to recognize that or consider what our marriage can be from now on. I just don't know."

Finn and Missy were subdued for the remainder of the drive. Jill was grateful that they didn't press her to consider letting David come home again. Although Liam was in favor of his mother's decision to start legal proceedings, she knew that Finn and Missy, having so recently taken their own vows, had mixed feelings.

As they entered the club where Chris was performing, they were greeted enthusiastically by Jill's students, who sat together at two tables near the stage. Everyone was there, except Joel. When their server appeared, Jill said, "The first round's on me."

"I'll just take a seltzer with fresh lime," Missy said. She looked pale as she sipped her water. Jill was immediately concerned. Missy hadn't spoken much in the car.

"Are you okay?" she asked, feeling Missy's forehead, as Finn's face broke into a grin. "You look a little bit queasy."

"She's a little bit pregnant," Finn said.

Jill nearly dropped her glass of red wine as Trish, Amy, Joni, Kristen, Meredith, and Pam shrieked in unison. Shelly's eyes were wistful, her congratulatory smile stiff as she watched the merriment around her. She took a sip of her iced tea and picked at the buttons on her sweater.

"I had no idea! Hey, everybody, I'm going to be a grandmother!" Jill turned to Missy. "How far along are you?"

"Not very," Missy answered. "I found out for sure today. I thought I was coming down with something. It never occurred to me it might be a baby."

Jill chuckled. "I remember being stunned when I found out I was expecting the twins," she said.

"My daughter and her husband had their first child last year," Pam said as she leaned across the table. "With all these new early home pregnancy tests, it seems like they announced she was pregnant as soon as they crawled out of bed."

Fortified by wine, the group was in high spirits as they waited for Chris to appear onstage. A few minutes later, he walked out from stage right to loud applause from his biggest fans down in front. His band of four musicians on bass guitar, keyboards, saxophone, and drums were already in place.

"Good evening," he said, bowing stiffly. "Thanks, everyone, for coming out tonight. It means a lot to see so many familiar faces in the audience." He shielded his eyes with one hand and grinned at his friends from class.

Taking the microphone in his hand, he said, "My first song tonight is one I wrote a few years ago called 'First Time for Everything.' It's a song about the amazing power of love, even when we believe we're past the point of amazement. Love is always new."

Chris closed his eyes and uttered the first notes of a song that brought a catch to Jill's throat. As she listened to the words he had written, she knew it was a love song for all ages, a song that had the potential to become a wedding classic. Chris's voice was inspiring in its depth and range as he sang the romantic lyrics. He didn't move around the stage much, but connected well with the audience, using his eyes and hands to reach out to them.

"I don't understand why he isn't already a big star," Jill said to Missy when the song was over and the audience clapped its approval. "He really is that good."

"He probably needs to understand that himself," Missy replied. "Can't you work your *feng shui* magic on him?"

"The real magic of *feng shui* is that we're each capable of achieving what we want on our own." Jill squeezed Missy's hand, feeling overcome with happy emotions. "I can't imagine a more wonderful evening than this. I'm overwhelmed—so proud of Chris, so happy that Finn will be a father, and so glad you're the mother of my first grandchild."

Missy's fingers returned the squeeze. "Finn was worried that we didn't have enough money saved and that we're still in an apartment. We might be rushing things." She smiled and shrugged.

"It's true that babies always mean new expenses and lots of changes, but they're reassurance that life goes on. That's what our family needs—a new start."

From the look on Finn's face, Jill knew everything was right with his world. Yet she experienced a pang, thinking about how she and David had always seemed to be such a stable, loving couple. What sort of message was she sending to Finn and Missy if she divorced him without trying to save the marriage? She resolved to strengthen the family area of her home to support her wishes for a happy family life—whatever that meant.

Chapter Twelve

Early Sunday afternoon, Jill drove to Chris's rental home in an older working-class neighborhood. After seeing him perform, she knew he was already well on his way to fulfilling his dream of success in show business, but that he needed a boost of self-confidence. As soon as she caught sight of his rundown house, she knew she had her work cut out for her. It was a tract house in a development of two-bedroom homes built after the war for returning veterans. Over the years, as owners remodeled to add value and individuality, each home had taken on a more distinctive appearance. But they were still quite small, often drab, and built too close together. Chris's house was nondescript—painted a dingy white with faded, peeling black shutters. In place of a porch, two cement blocks served as the entrance to the front door. A peeling wrought-iron front door cried out for a fresh coat of black paint, and the lawn was patchy, with more dirt and weeds than grass.

"Hey, welcome to my not-so-sweet home," Chris said in his jovial way. "You'll probably never see a place as un-*feng shuied* as this one."

"Now, now," Jill said, patting his arm, "every home has its charm and potential."

In response, Chris just laughed and shook his head. "I think you're about to find the exception."

Chris's house was decorated in what Jill could only describe as *early bachelor*, with bookshelves made of plywood planks stacked on concrete blocks, a grungy black futon sofa piled high with blankets and pillows, and an extensive collection of microbrew bottles lined up on a corner shelf as decoration. Stereo equipment, an electric piano, guitar, a drum set, and TV trays took up much of the space in the living room.

The fame and reputation area of Chris's home turned out to be a dining room overlooking a slab patio with an unsavory view of an old strip mall and gas station. Dead potted plants surrounded the perimeter, and more empty beer bottles were lined up near the two resin chairs outside. Chris's dining room table by the window was stacked so high with clutter, it was no wonder he ate on a tray in the living room.

"Balancing the energy and enhancing this general area will be easy, Chris," Jill assured him, hands on her hips. "First, it's really important to keep it clean and orderly. You don't want people trashing you, right?"

Chris laughed. "I never thought of it that way."

"We want to be known for how we present ourselves to the world. Plants are great, but get rid of the dead ones and those empty beer bottles on the patio, too."

Jill pushed open the back door and went out onto the patio. "Remember that the fame and reputation area needs fire, so a really easy fix is to move that red charcoal grill, which is a great fire symbol, into this area to represent the fire element. And that little black table? Spray-paint it green to match those plastic chairs. Black isn't a good color for this area because black represents water, and water puts out fire. Green is an important color in this area because it represents wood. It's also good that you have a big healthy tree, but try to keep the leaves raked."

"Doesn't fire burn wood? Wouldn't that be a destructive element?" Chris asked, scratching his head.

"Fire and wood are complementary in this area because wood feeds fire. Let's picture the creative and destructive cycle. In *feng shui*, we view wood as creative for fire, but destructive to earth because trees uproot soil."

Jill continued to survey the area with a critical eye. She knew Chris didn't have a lot of spare cash, so she had already promised to work with existing items. "Since you use this area for entertaining, you could add some lights. The porch has an overhead light, so turn it on!"

"I have some chili pepper lights I could hang around the back porch door," Chris chimed in helpfully. "The red hot peppers would be like a double dose of fire, right?"

Jill grinned. "Now you're getting the idea. I also want you to have something in this area that relates to your reputation as a singer. You want to display items that pertain to what you want to enhance in your life."

"I've got music awards I could hang on the wall. I could also move posters of my favorite musicians into the dining room—the ones that inspire me."

Jill clapped her hands together. "That's perfect. In *feng shui*, your intent is what matters most. Anything you can do to remind yourself of how good you are as a singer and where you want to go in your career will push you in the right direction. Have confidence in your dreams."

Chris looked thoughtful. "When I got eliminated from *Stars*, I thought I'd really blown my big shot at fame and fortune, even though I knew something about me must have caught the judges' attention in the first place. Otherwise I wouldn't have been picked to be on the show. Now I wake up every morning and picture myself on the stage performing and hearing the applause. I see myself jumping up in the air and high-fiving the other contestants because I've made it to the next round. Unfortunately, I can't go back on *Stars*."

"Maybe not, but I think it's great that you can still envision that scene, which in a way is like changing the outcome. You're very, very good, Chris. I mean that. The more you create a mental movie of what you want to happen in your career, the better your chances are of achieving it."

As Chris walked Jill to her car, she told him, "It's important to have dreams that we continually update as circumstances in our lives change. When one dream comes to pass, we automatically think up another one. In fact, I have a new dream where I host a television show about *feng shui*."

"Maybe I could write the theme song for you," Chris said, smiling.

"You're on, my friend."

DENNY PHONED LATE SUNDAY AFTERNOON as Jill was tossing a salad for dinner. "I'll be over in your neighborhood early this evening and wondered if I could stop by for a few minutes," he said. "I have something I'd like you to take a look at."

Jill's heart skipped a beat. "Of course you can stop by." She wondered what it was that he wanted to show her. "My son, Finn, is here grilling steaks, and my daughter-in-law, Missy, made a beautiful apple pie. Why don't you join us for supper? It's a beautiful evening to eat on the patio."

"I don't want to intrude on your family time," he said, but she could tell from the tone of his voice that he intended to accept her invitation. "I thought you might like to see some digital shots of a few new paintings, in case your clients need art for their homes. If sales go through the gallery, there's a considerable markup."

"I'd love to see more of your work," Jill said. "In fact, I'm looking for a painting for someone with a very special need. We can talk about it when you get here."

She ducked into the first floor bathroom to take a quick peek at her appearance and touch up her makeup. She dabbed a few drops of her favorite perfume oil on her pulse points and examined her outfit—a knee-length denim skirt and a long-sleeved V-neck tee shirt in her favorite periwinkle blue to match her eyes. Satisfied with how she looked, she went back out to the patio and set another place at the table.

"A friend from work is stopping by with something he wants to show me," she explained to Finn and Missy, who were already relaxing on the patio.

At five thirty, Denny arrived. He carried a bottle of red wine, along with a black art portfolio of photos.

"How nice! But you didn't have to bring anything," Jill said as Denny handed her the bottle wrapped in a cloth wine sack.

"Of course I did. I thought about flowers, but didn't want you to think I was overstepping the bounds of decency, bein' that you're still a married woman and all."

Jill blushed. "The wine is perfect. Thank you."

When Denny stepped inside, she offered him a quick, casual, one-armed hug around the neck. To her surprise, he leaned in and held her close for a moment in a way that nearly brought tears to her eyes—it was so comforting and safe. His hug was strong and reassuring, just the kind of hug she needed most from a man at a time when other male friends and colleagues seemed hesitant to touch her for fear of sending the wrong message. Her legs were unsteady as she stepped away from him. She met his eyes for a moment—long enough to see the attraction he felt for her. She had a sense that in a different time and place, this moment could have led to something more, and she was grateful for his sensitivity and restraint. They walked through the house to the patio, where Finn and Missy were drinking iced tea while reclining on the cushioned Adirondack chairs.

"This is Denny MacBride, a very talented artist I've gotten to know recently," Jill said. "He's doing specialty interior painting for our firm. But tonight, he's here to show us some of his artwork. Denny, this is my son, Finn, and my daughter-in-law, Missy."

They exchanged friendly greetings, but the meaningful look that passed between Finn and Missy didn't escape Jill's notice. Finn, especially, looked concerned. Missy, on the other hand, seemed more curious. Jill realized that in her customary way of entertaining others, coupled with her inexperience as a newly separated woman, she hadn't taken into account the reactions of others to Denny's presence. Of course her children would wonder why a strange man had been invited to dinner.

"I've got iced tea, red and white wine, beer, and mineral water. What will you have, Denny?"

"Red wine would be nice," he said. Jill fetched the corkscrew from the kitchen and returned to find Finn interrogating Denny.

"How did you meet my mother?" Finn asked in what could only be described as a fatherly, protective tone of voice.

Missy kicked him under the table. "We're glad you were able to join us tonight," she said, giving Finn a warning look.

"I was working at the home of one of her clients."

"That's cool," Finn said. "And you're an artist, too? What do you paint?"

"Mostly landscapes, but I'll consider an occasional portrait, if I happen to like the face."

Missy laughed and leaned in for a look at his portfolio. For the next several minutes, Denny paged through photos of his paintings as Jill, Finn, and Missy admired each one. There were landscapes of favorite locations around New England and a few mountain and seaside scenes painted from Denny's memories of Scotland.

"I like oceans and mountains," he said. "This one always makes me homesick for Scotland." He pointed to a painting of a white cottage in the hills, surrounded by mountains and a field of wildflowers.

"Oh, I like that one a lot," Jill said.

When they were finished with Denny's portfolio, Jill held up her glass. "Now, I'd like to propose a toast to my first grandchild, expected in May."

"Here, here!" Denny's eyes lit up as he clinked his glass to Jill's, then touched Finn's and Missy's glasses. "Congratulations! That's marvelous."

"Do you have any children, Denny?" Missy asked.

"As they say, 'none that I know of.'" Denny laughed. "I've never been married, either, although I was engaged when I lived in Scotland many years ago."

"How long have you lived in this country?" Jill asked as she sat down on a chaise lounge. She was anxious to know more about Denny, but careful not to seem more than merely curious. She could tell that Finn and Missy were watching her closely, wondering whether there was more to Denny's appearance at dinner than she let on.

"I left Aberdeen in 1985 to work for a fine man, James Thompson, who had a construction business here. His older sister was my teacher."

"But you're working on your own now," Jill prompted.

"Aye, James died about fifteen years ago and his son, William, is runnin' the business. He turned out to be a very different man than his father, and I ended up going out on my own. I've done well, though. I often think of Scotland and the family I left behind, but I've had a much better life here in America."

Over dinner, as they got better acquainted, Jill shared information about the class she was teaching and some of the students' reasons for wanting to know more about *feng shui*. "I have a student whose wife is recovering from cancer, but is still quite ill from the chemotherapy. I've helped them improve the health area of their house, but I think they need one more thing—a painting of a mountain. Triangles are a major symbol in *feng shui*, especially for the health area of the home. Denny, one of your paintings would be perfect in the stairway landing. How much would you charge for the painting of the turquoise and amethyst sky over the misty Scottish mountain?"

"To tell you the truth, I hadn't put a price on it yet," he said, scratching his cheek and looking thoughtful. "Let me think on it and get back to you. I'll make it reasonable."

After dessert, Missy helped Jill with the dishes while Finn and Denny remained on the patio, talking. Jill began to relax as she noted the lack of tension between Finn and Denny. After Missy and Finn headed home, Denny and Jill continued talking and drinking wine until the sun went down and the air temperature dropped at least fifteen degrees. Jill shivered and rubbed her arms. "Let's go inside," she said. "I'll light the fireplace and make some tea."

"Let me start the fire," he said. "It's a man's job to warm the home when a woman has provided such a fine meal."

As he lit the fire and tended it, Jill fixed a tea tray and set it on the coffee table. Then she sat at the far side of the sofa, curling her legs beneath her. She experienced a strange mix of nervousness and excitement being alone with Denny. As she watched him tend the fire, she remembered how she and David used to put the twins to bed and then relax together, often making love on the floor by the fireplace. Now here she was with this very attractive man who was capturing her attention in the same way. She felt a mixture of guilt, anxiety, and pleasure at the thought.

Denny sat down on the other end of the sofa, keeping a comfortable distance between them, before turning to her. "Jill, I know you've been through a difficult time of late. I'd like to get to know you better, but if it's too soon for me to say that, I'll understand. I don't want you to be nervous around me, especially since we work together. Is it too soon for me to say that I'd like to know you better?" The intensity of his gaze left no doubt about his intent.

Jill's cheeks grew warm. She hadn't expected this sort of candor. "I'm flattered, Denny. I'm still feeling a little off-balance at times, but things are getting easier. I'm legally separated now and have filed for divorce, but I still think it would be best if we take things slow on a personal level. I have no idea what will happen in the months to come. I'm sure I'll have some tough times. I wouldn't want you to get caught in the cross-fire, if there is any."

"I don't doubt you'll have your good and bad days. But are you sure the marriage is really over?" Denny looked at her with searching eyes. "I can imagine it would be a hard thing to accept."

"I'm beginning to understand that my marriage was probably over a long time ago, only I didn't know it," she said as she picked up her cup of tea. "As it is, the affair went on for at least a year before I found out. I'm apparently a little slow on the uptake." She sighed.

"Not if you had no reason to suspect anything. Ye canna blame yourself."

She reached for a dog-eared copy of the most recent *Celebrity* magazine and opened it to a photo of David looking handsome, as usual, in a tuxedo. Jill had viewed the page so often, the magazine opened naturally to that spot.

"Here he is at some kind of awards dinner, standing with this woman. I don't know who she is, and the article doesn't say he's her escort, but why else would she be in the picture?" Jill shrugged. "When I saw that photo, I had a strong feeling that she might be yet another in a long string of David's so-called distractions."

"She's not as pretty as you are," Denny said loyally, and Jill laughed. "We can start off as friends and see where things go from there."

Jill smiled, her cheeks growing rosy. "I definitely would like to get to know you better." She lowered her gaze. "In the meantime, I appreciate your friendship."

Denny glanced at his watch and then set his cup down. "And true friends don't overstay their welcome. I really ought to be going. Thanks for a wonderful dinner and great conversation. I really enjoyed meeting your kids and being part of the baby celebration."

"I'm glad you could join us," Jill said in a voice that was barely audible as she experienced a touch of vertigo. As they stood together, Denny touched his lips to her cheek and lingered for a moment before releasing her with a smile and a light caress of her cheek. He picked up his portfolio. "Thanks for letting me come over."

"I'm glad you called," she said honestly.

"I'll be in touch about that mountain painting," he said as he turned to leave. "Oh, and I wish you'd stop by the job site sometime late morning tomorrow and check out the library and the great room. I've got most of the painting done in there and just have to finish the enamel, so you can say if my work passes muster."

"I already approve of your work; you know that. But I'll stop by around eleven o'clock, just to admire what you've done," she said. "Be careful driving home."

He turned to wave before getting into his truck and driving away. She shut the front door and turned off the porch light, hugging herself as she remembered what he'd said and the way she'd felt when he hugged her.

"At some point, I'd better *feng shui* the romance corner of my own house," she said. "And this time, I'll make it foolproof."

Chapter Thirteen

As she watched Denny step out of his truck the next morning, Jill felt strangely shy, remembering his embrace the night before. Denny, on the other hand, flashed a confident grin as he made his way toward her. As he opened her car door, Jill's stomach did a flip-flop. He wore a black knit turtleneck and dark jeans that hugged his muscular thighs. His hair was still damp from the shower.

"Good morning," she greeted him as she stepped out of the car and shaded her eyes against the dazzling early morning sunshine.

"Aye, that it is." His eyes twinkled, taking in the sight of her.

Jill mentally kicked herself as she felt the heat rise in her face. They walked across the driveway to the front door of the Colver home and were greeted by the housekeeper, Pilar, who informed them that the homeowners were staying in a hotel until the project was complete.

"Mrs. Colver, she no like the smell," Pilar said. "She said she come back when this all done."

"I'm sure Mr. and Mrs. Colver will be relieved when the work here is finally complete," Jill told Denny. "This project has been behind schedule from the start, thanks to remodeling delays. They're anxious to get the new furniture, rugs, and art in place."

As they entered the library, Jill admired Denny's work and then showed him photos of other furniture, art, and upholstery design elements she planned to use to complete the room. "Now that this project has been so successful, there is another big interior painting job coming up in Westport. Maybe we ought to start talking about that project."

"Are you saying you want to spend more time with me?" Denny asked, flashing a teasing grin. "We *could* conduct all our business over email, you know. I don't normally spend this much time with interior designers."

"I could just add you to the Monday afternoon project memos. Then you wouldn't have to see me at all." She offered an angelic smile.

"I've a better idea. What are you doing at noon today?"

"I have a lunch meeting with Tom Becker." She tilted her head sideways, wishing that were not the case. "We always meet on Mondays."

"What about dinner tonight?"

Jill hesitated as thoughts flooded her head about what Tom Becker might say if he knew she was going out to dinner with Denny. "I don't know if that's such a good idea."

"We can discuss work, if that makes you feel more comfortable. What if I pick you up at six thirty? Let's go to Mario's. Have you ever been there?"

"No, but I read a good review about the chef. I've wanted to try it."

"The place is small, but it has an imaginative menu and a good wine list. I think you'll like it a lot."

They returned to Jill's car as a strong wind kicked up. Jill wrapped her sweater tightly around her while trying without success to keep her hair from flying in all directions. Denny smoothed a wisp of flyaway hair from her face, his hand lightly grazing her cheek.

"Six thirty it is, then."

"Okay," Jill said, shivering, whether from the wind or his touch, she couldn't be sure. Part of her sensed that she should have declined the invitation. But now that plans were made, she was excited at the thought of spending an entire evening with Denny over a leisurely meal.

After making a stop to pick up a set of framed prints for the Colvers' new home office, she drove back to Stamford to meet Tom at the deli where they usually had lunch. He had already ordered for her—a chai tea latte and a turkey on wheat berry bread, heavy on the guacamole, with sprouts. She slid into the seat across from him.

"Hey, thanks," she said, looking surprised. "You ordered exactly what I wanted."

"You've been eating the same sandwich for the past three years, Jill," Tom said, raising his eyebrows. "It's always turkey on wheat berry with guacamole and a medium chai latte with almond milk."

"I guess I'm sort of predictable, eh?"

"Not lately."

"What do you mean?" she asked, biting into the sandwich, which oozed guacamole.

"I used to think I knew you, but the past month or so has shown me a different Jill."

"The old Jill has been blown up and pieced back together, more or less," she said in what she hoped was an offhand manner. "Surely the new Jill isn't too foreign. Okay, so what's so different about me?"

"I'm not sure," Tom said, eyes narrowing. "I guess it's just that you're doing so much better dealing with the David situation than I thought you would. You've always had a blind spot where he was concerned. Admit it. I thought you'd be like that country song and stand by your man."

"I'm sure you aren't the only one who thought I'd pretend that what he did meant nothing. I'm betting a lot of his viewers think I should have swallowed my pride and given him a second chance." Jill frowned. "And they may be right. Perhaps I should have delayed the decision to separate. Maybe I shouldn't already have filed for divorce. But I think what still irks me the most is that he expected me to forgive him and continue on just like before the affair. A little counseling, a little more attention—maybe a trip or a piece of jewelry, and Jill would be fine." She paused. "I'm sure that's what he thought I'd do, and why wouldn't he think that? Liam says I've always given him a pass, and I have. Apparently, even you believe I've been spineless."

"That's not what I meant," Tom interjected, but she cut him off.

"Never mind," she said, holding up one hand. "As for my so-called blind spot, I couldn't very well have gone through married life expecting the worst, could I?"

"I thought you'd separate for a few days and then take him right back. You two have been together a long time."

"Yes, we have," she replied, stiffening. "And I'm still feeling my way through the grieving process and what my marriage meant to me. Nothing in my life is the same anymore, except work. But over the past couple of weeks, I've come to the realization that life goes on. It'll go on whether I accept the changes or not. Who knows? It might even be better."

They ate in silence for a few moments before she changed the subject. "Hey, did I tell you that Finn and Missy are expecting a baby in May?"

Tom slapped his hand on the table. "No, you didn't. That's great! It's sort of hard to believe, though." He chuckled. "I remember when the boys were real little. You used to bring them to the office and put them in that gigantic playpen—that is, until they learned to leapfrog over each other."

"I remember." Jill groaned at the memory of Finn and Liam racing around the office in diapers with other staff members dodging their movements and stepping over toys. "It's hard to believe how fast those years went by, and now Finn is married and about to become a father."

She sipped her tea and stared off into space, thinking. "Things certainly happen fast—not always the way I envisioned them. Children grow up. People grow apart." Her attention returned to Tom, who was looking intently at her. "What about you?"

"I thought my life would turn out much differently," Tom said, expelling a long breath. "I never imagined I'd end up a widower or that I'd stay in Connecticut this long. I always imagined myself living on a beach in Southern California. You, on the other hand, always knew exactly what you wanted. It was always David. And now I wonder whether you've given any thought to what you want in life now that David seems to be out of the picture."

"I don't have a plan, since I'm making it up as I go along. But I am learning that I'll be fine. I know that what David did was merely a symptom of a bigger problem we had. I excused him from marriage and fatherhood while I took on the bigger load. The balance of our relationship was often off kilter, and I didn't really have expectations of what I should be getting in return. I guess I thought that if I just kept believing in the good and setting forth positive intentions—rather than thinking or fearing the worst—all would be well. I thought if I could create the perfect home life for us, David would be happy, too."

Tom leaned his elbows on the table. "That's a pretty strong element of control you took on, isn't it? But then again, how could you *not* believe you had to make everything work?"

"What do you mean?" Jill's brow furrowed.

"As long as I've known you, there has been tremendous pressure on you to be perfect, to look perfect, act perfect. For chrissake, you're the daughter of America's favorite household advice columnist! Creating the perfect home and making it look easy was something you'd been groomed for. David couldn't have had a better, more perfect wife if the network had picked you out for him themselves. The trouble is, I don't think he ever really appreciated who you are."

Jill smiled at the unexpected compliment but she also took in a slow breath in an attempt to maintain her composure. "I wonder now if I was so focused on creating the perfect life that I overlooked what was right in front of my face. Clearly, David wasn't happy with me or he wouldn't have cheated."

The distress on her face was evident as she glanced quickly out the window, unwilling to let Tom see her cry. "I'm wondering if our marriage was more about looking and acting perfect, part of the public relations package that David's career required of him, than creating a happy life together. We were expected to be the perfect couple, and we couldn't behave otherwise without affecting his career. The trouble was, I thought we really were the perfect couple."

Tom reached for her hand. "I'd venture to say that there is an element of superficiality in the way most married couples present themselves to others. In your case, though, I wonder if any marriage could survive the kind of pressure you were under."

Jill removed her hand from Tom's and dug through her handbag for a tissue. Tears welled up. When she could speak again, she began slowly, choosing her words with care. "I think what I'm saying is that it's possible David got caught up in a life he didn't want. In a way, so did I. I wanted a happy family life similar to what I had growing up, without all the drama his career brought to our lives. Oh sure, at first it was exciting. But then it was just really, really hard. Maybe he wanted something different, too, and just didn't know how to say it. Maybe he was afraid to make changes because of how others would judge him."

"Did you stay, too, because it was easier than leaving?" Tom's eyes never left hers.

Jill shook her head. "It never occurred to me to leave. I believe in fixing things, not breaking them. David made a choice to find love elsewhere, and although I don't agree with what he did, I now understand that it's not something I could fix even with the best of intentions. *Feng shui* can fix a lot of things, but it can't change another person, especially if that person wants something entirely different."

Tom shifted in his seat and then leaned forward, meeting her gaze. "David had it all, Jill. I've watched you give everything you had to him over the years, and all he did was take. If he was unhappy—and God knows, I have no idea why or how he could be unhappy with you—he could have been honest about it. Instead he chose to be dishonest. It's unfortunate that you were the last to see it."

She gave him a warning look. "Well, the time has come that I'm able to imagine a different, happier life. But I still want the same things I wanted when I was younger—to find a partner to share a home with and to continue growing in my career. I've loved teaching this class, and I'd like to keep doing that, too." She shrugged. "Correction: I *thought* I had it all, but I was mistaken."

Tom leaned forward. "I never thought I'd see the day you'd be a free woman, Jill. Wherever David led, you followed. You couldn't even see who he was, and you never wanted to hear anything that didn't fit in with your view of him. I was his fraternity brother and his friend, so I knew he wasn't who you thought he was."

"I know you had concerns about him before we got married. You told me you didn't think he would be the kind of husband I wanted or needed. Turns out, you were right. But I'm not sorry for loving David or being his wife for so long, or having his children. I saw what every other person who has met him or seen him on television saw—a good looking, intelligent man. Did his character really change? Or did I simply not see his true character, only the one he wanted me to see?"

"And can you really imagine life with someone else?" Tom looked earnestly into her eyes.

"Yes, I can. But it's too soon to think about that." Jill pushed her sandwich away, sensing an uncomfortable shift in the conversation that left her feeling vulnerable and anxious. It wasn't like Tom to press on a personal subject this hard. They usually talked about business.

"What I really want to know, I guess, is whether our friendship could ever become anything more than what it's been since the day we first met. Don't I deserve my chance with you?"

The plaintive look on his face stabbed Jill in the pit of her stomach. Her throat constricted as a choking sensation overcame her. She took a quick drink of her latte. "Tom, this is such a surprise. I-I'm so touched that you would think of me that way. You've always been my best friend; it just never occurred to me to want or expect anything more with you. I was with David and you were with Janice. Janice was my friend, too."

"I've been alone for several years, and now that you're single again, what's to prevent us from exploring another dimension of our relationship, when you're ready, of course?"

She blinked, wondering how long he had felt this way. "I think we need to consider that we're business partners and friends, and we don't want to risk ruining that. Tom, you're a wonderful man and I love you dearly. But we have too much to lose if we were to start a romantic relationship and it doesn't work out. We'd lose the 'us' we've always been to each other. I'm not sure I can go through the loss of another relationship that has been part of my life for so long."

She saw the pain in Tom's eyes and was heartsick. He gathered up his untouched lunch and tossed it in a nearby trash bin. "Well, I had to give it my best shot," he said. "I hope this won't change the dynamics of our friendship or our working relationship." He pushed open the front door and turned to look at her. "Of course, it will."

"Tom, wait!" She leaped to her feet and sprinted to the door. She grabbed his forearm, fighting back tears. "I feel terrible.

I never saw this coming. Surely you know I'd never say or do anything to hurt you, not intentionally."

"I do know that," he said, meeting her eyes before turning and walking out.

She took double steps to keep up with him. "Please try to understand. I meant it when I said I can't bear the thought of risking what we've meant to each other all these years, especially now."

Tom offered a half smile. "And I thought what we already had together all these years might provide a better start than what most new relationships offer."

Jill stopped, watching his retreating back as he continued along the sidewalk to their building. Now that the cool air was clearing her head, she thought about corralling him in his office until she knew everything was okay between them. At the same time, she was angry. *How dare he lay this at my doorstep when I'm just weeks out of a long marriage and the worst heartache I've ever endured?* Yet, she had to admit that this was exactly what Denny had asked her to do, and her reaction had been completely different.

For the rest of the afternoon, she agonized over her conversation with Tom, straddling the line between guilt at hurting his feelings and annoyance that he had altered their relationship with his request. But more than that, she felt sadness at this strange turn of events, as if she'd already lost him as a friend. They avoided looking directly at each other, sidestepping in the hallway, until Monica asked if anything had happened at lunch.

"Okay, spill. What's going on with you and Big T?"

"Just a different viewpoint on something," Jill said quickly and retreated into her office.

She wished Tom had never brought up the subject of a romantic relationship, and she wished even more that her response hadn't hurt him. The truth was that she couldn't even imagine a romantic relationship with Tom. Although he was a smart, attractive man with a witty personality, she had never felt anything remotely resembling chemistry with him. Theirs had been a supportive, easygoing friendship with none of the male/female complications that could trip up working relationships between men and women. Embarking on a romantic relationship could be deadly to their business partnership as well.

On the other hand, a similar personal/professional struggle might present itself where Denny was concerned. Jill wondered how Tom would react now if he learned she was going out for a friendly dinner tonight with the painter he had just hired. No doubt he would be offended. There might even be repercussions.

"Ugh," she said, "this is a nightmare."

She struggled all that afternoon with regret over her unexpected conversation with Tom, considering ways that she could resolve any potential issues without hurting him further. The situation was less dangerous with Denny than with Tom, but it was still a risk. If her relationship with Denny went south at some point, the company might lose a valuable contractor. But this was less likely to present a problem than if she and Tom were unable to work together. In that case, she would feel pressured to leave the company.

The entire situation was surreal. Had it been only six weeks since life as she knew it changed forever? And now two men— who were not even her husband—had expressed their desire to have a romantic relationship with her. "Go figure," she said out loud.

She hadn't realized until Denny put his arms around her when he came to her home for dinner just how attracted she already was to him. Yet she also understood the ramifications of spending time with him, especially while she was still technically married. He was becoming a frequent subject of her daydreams. She wondered if it was a wiser course of action to put the brakes on the personal side of their relationship before anything of a more intimate nature happened and one of them got hurt.

After the unsettling experience with Tom, she wondered if going out to dinner with Denny was even such a good idea. But the truth was that she was looking forward to seeing him again. Sighing deeply, she had to acknowledge that no matter what happened with Denny, there would be a shadow over her relationship with Tom for the foreseeable future.

Chapter Fourteen

WHEN JILL RETURNED HOME FROM the office that evening, she found a message on her answering machine from Liam. "Hi, Mom—just wanted you to know Brian and I are back. Finn told us about the bun in Missy's oven. Sounds like good times all around. Give me a call when you can. Love you!"

Jill chuckled and returned Liam's call, only to get voicemail. After the beep, she said, "It's your mother. Glad you guys are back safely. I'll be out this evening, but I'll call you back tomorrow." She didn't provide any other details of her plans, although she knew Liam would approve of her dinner with Denny.

She showered and dressed carefully, selecting a pair of figure-flattering gray slacks, a black silk shell, and black boiled-wool cardigan. She donned pearl earrings and touched floral perfume oil to her pulse points. Promptly at six thirty, Denny rang the doorbell. When Jill answered the door, she spotted a sporty red Mazda Miata in the driveway, its top down.

"I love convertibles!" she exclaimed. "It's even red!"

"It's my favorite new toy," Denny said with a grin. They walked to the car, and he held open the door for her to slide in.

"I bought it as a present to myself for my forty-ninth birthday this year."

"We're the same age." Jill admired the leather interior with its attractive red-and-black tartan seat covers. "I probably shouldn't ask about your birthday."

"In case my horoscope isn't a match?" he asked with an impish grin. "I'm a Pisces, by the way—February twenty-fourth."

"No, in case I'm older than you," she corrected him with a coy glance from beneath her lashes. "I'm a whole month older than you, so remember to respect your elders. By the way, Pisces and Capricorns get along just fine." She cast her eyes around the car, admiring it. "Gosh, I haven't been in a convertible since, well, I can't remember." Actually, she did remember, but decided not to mention the Triumph Spitfire that David had owned for many years.

"Will it be too breezy for you if I leave the top down?" Denny asked as he started the ignition, cruised onto Jill's street and then pulled out onto the main road.

"Nope, this feels great," Jill said as the wind played havoc with her hair. The crisp autumn air smelled of burning leaves, and she had a strong desire to ask Denny to forget dinner and just keep driving. Who cared where they ended up?

"Before this evening officially begins, I'd like to say that I fancy you, Jill. That might make me say or do something stupid, especially after a glass of wine. Forgive me if that happens." He grinned, not looking at all apologetic.

"I doubt there is anything you can say or do that I haven't thought of myself," she said, shocking herself. "But I appreciate your restraint."

"Well, all right then," Denny said and stepped harder on the gas pedal.

Being with Denny was like swirling in a whoosh of colorful energy. He had a sharp mind and a quick wit coupled with a genuine interest in other people. He was a good listener, and they conversed easily as they drove to Mario's, a restaurant nestled in a quiet, wooded area near a small lake.

"Tell me about your family," he said. "Are your parents still with us?"

"They're both alive and well, thank you for asking. My dad, Hal, is a retired dentist who plays golf every chance he gets. He also happens to be the alter ego for my mother, Nancy Brenneman, otherwise known as *Nancy Knows*."

"Go on! I read her columns every day. She's verra funny."

"She's a character," Jill acknowledged wryly. "Thank goodness my dad isn't anxious to be in the spotlight, although my mother mentions him in just about every column. Actually, I don't remember a time when my mom hasn't been a household name. She started writing her columns for the local newspaper just for something to do. It was so popular, the column ended up getting syndicated. Her writing career really took off after that. My dad just takes it all in stride. Of course, Mom was always there when I got home from school, and she was a stickler about family meals. We ate together as a family every night."

"My maw didn't have much time for any life other than raising seven children," Denny said. "Da worked hard to provide for us, and we always had enough to eat, but Maw didn't have many conveniences. It was a hard life for her."

The evening air smelled deliciously of wood smoke, charbroiled meat, and cinnamon apples as they made their way inside Mario's. Jill was delighted that Denny had reserved a table nearest the fireplace. As he reviewed the restaurant's impressive wine list, Jill studied his face, admiring his hair, a lock of which fell boyishly across one side of his forehead, the nose that had a slight bump on the bridge, and the strong chin with the merest shadow of a beard. Tonight he wore pressed khakis and a light blue dress shirt with a navy cardigan. She had never seen him look anything other than immaculately dressed. As he glanced over the menu, she admired his hands with their clean, closely trimmed fingernails. Strong hands that could do a day's work and still be gentle—or so she imagined.

"Jill?"

"Oh, I'm sorry. Yes, I would like wine, thank you. I was just thinking ... never mind. I guess I'm just reveling in the fact that it's been so long since I was out to dinner without a care in the world other than what to order for dinner. But it's also the novelty of being here and feeling normal."

Denny poured wine in Jill's glass and then his. "After what ye've been through, I can imagine it's nice to relax a bit. But trust me, the pleasure is all mine."

"I hope you realize that by having dinner together, we've taken a huge step toward creating a potential conflict of interest at Becker, Hennessy and Johnson," Jill said with a mischievous glint in her eye. "We have to agree that no matter what happens after this, we still have to work together and act nice."

"I'm not concerned." Denny held up his glass. "It's just dinner, Jill. We haven't gone to bed together yet, although I imagine that will happen soon enough."

Jill sputtered and set her wine glass down on the table. "You *are* confident, aren't you?"

"I'm a man who knows what he wants, and I don't believe in playing guessing games. And now, I recommend we do something really dangerous and have the Caprese salad. No telling where things will go from there. We might even end up having dessert, and wouldn't that be scandalous? Now, tell me what on the menu looks good to you."

Suddenly Jill was ravenous. "The coconut macadamia-encrusted shrimp looks great."

"There's a lot of heat in that dish, as I remember. I'm thinking of the sea bass. It's got a nice lemony sauce."

"Do you come here often?" She hoped she sounded nonchalant. Denny's familiarity with the menu led her to wonder how many times he had dined here, and with whom. *Stop that*, she scolded herself.

"I come here about once a week. I live not far." He glanced up in time to see one of the servers blow him a kiss. His face colored deeply as he nodded in her direction. "I like to cook, but by the time I get done on a job site, clean my brushes and rollers, and prepare for the next day, I'm often too tired to fix a decent meal. Do you like to cook?"

"I love to cook, actually. When the boys lived at home, I made dinner nearly every evening. They complained that their friends got to eat fast food, but I never wanted my career to deprive them of home-cooked meals like I remember from my childhood. Sometimes David was there for dinner, but most of the time, that wasn't the case. I still thought it was important for us to have family time."

"My maw felt the same. Our meals were simple, but all seven of us were expected to use our best table manners and talk nicely with one another."

"Seven children, my goodness," Jill said, shaking her head.

"Aye, Maw is a saint."

"Tell me about your parents, Denny. What did your father do for a living?"

"Da was a stonemason. He's not alive anymore, but my mother still lives in the thatch-roof cottage where I grew up in Aberdeen. I get back once a year to visit, sort of like the prodigal son." He paused and sipped his wine. "When I left, it wasn't under the best of circumstances."

"Horse thief?"

"Sheep stealer, actually." He grinned and refilled her glass.

"What really happened, if you don't mind the nosy question?"

While she waited for his response, Jill took a bite of her Caprese salad, which was delicious. The tomatoes were ripened perfectly, and the basil was pungent, the mozzarella creamy and full of flavor. After several weeks of eating meals while standing up at the kitchen counter or in front of the television, she was glad for a leisurely meal in a restaurant. She also hadn't expected to feel this at ease with a man she barely knew.

"I was engaged to a girl in Aberdeen," Denny explained. "I worked for her father's construction company. When I decided to come to America, I'm afraid no one was very happy about the way I did it. Of course, I wouldn't have made it here if I'd done it any other way. You see, I was given an incredible opportunity, complete with a generous loan that allowed me to buy a plane ticket to get here. Thanks to my teacher, Maeve, whose brother James lived in Connecticut. She believed in me, you see. I did it fast before I could change my mind. When I told Cara, my fiancée, she made quite a fuss, as well you would expect, since the *banns* were just weeks away. Her father let it be known that he'd kill me if I *didn't* leave. He had quite a temper, Ian did. I said goodbye to my parents and stayed at my teacher's house until I left Scotland."

"That must have been hard to walk away from your fiancée, not to mention your homeland. You obviously loved Cara or you wouldn't have planned to marry her."

Denny sighed. "I did care for Cara, but I didn't love her the way she deserved. She was verra beautiful and would have made a fine wife and mother. And I doubt our temperaments would have suited in the end. I admit it; I chose my own happiness." He shrugged. "You might say that was selfish, and you'd be right."

"Selfishness is taking care of one's self, which doesn't seem so bad, if you think about it," Jill said. "I've been thinking that if I'd been more selfish, David and I might have had a happier life together. If I'd told him I wanted him home more often and insisted that we spend more time together and with our boys, he might not have done what he did."

"When a man decides to cheat, there isna much a woman can do to stop him," Denny said as he offered Jill a bite of fish. "He's a scoundrel, that's a fact, and there'll be no excusin' David's behavior. I'm just saying you ought not to blame yourself."

Jill accepted the forkful of flaky sea bass, savored it, and swallowed. "Thanks for saying that. Now I want to take my time and make careful decisions. The divorce is in process and will be finalized, I think, after the first of the year. I'm moving in that direction because I can't imagine ever returning to married life with David. So far, things have gone well in mediation. David has already agreed in principle to most of the usual conditions my attorney wrote into the agreement. I didn't ask for much." She gave a rueful laugh.

"Would he like to be back in your good graces, I suppose?"

"That's a sore subject," Jill said. "Let's not talk about David anymore. I want to know more about you and your art career. My clients have been thrilled with your paintings. I'm happy to recommend your work."

"I appreciate that. By the way, I meant to tell you that the Scottish mountain watercolor you admired for your student's home can be delivered any day now."

"That's great. I ought to tell them how much you're asking for it, though, and allow them to decide if it's in their budget."

"I'd consider it my privilege to let them have the painting as a gift. If they hate it, they can give it back. If they love it and the young wife recovers her good health, it'll be payment enough."

"Denny, that's very generous." She was deeply touched. "I'd love for you to meet them. Then you'll understand what a good thing you're doing."

"When you've been blessed with as many lucky breaks as I have, it's important to give back. I haven't been able to get their story out of my mind since you told it to me."

They finished their meal as the dessert cart appeared at the table, and listened as their server provided elaborate descriptions of the five offerings. Jill saw a deep dish caramel-drizzled apple pie, dense chocolate ganache tart, chocolate-cherry cannoli, fresh berry shortcake, and peach cobbler. "Everything looks delicious," she declared, "but I don't believe I need anything else tonight."

Denny flashed a wide-eyed *Are you crazy* look and said, "I'd like the cannoli, please, and bring two forks. I'm feeling reckless tonight, and she's not getting away with being cautious."

Jill laughed. "It's a Monday night. How reckless can we possibly get?"

"Don't tempt me or you'll find out."

When dessert came, he offered the plate to Jill first. "You really have to try it," he said. "These cannoli are a wee bit of heaven on earth."

Jill bit into the forkful of sweet mascarpone filling, dark chocolate shavings, and tiny bits of cherry in a crunchy shell dusted with powdered sugar. Denny was right: to hell with her diet. They finished both cannoli in record time, punctuating their oohs and aahs with satisfied sighs. When the check came, Denny accepted it from the server and pulled a pair of readers out of his pocket. Jill couldn't help smiling when she noticed they were decorated in bold primary colors. She knew few men secure enough in their manhood to pull off that look, much less with such panache.

He waved off her attempt to pay for her own meal. "Don't be silly. I'm making a small fortune off your company."

The sun had already gone down as they made their way through the chilly night air to Denny's car. Even though the top was up on the car, Jill wrapped her wool sweater tightly around her as he started the engine. She glanced over at his profile, and her heart skipped a beat. She found him every bit as handsome as David—more so.

"Would you consider coming over to my house for a cup of tea or a nightcap?" he asked. "I promise to behave myself. I'd like to show you my koi."

"Now that's an interesting proposition." Jill wasn't sure she had heard him correctly. "Did you say koi, as in goldfish?"

"Yes, I have four big, beautiful koi: Flopsy, Mopsy, Cotton-tail, and Peter."

"Now I know I shouldn't trust you."

"I'm serious. I couldna think of any other names that had quite the same ring to them. And it is no' like they come when I call, anyway."

Jill laughed, shaking her head. The man was adorable. As they parked in front of Denny's craft-style bungalow, Jill was struck speechless by the rich color of the lapis lazuli blue door on the reddish-orange brick house. The bungalow was exactly as she guessed it would be: stylish yet unpretentious, decorated in a mix of bold color and sophisticated accents. She admired his coastal-style living room with its soft palette of creamy vanilla and cerulean blue hues highlighted by a large globe and atlases. The bookshelves and walls were adorned with seashells and starfish. The combination of an overstuffed, cream-colored sofa, blue cushions, and distressed wood furniture appeared almost feminine in design, yet there was a strong masculine element in the placement of each object.

A four-season porch attached to the living room was painted a rich hydrangea color that complemented the white and blue décor of the living room. This was Denny's art studio and included a large table with mason jars filled with paintbrushes and trays of watercolor tubes arranged by hue. Several easels displayed finished paintings. The effect was surprisingly neat and orderly. The dining area was a spectacular mix of autumn colors—shades of muted and burnt orange, pine green, and creamy birch white with a huge pine trestle table and benches. An oversized painting on the wall above the dining room table depicted a peaceful lake with a blue sky and jewel-toned autumn trees reflected on its surface.

"This is gorgeous!" Jill said in astonishment. "I love all the color."

"There's one more room I want you to see. This is my newest creation." Denny pushed open the door across the hallway to the master suite.

Jill's jaw dropped. Stepping into this room was like walking into a mountain masterpiece with a mixture of serene colors from yellow and dusky violet to the lightest pearl gray. A dark gray stone color accented one entire wall. This room featured spectacular mountain paintings displaying the grandeur of craggy rocks in concert with seasonal trees, spectacular sunrises, and sunsets. It was the headboard of the king-size bed, however, that brought a gasp of admiration from Jill. The bed, which was arranged diagonally in the corner, was topped with a headboard in colors of stone, pearl gray, and dusky violet that Denny had built himself to give the illusion of a mountain range.

"This is unbelievable!" Jill touched the headboard as if expecting it to be made of real stone. "I don't know if you realize it, but these colors and the design you've chosen for this area of the house are ideal *feng shui*, because this is your health area. You've got lots of earthy tones and that candle garden to represent fire. Even the headboard is ideal. This room is perfect, Denny."

As they walked down the hall through the bungalow, their last stop was the kitchen, which was painted a rich tomato red with a sage green ceramic tile floor and charcoal granite countertops. Shelves along the backsplash displayed whimsical hand-blown glass ornaments of various fruits and vegetables. More original paintings by Denny were on display in this room—still life watercolors of wine bottles, wineglasses, fruit, and cheese platters. The overall effect was sophisticated, yet warm and inviting—perfect for the romance area of his house.

"We're not quite through yet," Denny said and drew her out the back door to the red brick patio built on two levels.

Tucked in the center of vibrant red Japanese maple trees that lined the perimeter was the koi pond, a bamboo table, and four chairs. "Have a seat and enjoy the koi while I get us something to drink," he said and disappeared into the kitchen.

The air was too cool to remain outdoors for long. Jill shivered and was surprised moments later to feel delicious, unexpected warmth on her shoulders. Denny had turned on a tall outdoor heater by the table. He stepped outside carrying a bottle of wine and two stem-less wineglasses.

"I've always loved the outdoors and thought it a shame that

I couldn't use this patio earlier in the spring and later into the fall," he said as he poured her a glass of zinfandel. "The Japanese theme out here pleases me."

"It's heavenly," Jill said, leaning back on her cushioned chair to gaze up at the moonlit, indigo sky. "This would be where I'd choose to meditate. It's so serene."

"Aye, I've spent many a quiet early morning out here, dreamin' and plannin.' "

They drank their wine and talked, forgetting about the time until Denny glanced at his watch.

"I ought to be getting you home now." He took her hands and brought Jill to her feet. "To be continued."

Jill allowed Denny to wrap his arms around her for a moment. She shivered again, this time in anticipation, as he tipped her chin toward him and kissed her lightly. The sensation of his lips, so warm and soft, left no doubt about his feelings for her. Suddenly, the kiss deepened, and Jill tasted the sweetness of the wine on his tongue. She returned his kiss with a passion she knew couldn't be contained for long. Whatever happened now, it was pointless to ignore the deepening attraction she experienced whenever he was near.

"So much for mere friendship," she said lightly, when they stepped apart.

"I can't say I'm sorry," he admitted. "I've wanted to do that since the first day I saw you at your house, wearing those captivating elbow-length blue cleaning gloves." He grinned.

"Not such a good memory for me, I'm afraid," she said, wincing. "I was mortified that you caught me like that. It is definitely not my best look."

"Oh, I thought you looked fine," he said, lifting his eyebrows. "In fact, I'd like you to wear that outfit again for me someday. Then I'll get to live out my initial fantasy."

She colored deeply, but couldn't restrain the laugh that escaped her lips. "And with that comment, I think you ought to take me home. It's a school night, after all."

"Aye, it is," he said, laughing.

Later at home, as she removed her makeup and patted moisturizer on her face, she noticed the rosy glow emanating from her skin and thought of the way she had looked as a young bride, happily in love, with nothing but high hopes for the future. She removed her wedding rings to apply lotion to her hands and then, humming to herself, placed them in the jewelry box on her dressing table. Then she opened the hall closet and rummaged through several boxes. She retrieved a velvet red heart-shaped box and placed it symbolically in the relationship corner of the house.

"Let this serve as my intention for love," she said with a satisfied smile, as Chris's lyrics "Love is always new" ran through her head.

Chapter Fifteen

❧

Family was the subject of Tuesday evening's *feng shui* class. To everyone's delight, Joel arrived, looking tired but happy. He reported that Diana was home again and starting to eat a little. Jill couldn't wait to tell him about Denny's generous offer of a painting. She walked over and began explaining the colors in the painting, how the scene depicted a Scottish mountain range, and how nice it would look in his stairway. She finished by telling him that the artist wanted to give them the painting so that Diana could regain her health.

"Joel, this painting is perfect for your health area," she said. "You'll love it."

"Wow, I don't know what to say." Joel raked his lower teeth over his upper lip, looking as if he might decline the gift. "Why would he do something that nice for people he doesn't even know?"

"I think he's paying it forward in thanks for his own good fortune. Trust me, he really wants you to have it."

"I hope we can thank him personally," Joel said.

"Actually, I'm pretty sure he'll insist on hanging the painting himself to make sure it's displayed to best advantage." They headed into the classroom. "Let's aim for this weekend, if that works for the two of you."

As she began her remarks for tonight's talk on the family square of the *bagua*, she remembered her student Joni's earlier comment that the family area was what she most wanted to enhance in her home. Jill knew from a quick conversation in the parking lot one evening that Joni's parents had divorced and remarried, and were now divorced again. Joni had alluded to substance abuse issues with one of her parents, as well. In addition, an elderly, wealthy uncle created havoc in the family with his constant threats of cutting family members out of his will if they didn't abide by his wishes or agree with his ultra-liberal politics.

"For most of us, family is the source of our greatest joys, but also some of our most painful moments," Jill began. "Family is supposed to mean security and unconditional love. That's what we believe and what we want, but it's not always the reality."

She held up the *bagua* and pointed to the family area, which was located in the middle left hand square. "The family area in *feng shui* borders knowledge and skills, prosperity, and health. Remember, these areas all overlap in important ways. If you're trying to learn something, family members are often willing and able to help. We need to learn about one another so that we can interact most effectively. When we're in trouble financially, family members often come to our rescue. When we hit the jackpot, we usually take care of family first. When stress occurs within the family, we can become sick. We suffer when a family member is ill. You get the picture."

"Some families won't help each other because it would mean having to actually communicate or compromise," Joni said with an edge to her voice. "I keep hoping things will change in my family, but it seems unlikely. *Feng shui* can't change how someone else behaves." She paused. "Can it?"

"If it's your intention that relations be better within your family, then *feng shui* can help," Jill insisted. "It can't change difficult personalities, but it can change how we view them. Often, that change in ourselves gets reflected back to us by the other person. If it doesn't, it may not be in our best interests for that relationship to continue." She paused as she realized the significance of those words in her own life.

"Let's review the creative elements for this area, which are wood and water. The most important shape is the rectangle. This gives you a lot of creative possibilities with photos and art. Hang family portraits in rectangular wood frames. Put a nice green plant in this area, but be sure to keep it well watered. Dead plants aren't good in any area, by the way. At holiday time, if you have a Christmas tree, place it in this area and arrange gifts for other family members under it. I know someone who hung family snapshots with green thread on a ficus tree." She grinned. "Maybe that's not your decorating style, but if you want to fix a family argument fast, hanging their photos together on that tree would certainly do the trick from a *feng shui* perspective."

"I was thinking more of a wooden dartboard decorated with their photos, but that probably wouldn't show good intent," Joni commented, rolling her eyes.

Jill shook her finger at her. "Shame on you," she said, laughing. "Those metal darts would be an even more destructive element, since metal cuts wood. Don't do that."

"What about colors?" Trish asked. "What if you don't want to paint the room green?"

"Green really is the best color in this area, I believe, but there are so many shades—even whites that have the merest touch of green. Black is another power color because it represents water, but you definitely don't want to paint a room black. Just avoid stark white, which is metal. If you do have any metal or white in that area, you can fix those elements by adding the color red for fire, which melts metal. My mother had a white bedroom in her family area, and she really liked the airiness of the room, so I painted the walls a shade of white that had a subtle green tint. It's called 'woodland white,' which made her happy, but even the name of the paint was good because it brought trees to mind. She had a white cloth-covered headboard on the bed, too, so we reupholstered it in a muted red, gold, and green print. Then I helped her pick out a lot of green hanging plants for the windows. I'm happy to report our family is very secure in my mother's love for us."

She grinned. "If you knew my mother, you'd also know that it was quite a stretch for her to accept my help. I'm not even sure she believes in *feng shui*. She's a very self-sufficient, super-resourceful person who takes pride in helping other people fix their problems. By the way, my mother is Nancy Brenneman of *Nancy Knows*."

Members of the class reacted to the news with surprise and excitement. Even the men were well acquainted with *Nancy Knows*. Over the course of her life, Jill had grown accustomed to having a well-known mother, although Nancy never flaunted her fame. In fact, life in the Brenneman household had always been relatively normal, with both parents home for dinner each night and Nancy leading Jill's Girl Scout troop and singing alto in the church choir.

This familiarity with celebrity life contributed to Jill's comfort level when David's star began to rise. The only difference was that David reveled in his celebrity status. Jill's mother handled her renown differently, which is what Jill had expected from David. It didn't hurt David's star status, either, that his mother-in-law was a celebrity. Jill preferred privacy and quiet times at home, just like her mother.

"Geez, Jill, with all the celebrities in your life, I don't know how you can be so down-to-earth," Meredith said, shaking her head. "You're one of the most calm, together people I've ever met."

Jill rolled her eyes. "Hah! If you only knew the truth, Meredith—but that's nice of you to say. For the sake of our discussion, let's chalk up my temperament to *feng shui* and the feeling of calm and order that it brings." She passed out a drawing outlining the elements important in tonight's discussion. "And if you honestly believe I have everything under control after events of the recent past, look again. Like everyone else, I'm learning to adapt. I'm making improvements to my own home and thinking up good intentions for the future."

After class, she walked to the parking lot with Joni, a tall, elegant woman who rarely spoke up in class. When she did, it was usually a word of support for what others were experiencing. Jill knew that Joni valued family, even if her own extended family brought pain.

"I don't want you to get the impression I'm unhappy," Joni told her as they stood in front of Jill's Subaru. "I've got a good life with my husband and our two teenage daughters. My husband provides well for us, and I have a successful business on the side doing what I love. I'm certainly not scarred by my past or anything as dramatic as all that. It's more about wanting to help bring my family together. Either that, or cut the ties as much as possible."

"Cutting all ties with blood relatives, no matter how much it may feel like a bloodletting, seems rather drastic. Let's try some *feng shui* and see if we can bring about a more positive outcome." Jill patted Joni's arm. "See you Thursday."

As she drove home, Jill thought about how much she enjoyed teaching the class and how glad she was that she no longer felt nervous or awkward in front of a group. Maybe it was because she believed so strongly in the power of *feng shui* to bring about change. It was easy to be enthusiastic when the subject was second nature to her. She'd begun to think more often of a television show about *feng shui*, but wasn't sure how to make that happen. Perhaps, next time they talked, she could ask David whether he knew anyone at the Home and Hearth television network.

These days they spoke about twice a week to maintain lines of communication and keep David in the loop about house expenses, their sons, and Missy's pregnancy. She continued to hope he'd make an effort on his own to improve those relationships. Earlier in the week, there had been discussions through their attorneys about the house. As a result, Jill was guaranteed that she could continue to live in the home as long as she wanted, but if she sold it, David would receive a percentage of the equity. David, of course, wanted her to sell the house sooner rather than later, but had agreed in principle to this arrangement. With David in agreement on all other matters regarding taxes, retirement assets, and investments, finalizing the divorce was just a waiting game. Jill still had to make a final decision that this was what she wanted.

"I can't believe you'll want to stay in that big house all alone the rest of your life," David said one evening over the phone.

She chose to ignore the part about *all alone the rest of your life*. "I'm not ready to move," she said simply. "I'd like to take a year or so to consider my options. There have been too many changes, and I want to get used to the way things are now."

"Jill, you know I never intended to hurt you." It was as close to an apology, she knew, as David would ever get.

"I do know that," she answered quietly. "On some level, though, you must have known what you were doing would hurt me, if I found out." When he didn't respond, she continued, "Whatever happens, it's important for us to have only best wishes for each other. After so many years together, it wouldn't have been easy to split up, no matter how it happened. What's important now is that we don't forget about the kids' feelings."

"Liam won't speak to me at all," David said.

"Liam might find it easier to accept who you are if you try to accept who he is," Jill said mildly. She heard a long outpouring of breath on the other end of the line. "Talk to him, David. You're his father, and no matter what happens, he loves you and needs to feel that you love and support him, too."

That night, before crawling into bed, she reviewed the family areas of her house: the den on the first floor and a guest bedroom on the second floor. She put all the wedding photos into a box in the hall closet, but left photos on display of David with the twins and with Missy. Because of their sons, David would always be family, especially with a baby on the way. Jill believed it was important to embrace every member of the family—to heal past hurts and nurture healthier new relationships. She wanted Finn and Liam to grow closer to their father, and this was the intent she set forth as she enhanced the family areas of the house.

As she dusted and vacuumed the family areas on both floors of the house, she hummed along to a popular song on her iPod. A sense of contentment and well-being washed over her. She continued clearing out the old to make room for the new, realizing that it was a relief to put away old family photos that had caused pain in light of David's affair. Many of these photos showing them as a perfect couple with the perfect family had been taken while David was having his affair. With David gone from their home, she could display photos of Liam and Brian in plain view. In the family area downstairs, David's den, she decided to box up his books and put them in storage. Her grandmother's collection of teapots would look lovely on those shelves. While David lived there, it had never been an option.

She wondered if Tom was right. Had there been so much pressure on her marriage that it was a relief to finally end the pretense? Had she and David simply grown apart?

WHEN JILL ARRIVED THAT THURSDAY at Joni's home in Westport, it was obvious from the size of the house and the manicured grounds around it that Joni and her husband, Pete, were quite wealthy. She parked behind Joni's Lexus SUV in the driveway, noticing a sleek gray Porsche parked near a private tennis court. She rang the doorbell and waited until Joni appeared, dressed in a pale blue cashmere sweater and navy dress slacks. Diamond earrings even larger than the enormous diamond wedding rings on her manicured hands twinkled in the afternoon sunlight.

"Please come in," Joni said, leading Jill through a house that could only be described as opulent. Vaulted ceilings with enormous crystal chandeliers, richly colored Oriental rugs, and valuable antiques were on display in every room. Yet the main living areas were comfortable and surprisingly casual.

"Everything looks spectacular, Joni," Jill said. "Are you in the antiques business?"

Joni laughed self-consciously as her face reddened. "I'm in the chocolate business. I make and sell specialty chocolates."

"I didn't know that! Would I have seen your candy in a store?"

"My candies are called Joni's Delights. They're available by mail order or through a few specialty shops," she said. "I make candy in a kitchen at the back of the house and sell it online and through catalogues. I'll give you a sample of everything before you leave."

"I'd love to try them. I didn't know about this side of you." Jill was intrigued. "You're usually so quiet in class."

"I'm accustomed to keeping a low profile, I guess—safer that way. Anyhow, in answer to your question about the antique furniture, a lot of what you see has been handed down through the family. This house was built by my great-grandfather. I grew up here because my grandparents, who inherited the house, insisted I stay with them from the time I was about ten until I graduated from college." She shrugged unselfconsciously. "My parents were always fighting, and my father is an alcoholic who abuses painkillers. He was thrown from a horse during a polo match in college, and it caused a lot of back pain. It affects his personality. Or rather," she said carefully, "the manner in which he chooses to medicate himself affects his personality."

"Did you enjoy living with your grandparents?"

"I adored Nana and PapPap. The only trouble was that it became just another resentment my mother piled up against her parents. She knew better than to fight my grandmother, though. Too much was at stake."

Jill raised an eyebrow in question. "It's such a shame that your mother couldn't get along with her own parents, and now that's spilling over into the next generation. But why?"

"Inheritance." Joni spit the word out. "It's always about the ever-lovin' money."

They walked down the hallway into the music room, where the most enormous grand piano Jill had ever seen was clearly the centerpiece. There were a few paintings on the walls—obviously originals—and an elegant crystal chandelier on the piano. But other than the piano and its green velvet-covered bench, the room held no other furnishings.

"This is the so-called family area of the house," Joni said. "As you can see, it isn't used for anything other than a place to store this piano, which is my mother's. She was a concert pianist, but she stopped playing many years ago. My husband doesn't play, and neither do I. Our daughters were never interested in taking lessons, so the room isn't really used by anyone. It's just a place to display my mother's piano." She shrugged.

"This is definitely not good *feng shui*," Jill observed, wondering how such a gorgeous grand piano could remain untouched. "The family area is supposed to be about positive relationships. There ought to be life in this room: people playing and milling around the piano, enjoying time together. I can think of all kinds of ways to enhance this room, but I'm curious why you don't have other furniture or personal photos in this space. Is there a reason why there's nothing but a piano?"

Joni screwed up her face in a grimace, "Not really. I guess I just don't like this room very much. It has a lot of bad memories, so I don't care to spend time in here." She frowned. "I should probably explain. This house was supposed to go to my mother after my grandparents died, but they left the house to me, instead. My husband and I had a small starter home over in Darien that suited us just fine. Of course, he and I were thrilled to get this house after my grandfather died, but there were a lot of hard feelings that it was given to me. Finally, though, we decided to accept it and move in because we realized we were fulfilling my grandparents' wishes."

She sighed deeply and blew out a long breath. "All these years, the house has been at the heart of a lot of my family's squabbles. I have a much older sister and brother who thought the house should be sold so that each of them could benefit as well. But that wasn't what my grandparents wanted. They were angry at my mother for marrying my father, to begin with, and then divorcing and remarrying him. They didn't want her to have the house because they didn't want *him* living here or getting his hands on it. The reason they gave it to me was because I lived here for so many years with them and because they didn't want the house to be sold to strangers. I guess they trusted me to honor their wishes and keep this house in the family."

The truth of what Joni was saying was evident from the pained expression on her face. Jill sat down on the piano bench and waited silently for Joni to continue. Joni surveyed the room, her eyes glittering with emotion. She seemed to be lost in thought, reliving some past, sad time.

"My uncle thought it was wrong that I got the house, so he included my siblings in his will and cut me out entirely. That seems fair, and I truly don't care. The trouble is, every time my brother or sister disagrees with Unc's politics or intervenes when he behaves badly at family gatherings, he threatens to change his will. Then they start in again about the house. That opens the door for my mother to say that this is really her house, not mine."

She stopped for a breath. "Before my parents' second divorce, my father pressured me to sell the house so that everyone in the family could benefit. But Jill, I don't want to sell it because it really *is* my home. I've lived here for many years, and I've raised my children here. Plus, I really do care about honoring my grandparents' wishes."

"Would it help if the piano was gone? Would your mother want it in her own home?"

"I've already offered it to her. She's adamant that it belongs in this house and that it could be damaged in a move, which is entirely possible." Joni blew out a breath.

"Well, then, let's *feng shui* this room." Jill rubbed her hands together. "First, I want you to gather as many happy family photos as you can. Make sure they are framed in wood, not metal."

Joni pulled open two louvered closet doors and lifted out a large box containing framed and loose photographs. "There are some beautiful photos of my parents with my brother, sister, and me when I was little. There's another one somewhere in here of my mother and Unc." She began rifling through them.

"Arrange your favorites, the ones that bring you pleasure, all around the room at eye level," Jill said. "You want to feel happy when you see them. That's part of the good intention you're setting forth."

Joni looked intently at a photo of her mother sitting at the piano in a full-skirted black evening dress, a string of pearls about her long, graceful neck. "She looks so happy in this photo. This was before she married my father the first time." Joni looked up at Jill. "What else do you think I ought to do besides hang these photos?"

"The colors in this room need to be serene, warm, and inviting. You've got a beautiful, creamy-vanilla color in here, but it needs to be something other than such a light shade of white. Remember, white is metal. We want wood and water to be center stage. I'm going to ask a color specialist for his opinion on this, but I see a warm olive green, which represents trees and plants. You've already got gorgeous hardwood floors, but I want you to take up that white rug right away. Use it somewhere else, like in your creativity and children area, or perhaps the knowledge and skills room. The piano is black, which is the color of water, so the place it holds in the room is actually a strong, supporting element to the wood."

Jill put one finger to her lips as a new thought formed. "It would be nice if your mother could see the room after you're finished enhancing it. Does she still like to play this piano?"

Joni let out a harsh laugh. "The only one who touches this piano is the housekeeper, whenever she dusts it."

"Wouldn't it be nice if your mother could sit down to play this piano at a family gathering?"

Joni's eyes suddenly filled with tears. They trickled down her cheeks, leaving traces in her otherwise perfect makeup. She wiped them away with her fingertips and paused for a few moments to regain her composure. "I remember when I was a little girl and she sat down to play "Greensleeves" for my grandfather. He always stood near the piano, sucking on his cold pipe. He didn't actually smoke." Her breath caught as she fought back a sob at the memory and then let out a choking kind of laugh. "He sucked on that pipe when he was thinking extra hard about something. He would listen to her play with such pride. Afterward, he would always say the same thing: 'I have never heard you play that song so beautifully, Paget.' That's my mom's name: Paget."

"What a sweet memory, Joni. It's one that you ought to keep in mind as you enhance this space. I hope you'll find this to be a healing process and that you'll actually enjoy fixing this room. I'd love to see it when you're done." Jill picked up her handbag in preparation to leave.

"Please don't go just yet." Joni reached out and placed her hand on Jill's arm. "I'd like for you to come into my kitchen studio, as I call it, and let me treat you to some of Joni's Delights."

"That sounds wonderful. Thank you," Jill said. She followed Joni down the stairs and through a long hallway to a lower level of the house that was equipped with commercial kitchen equipment, including a large gas stove, double oven, dishwasher, and walk-in refrigerator. Long tables were covered in trays of fresh chocolates ready to be boxed. Colored foils and tissue-filled boxes were lined up on nearby shelves. The rich smell of chocolate hung in the air until Jill was sure she would smell it on her skin for days.

"You have your choice of espresso truffles, cherry cordials, caramel and sea salt squares, blueberry crèmes, thin peppermints, pecan turtles, peanut butter melts, and almond clusters, all freshly made, of course." Joni washed her hands, pulled on latex gloves, and donned a white lab jacket with embroidery on the breast pocket that read, "Joni, Chief Chocolate Artist."

Jill's eyes were wide with amazement as she surveyed the display of candy. "I don't think I can decide. May I try one of each?"

"You certainly may." Joni deftly began wrapping chocolates in colored foil and shiny paper wrappers and placing them in a three-pound box. "One is never enough, you know. With this many, you can share."

"I'd better share if you're giving me that much chocolate," Jill said, laughing. "I have to ask, though. Whatever led you into the chocolate business?"

"I came by my interest in chocolate genetically, you might say," Joni answered with a twinkle in her eye. "Nana's family owned a large candy business in New Jersey, and she taught me how to make candy when I was just a little girl. I'd stand on a stepstool at the kitchen island, and during the holidays, help her make chocolates for our family members and friends." She handed a turtle to Jill, who bit into it and closed her eyes in bliss.

"Joni, this is divine."

"Why bother eating it if it's not? That's the whole point. Chocolate-making is an art and a science intended to produce pleasure," she said, looking up from her task. "Nana told me you have to love your work. If you don't really love making candy, it won't taste as good." She handed the box to Jill with a flourish.

"This is such an unexpected treat," Jill said, pretending that her knees were buckling under the weight of the heavy candy box. "I can't help thinking that between decadent chocolates and that concert piano, your family ought to share only happy times together. I'd love to hear how things go after you make those enhancements to your music room upstairs."

Joni grinned widely and gave Jill a spontaneous hug. "You just gave me the best *feng shui* idea of all."

Chapter Sixteen

Sunday dawned cold and overcast with a chance of rain. Jill crept out from beneath her down comforter and stood shivering in a gray jersey nightshirt and thick socks. Denny had said he would pick her up at ten thirty to deliver the painting to Joel and Diana, and she wanted to bake a pan of whole-grain tart-cherry muffins to take along.

So far, Diana's cancer seemed to be in remission, and she was scheduled to see the oncologist in two weeks for another consultation. In the meantime, Diana's mother returned home to Hartford until she was needed again. That meant Joel had more childcare and household responsibilities, in addition to his job. But Jill had to give him credit; he bore his duties like a champ.

"It's just Diana, Zoe, and me together again," he said, when Jill called to arrange their visit. "We're managing okay, except Zoe doesn't like my cooking."

As she stirred dried tart cherries into a mixture of cornmeal, oatmeal, and whole-wheat batter, Jill thought about the hopes and wishes that fed the various *feng shui* enhancements in her students' homes, and decided it was time to tackle the creativity and children square of the *bagua* at the next class. Later in the day, Liam, Brian, Finn, and Missy were coming over for dinner. She wanted to talk with Missy about enhancements to the creativity and children area of their apartment in preparation for the baby's arrival.

"Will Denny be there for dinner?" Missy asked.

"Denny and I are just getting to know each other," Jill said. "I like him a lot, but I want to take things slowly."

"I like him," Missy said. "So did Finn, although he won't tell you that."

Nancy's reaction to hearing that Jill had gone out to dinner with Denny was positive and predictably maternal. "I'm glad to know you're getting out and having a good time, instead of sitting at home alone crying over David. Just keep your knees crossed until you know he isn't one of those—whaddya call them—players."

"For heaven's sake, Mom! I'm glad you approve, but I hardly need your advice in that regard," Jill said, rolling her eyes. Yet she realized her mother's point was well taken. She didn't know Denny very well, and he was a longtime bachelor, after all. She knew it was possible that she was playing with fire.

Denny soon arrived in his truck, the mountain painting for Joel and Diana safely tucked into bubble wrap and brown paper in the back seat. They drove forty minutes to the Fosters' home, enjoying the crisp Sunday morning and the sights and smells of autumn. Already, most of the jewel-toned leaves had fallen off the trees, and roadside stands were well stocked with pumpkins, gourds, dried corn, apples, and cider. Autumn was Jill's favorite time of year, a season when she enjoyed flea markets, cooking and baking, chilly evenings by the fireplace with a good book, and biking along the country roads near her home.

"Mm, it smells delicious outside," she said, breathing in the woodsy outdoor scents.

"Aye, it does," Denny said, smiling to himself as he accelerated.

When they arrived at the Fosters' home, Diana was wrapped in a shawl on the sofa, sipping a protein shake. Over her bald head she wore a pink-and-white silk scarf that matched her pink robe and fuzzy slippers. Her blue eyes looked enormous and unprotected minus eyebrows and eyelashes.

"It's so nice to finally meet you, Jill!" she said, standing with difficulty to offer Jill a fragile hug. She accepted the straw basket of muffins in the blue-checked cloth. "These smell wonderful." She handed the basket to Joel, who immediately picked out a muffin and bit into it.

"Mm, food that I haven't cooked," he said with relish, devouring the rest of the muffin in three bites.

Diana held out her hands to Denny, who grasped them gently as a look passed between them that was palpable in its meaning. "I can't thank you enough," she said. "It's a thrill to meet you and have one of your paintings. I'm sure it's quite valuable."

"A painting is only valuable if it's well loved."

Denny unveiled his painting to sounds of appreciation from Jill, Diana, and Joel. A whitewashed stone cottage stood in a rocky field beneath tall, craggy mountains. The peaks of the mountain were misted in swirling white, heather, gray, blue, and violet.

"This is the Buachaille Etive Mor," Denny said. "That's the Gaelic name. It's the prettiest summit in Scotland, as far as I'm concerned."

"It's lovely," Diana murmured as Joel put his arm around her.

"Diana, the mountain represents earth, and the triangular peak is a strong symbolic shape in *feng shui*. Look upward to the summit and believe that good health is yours," Jill said as Denny began hanging the painting in the stairway.

Zoe woke up from her nap when she heard the gentle tapping of Denny's hammer on the wall. Joel headed upstairs to retrieve her from her crib before she put up a fuss. As they descended the stairs, he pointed to the painting. "See what our friends have brought Mommy to help her feel better."

Zoe had her mother's prosthesis tucked tightly against her body. Wordlessly, Diana held out her hands as Joel gently transferred their daughter to her waiting arms.

"Are you sure you can manage?" he asked as Diana's eyes widened in surprise at Zoe's weight.

Diana juggled her on one hip. "I'm okay, but I believe my next challenge will be getting this thing away from her," she said with a wry grin as she held up the plastic breast.

"I'm sure there are many men who would like to have that for their sleep toy," Denny joked.

They all laughed. Jill blushed when her eyes met Joel's, and a mischievous grin spread across his face. She knew from his expression that she was in for some good-natured teasing.

On the way home, Denny and Jill stopped for lunch at a rustic lodge, where he promised that mulled wine and the best crab cakes in the state were on the menu. "In fact, this might be a nice place to spend a bit of time some weekend," Denny said with a wink. "Not that I'm trying to put the rush on you or anything. Just stating my interest."

"Duly noted," Jill said, lowering her eyes as they went into the dining room. "But it's not going to happen this afternoon, so don't get your hopes up."

"Aye, I dinna think so." He grinned and picked up his menu. "Canna blame a man for trying, though."

Jill noticed with amusement that Denny's Scottish brogue became more pronounced when he flirted or became nervous. It was one of the qualities about him she found most endearing—his total lack of guile when it came to sharing his thoughts or feelings. He was a man who spoke from the heart.

As their mulled wine was served in steaming glass mugs, Denny leaned across the table and took her hands. "Honest, I dinna mean to make you uncomfortable with that remark about spending a night here. You're a beautiful woman, Jill, and I would no' be a normal man if the idea dinna cross my mind to think of us together that way."

Jill's eyes softened and she reached across the table to take his hand. "Although it sounds wonderful, and I'm definitely interested, I'm not ready yet, Denny," she said firmly. "I was married for twenty-five years to the same man—who I also dated for three years before we married. I'll know when the time is right. I appreciate your patience." Jill smiled. "I don't see anything that could possibly happen to slow things down or stop the divorce, but I need to move carefully. I could hurt you without intending to."

Denny nodded. "Why doesn't it surprise me that you'd be worried about my feelings?" He paused to give their order to the waiter before continuing. "I care for you, Jill. I know I might seem to be a man who has avoided commitment all his life, but it is no' true. I never wanted to settle for less than my heart's desire. There's something about you that speaks to my mind, soul, and body. You're a good woman with a heart that cares for others. From the first day I laid eyes on you, I knew that."

"Then we have a good foundation to build on, because I feel the same about you." Suddenly embarrassed, she cleared her throat. "Giving that painting to Joel and Diana was such an incredible gesture. It means a lot to me that you cared enough to do that."

"They're fine people, and someday I'd like to paint the little girl. She reminds me of the storybook *The Littlest Angel*.

AT DINNER THAT EVENING, MISSY nibbled oyster crackers and took slow spoonfuls of chicken broth. Bluish circles were visible under her sunken eyes, and her lips were nearly bloodless.

"This won't last forever, honey," Jill assured her. "I had about three weeks of morning sickness with the twins, but then one day I woke up feeling fine, and I never had another moment of nausea the rest of the pregnancy."

In response, Missy smiled weakly, wiped sweat from her upper lip, and made a beeline to the bathroom. It was the third time in less than an hour. Finn, looking worried, got up to check on her, as he had done each of the previous times.

When he returned to the kitchen, he said, "It isn't just morning sickness, Mom. She's been sick pretty much twenty-four/seven, but she doesn't want meds for it, and she won't stay home from work, either." He shook his head. "I can't believe she worked every day last week. Just the smells alone in a pediatric office would do me in, if I was pregnant."

Jill got up from the table and pulled out a large Nordstrom's bag. "Maybe this will help her look past this not-fun stage and focus on the future," she said, setting the bag on Missy's chair.

While they awaited Missy's return from the bathroom, she updated Liam, Finn, and Brian on her *feng shui* cast of characters. "I just visited the most fascinating woman, Joni, who has a chocolate business in her home. In fact, there's a huge box of her candy on the kitchen island that you ought to sample," she said. "I'm not planning to eat them all myself, that's for sure."

"Why were you visiting her?" Brian asked. "Are you redecorating her house?"

"She's one of my students, and I'm helping her *feng shui* her family area," Jill responded. "Oh, Brian! I have to tell you about the gorgeous piano in the center of the room that her mother, Paget, used to play when she was a concert pianist—back when she lived in the house many years ago."

"Paget Weintraub? Are you saying that your student's mom is Paget Weintraub?" Brian could barely contain his excitement.

"I don't know Paget's last name, actually. Her daughter's married name is Silversmith. Brian, how do you know Paget?"

"I don't know her that well," Brian admitted. "I've been introduced to her at benefactor parties. She's quite the diva—a real legend from when she performed many years ago. Now she's a benefactor to the arts. I sometimes see her at receptions and shows."

When Missy returned and saw the Nordstrom's bag, her eyes

lit up. "What's this?" she asked as she peered inside. She lifted out a plush brown teddy bear and said, "Oh, he's adorable!" A little color returned to her cheeks. "Thanks, Jill. This will be the first thing to go into the nursery. Will you help us decorate the baby's room?"

"Just try and stop me."

"I'd love an animal theme," Missy said. "And I'd prefer the colors not to be pink and blue."

"The room in your apartment that you're planning to use as a nursery isn't in the creativity and children area of your apartment. Your bathroom is. So I thought we'd add some yellow and white to your bathroom to strengthen that area. We can do whatever you want color-wise in the actual nursery, since it's in the prosperity area, and most colors work great in there."

"She probably already has a dozen designs for us to look at," Finn teased.

"Just two," Jill admitted. "I couldn't resist playing around when I found out you were pregnant. One idea is to decorate the nursery, which is your prosperity area, in greens, reds, golden yellows, and purples. We could do a rainforest theme with giraffes, elephants, and any other animal you want."

"I love that idea!" Missy's face lit up.

As they discussed furniture for the baby's room, the doorbell rang. "I'm not expecting anyone," Jill said, starting to rise.

"I'll get it, Mom," Liam said and headed to the door.

There were low, muffled voices and then footsteps in the hallway. Suddenly David was standing before Jill, a bottle of red wine in his hand. Liam quietly returned to his chair, his face stony.

"David, I didn't know you were coming over tonight." Jill rose quickly to accept the wine from him, but turned her face so that his kiss landed on her cheek. "Th-thank you," she stammered, unable to meet his eyes. "I'll be glad to set another place, if you haven't eaten yet."

The tips of David's ears turned red. "That'd be great. I figured everyone would be here for dinner, so I thought I'd take a chance and stop in."

It was the first time Jill had ever seen David appear out of his element. He was dressed casually in a navy argyle sweater and dark jeans, and his hair was noticeably gray. He shifted his weight from one foot to the other as Liam, Finn, and Missy exchanged subtle and not-so-subtle looks.

Missy was the first to break the silence. "It's good to see you, David," she said shyly. She stood and gave him a hug.

David held her tight, his hand caressing the back of her blonde head as he touched his lips to her hair. "How are you feeling, Missy?" he asked.

"Not great, but I'm sure this morning sickness thing will be over soon." She eased herself gingerly down into a chair.

Finn stood to give his father a swift hug, one arm slung over his shoulder, bodies barely touching as they slapped each other on the backs. "Hey, Dad," he said.

David grinned. "Congratulations on becoming a father! I hope you and Missy enjoy this baby as much as your mother and I enjoyed you and Liam."

"Thanks, Dad. We're excited."

Liam remained seated, his mouth a solid line, as Brian stood to offer his hand. "I'm Brian," he said. "It's nice to meet you, sir."

"Same here," David said, clearing his throat as he took the proffered hand. "I understand you're in the music business."

"More music than business, actually. There are other people who handle that side of things," Brian said easily. He seemed completely comfortable, despite the tense glances passing between the others.

Jill went into the kitchen to fill a plate for David. As she arranged baked lemon chicken, wild rice, and sugar snap peas on his plate, her mind spun with troubling thoughts. Would David want to stay after dinner to talk with her alone? Or was this unexpected visit solely to ensure he had a chance to see Liam? She hoped so.

"Smells good," David said, as he slid into the chair at the head of the table, his usual spot. "I lucked out getting here in time for your famous chicken." He dug into his dinner with gusto while Liam picked at his food.

Jill was adrift on a sea of conflicting emotions as she watched David eat as though nothing was out of the ordinary. On the one hand, it felt familiar having him in his usual place at the dinner table—rather like old times. On the other hand, she was unable to feel any joy at his unexpected visit. The thought was somehow more troubling. This was so like David … to be oblivious to the undercurrents in his own family.

Dinner conversation was easier than Jill thought it would be, however, thanks to Brian's gift of gab. Still, she was unable to meet David's frequent glances in her direction or offer many responses. She was taken aback that he hadn't called first to let her know he was coming, and she realized that this, too, was typical. He assumed whatever he wanted would be fine with her, and she had done nothing over the years to change that pattern. She had always made allowances for his behavior. Would these unannounced visits continue? She flinched and thought about how her relationship with David was changing. Even a few months ago, she would have welcomed his being home with her and their sons. She thought how fortunate it was that after spending the afternoon together, she hadn't invited Denny to stay for dinner. His presence would have complicated what was already a difficult dinner.

Now that the initial surprise had passed, she began feeling more and more resentful. Since David's departure from their home, Sunday family dinners had become a respite from stressors of the week. Liam and Brian drove in from the city and spent the entire evening. Their conversations were full of carefree banter, and Finn and Liam had brotherly time together. Without David's presence, there was less strain in discussions, no need to validate one's opinion with the most recent published research or risk being debated into submission. Even the meals Jill cooked were simpler, with no need for the multiple courses David preferred. Yet, she reasoned, it was a good idea for them to have dinner together with their children. Doubtless, there would be many more times in the future, especially after the baby was born, that they would see each other. *Best get used to it now*, she thought. She picked at her food, which had grown cold.

Giving up entirely on finishing her dinner, Jill rose to make coffee, which she served with thick slices of homemade coconut cake and scoops of dulce de leche ice cream. This, too, was filled with memories, a dessert she had served at many family meals. It was David's favorite indulgence, even though he followed a restricted diet in an effort to look as trim as possible on television. Given his present gauntness, Jill thought he needed to put on a few pounds.

"This is so good, Jill," David said, closing his eyes in bliss at the first bite.

Liam still hadn't said a word, just watched his father warily out of his peripheral vision throughout the rest of the meal. Jill could see that he was seething, and she was uneasy about what might happen next. Brian continued to keep the conversational ball in the air, answering David's polite questions about his upbringing and career.

"I majored in piano in college. I was there on scholarship, but not for music, for baseball. My dad wanted me to play professionally—baseball, that is, not piano—and I guess I wanted that, too. During college, I went the amateur route because it seemed the thing to do. Hard to break with expectations, but by then, I knew I didn't want to play pro ball." He took a bite of cake.

"You're an athlete and a sports fan," David said with obvious surprise, but recovered nicely at the look of reproach that crossed Liam's face.

"As big a fan as they come. I pitched after college in the minors, but I wasn't really good enough to go to the majors. After I got my first job composing for an off-Broadway show, I stopped playing ball, although I still coach a little for fun. I don't miss many Mets home games if I can help it."

"Liam, you've never said anything about enjoying the Mets." David took a sip of coffee and looked at his son.

Liam looked his father squarely in the eye and paused for dramatic effect. Jill groaned inwardly, guessing what was coming. Liam picked up his coffee cup, extended his pinky, and replied, "I prefer to cook and care for our home."

Finn's face flushed beet red and he shot Liam a black look. Missy and Jill exchanged looks of dismay, and Jill dug her nails into her palms to keep from reacting. David's fork was suspended in mid-air while he considered how to respond. His ears reddened again, but he said nothing, just looked from Liam to Jill to Finn and back to Liam again. Then he stared at Jill, a look of clear expectation on his face. Was she supposed to handle relationship situations with the family as she had in the past? *Probably*, she thought, but she didn't want that responsibility. Enough was enough.

Brian's face was a study in self-control, although one eyebrow arched in disbelief. He elbowed Liam. "That's funny," he said. "Who knew? Now I know what to buy you for Christmas: a new mop."

"More coffee for anyone?" Jill asked and escaped into the kitchen to retrieve the carafe.

The tension between Liam and David remained high. It was thanks only to Brian's grace under pressure that the rest of the meal passed in relative calm. After dessert and coffee, Brian and Liam prepared to drive back into the city.

"It was nice to meet you," Brian said and extended his hand.

David hesitated for just a moment before taking Brian's hand. "Same here," he said, clearing his throat.

Liam kissed Missy, gave Finn a quick hug, and hugged Jill

before taking off like a shot for the front door. David watched his angry son's retreating back, looking uncertain and hurt. Jill wanted to run after Liam, but her body seemed rooted in place.

"We need to get going, too. I'm really beat." Missy leaned her head against Finn's shoulder. He nestled his cheek against her hair.

"Okay, I guess I ought to get the little mother home." Finn picked up the shopping bag containing the teddy bear.

"Missy, we'll shop more for the baby's room when you feel better," Jill said, standing up to hug her.

She stood back while David embraced Missy and Finn. Then they were gone. That left Jill alone with David, a gulf between them the length of the dining room table.

"Would you like anything else?" she asked politely as she began to clear the table.

"Thank you, but I've had plenty. Dinner was great, as usual." Picking up his dessert plate and fork, he followed her into the kitchen. As she loaded the dishwasher and washed pots and pans, he poured each of them another glass of wine and then sat companionably on a stool at the kitchen island.

"You look good, Jill," he said. "Your hair has gotten longer."

"A little, I guess," she said, plunging her hands into the dishwater. She needed to stay focused. If she looked at him directly, she might lose her composure and lash out at him— the last thing she needed or wanted to have happen today. Besides, it could escalate into an argument and cause problems in the divorce mediation. An angry David could be a vindictive David.

"You said you're teaching a class. Are you still enjoying it?"

"Very much. I might do it again next semester."

"That's good," he said and came over to the counter, leaning against it. "Jill, we need to talk."

"Okay." She dried her hands and faced him, her heart pounding.

"I'll be honest. I don't want this divorce, and I'm willing to do whatever it takes to win you back. I know what I did hurt you and that you've had a difficult time trying to forgive me. I don't blame you for that, but how can we throw away twenty-five years of marriage without trying to save what we had?"

Jill took a deep breath and looked into his eyes. "David, to tell you the truth, lately I'm not totally sure what we had. Our marriage was about my accepting your life, supporting what you wanted, and trying to mold myself around you. That's not your fault, by the way. I was willing to do that because I loved you and thought that if you were happy, I'd be happy, too. I thought that would make both of us content. But now that I know you weren't happy, it all seems so sad, as if we wasted our time. I want more. I'm not sure what a relationship with me would mean to you. And to be honest, David, I don't believe I was happy living the way we were."

"You said 'loved,' past tense. Can you honestly say you've stopped loving me?" David lifted her chin and looked into her eyes. Then he leaned forward and kissed her, a surprising kiss, his lips fitting over hers in that way that evoked an automatic flutter deep in her lower abdomen. It had always been like that, and she found the sensation bittersweet.

She felt her resolve to remain cool and detached rapidly deteriorate as David took her into his arms and continued kissing her. She returned the kiss, with reservations, as the familiar scent of expensive soap and Grey Flannel cologne filled her senses. Almost immediately, she also became aware of an inability to fully relax as an undercurrent of something she couldn't identify gathered strength and rose up from inside.

"David, I can't," she said and stepped back. "You showed up tonight without any warning. I'm just starting to get my feet under me again. I'm not sure what you wanted when you came by for dinner."

"What I wanted was to see you, Jill. I wanted the chance to tell you that we can change the way we've lived. We could start a new life together."

Jill could hardly believe her ears. "David, I don't know what to say. What would that new life look like?" She waited anxiously, willing him to answer that they could have more time together, better communication, or more time with Liam.

"For one thing, it wouldn't involve this house. We could sell it and get a really nice apartment in Manhattan."

Jill's stomach flopped. "You think that we should begin to start a new life by selling the house?" Was that all he could say? "David, when you and I made the decision to live here, neither of us wanted to live in the city because of the boys. When did that change for you?"

"Jill, let's face it: my career is in the city. The commute can be a killer, and everything we enjoy is in the city: restaurants, museums, theater, the whole social scene. I know you've got your job here, but you could start your own interior design company. Don't tell me you've never thought about what it might mean to design multimillion dollar properties in Manhattan. Besides, there is such excitement there. Remember our dream when we were kids to live there?"

"David, I already design multimillion dollar properties. Although I like going into the city for dinner or to shop on the weekends, I don't really want to live there." She did not add that living in New York City had been more his dream as a young man, and she had gone along with it. After they were married, they settled in Connecticut, which had been his decision as much as hers, since they both worked there. The invitation to join the network in Manhattan had come after they already had the twins and their big home in Connecticut. Jill waited for David to amend his suggestion—perhaps suggest a second, smaller apartment in the city for weekend fun. That would be a nice compromise.

David ran his long fingers through his immaculate hair. As she had observed earlier, it was shot through with more silver than she remembered, and he had lost a considerable amount of weight; his expertly fitted jeans hung low on his hips. In just two months, he had aged at least ten years. He was quiet for a few moments, and she knew he was contemplating how to respond. He held one of her hands between his, studying her fingers.

"You're not wearing your wedding rings." When she said nothing, he looked pained. "Is it that easy for you to just … detach?"

She shook her head. "Nothing about this has been easy. You surely know that. Taking a step back from this very difficult and public situation is the only thing I can do, since I can't seem to put aside what happened. I am still trying to understand why and how it happened. David, I still haven't heard from you why you think you had an affair. It matters to me." She paused. "What about the woman I saw you with in the magazine?" She asked the question calmly, not wanting to provoke him. That argument could end with a complete breakdown in communication between them, more family tension, and even escalate into a contested divorce. She had been warned by her attorney not to do anything that might delay finalization of their case for months or even years. Yet she wanted—no, *needed*—to learn the woman's identity.

"Jill, she's a friend and colleague. I took her to an awards dinner. There's nothing between us."

"What about Amber?"

"Amber resigned. I have no idea where she is."

"David, finding out the way I did was the worst day of my life."

David flinched. "Jill, I'm asking you to think about giving me another chance. We can start over, maybe renew our vows and take a second honeymoon. I promise things will be better. We can talk about what our future would look like. Jill, I need you in my life. I need my wife back."

Jill was silent. This was not precisely everything she hoped to hear from him, but when he expressed need for her, she had a moment of déjà vu, remembering the early years and becoming confused. She was torn between asking David to leave and wanting to hear more—something that might help her better understand what had gone wrong between them. What if she never learned the reason he betrayed her? Was it possible to just forgive and forget?

"All I want to do is be alone with you," he said. "Let me prove how much I love you."

She knew exactly what that meant, and a fleeting thought of making love led her to wonder if it might fuse the great division between them. Their lovemaking had always been the primary way they communicated, but when he had the affair, she wondered if even that part of their lives was a lie. What did that say about them as a couple—that the connection was mostly physical? Yet she knew that if she did invite him back into their bedroom, there would be no turning back, and she would agree to let him come home. Everything could return to normal … a thought she now found inconceivable.

Steeling herself, she picked up his leather jacket, catching a whiff of that beloved David smell. Handing it to him, she said, "David, I can't give you what you're asking of me, at least not now. The divorce won't be final for some time. Between now and then, we'll both have plenty of time to think and talk." She walked him to the door. "That's why they call it a cooling off period."

As she placed a hand on the front door knob, he reached out and took her hands, drawing her close. She did not make eye contact, fearful that he would kiss her again. Her legs were weak and unsteady, and she knew she was on the verge of tears. "David, I can't—"

"I can be a better man. Just give me a chance to prove it to you."

She wondered now what it would mean to give David a second chance, or even how to go about it. If David wanted a second chance, he'd have to begin making some kind of effort. There was time to wait and see what his next move would be.

Chapter Seventeen

"**M**OM, I HAVE NO IDEA what I'm going to do!" Jill began in a quavering voice when her mother answered the phone later that evening.

"My goodness, what happened?" Nancy's voice was as calm and reassuring as always.

Jill could picture her mother and father sitting together in the den, enjoying a cup of tea and watching back-to-back episodes of *Law and Order*, as they had for years. She had thought fleetingly of driving over to see them, but it was getting late. Lord knows, her parents had better things to do than listen to yet another anguished phone call from their middle-aged daughter. Jill had decided, instead, to take a hot bath, put on her robe, and try to get her bearings. Yet, by nine thirty, she knew she wouldn't sleep a wink if she didn't talk with her mother, who would be able to put the evening's events into perspective.

"David stopped by unexpectedly at dinnertime and asked me to put the divorce on hold," Jill announced. "He wants me to give him another chance."

"He hasn't wanted the divorce all along, honey. You've surely been expecting this. What did you say?"

"I said there will be plenty of time to consider things as we go along," Jill said, wincing as she replayed the memory of their passionate kiss. "I'm not going to just stop the divorce now that it's this far along. On the one hand, I feel like a failure for not trying to put everything back together. You know I always try to fix things. On the other hand, I can't imagine being married to him anymore."

"It's understandable you'd feel that way, given how long you've been together."

Jill chewed on a hangnail, wincing as it started to bleed. "I've been handling things so well the past few weeks; I've actually been happy. I didn't intend to meet someone else so soon, but now that I've started spending time with Denny, I actually feel hopeful about the future."

"Denny must seem like a sure sign that there's life after David."

Jill paused for a second, amazed at how easily her mother could size up any situation and express how Jill was feeling. "That's it, exactly, Mom. How do I know the best course of action now? I'm upset with David for making my life even more difficult by asking me to save a marriage that feels like it's over—apparently has been over, without my knowledge, for quite a while. If all my efforts in the past weren't enough, why would they work this time? Wouldn't we eventually break up, anyway? Then I'd have to go through this all over again."

"That's a legitimate concern, and of course you'd feel that way," Nancy said. "Dad's sitting here with me, by the way. He sends his love. He's thought all along that David would ask you to stop the divorce, didn't you, Hal?" She paused. "Dad says yes. After what David did, I think you're justified in taking whatever steps you think are best for your life."

"I'm not planning to stop the divorce. I can't help feeling guilty, though, as if I'm letting everyone down."

"Jill, it might be a good idea to ask yourself one question and let that be your guide."

"What's that?" Jill flopped on her back across the bed.

"What reasons would you have for wanting David back as your husband? I think if you seriously consider that question, you'll know what to do. Don't worry about what anyone else thinks. It's not their lives we're talking about."

"Thanks, Mom." At that moment, Jill felt much as she had as a teenager when her mother patiently guided her through problems regarding boys, college, or career decisions. "I'll talk with you later. Give Dad a kiss for me."

TUESDAY'S *FENG SHUI* CLASS FOCUSED on the creativity and children area of the *bagua*. This square was located in the right-hand side of the bagua in the center square, vertically between love and relationships and benefactors and travel. Jill came to class loaded down with books and handouts for her students, including photos of rooms she had designed for clients. This area of the *bagua* was one she enjoyed designing most because there was so much scope for the imagination.

"Tonight we're going to learn about one of my favorite areas—the square dealing with creativity, fertility, parenthood, and youthful thinking." Jill passed out notes for discussion. "If you want to feel like a kid again in this game called life, this is the square to land on."

Shelly's pen was poised over her notebook, a mixture of hope and despair in her eyes. Jill's heart went out to her. She was aware that Shelly had recently asked her husband to go for couples counseling in an effort to convince him to agree to fertility testing. He had flatly told her no—that the problem was with her body, not his.

"The creative elements for this area of the home are metal and earth," Jill began. "We want to use white for metal and an earthy color, such as yellow or brown, whenever possible. In my house, the kitchen is my area of creativity and children, so I chose a buttery color for the walls, high-quality metal pots and pans that help me create delicious meals, and white cabinets with brushed stainless steel knobs. There are photos of my kids on the refrigerator, and I've got a bouquet of Tootsie Pops on the counter. On the second floor, the creativity and children square happens to be the guest bedroom, which is where I intend to put the crib when my grandchild comes to visit."

Shelly fidgeted constantly, crossing and uncrossing her legs, fingering her cross, and playing with her hair. As Jill illustrated a point on the chalkboard, Shelly made an effort to sit still, yet one knee continued moving involuntarily. Jill saw her blink back tears as she took deep breaths.

She smiled kindly in Shelly's direction before saying, "Children and creativity go hand in hand, which is why they are included in one area of the *bagua*. It's no accident that conception of a child, the most amazing act of creation of all, can be affected by enhancing this square. But it's important to consider in the case of infertility that opening up one's heart by adopting or fostering a child in need can also be encouraged by enhancing this area."

Shelley looked away. On break, she confided to the other women, "My husband, Joe, thinks it's my fault, my lack of faith in God. I've been through testing, and there's no reason for me not to be able to get pregnant. Joe won't get tested. I think he's afraid he'll be the one with the problem." Her mouth was set in a white line. "It doesn't help that his family, especially his dad, makes comments that hurt his pride."

"That's just mean spirited and stupid," Pam said. "It might be a simple matter of changing from briefs to boxers … or trying new positions."

Shelly got a blank look on her face for a moment before blushing beet red. The other women laughed. Jill rolled her eyes at Pam and shook her head in an effort to get across the message that Shelly might not be open to Pam's sexual coaching.

"Perhaps Joe can't deal with the thought of being sterile or having a low sperm count because he knows it means so much to you to have a baby," Jill suggested and watched Shelly's face fall. "His feelings are probably very complicated. Even if he did agree to adoption, would you be happy not having a biological child?"

"At this point, I want to try *in vitro* fertilization, but Joe says we can't afford that, that we just need to have faith and keep trying. I'm not ruling out adoption, but I can't give up trying to get pregnant yet."

"It took me almost a year to conceive my first son," Meredith said. "The next two were big surprises—no work at all. Maybe if you just relaxed and enjoyed the process …."

Shelly flushed. "My husband believes sex is for procreation, not recreation. He comes from a very strict religious background."

"Oh." The other women exchanged astonished yet sympathetic looks.

"I miss that—sex, I mean." Meredith's dark eyes spoke volumes. "I've been completely alone for five years." She raked a slender hand through her long dark curls. "It's a good thing I love what I do because work has become my entire life."

Jill had arranged to meet with Shelly at her home the following week. As Jill and the other women returned to the classroom, Shelly stayed behind, staring out the large window in the hallway. Jill could see a war going on inside her and wondered what the outcome would be. Shelly had asked Jill to visit her house while her husband, Joe, was at work. Jill thought it was better for Shelly to be open with Joe about wanting to *feng shui* their home, but Shelly was adamant.

"He thinks anything that isn't in the Bible is evil. Let's face it; nowhere in the Bible did the Lord say, 'Let us *feng shui* this house.' "

Jill chuckled. "I'm glad you haven't lost your sense of humor."

During the last half of the class, Jill displayed several photos of rooms she had designed in the creativity and children areas of clients' homes. The most important thing for people to remember about this area, she believed, was that it was just as important to find and nurture one's inner child. She often suggested turning it into a fun activity room for all ages.

"Many people turn the creativity and children square of their home into their child's nursery or bedroom, for obvious reasons. But it isn't necessary. Remember, all the areas flow together. You might consider making this an arts area, and enjoy your favorite craft or hobby there. Or turn it into the game room where you play the games you played as a kid."

As CLASS ENDED, JILL TURNED her attention to Joni as they walked together to the parking lot. "Is your mother's last name Weintraub?" she asked her.

"Yes, that was my maiden name. Why do you ask?"

"My son's partner, Brian, is a pianist and songwriter on Broadway, and he says he knows your mother. I showed my kids the big box of chocolates you sent home with me. That led me to tell Brian about the gorgeous piano in your house, and I mentioned your mother's first name and that she was a concert pianist. Of course I didn't know her last name, but he knew the name Paget immediately."

"What's Brian's last name?" Joni asked.

"Baker; he's written scores for several shows."

"I'll ask my mother about him when I talk with her this week. Actually, I'm calling her tomorrow because I'm planning a special gathering to celebrate the new family area of the house. You gave me the idea, actually. I'm thinking of a death by chocolate theme. That way, if they kill each other, at least they can have dessert first."

Jill laughed. "I love that idea!"

"I really wish you could be there, too, Jill—sort of for moral support. My family behaves better when strangers are around. Now that I know my mother knows Brian, maybe I could invite him, too, and your son, of course."

"Actually, that sounds like a wonderful evening. Brian's fingers will be itching to play that piano. I hope your mother won't mind sharing."

"As long as he doesn't upstage her, it should be fine," Joni said, rolling her eyes. "I'll be sure to get the piano tuned. No one has played it in a long time."

JILL KNOCKED ON TOM'S OFFICE door, which was ajar. When she peeked through, she saw that his enormous leather chair faced the window. He was surveying the wooded hill behind their building, apparently deep in thought. Suddenly he whirled around, startled to see her.

She smiled brightly. "May I come in, or am I interrupting a brainstorm?"

"Yeah, sure, come in. What's up?" Tom looked distracted and ill.

"I just wanted you to know that we're completely finished at the Colver house, and Denny MacBride just got started on the Weissmuller house over in Bridgeport. I've finished designs on the two other new jobs, too."

"That's good. Were you able to come in on budget on that old millhouse?"

"Give or take a few hundred. Denny's bid was a little higher than I thought, but he's definitely the painter for this job. The homeowners already know his work and insisted on waiting for him to be available."

"Well, as long as he doesn't get too out of line with his bids."

"I'm sure that won't be a problem," Jill said, growing alarmed at Tom's gray pallor and the beads of sweat forming at his temples. His lips looked slightly blue. "Tom, you don't look well," she said. "What's going on?"

"Just a little indigestion," he said, pounding lightly with his fist on his chest. He rubbed his jaw as Jill waited for him to speak, then grabbed his left arm in pain and leaned forward against the desk, clutching his chest and breathing hard.

"Monica, call 911!" Jill shouted. "And then get the AED kit on the wall by the kitchen! God, I hope it doesn't come to that," she mumbled.

She pulled Tom back into a sitting position as several coworkers rushed to assist. "I need two aspirin!" she said. One of the architects ran to find the first aid kit.

Tom was conscious and in a lot of pain. His breathing was labored, and sweat poured down his face. "This can't be happening," he panted.

Jill was terrified, but managed to stay calm, reassuring him as she held his hand and patted his face. "The ambulance will be here soon. Just stay with me, Tom." She put both aspirin in his mouth, her hand against his face. "Chew and swallow," she said, giving him small sips of the water one of the architects had supplied from the cooler in the hallway. She prayed he wouldn't lose consciousness. Then she would need to do CPR and use the AED to restore his heart rhythm.

He winced at the taste of the aspirin and shivered, but did as he was told. Two of the men helped Tom onto the floor, and Monica held his head in her lap. It took no more than ten minutes for the ambulance to arrive, but it seemed much longer to Jill, who kept up a constant litany of prayers in her head as she looked into Tom's frightened eyes and held his hand.

"Just a few more minutes, big guy. Hang on."

"Jill …." Tom started to say, but was interrupted as the ambulance crew barreled into the office and surrounded him.

One paramedic hooked up an EKG while another administered oxygen and inserted an intravenous line. They gently lifted Tom onto a stretcher and tucked a blanket around him. Jill stayed as close as she could and then backed away as Monica put her arms around her.

Tom's eyes were clear, his voice surprisingly strong now. "Jill?" He turned his head back and forth, looking for her.

"I'm here," she said, walking along beside him. "I'm coming with you."

Monica handed Jill her coat and her purse. "Do you want me to meet you there?"

Jill looked at her gratefully. "Yes, please."

They accompanied the stretcher to the ambulance. Jill gave Tom's hand a squeeze as a paramedic adjusted the intravenous line and kept his fingers on his pulse. She wanted to get in the ambulance, but was told to follow in her own car. It was at that moment she realized that Tom could die on the way to the hospital. The ambulance crew didn't want her in their way.

"I'll meet you there," she told Tom, reluctant to let go of his hand.

It was about a fifteen minute ride to the nearest hospital, where Tom was whisked into a cubicle in the emergency room. Jill parked her car and waited for Monica. Then they entered the emergency entrance for visitors and took a seat just outside the area where Tom was being treated.

"I need a little information about Mr. Becker," a nurse said.

Jill answered the nurse's questions as best she could about Tom's health history. Janice, his wife, had always kept detailed family health records. Jill knew where they were located in Tom's house and offered to retrieve them, if necessary. The fact was, though, that Tom rarely took sick days and had always seemed healthy as a horse.

"This is just so unexpected," she found herself saying over and over again to the nurse.

Meanwhile, Monica fetched Jill a chai latte from the lobby coffee bar. "Sustenance," she said. "So, how's he doing? Everyone at the office wants me to call as soon as we hear anything."

"He's being stabilized now. The nurse said he'll probably be going to the heart catheterization lab as soon as they can take him." Jill sipped her drink, which helped her to feel less light-headed and shaky. "He probably has a blockage somewhere."

"With *his* diet? His arteries are probably clogged with fat. He's lucky he isn't a complete solid," Monica said.

As they sat together in the waiting area, Jill's thoughts darted from anguish at what had happened, to gratitude that Tom was alive and in good hands now, to worry about his future. "He might not have made it if he'd been at home alone," she told Monica, and burst into tears, covering her face with her hands. "Since Janice died, Tom hasn't been taking care of himself. He's got to start eating healthier and exercising more."

"I'm glad you were there with him when it happened," Monica said, patting her back. "You knew just what to do, and he trusted you. I was freaking out."

"Tom and I go back a lot of years," Jill said, wiping her eyes and dabbing at her nose. "He's one of my oldest and dearest friends. I wouldn't know what to do if anything happened to him."

"I know. That's why it's been so hard watching the two of you tiptoe around each other lately."

"I was hoping it wasn't so obvious. It's nothing, really. It was just a discussion that got out of hand. It isn't important now."

A male nurse came out of the double swinging doors of the emergency room. "Which one of you is Jill?"

"I am." She sprang to her feet.

"We're taking Mr. Becker upstairs to the cath lab now. It'll be about two hours or maybe a little longer until he gets in there and is finished with the procedure, and then he'll go to recovery for a little while. He's doing fine right now. He wants you to go home."

Jill breathed a sigh of relief. "Thank you. But tell him I'm staying right here."

"He said you'd say that. There's a waiting area on the fourth floor as you step off the visitors' elevator."

"Monica, why don't you go back to the office and tell everyone what's happening? I'll be fine here," Jill said. "I need to be here."

Monica gave her a hug. "Don't worry. Tom's a tough guy. Call me if you need anything."

"Thanks for staying with me. I'll call you as soon as there's news." Jill grabbed her coat and purse and followed the signs to the public elevator. As she pushed the button for the fourth floor, she was suddenly exhausted.

She drank a cup of dishwater coffee from a vending machine while she waited, watching the second hand of the wall clock tick off the minutes. After she had paged through every magazine in the waiting area, including *American Auto* and *Hunting World Digest*, she checked her cellphone alerts and found a message from her mother. She hit the talk key.

Nancy answered on the second ring. "I was wondering why I hadn't heard from you since Sunday. Is everything okay?"

"Not really. I'm here at the hospital. Tom had a heart attack this afternoon, and he's in the heart cath lab now."

Jill heard the gasp on the other end of the line, followed by her mother's comment, "But he's so young!"

"He's fifty, Mom. He's going to be fine, I'm sure of it, but it was so scary," Jill said. "I was there when it happened."

"That must have been awful. How are you holding up?"

"I'm fine, just anxious to hear that he's in the recovery area and okay. I don't know how we're going to keep him down long enough for him to rest and heal, though."

"I'm sure you'll think of something. He always listens to you."

"Mom, do you think it would be, I don't know, *weird* to insist that he stay at my house after he gets out of the hospital? I don't trust him to follow the doctor's orders, and I could make sure he eats properly and rests. If he wants to work, we could work at my house or I could drive him to the office."

"I think that idea sounds divinely inspired. Please call us when you have time, and let us know how he's doing."

"I will. Thanks, Mom."

By six o'clock, Tom was taken from recovery to his room. Jill waited outside while a nurse and the surgeon's physician's assistant settled him in his room. Finally she was allowed to enter.

"Hey, you don't look too bad," she said as Tom turned his head toward her. "Your color is much better. Blue gray is not your best hue."

Tom grimaced and attempted to smile. He wasn't able to move around much with so many tubes and wires in place, but he held out the free hand that wasn't hooked to an intravenous line. She took it, warming it between hers. There were no words to describe the relief she felt at seeing him.

"Jill, thanks for everything. You knew just what to do—the aspirin, I mean."

"I was so scared," she said, tears welling up. "Don't ever do that to me again. I mean it."

Tom smiled. "I'll try not to." He winced again.

"We'll all help you get healthy. No more fatty, greasy, salty foods, no matter how good they taste."

"I thought you were supposed to give me reasons to live." He shifted slightly in the bed to face her. "Jill, I need to say something to you, and I want you to listen and not interrupt."

"Okay." She settled on the edge of his bed, careful not to bump anything.

"What happened between us … well, what I said was unfair," he said. "I shouldn't have been so selfish. You've got a lot going on in your life, and I added to your troubles. I'm sorry."

"Tom, this isn't necessary."

"It is, Jill. I'll feel better once I get it off my chest." He smiled at his own unintended joke. "I care for you, and I always thought David was an idiot for not loving you the way you deserved. But I know what you mean when you say a relationship between us is risky. I wouldn't want anything to come between us. Your friendship means too much to me."

"There's no harm done, and anyway, I was flattered," she said, blinking away tears. "All that matters is that you get better. We can have soup and salads for lunch and take a walk every day. It'll be good for me, too."

She stood by his bed, watching the slow drip of the

intravenous solution and watching the monitor that registered the steady thump of his heart, until his eyes began closing involuntarily.

"I'll be back tomorrow." She kissed his forehead. "Don't worry about anything at the office, either. We've pulled together a good team."

As Tom's eyes closed again, she slipped silently from his room and decided to go straight home. Tom's heart attack had shaken her to the core, and all she wanted was a hot bath to relieve her aching lower back muscles. When she arrived home, she slipped off her shoes and put her feet up on the coffee table for a moment while she read the day's mail. Then she closed her eyes, resting her head against the back of the sofa until her cellphone rang.

"Hello?" she said when she saw Denny's name and number come up on the screen.

"Hey, I just wanted to say hello. Are you, by any chance, thinking of stopping by first thing tomorrow on your way to work to see what's been accomplished today?" Denny asked in a hopeful voice. "Our favorite client, Mona, was hoping to get your opinion on something. May I suggest that you not wait too long to see what she has in her mind, if ye know what I mean?"

"I can make it late morning. There's a lot going on." She told him what had happened to Tom.

"Man, I'm sorry to hear that. Please give him my best," Denny said. "How are you holdin' up?"

"I'm more than a little shaken. Tom and I have been best friends since we were eighteen. I can't believe what just happened to him. There's something so surreal about having your friend keel over from a heart attack. It really brings the reality of middle age to your doorstep. He'll be fine, according to his doctor, but we could have lost him today."

"Well, don't worry about anything else, then. We can catch up later on the job site."

"Thanks. If you have some ideas for paint color to keep Mona from going too far over the edge, I'd appreciate it. I'll call you tomorrow and let you know what time I can be there."

"No problem. I'll handle Mona," Denny said. "I'll give her some color options and stall until you get here. See you tomorrow."

Jill ran water in the wide Jacuzzi tub and retreated fully into the comfort of her Santa Fe bathroom. She poured a glass of merlot, lit a jasmine candle, and undressed, stepping into the tub with a satisfied groan. Flipping the switch to start the motors, she reveled in the soothing hot blasts of water on her aching lower back muscles and reclined against the terrycloth bath cushion. Alone with her thoughts, she couldn't help replaying in her mind what had happened to Tom and the fear she had experienced, not knowing if he would live. His words of apology in the hospital room had been comforting, too, and his courage in speaking them had set their friendship back on firm footing.

She remembered back to the day four years ago when Tom's wife, Janice, had died alone at home from a ruptured brain aneurysm. For over a year he had been inconsolable. Jill had grieved alongside him, for she and Janice were friends, too. Since Janice's death, Tom had lived alone, spending most of his time working at the office or around his house. His only daughter, Meghan, who lived in San Diego, frequently asked him to consider moving there, but he had remained in Connecticut. For years, Jill believed it had been the business that kept him firmly rooted there. Now she wondered if Tom had remained in Connecticut to be close to her. It was an unsettling thought.

Chapter Eighteen

DAVID CALLED JUST AFTER NINE o'clock that evening as Jill was getting ready to crawl into bed. "Hey, I haven't heard from you since Sunday evening," he said without preamble. "I thought we might have a chance to talk again about, well, you know."

"I'm sorry," she started to say, and stopped herself. She had no need to apologize for anything. It was her habit with David to begin most responses with an apology. "I'm afraid I've had other things on my mind today. Tom had a heart attack this afternoon."

David was silent, shocked, as Jill gave him the details. "He'll be fine, but he's got to make some serious lifestyle changes."

"I know we're at an age where this stuff happens, but it still throws me when someone we've known for years has a life-threatening event," David said.

"It doesn't seem like any time at all since we were in college," Jill admitted. "But we *are* 'at that age.' I'm just grateful there were so many people around when it happened, and that he's going to be okay."

"This is all the more reason to consider where we go from

here," David said. "We don't know what twists and turns life will throw at us. We need to appreciate each day we have. It's time to remember what brought us together."

She was silent, considering whether it might be possible that David had done some serious soul-searching. In time, could she really forgive him and forget the past? Could she learn to trust him again without waiting for the other shoe to drop? Would she ever get the image of David with another woman out of her head?

"Honey, I want us to start over again," David said. Let's have dinner Saturday evening and get reacquainted. It can be just the two of us, just like the old days."

"Okay," she said, vaguely considering the pros and cons. "I could come into the city."

She wanted to avoid the likelihood that David would insist on driving to Connecticut, which might result in him being too tired to drive home. The idea of making love with David was too painful to contemplate. She wanted to keep him at a safe distance until she figured out what to do next.

"Why don't you meet me at my apartment, and we can walk over to Anthony's? You like that place," David said. "We'll have a nice dinner and see what happens after that. I'll make reservations for seven fifteen."

Jill was fairly certain she had never been to Anthony's, but chose not to comment. She also had a clear picture of what David intended to happen after dinner. She wasn't sure that if things went well, she'd be able to resist his charms. Whatever happened next in their lives couldn't be solved by sex. Of that she was quite sure.

She paused for several seconds before answering, "Okay, I'll see you around seven. But I'll need to drive home, so let's make it an early evening."

AFTER LUNCH THE NEXT DAY, Jill met Denny at Dr. Mona Gagnon's home in Greenwich. Mona, an attractive, vivacious flaxen-haired chiropractor with a lucrative practice, had decided to build another wing onto her home for a workout room and spa. To say that Mona's vision was grandiose was putting it mildly. The project was estimated to cost $250,000, and constant add-ons were raising the price tag even higher.

Jill's heart jumped when she saw Denny standing by his truck in front of Mona's home. Her chest thumped wildly at the sight of him as she brought her car to a stop in Mona's wide driveway. She knew it was time to be honest with him about what was happening with David, but dreaded speaking the words. Stepping out of her car, she tried to smile and failed miserably.

"Your face matches this cloudy mornin', lass," he observed. "Is everything okay with Tom?"

"He's fine. Thanks for asking. In fact, he should be released from the hospital on Sunday," she said, steeling herself as he approached her. "Denny, I need to tell you something—not about Tom. I feel terrible that I waited until now, when I should have told you earlier this week."

"What's the matter?" Denny's expression was patient, his eyes kind. He looked worried, however.

The words spilled out in a flood. "David unexpectedly showed up for dinner on Sunday evening. After the kids went home, he asked me to reconsider the divorce. I know I told you my marriage is over, and I still believe it is. It's just so hard right now to figure out what's best for everyone." She pressed her fingers hard against her eyes. "We're going into the final stages of the divorce, so it's now or never."

"That's a reasonable request, I'd say. You might have regrets, otherwise."

"Thank you for understanding. So much has happened so quickly." Jill released the pressure of her fingers, causing wild colors to swirl across her field of vision. "I know it's the right thing to do. I just wish I felt happier about it, or at least more hopeful."

"But it's important to know for sure."

"I haven't called my attorney to stop the divorce from moving forward." Jill looked into Denny's eyes, expecting conflict, but saw only acceptance. "I know I can't go back to the way things were. Too much has happened. But I said I would have dinner with him this Saturday, which will give us a chance to talk. Maybe things will be clearer after that."

"And you need me to back off." There was no bitterness in Denny's voice. He shifted from one leg to the other.

To Jill, the slight space he put between them was the same as if a wall had gone up. "Don't say it like that. I've got to take these next few weeks to consider what's best for everyone, not just me. It isn't right for me to string you along and put your life on hold, too, while I figure out what comes next."

He was silent for a moment before clearing his throat. "Jill, you're behaving as if it's the end of the world. It's no' that bad. Do you honestly think I'm that shallow, that I wouldn't understand? If my opinion matters, which it shouldn't, I think you're doing the right thing." His face was full of compassion.

She looked into his clear brown eyes as the moment lightened. "How can you be so understanding and rational about this?"

Denny chuckled. "I knew the timing of meeting you wasn't ideal," he said, "and I've expected that I might need to hold back for a while. It's okay. Do whatever your heart says to do," he said quietly. "I'll be here, if you still want me. If you choose David, we'll still be the greatest of friends."

As she looked into his eyes, she saw that he meant what he said.

Jill dressed carefully for dinner with David, selecting gray flannel slacks and a rose-colored cashmere twinset that brought out the natural color in her cheeks. She donned the amethyst pendant and earrings he had given her early in their marriage and then drove into Manhattan, arriving at his apartment a few minutes before seven o'clock. She thought that if he saw the jewelry he had given her, it might result in a deeper discussion between them. That pendant and earring set had been his housewarming gift to her. At the time, he had loved their big, new home.

He answered the door in his bathrobe, giving her a quick peck on the lips. "Give me just a second to throw on some clothes," he said as he towel-dried his hair. "I just went for a run in the park."

"No problem," she said and plunked down on the sofa, picking up an *Architectural Digest* magazine and skimming through it quickly.

The apartment was furnished with a woman's touch, she decided immediately, noting the damask furniture, soft wool throws, tufted cushions on the sofa and chairs, and slightly kitschy accessories. There was a bookshelf filled with broadcasting journals, along with an impressive display of romance novels. She wondered about the identity of the woman who lived here. David had said he was subletting from a colleague.

"You can come back here and talk to me," he called out to her from the bedroom.

Jill raised her eyebrows and picked up a food and wine magazine. "Take your time. I'll pretend we're back in college and I'm sitting here waiting for you. I never knew a man could take longer than a woman to get ready for a date."

She heard his quick laugh. "Oh, come on," he retorted. "I wasn't always late."

Yes, you were, she mouthed the words silently in an exaggerated fashion before commenting out loud, "You were fortunate that no one else in your fraternity cared about hygiene."

When he emerged about ten minutes later—record time for David—he looked as handsome as ever. Jill took in a quick, appreciative breath before reacting. "I guess you were worth the wait."

"Aren't you the little smart aleck tonight?" he teased as he drew her to her feet and enveloped her in his arms.

He smelled good, too. It had never taken much for Jill to respond to his attentions, but tonight, she preferred to keep a safe distance. Too many questions remained unanswered, and she wasn't sure this evening was even a good idea.

"I thought we had reservations for seven fifteen," she said. "I don't know about you, but I skipped lunch."

"Well, then, I guess we'd better get going." He took her hand as they walked to Anthony's, an elegant and expensive trattoria specializing in seafood and fresh pasta. As they walked, Jill decided to risk dampening the mood by asking the identity of the woman whose apartment David was subletting.

"She has nice taste," she said.

"Who are we talking about?" he asked in a clipped, polite tone that told Jill he knew exactly what she wanted to know.

"The woman whose apartment you're subletting. I like what she's done with the place."

"How do you know it's a woman?" David's eyes met hers.

"Furniture style, romance novels, feminine design touches." Jill shrugged. "No pool table in the dining room. No old couch with camouflage upholstery. No craft beer bottles as decoration."

David laughed out loud. "No guy I know would decorate like that. But yes, you're very observant," he said as they paused at a street corner for the crossing light. He kept his hand firmly on her elbow. "Her name is Andrea Colson. She's on assignment in the UK, so I'm living there until she gets back."

Jill recognized the name of the correspondent, but could only vaguely recall seeing her on television. She wondered how well David knew Andrea, since she obviously was comfortable enough to sublet her apartment to him. They arrived at Anthony's—a small, elegant restaurant co-owned by two up-

and-coming chefs who also happened to be married to each other.

"Ah, Mr. Hennessy," the maitre d' said. "We're happy to have you dining with us tonight. We've got your table in the back all ready for you. Good evening, Ma'am." He smiled noncommittally in Jill's direction and then averted his eyes discreetly. David obviously had been here before with other people.

It was a reality of life with a celebrity that anonymity and privacy could never be guaranteed. She was reminded of this as they were ushered to their table in the rear of the restaurant behind a curtain. Other diners looked up as David passed, and there were whispered comments and curious stares in her direction.

Jill sat down in the chair David held out for her before taking his own seat. He accepted the wine menu from the maitre d' and flipped it open, studying it carefully. David prided himself on his knowledge of wines, a skill Jill had appreciated all these years.

"I think a nice cabernet is in order, don't you think?" he asked, glancing up at her and smiling.

"Whatever you think," she said out of habit, and then caught herself. She actually preferred cabernet sauvignon to other red wines, but was all too aware of her habit of acquiescing automatically to David's wishes. This time she decided to let it go, thinking he might have suggested a cabernet because he remembered her preference for it. They ordered the house *insalata* prepared tableside as they chatted companionably about their jobs, Finn and Liam, and Missy's pregnancy.

"I'd like to give the kids nursery furniture for their big Christmas gift," she told him. "Maybe you'll go in on that with me."

"Let's do it," he agreed.

"Brian and Liam could use a new desk for their office."

"Fine with me. I'm sure you know what they'd like—what would look good in their place."

It felt so natural to hear him respond this way. To her relief, the conversation flowed without much effort, and by the time their entrees arrived, Jill recognized that David was making more of an effort to engage her in conversation and to solicit her thoughts. Usually he listened passively, his attention elsewhere until she called him on it.

She told him about her *feng shui* class. "They're such a great group of people. I can honestly say I'd choose any one of them for a friend."

"It surprises me that you're teaching. You used to be so afraid of public speaking. Remember how you practiced over and over when you had to make a presentation in school until you'd memorized everything?"

"I do remember." She chuckled at the memory. "I was nervous the first two weeks of this class, but then I realized that I love talking about *feng shui* in design work, and the information just seems to flow. In fact, I've been thinking how nice it would be—don't laugh—to have a television show about *feng shui*. Can you believe it's me saying that?"

David looked thoughtful. "Anything is possible, if you want it enough."

Jill smiled as their eyes met. "You should know, since you made all your dreams come true."

"How's Tom?" David asked, changing the subject. "I can't stop thinking about what happened this week." He shuddered and took a gulp of wine.

"He's getting out of the hospital late tomorrow morning. I'm bringing him back to the house for a few days so I can keep an eye on him. He isn't supposed to be alone, and he's refusing home health care."

David raised his eyebrows, opened his mouth to speak, and stopped. His eyelid twitched—a sure sign that he was holding something back.

"What?" Jill looked intently at David.

"Nothing."

"What were you going to say?" Jill put down her salad fork.

David chewed and swallowed. "One of your most endearing qualities is that you give a hundred percent of yourself, but you don't always see the big picture."

"Which is?"

"Tom has had a 'thing' for you as long as I've known him. Do you think having him stay at the house is such a good idea?"

Jill quickly lost her appetite. She wasn't about to tell David what had happened between her and Tom a few weeks earlier. Besides, since she and David were legally separated and in the process of divorcing, it was none of David's business whether or not she allowed Tom to recover at her home, or for that matter, whether she and Tom carried on a torrid affair. For the sake of civility, she decided to keep her thoughts to herself.

"The reality is that he can't go home alone, David. He just had two stents put in. If you think we're going to engage in wild, passionate sex, think again." She laughed to soften her message.

"He can't like me very much these days," David observed wryly, taking another sip of wine.

"Well, you can certainly find out. He'll be at the house for dinner tomorrow evening, if you'd care to join us."

David let out a long breath. "Jill, all I care about right now is getting our lives back on track as a married couple. I hope there won't be other people with their own agendas who want to derail us. That's all I'm saying."

Jill wondered what had happened to his earlier suggestion that they have a fun evening together and get reacquainted. If he was trying to win her heart, this was not the way. He was assuming they'd reconcile. He was even setting the terms.

Indignation surged through her, but she contained herself, aware that the few other diners in their section seemed to be craning their heads to listen. "There are obviously people with strong opinions," she said quietly. "We can't insulate ourselves from everyone who has a thought about what happened. Those people who truly care about us will be in our lives supporting what is best for each of us."

As they finished the rest of their dinner, Jill realized that once again she was censoring herself. Just when she thought she couldn't keep up the pretense any longer, the check came. As David paid the bill, she considered how best to tell him that she was not going back to the apartment.

As they stood to leave, he took her arm. "Let's walk a little," he said. They covered several blocks within a few minutes, barely speaking except to comment on the aromas of New York City on a Saturday night—the smells of roasting meat, garlic, popcorn, and freshly ground coffee emanating from restaurants and storefronts. "It's been too long since we did this kind of thing," David observed. "We're out of practice just hanging out together."

"It does seem like forever." Jill thought for a moment and realized that it had been at least three years since the last time they'd spent a Saturday evening walking the streets of Manhattan. On the rare occasions they went out for dinner together, David insisted they stay in Connecticut.

Rounding the corner, Jill noticed a sign for the gallery where Denny's paintings were on exhibit. She kept her eyes focused ahead and quickened her step, but David slowed down to linger in front of several paintings arranged on brass easels. He studied them at length, commenting on the color and style.

"This guy is good," he said. "I'm no expert, but his water looks really wet."

"I've recommended this artist's work to several clients. He also does specialty interior painting for us." She pulled David along by the hand before he could make another comment.

"Are you tired?" he asked after they covered another couple of blocks. "Would you like to head back to my place?"

"I need to think about getting back to my car. It's late." Jill glanced at her watch.

"You could spend the night." He squeezed the back of her

neck lightly, and she felt an involuntary shiver.

David now had his arm possessively around her waist, his hand resting low on her back, in what she recognized as his customary proprietary hold. She knew he expected her to go along with the idea. To make matters worse, she still couldn't get out of her mind the thought of him with Amber. The graphic mental image made her slightly ill. Again, she wondered what kind of relationship David had with Andrea that she allowed him to live in her apartment. But more than these troubling thoughts, it was Denny and their last kiss at his house that was foremost on her mind after seeing his paintings in the gallery window.

"It's not a good idea," she said, and David's eyes opened in surprise.

When they reached her car, he wrapped his arms around her and kissed her. "Jill, I love you," he said. "I wish I could turn back the clock and make everything that happened go away."

"David, I will always love you for all the history we have and the fact that you and I made a family together," she said, giving him a squeeze. She stepped back. "No matter what, you have to believe that." She unlocked the car and got in. "I meant it when I said you should come by for dinner tomorrow night. That's a good next step for the sake of everyone in our family."

David's smile was noncommittal. "Sure," he said.

As she drove away from the curb, she caught sight of him in the rearview mirror. He looked drawn and uncertain, standing alone. There was a faint stirring in her heart—a fondness she knew could never be extinguished. But now in place of a deep connection, she felt little more than a vague sort of familiarity. More significantly, as she drove home to Connecticut, her thoughts were not on David.

Chapter Nineteen

Tom was released from the hospital late Sunday morning. He was embarrassed at so clearly needing the wheelchair the nurse brought to transport him from his room to the circle driveway. More concerning was his fragility. He was noticeably shaky as the nurse assisted him into Jill's car.

"I can do this myself," he insisted in a subdued tone. Jill and the nurse exchanged glances.

He was unusually quiet on the drive to his house to pack a small suitcase. While he went upstairs to pack, Jill cleaned out his refrigerator, grimacing at what passed for groceries in Tom's mind: cheese brats, Danish, a few slices of congealed meat lovers' pizza, and beer.

"I'm sure I'll be fine here at home," Tom insisted again as he came into the kitchen. "I don't want to be a bother."

"Tom, you are anything but a bother, and I have plenty of room. Let's put it this way: you either stay with me, or your daughter will be on the first plane here. I *will* call her."

"Okay, you're right. Meghan has a busy career. That would be tough on her." He offered no further resistance.

"Besides," she added, "Saturday night is the annual Halloween party, and I could use your moral support."

"I'm surprised you're still having the party, with everything that's been happening."

"Tom, that party is tradition—not just because David and I gave it. It's tradition because it brings the people I care most about together. That's important to me now."

"Well, then, count on me as your bartender."

When they arrived at Jill's home, she settled him into the downstairs guest room. "It won't hurt you to chill out for a few days," she said as she turned down the comforter and plumped the fat pillows. "Besides, you'll be company for me. It's too quiet around here these days."

"If we get on each other's nerves, I'll leave."

Jill laughed. "Tom, if we haven't gotten on each other's nerves in all these years of working together day in and day out, it's not going to happen now. Besides, if I let you go home, you'll find bad things to eat. I swear, my friend," she said in her most threatening tone, "if you consume anything that isn't heart-healthy and I find out about it, I'll kick your ass."

"Just sticks and straw?"

"Carrot and celery sticks and high-fiber cereal, yes," she answered in a firm voice that allowed for no argument. "Nothing fried or high in sugar, Tom. I mean it. You'll eat whole grains, vegetables, and fruit for dessert." She patted his arm. "We have to get you well."

With his energy level at an unaccustomed low, Tom slept and caught up on his reading. By late afternoon, he sat at the kitchen island as Jill prepared dinner and set the table. "So you're really letting him come home," Tom said as he observed her setting a place for David at the head of the table.

"I don't know the answer to that, Tom. I want him to spend more time with Liam and Finn, no matter what. He's still their dad."

"It's not up to you to manage David's relationship with his kids," Tom pointed out. "If he wants to be close to them, he'll have to make the effort on his own."

Jill had to acknowledge the truth in that statement. "In some ways, it would be easier if I let David come home. But to tell you the truth, it's as if the door has been slammed shut and locked on that chapter of my life. I'm struggling to find the key to let him back in."

"For once in your life, don't listen to the 'shoulds' or the 'what ifs.' If you make a decision because you think it's in the best interests of anyone else, you'll end up miserable," Tom said. "A leopard can't change his spots, and it seems to me you've earned the right to be happy."

"DAD WILL BE HERE A little later, I guess," Jill told Finn, Liam, and Missy as it neared six o'clock and there was still no sign of David. He had not responded to a phone call or text, either. A knowing glance passed between Liam and Finn. Jill was embarrassed, more for David than herself.

She addressed the twins. "I want everyone to be on their best behavior. Tom doesn't need more stress in his life right now."

"Then you shouldn't have invited Dad," Liam said.

Brian flashed a look that silenced him. Missy and Finn joined Tom in the den in front of the evening news while Brian and Liam stayed in the kitchen with Jill. While she put the finishing touches on a pan of roasted salmon with lemon and fresh dill, Jill told them about Joni's plan to have a death by chocolate party to bring the Weintraub family together.

"It's the Saturday after Thanksgiving, and you and Liam are invited since you know her mother, Brian."

Brian's eyes lit up. "I wonder if Paget will let me play her piano." He grinned and rubbed his hands together.

"I wonder if Paget has any choice," Liam teased. "I've never known you to pass a piano without an impromptu performance."

As she watched Brian pantomime stepping up to the plate and hitting a fly ball straight at Liam, Jill shook her head. "Joni is trying to bring harmony back to her family, and I'd like to help her," she said. "Sometimes it takes the good intentions of several people to mend fences." She hadn't meant the remark as a reflection on what was happening with her own family, but the inference didn't fall on deaf ears.

"I know that's what you're trying to do with Dad," Liam said. "I just don't think he's capable of that kind of change."

Jill gave him a pleading look. "No matter what has happened, I still have a long history with your dad and some good memories. He has asked me to reconsider, and I want no regrets later on." She looked Liam straight in the eye. "Don't turn your back on your father or you may end up with your own regrets."

Liam's face turned stormy. "Unlike you, Mom, I have almost no fond memories," he said, turning on his heel to leave the room.

"Excuse me," Jill said, exchanging looks with Brian as she left the kitchen, following Liam into the living room.

He was sitting at the piano, plunking one key at a time, when she slid onto the bench beside him. "Hey, I realize that you're upset, and I have a feeling that it's as much about me as it is about your dad," she said. "I know that you don't want me to reconcile with him, and if I had to wager a bet, I'd say chances aren't good. But he asked me to reconsider, and this is part of a healing process I need to move forward. I'm saying what I need to say to him now, whether he likes it or not."

"How's that going?" he snorted.

She ignored his sarcasm. "Not well. I won't mince words. I doubt your dad and I can ever be happy together again. We're very different people, and I won't reconcile with him unless all of my concerns about his behavior—toward you, too, not just me—are addressed."

Liam turned to her. "I just don't want you to be hurt again, Mom." A lone tear dribbled down his cheek. She held him close to her, kissing away his tear, just as she had when he was a little boy.

"Everything will work out as it should," she said. "I promise you, Liam, that I will end this marriage if I'm not sure it's what I want and what's best for all of us."

"Okay," he said in a barely audible voice. "I'm sorry for creating a scene with Tom here."

"Tom gets it. Don't worry about that. Now let's finish making dinner before the fish gets cold."

As they made their way back to the kitchen, their arms around each other, Jill thought again how much Liam was like his father—more than he would ever admit. He had a sensitive, stubborn nature that during high school and college often led him to retreat into moody silences. He was quick to carry a grudge and rarely apologized—very much like his father. She was thankful for Brian's more mature, laid-back temperament—so much like Finn's—and hoped that in time Liam would come around to a less angry point of view.

"Jill, I'm sorry about Liam," Brian said, squeezing her shoulder gently as she heaped salad onto plates. "He's behaving badly tonight."

"He's always been the one to chew on hurts and slights," she said. "In this case, though, he's got a misplaced sense that he's trying to protect me."

As Jill finished preparing the main course and spooned vegetables into serving dishes, she began to feel disgusted. Where was David? Surely he wouldn't miss this opportunity to show that he cared about family life. By six thirty, Jill knew that he would not be there and began serving.

"How did dinner with David go last night?" Missy asked curiously, coming into the kitchen to help.

"All things considered, I'd say it went better than expected," she said. "It was a little tense at times, but overall, we had a nice meal. Then I drove home."

"But David still isn't here for dinner tonight," Missy pointed out, her small face serious and drawn.

"No, he's not." Jill sighed.

* * *

SHELLY WAS WAITING ON HER front porch when Jill arrived for her *feng shui* consultation. For the past week, Jill had dreaded this particular home visit, knowing that Shelly's husband was being kept in the dark about Jill's purpose in being there. When making *feng shui* fixes with positive intention, deception was never a good idea. Shelly looked nervous and was jumping from one foot to the other in her excitement. Jill's anxiety increased as she viewed the exterior of the house, which had zero curb appeal. The house looked sterile. The irony of this thought wasn't lost on her.

"Joe got home early from work," Shelly said in a whispered tone. "We'll need to be careful what we say in front of him."

"I could come back another time." Jill wanted nothing more than to leave.

"Oh, no, you can't go! I mean, I've looked forward to …. Please stay. I've been so excited about this, and Joe probably will be glued to the evening news."

Jill followed Shelly into the house, where she was introduced to Joe, Shelly's husband of seven years. He didn't look at all the way Jill had imagined him: a big, burly, loud man, overbearing in his mannerisms. Quite the opposite. Joe was of medium height, slightly built, his sandy hair already receding. He had a studious, almost mousy air about him. His eyes were the lightest shade of blue, yet cold and furtive. He resembled a rodent, she thought.

"It's nice to meet you," he said in a soft, flat voice as he shook Jill's hand. "Shelly certainly enjoys your interior design class— says she wants to make a few changes upstairs. I reminded her that she's married to a working man, not some rich celebrity like you're used to, Mrs. Hennessy." His eyes bored into Jill's, and she shivered.

Jill cleared her throat, hoping her dislike of the man wasn't written all over her face. "I'll be glad to offer her some budget-friendly ideas."

"I'll be downstairs until you get dinner on the table," Joe

told Shelly, giving her a look that was nothing short of a direct order. Jill wondered what the consequences would be for Shelly if she displeased Joe.

"I've got your favorite chicken casserole in the oven," Shelly told him. "It'll be about another hour until everything is ready. Jill and I will be done by then. Jill, can you stay for dinner?"

"Oh, that's nice of you, but I have a house guest this week. Maybe some other time."

Once they were on the upstairs stair landing, Shelly whispered, "Remember, he doesn't know the class is about *feng shui*. I told him it was an introduction to interior design. If he knew the truth, he'd think it was evil."

Jill let out a soft laugh. "I still hear that occasionally. There are people who have the same beliefs about yoga and meditation. But fine, your secret is safe with me."

She followed Shelly into the creativity and children area upstairs, a guest bedroom Shelly planned to use as a nursery. It had medium blue walls, beige carpet, and cheap cream-colored drapes. A crucifix hung on the wall above the bed, which was covered in a white chenille spread. Other than the crucifix, there was no art on the walls. A round pillow in cream with The Lord's Prayer in skillful needlepoint adorned the bed.

"We need to look at the main floor area," Jill reminded her. "It's fine to *feng shui* the upstairs, but that's the primary living space we need to enhance."

"I can't make any changes downstairs," Shelly said abruptly. "That's Joe's television area. He'd have a fit."

Jill's eyes opened wide as she looked curiously at Shelly. This was way beyond controlling behavior, in her view. She wondered what would happen if Shelly asserted her wishes for the room's décor. Surely, the man wouldn't strike her.

"He's just opinionated," Shelly said. "All the men in his family are like that. If I disagree, he gives me the silent treatment. If I argue with him, I always end up wishing I'd kept quiet. He's the man of this house."

"Shelly, you're a smart woman. You're an office manager, right? You ought to be an equal partner in your relationship and in your own home." Jill willed herself to stop talking as Shelly's face turned stormy. "I know I have no right to tell you what I think, but what you want matters, too. Doesn't it?"

"I want a baby, and one way or another, I'll have one. I don't care what I have to do."

Jill's stomach lurched. Fighting off an urge to tell Shelly exactly what she thought, she asked, "Do you have a support system, perhaps your minister?"

Shelly snorted. "It's useless to say anything to Reverend Don." She drew out the name 'Don' with contempt. "He's Joe's older brother, and the entire family thinks it's my fault we haven't had a baby because I work outside the home."

Jill wanted to say something, but decided to let the comment go. She had wanted to sit down with Shelly the previous week and ask more personal questions, but there was something about the woman's demeanor that stopped her. Despite the obvious issues with Shelly's marriage, it was up to her to speak up to her husband or tell him what she expected. Jill knew this from personal experience.

Shelly looked down at her own hands, turning them over. "My parents didn't want me to marry Joe, so I just keep quiet. They don't know everything that's been happening."

"It's a shame that your family isn't able to be more supportive," Jill said, placing her hands on Shelly's thin shoulders and looking into her eyes. "Isn't there anyone you can talk with?"

Shelly was silent for a few moments before answering. "My sister, Jody, would understand. I don't get to see her very much. Joe doesn't want me to spend time with my family and friends, especially Jody. He can't stand her because she divorced her husband a few years ago. Oh, and Jody doesn't like Joe, either, and she lets him know it."

Closing the bedroom door so she wouldn't be heard, Jill asked, "Would you and Joe really be that much happier if you had a child of your own?" She couldn't imagine how that could be the case.

"Oh, yes! A child would bring so much meaning to our relationship, and I think Joe would be nicer. He thinks women ought to be mothers."

Jill sighed. She no longer wanted to help Shelly enhance the creativity and children area of her home. Half-heartedly, she began her assessment of the room. "Metal is the power element for this area, and you've already got a brass daybed, so that's a good start. The walls are blue, so I'd start with a soft yellow on these walls."

"Joe painted this room blue," Shelly said. "He won't like it if I change the color."

"Shelly, the fixes have to be made by you in order to work." Jill shook her head and then decided to let it go. "Okay, then let's strengthen the earth element in this room since earth is creative with metal. Find a round, terra cotta clay pot with some kind of yellow or white flowers. You could paint the pot yellow, too, which would get a stronger yellow element in here. There are some really cute daybed covers in yellow patchwork that would be pretty. Or at least put a yellow pillow on the bed." Her voice trailed off. She wanted to suggest a white crib for the baby, but she kept quiet. She could hardly stand the thought of an infant in this home.

Jill sat down on the bed, hoping to think of something else that would be helpful, but all she wanted to do was find a way to get through to Shelly. Perhaps she wasn't the one to provide the help Shelly needed, but she would figure out who could. If Shelly was being abused, she needed help now. Jill couldn't imagine how the situation could get better, given Joe's personality.

"How did you meet Joe, anyway? Was he like this from the first?"

"We were introduced at church camp when I was in high school, and he was in college. He was my counselor. I've always been shy, and I had trouble making friends that summer. I didn't fit in with the other kids, and I didn't want to be there, either. He sort of took responsibility for making sure I wasn't alone. After camp was over, he became my first boyfriend—my only boyfriend." Shelly smiled grimly at the memory. "He had so much confidence. I felt special that he chose me. My family doesn't like him much. When we got married, Joe said he didn't enjoy being around them, so we only see them at Christmas."

Jill bit her tongue. "I wouldn't know what to do if I weren't so close to my parents."

Shelly looked down at the floor. "I've made my bed. Now I have to lie on it."

From an ethical standpoint, Jill knew that she was called to provide honest assistance, even though she believed strongly that *feng shui* fixes might not work in this case. The only positive to fixing the creativity and children area was that Shelly might decide she wanted more joy in her life with a man who could give her children, and eventually leave Joe. Perhaps the Women's Help Center could get through to her in ways that Jill could not. She resolved to get the name and number of a counselor and give it to Shelly.

Although Shelly's situation was far more extreme than her own, Jill realized that she had bent to David's wishes in much the way that Shelly did with her husband's demands. Jill didn't believe in coincidence—random events happening for no reason. Rather, she thought each life event brought new lessons to be learned and shared. Now that she understood better how injurious this kind of relationship could be—not just to the survival of a marriage, but to the individual's self-esteem—she had a sense of destiny. She and Shelly had been brought together so that a lesson could be shared.

Chapter Twenty

Halloween week started out with heavy rain and strong winds. Jill was glad to have a reason to work from home as she served tea and toast with cinnamon and honey to Tom in front of the fireplace. Although he had been a courteous, undemanding patient the past two days, he insisted that he would feel less stressed if he could go into the office for just a few hours every day. Reluctantly, Jill agreed, but told him they would work a half-day and return home for lunch so that he could have an afternoon nap. So far, it had worked out well, and Tom said he felt much better. He certainly looked better.

As she reviewed costs for a new home project design that afternoon, she received a text from Denny. *Mona has chosen new colors for the spa and exercise room in honor of the holiday. I hope black and orange are good colors in feng shui.*

Very funny; not budging until tomorrow, she texted back, but added an emoticon wink.

That evening, while she and Tom ate dinner at the kitchen table, she nudged him with her foot. "Why don't you come with me to *feng shui* class tomorrow night? You've never seen me in action, and the subject is prosperity. Who doesn't love hearing how to make more money? Plus, you'll get a kick out of my students."

"If you insist," he said blandly, but looked interested nonetheless. "Can I do a short spiel about the company? Or maybe I could give them a pop quiz?"

"Can you say, 'This is Jill's class'?" she asked, giving him a stern glance.

"Sorry. I promise to be on my best behavior."

David called that evening as Jill did the dishes. "Answer that, will you?" she asked Tom. "My hands are wet."

She heard Tom say, "I'm doing much better, buddy. Thanks for asking. And you?" He listened for a moment before saying, "I'm giving you to Jill now." There was no expression on Tom's face as he handed her the phone.

She took the phone into the laundry room and shut the door. "Hey, what happened to you last night?" she asked. "I expected you for dinner."

"I got hung up doing some reading," he said, before launching into the reason for his call. "This Saturday I thought we could head over to Block Island," he said. "We'll stay at that little inn you like so much."

"It's a lovely idea, but Tom is still here, and in case you've forgotten, it's Halloween. I sent you an email invitation to the party, in case you haven't seen it in your inbox yet."

There was silence on the other end of the line. "I didn't think you'd want to have a party this year," he said, "considering what's been going on."

"The Halloween party is tradition," she said. "I wish you had talked with me first."

"I wanted to surprise you."

"I appreciate that, but even so—"

"Jill, I'm making an effort here."

"Are you? Sunday dinner was a chance for us to spend time together with our sons and daughter-in-law."

"Let's not forget about Tom. He's in the picture now, too. I guess I just didn't feel like competing."

She paused and bit her upper lip before saying, "Tom is not your competition."

ON TUESDAY EVENING, TOM INSISTED on driving Jill to the community college. She knew he was restless, even though he had been to the office a few hours that day and the day before. He scooped the keys up off the kitchen counter before Jill could reach them.

"I feel fine. I'm getting edgy from being cooped up so much."

Jill rolled her eyes. "First, you aren't really supposed to be driving yet. Second, considering that we've been to the office two days in a row, I don't think that qualifies as being cooped up."

Tom grinned. "Good thing you already fed me dinner. Otherwise, there's no telling what kind of fast food I'd crave on the way over there."

Jill gave him a stern look. "I assume you have reasons to live."

When they got to the classroom, Jill was elated to see that all of her students were present. She especially was glad to see Joel back again. He stood up to greet her.

"Hey, there," she said, giving him a hug. "Glad to see you in class. This must mean Diana is doing better."

"Two of her best friends came over this evening to hang out with her." He gave a casual shrug, but the delighted look on his face told her that everything was better than fine. "She said I should come back to class and see what else I can learn."

"That's a good sign." Jill made introductions all around. She suggested that Tom take a seat beside Trish.

"Tonight, we're going to discuss the prosperity square of the *bagua*," Jill said. She pointed to the square in the upper left-hand side. "If you want more money circulating in your life, as well as an overall feeling of abundance and well-being, this is a very important square. Remember that abundance isn't just about money, though. You can be wealthy and still not have happiness or health or loving relationships. All the areas work together. I feel prosperous because I have so many wonderful friends."

She pointed to the square and on the blackboard wrote a list of the colors best for this area in chalk. "I like to use purple, green, red, and gold in this corner because they're power colors symbolic of wealth and energy."

"I get why you use green and red, but why purple?" Shelly asked.

"Purple is the color of royalty. Kings and queens wore purple robes," she said. "But it's also a very spiritual color in any tradition. It's our faith in something higher that allows us to believe in the flow of abundance. For that reason, I like to keep a huge amethyst geode in my prosperity area. The wall color in that area of my house is lavender—very subtle. I needed to use purple, since that room is a laundry area and I didn't want to paint it green or red. Of course, I also have green plants hanging in the window. For the red element, I bought a red washer and dryer. To tie all the colors together, I found a Navaho cloth with purple, red, and green stripes that I draped across the top of the appliances. The whole effect is quite striking."

Trish raised her hand. "What about a red candle?"

"Great question," Jill said. "A symbol of fire isn't a good idea in this area because it can symbolize that your resources are going up in flames. Water is the important element in this area because prosperity flows. However, if you're using a fountain to symbolize the flow of resources, make sure to change the water regularly."

"I'm still worried that my prosperity area is located in my bathroom," Trish said. "I could be flushing away all of my resources." She and Tom exchanged shy smiles.

"I'll be seeing you later this week, Trish, and we'll make sure we add enough positive elements to counteract any negatives from the toilet. You're right, though. A toilet is definitely not good to have in the prosperity area because of the symbolic flushing-away aspect."

On break, Tom and Trish continued talking in the classroom. After a few minutes they left and walked down the hall toward the cafeteria, still engaged in animated conversation. Jill watched them as they walked together, stopping now and then to look at each other as they talked. She hoped that Tom was having a good time.

"Trish has a new friend," Kristen observed with a grin. "I hope he's single and available."

"Very." Jill watched as Tom and Trish turned a corner and disappeared out of sight. "He's a widower. I'd love to see him settled down with someone as sweet and grounded as Trish."

After class, Jill reminded everyone about the Halloween party at her home that weekend. "Come in costume, if you want. You don't need to bring anything, except your appetite. Our very own Meredith will be catering the festivities."

Meredith smiled, and her cheeks colored as the other students reacted to the news. "Thank you again, Jill," she said. "I'll make it a feast!"

"Will you be there?" Tom asked Trish, whose eyes lit up in response to the question.

"I wouldn't miss it for the world," she said.

BY FIVE THIRTY ON THURSDAY, Jill was on her way to meet Trish at her apartment in an older section of town. Before leaving the house, she'd prepared a plate of steamed vegetables and broiled lemon tilapia for Tom to heat up for dinner, promising not to be late. She got the distinct impression that Tom wanted to tag along, but she needed Trish's undivided attention as they applied fixes to her bathroom.

"I won't be late," she promised. "Why don't you call your daughter and let her know how you're doing?"

"I already did that," he said. "She had some big news of her own: she's pregnant, due in June."

"Tom, that's fantastic!" Jill said. "Both of us are going to be grandparents next spring."

"The times, they are a changing," Tom answered quietly. "A heart attack and now news of a grandchild make me realize that while I wasn't paying attention, the next phase of my life began."

"That goes for both of us," she said and watched as Tom's eyes grew distant. As she got into her car, she wondered specifically which thoughts about his future were now going through Tom's mind.

TRISH'S APARTMENT WAS ON THE third floor of a rehabilitated motel badly in need of more renovation. Beige paint on steel beams and supports was peeling, the orange brick needed tuck-pointing, and the black metal railings were rusty and splashed with bird droppings. As she climbed the concrete steps to the third floor, Jill noticed cigarette butts and trash in corners. Strong, unpleasant cooking odors wafted into the air from apartments along the way. Her heart went out to Trish, who had taken great pride in her home before being forced out of it. This place was the pits. She rapped lightly on the door of 3-B.

Trish answered promptly, a huge smile on her face. "Jill!" she exclaimed, enveloping her in a warm hug. "Please come in."

When Jill entered the apartment, she was struck by the imaginative style and creativity Trish had taken with what could have been a lackluster rental space. Although the walls were neutral and the carpet bland and threadbare in places, Trish had covered areas of the floor with attractive patterned rugs. Her furniture was tasteful and expensive, and she had added bright splashes of jewel-tone colors. There were lush, healthy plants arranged in decorative, hand-painted pots, whimsical hand-blown glass figurines, and tasteful paintings to enhance a space that otherwise would have been depressing.

As Jill surveyed each room, she almost forgot that she was

in a renovated motel. "This is lovely," she said, and sank into a yellow floral chair with a hand-crocheted blue-and-white throw.

"I was able to keep some of my favorite things," Trish said. "Of course, I had to sell a lot of my furniture, but it doesn't matter; I'm doing okay here. If it weren't for the location, I'd consider staying a while. But the neighborhood isn't all that safe, and I really want my own house again, even if it's tiny." She looked wistful. "Would you like to see the bathroom? That's my prosperity area."

When Jill saw the bathroom, she held back a grimace. The space was drab, the sink and tub chipped, and the commercial fixtures cheap and utilitarian. It was a credit to Trish's decorating abilities that she had been able to do anything at all with this room.

"It's not bad at all," she lied, squeezing Trish's arm reassuringly. "I think you need to go bold with the space, though. We want to enhance wood and water, and the toilet and these pipes are taking water away. Water represents flow of resources. But I see you've already taken care of that." Trish had tied red silk ribbons around all the outgoing pipes. "That'll do it." She grinned.

Trish sat on the toilet seat. "I can't keep real plants in here because there's no natural light, and it's dark most of the time while I'm at work. There isn't any wood in here, either."

"Ah, grasshopper, have no fear," Jill joked. "All we need is a wood toilet seat—oak, I think. I wouldn't normally choose that; it's very 1980s. But in this case, it seems ideal."

Trish laughed out loud and then covered her mouth with both hands. "Why didn't I think of that?"

"That's one quick fix. But I also have another idea." Jill grinned. "I have some plush forest-green towels that my mother-in-law gave me last year for Christmas. They're still in the package because I hadn't yet found a place for them. I'm sorry to say, I don't value them as much since her son broke my heart." Jill rolled her eyes toward heaven dramatically and clasped her hands over her heart. "Please let me make a gift of the green towels to you. Green would really do it for this room."

"I'd appreciate that very much, but only if you agree to stay for dinner. I picked up a nice bottle of pinot grigio for the occasion, since I feel that this is a kind of celebration of new beginnings. I also made a panzanella salad for supper with my sister's beefsteak tomatoes and butter lettuce. I toasted homemade bread croutons with olive oil and garlic to toss in there, too. Please stay."

The earnest look on Trish's face gave Jill little choice but to accept. "I haven't had a panzanella in years. I'm sure Tom can fend for himself this evening."

"How long will he be staying at your home?"

"Probably just until Sunday. He had a heart attack last Thursday and ended up having a catheterization and two stents. He's been staying at my house until he recovers enough to be at home on his own. Fortunately, he's doing really well and feels much better."

"That's nice of you to invite a colleague to share your home while he recovers." Trish looked as if she wanted to ask another question, and Jill guessed what it might be.

"Tom and I have been the best of friends since college," she explained, "and of course we've worked together for many years. We're partners in the business. I know him too well to let him alone at home. He's got some lifestyle habits that need fixing."

"He looked fine last night at class. He didn't seem sick."

"He still needs to rest. By the way, he'll be at the Halloween party Saturday night."

"He's such a nice-looking man." Trish blushed as soon as the words were out of her mouth.

"He's just as nice on the inside. You'll have a chance to get to know him better at the party."

"I appreciate the invitation since I don't have a lot of opportunities to go out," Trish said as she set the table. "Money has been pretty tight for the past year." She shook her head. "But I'm getting my feet under me now, and I'm making new friends, too. It feels good to know that I'm doing it on my own."

"It's important to be self-reliant, especially in this day and age. Any woman who suddenly loses her husband through death or divorce can be vulnerable." Jill took a sip of the pinot grigio, which was excellent.

Trish plated the panzanella and served Jill. "Not you," she observed. "You're so strong and resilient."

"So are you, Trish." Jill was quiet for a moment. "I've done my fair share of suffering and soul-searching since David's affair," she admitted. "He wants me to reconsider the divorce, but I haven't stopped the legal proceedings. Maybe it's just too late. I may be too far gone from the life we had, or rather, what I *thought* we had. So much of our life was based on appearances. Now that I see the truth, I think maybe you have to experience the contrast between what you don't want in order to know what you do want."

Trish swirled the wine in her glass. "Or another way of putting it is that you've just *come* too far," she said. "That might be a better way of looking at the situation. Maybe this had to happen for you to realize what you really wanted in life." She let out a short laugh. "I remember sitting on my sofa in this apartment in August, right after I moved in, thinking *how will I manage*? The apartment was so terrible, and I cried all the time. But after I started your class, I began to think that maybe everything would be okay. I know it's up to me to make that happen, but your class has really helped. I do believe there's a better life ahead for me."

Jill held up her glass. "To happier times," she said as they clinked glasses and toasted the future.

As they talked over white wine and salads, Jill couldn't help comparing how she found out about David's affair with the way Trish learned of her husband's betrayal. Trish's husband already knew he had lost the business before he told her, and they were in massive debt. Trish learned the truth about their financial situation when her credit card was declined for a relatively minor purchase.

"When I found out why the card was declined and confronted him, he confessed what was going on. I said we would figure out how to make things work together. Then he told me he was leaving me. I was the last to know."

"I wonder how many smart women out there have experienced what we have," Jill mused. "I mean, being totally surprised by the actions of a spouse."

"At first, I thought no one else could be that dense," Trish said, refilling Jill's glass. "Shouldn't I have known that something was wrong? Was he that good at hiding things from me, or did I just not want to see what was happening?"

"I've asked myself the same questions, believe me," Jill said. "I did know there were troubles in my marriage, but I thought they were things everyone experienced, and all I had to do was keep him happy when he was home."

"Did you have a good love life?" Trish asked and blushed. "I'm sorry, that was a very personal question. Forget I asked that."

"That's okay. It was the one area of our marriage where I have no regrets," Jill said. But now, I think it was the only way we could communicate. If our sex life was good, I figured everything else would work itself out."

"But you can't spend all your time in bed," Trish said. "Did you try to talk to him?"

"I would broach topics very carefully," Jill admitted. "For example, one of our sons is gay, and David won't accept it. I'd try to talk to David about how important it is for him to support Liam. He's our child. But David always shut down, and I let it go. Now I think I was afraid that if I was more assertive, for our son's sake, things would spin out of control and I might lose him—David, I mean. But then, everything *did* spin out of control. If I had talked with him more openly, I would have known we were in trouble."

"Same here. I remember how my husband didn't want me to open bank statements or credit card bills, claiming he was the breadwinner and liked to open those things himself. Part of me thought that was fine. I trusted him. But if I had said that was ridiculous and told him we needed to pay bills together, I would have known sooner." Trish stood up and took their empty plates to the sink before turning to Jill. "I still feel ashamed that I was so clueless. I would never let that happen again, and I'm on top of my own finances now."

"That's important for achieving prosperity, and it'll serve you well as your financial life improves. Strange as it may sound, I have this strong sense that things happen for a reason, and that our own desires, conscious or unconscious, lead us forward to learn and grow." Jill took another sip of wine. "If negative events didn't happen, we'd never take new chances or leave situations that made us unhappy."

"Are you saying we might actually *want* something bad to happen like a divorce, even unconsciously?" Trish raised her eyebrows.

"Not *want*, exactly. But life does tend to propel us forward in interesting ways, and sometimes in order for something really good to happen, something not-so-good has to first. We can't possibly know whether that *something* will lead to a better life. Challenges can be blessings in disguise, I think."

"That's a very positive way of looking at things. So, after what happened with your husband, do you want to fall in love again? I'm a little scared to try it. But I still want to."

"So do I," Jill admitted, "and I intend to have the relationship of my dreams, whatever happens." Her thoughts turned to Denny as her stomach did a flip-flop. She wondered if it was her gut instinct telling her something important about him.

Glancing at her watch, she realized that it was nearly time to go. But before she left, there was another important thing she could do for Trish. "While I'm here, let's *feng shui* your romance corner, too," she said. Trish's eyes lit up. "The prosperity and relationship areas are across from each other, but we'll see if we can bring them closer together."

Chapter Twenty-One

ON FRIDAY AFTERNOON, JILL MET Denny at Dr. Mona Gagnon's house in Greenwich. Mona lived in an enormous two-story home flanked with white columns and southern architectural details that at first sight led Jill to think of the grandeur of Tara in *Gone with the Wind*. The interior of the home was every bit as grandiose as its exterior. There was little doubt that Mona had a flair for the dramatic.

This morning the attractive blonde chiropractor was dressed in a sleek, low-cut leotard that left almost nothing to the imagination, including her impressive surgical enhancements. Despite the casual ponytail and workout attire, breaking a sweat in her new workout room didn't appear to be part of the morning's plans.

"Jill, I'm so glad to see you!" Mona touched both cheeks to Jill's. She exuded an obviously expensive, cloying scent. "I've been giving some thought to a new color in the workout room, something a bit snazzier. Of course, Denny has provided me with wonderful counsel. What a find he is!"

Jill glanced around, but Denny was nowhere in sight. "Denny!" Jill called out, but got no response. "Mona, I understand you've got a rather bold shade of orange in mind."

Mona handed her a panel of orange colors. An 'x' was scrawled beside a tangerine shade. Trying to keep the concern out of her voice, Jill said, "We don't want paint colors that will clash with the tile or countertops."

Instead of looking over the color palette with her, Mona grabbed Jill's arm. "He's adorable," she gushed.

Jill paused to consider her measured response. "Who are we talking about?"

"Denny, of course." Mona gave her an exasperated look.

"Yes, he's very nice-looking. He's got a great eye for color."

"Oh, come on, Jill. You're not dead yet!" Mona's boisterous laugh ricocheted around the empty space.

Jill smiled in her most professional manner. "I'd love to see the colors he thinks you should consider. I completely trust his judgment."

As they discussed Mona's wishes for a color change from a tasteful buttery yellow to bright orange, Denny returned with yet another stack of orange color samples. "Since you've got your heart set on orange, Mona, I thought you might want to see this new shade. It's technically an apricot—quite soothing, I think. I can mix it with a creamy pearl that will give it a nice luminescence and transition into the freshwater pearl color in the spa. It'll go beautifully with the countertops and floors."

Jill flashed him a look of gratitude. Clearly, anything Denny said would be well accepted by Mona. "What do you think, Mona?" she asked.

"It's perfect. You're a genius, Denny!" Mona's throaty voice oozed pure sexuality as she laid a French-manicured hand on his bicep. Denny raised his hands in the air in a gesture of humility, but his eyes twinkled.

Bile rose in Jill's throat. "So, Denny, it looks as if you've saved the day," she said crisply, replacing the color samples in her briefcase. "Mona, is there anything else about the original plan you'd like me to revisit while I'm here?"

"I think that's all for now," Mona said, her gaze fixed on Denny. "Will you do a broad swath of that color on the wall so I can make sure it's what I want? I'm not able to visualize things like you are. My profession makes me more of a hands-on kind of girl."

"I'll check in with you later," Jill said to Denny between tightly clenched teeth.

She saw that Denny and Mona weren't paying any attention to her, anyway. The rest of the day, she felt out of sorts, replaying in her mind the way Mona touched Denny and what she thought she saw reflected back to Mona in his eyes. And why shouldn't he return Mona's interest? He was single, after all. There was no reason for him to put his life on hold just because hers was in limbo.

"How's the project coming along in Greenwich?" Tom asked that evening during dinner. "From the way you're picking at your food, I'm guessing things aren't going according to plan."

Jill looked up and blew out a long breath. "The client wanted orange walls. Denny MacBride found a more tasteful apricot that suited her. It's quite lovely, as you would expect."

"So all is well."

"I guess so." Jill rested her head on her hand.

"And you're getting along okay with MacBride? With his reputation, I expect he has a real ego."

Jill looked up and her face colored. "Nothing could be further from the truth, Tom. He's wonderful to work with."

"We still have other painters you can use, you know."

"I prefer Denny," Jill said as Tom raised his eyebrows but said nothing more.

On Halloween night, with the bar well stocked and a lavish buffet ordered from Meredith's catering business, Jill turned her attention to the final details of her costume. She enjoyed every part of the costume design process and usually spent weeks thinking up ideas. Halloween was her favorite holiday.

"Stay out of the kitchen for a little while," she told Tom. "This is bloody work."

Tom, who was feeling much stronger after his week of rest, decided to dress up as a pirate. He spent the afternoon designing his costume and devising a corrugated cardboard peg leg. He had even raided Jill's closet for a scarf and a clip-on gold hoop earring.

Jill pinned single serving-size cereal boxes to a long white nightshirt. Then she stabbed plastic knives through the cereal boxes so the knives stuck out at various angles. For the finishing touch, she dripped fake blood liberally all over the knives and cereal boxes and allowed it to coagulate.

"Who the heck are you supposed to be?" Tom asked, when she allowed him back into the kitchen.

"I'm a cereal killer."

Tom chuckled. "Very clever. Then I guess I'll be Captain Crunch. Hmm, I don't think we've matured much since college."

"Probably not," Jill agreed.

Every year, Jill and David hosted this Halloween party for family, friends, neighbors, and co-workers. While Jill preferred to remain mostly in the background visiting with guests, keeping serving bowls and trays full and restocking glasses and plates, David had relished the opportunity to play gregarious host. With or without David in her life, Jill intended to continue the tradition of entertaining. With Tom's help, it wasn't as daunting a task as she had imagined.

Meredith arrived at five thirty to set up the buffet, accompanied by one of her sons. "This is Todd," she said, introducing Jill to a gangly young man of about fifteen with a grin as delightful as his mother's. "He's the only one of my three boys who has an interest in the business. I couldn't get as much accomplished if Todd wasn't willing to help me out."

Meredith and Todd set up a buffet that included crunchy chicken baked in panko crumbs, vegetarian spring rolls with assorted dipping sauces, red-skinned potato salad, mixed greens with marinated vegetables, and bowtie pasta with an artichoke-marinara sauce. She also assembled a relish tray with hummus, ranch dip, olive tapenade, and assorted crackers, and a platter of brownies, cookies, and nut rolls. She arranged black-and-orange cloth napkins next to a stack of square black plates. Then she mixed up a punch out of fruit juice, ginger ale, and vodka and added a floating ring of bulbous frozen green grapes resembling eyeballs.

"Totally gross, but I'm sure it'll pack a punch," Jill remarked as she noticed the empty vodka bottle and admired the pale pink concoction. "Meredith, I'm really glad you took my class. Otherwise, I wouldn't have known about your business. This is really wonderful. Thank you."

"I'm supposed to be thanking you for your business." Meredith held out her hands to Jill, who took them in hers. "And thanks for taking so many of my business cards to pass around. That was a big help."

"You'll have no trouble getting enough business if you just believe in yourself. Aren't you staying for the party?"

Meredith grinned. "Thanks, but I have another catering job tonight."

At six thirty, Jill heard one of the garage doors go up and realized that David had parked his Range Rover in there. She hadn't remembered to ask him to return the other garage door opener. When he entered the kitchen, where Jill was polishing wine glasses, she took one look at his costume and groaned. A large round picture of the earth was pinned to his olive Henley shirt, and he had a red stadium blanket over his shoulders.

She sighed. "That might be your most frightening costume yet."

"Oh, good, you got it. Don't you think it's funny?" He leaned in and gave her a peck on the cheek.

She rolled her eyes. "David, I feel certain that environmentalists and climate experts all over the world would be horrified at your light-hearted approach to global warming. But, yes, I think it's very clever. Go make sure Tom isn't doing too much, will you?"

David headed for the living room to say hello to Tom, who had the bar set up and was perched on a high-backed stool. Jill had made him promise not to overdo it. She figured that seeing Trish would be about all the excitement the man could handle for one night.

Within minutes other family members arrived. Missy and Finn were dressed as babies, complete with diapers, bibs, bottles, and pacifiers. Liam and Brian were glam rock stars wearing platform shoes and black wigs. Even Nancy and Hal Brenneman got in on the act and made their royal entrance as King Henry VIII and one of his doomed wives.

"Mom, that's disgusting," Jill said to Nancy, whose head appeared to be fastened on her bloody neck with black yarn stitches.

"Hi, Dad," she said, hugging her father as tightly as her cereal boxes would permit. "Nice tights. I see Mom overcame your usual resistance to dressing up."

"As usual, I had no choice." He chuckled as he took his wife's coat to the guestroom. With his laidback good humor and inexhaustible patience, Hal Brenneman was the perfect mate for someone as strong-willed as Nancy. They had celebrated their fiftieth wedding anniversary over the summer, just before Hal retired from his dental practice. Now the two were rarely apart.

Joel and Diana were also among the first guests to arrive. They were dressed as rosebushes in dark green turtlenecks and pants with silk roses pinned to their shirts. Joel had added cardboard thorns to his costume. Zoe was an adorable bumblebee with springy gold antennae.

"It's nice of you to invite us," Diana said, embracing Jill. "Joel and I haven't been anywhere in ages. My mom isn't with us this week or we would've left Zoe with her."

"My daughter-in-law, Missy, will be thrilled to meet Zoe. She's expecting her own baby in May, and she's a pediatric nurse, so Zoe will be in good hands." Jill stood back to take a good look at Diana. "I'm so glad you're feeling well enough to come, Diana. You look wonderful, by the way."

Diana did look well in a short, wispy blonde wig that gave her the appearance of a wide-eyed pixie. "So far, so good," she said with a smile and a quick thumbs-up.

Joel's eyes opened wide when he saw David standing by the bar talking with Tom. "I guess I'm behind on all the big news. Are you and David together again?" he asked under his breath as Jill ladled cups of punch.

"David and I are in a sort of transitional time," Jill said carefully. "We always have this Halloween party, and after so many years, I didn't want to give up on tradition." Her response sounded hollow even to her own ears.

Missy gravitated toward the group when she saw Zoe. "Is it okay for me to give her juice and cheese crackers?" she asked Diana.

"She'd love that. Thank you." Diana accepted a glass of punch. "I hope this is fortified," she said. "It's time to live again."

"Well, just be careful of that stuff. It's stronger than it tastes," Jill said. "There's also wine, beer, and soda, if you'd prefer. Or Tom has just about every other liquor behind the bar."

Joel went in search of a beer. When he returned, he sidled up next to Jill. "What about Denny MacBride?" he asked in a stage whisper behind his hand.

"Joel, it's none of your business." Diana elbowed him. "Don't mind him, Jill."

Jill glanced over at David, who was engaged in conversation

with a few of Jill's neighbors. He was punctuating what looked to be a serious discussion with broad hand gestures. She wondered what he was saying, since several of them kept giving her surreptitious glances.

"Denny is a good friend," she explained, and added, "We work closely together."

"Will he be here tonight?"

"Not tonight," Jill said. "It would be fun to have him here, though."

"Apparently, things are going well with David, or he wouldn't be here," Joel persisted.

Diana rolled her eyes. "Joel, for heaven's sake, stop it. Jill, please forgive his nosiness."

Jill brushed off Joel's observation with a quick smile as David made his way across the room to stand beside her. She introduced him to Joel and Diana, and then to Trish, who had arrived dressed as a Southern belle. Pam, who appeared just behind Trish, wore a witch's costume, with red-and-white striped stockings and glittering red shoes.

"I'll get you, my pretty, and your little dog, too," she said to Jill with a cackle.

David laughed, flashing his newsworthy megawatt smile. "It's nice to meet all of you. Sounds like you have quite an interesting bunch in that class."

When Tom saw Trish, his face lit up, and he motioned her over. Jill was delighted to see him greet her with a quick hug. Trish beamed as Tom handed her a glass of white wine, his gaze never leaving hers.

I'm glad all the enhancements to my romance area have worked for someone, Jill thought as she observed fondly, and a trifle wistfully, the glow of budding romance. She was relieved that the party was a success so far, despite a few awkward silences and the inevitable questions about David's appearance, especially from the neighbors. She hadn't expected David to show up at all. As the evening wore on, and he continued to refill his glass of scotch at the bar, she wished he hadn't.

"Hey, buddy, why don't you get something to eat and then I'll fix you another one," Tom said, meeting David's eyes with a look that didn't allow for discussion or argument. Tom's imposing height was deterrent enough.

"You're a guest in my home," David said. "Don't tell me what to do."

In response, Tom picked up a bottle of wine, made firm eye contact with David, and poured a glass for another guest. David turned and walked unsteadily toward Jill, an anesthetized glaze in his eyes. Tom's face registered disapproval and something more that Jill couldn't quite identify as he turned and said something to Trish.

"Tom sheems to think he's the co-hosht of this party," David remarked thickly as he returned to Jill's side, latching onto her arm.

"David, just let it go." Jill's face reddened. "It's been good for him to be here this week."

"Don't ge' mad," David said. "I didn't mean anything by that. What you did for him was a nice gesher … gesture."

He belched slightly into his fisted hand, then excused himself and headed unsteadily toward Liam and Brian, who were standing in a group that included Nancy and Hal. Jill saw Liam's back stiffen noticeably when David slapped Brian on the shoulder. Embarrassing Liam by drinking too much was *not* a good way for David to make amends with his son.

Jill caught the look of alarm on her mother's face as David's knees swayed and quickly fixed a plate of food. Placing it next to David on a table, she said, "David, please sit down and eat something. This buffet is too good not to taste a little of everything."

Jill's eyes opened in alarm as her mother silently mouthed the words, "He's hammered."

"David, would you come with me for a minute?" Jill took

him by the elbow and guided him to his feet and toward the hallway.

"Hey, honey," David said, laughing. "If you want me that much, we can go upstairs."

"You're behaving like a complete jerk!" Jill said. "You need to stop drinking and eat something before you make yourself sick."

She body-blocked him as he leaned forward, nearly falling. David placed his hands on the sides of her face and tried to kiss her, but Jill pushed him away. Her anxiety increased as he laughed and swayed, bumping twice against the wall. Holding onto his arm, Jill guided him down the hall into the den. Perhaps she could get him to lie down in there. His arm was around her as he patted her on the backside.

"Nice ass. You've always had such a nice ass," he said.

"Dad, let's go." It was Liam's voice Jill heard now. Relieved, she turned and saw Liam and Brian coming up behind them. They each took one of David's arms.

"I think he needs some air," she said weakly, relinquishing her hold on him.

"And he'll get it," Brian said as he and Liam escorted David back down the hallway to the kitchen and onto the back patio.

Tom excused himself to join Jill in the kitchen. "He can't drive back to the city like that. He'll have to stay here tonight."

"I know. This really isn't like him, Tom. He's usually in complete control of himself." Jill knew that she had no need to apologize for David, but the truth was, this was uncustomary behavior. David had a public reputation to uphold.

"I haven't seen him like this since freshmen days at rush," Tom said. "Are you okay?"

"I'm fine. No, actually, I'm not fine. I'm mortified."

"You're not the one who ought to feel embarrassed." Tom laid a large, steadying hand on her shoulder.

"Is there anything I can do?" Trish asked, joining them in the kitchen.

"Thanks, but I think this is my problem to deal with." Jill let out a deep breath and headed toward the patio to assess David's condition. She was intercepted by Brian.

"He's past saving, and unfortunately, so is that butterfly bush beside the porch where he just puked," Brian said. "Liam and I are taking him home. I'll drive David's car."

"Liam is driving David home all by himself?" Jill's eyes widened with surprise.

"Don't you think he should? David's his father, not mine." He rolled his eyes. "Thank God."

"Actually, I think that's the best of all possible outcomes," Jill said, shaking her head at this unexpected but welcome turn of events. She grabbed David's keys from the kitchen counter and handed them to Brian. "Thank you. I'm sure you had something to do with this."

Brian hugged her. "Actually, it was entirely Liam's decision. Don't feel bad about what happened tonight, Jill. David messed up, and he knows it. What's making him crazy is that he can't control what's happening in his life. Men don't handle that very well."

Jill looked into Brian's kind gray eyes. "Control is an illusion, anyway," she said grimly.

A few minutes after David was whisked away, Tom said, "I think I'll head home tonight instead of tomorrow morning. Trish has kindly offered to drive me back to my house. Besides, I think you probably deserve a little time to yourself after putting up with me all week."

Jill embraced him. "Don't be silly. I've loved having you around, and I'll miss our dinner conversations." She leaned into him and whispered, "Trish is a good woman. Be nice to her."

"Count on that. You're a good woman, too," he said, his expression pained. "Don't settle for less than the man you deserve, pal." He went to pack his bag.

Nancy and Hal came in search of her. "We're going to head out now, too. Dad is homesick."

Jill hugged her parents. "Sorry about what happened with David. I've never seen him behave like that. Liam is taking him back to his apartment now."

Nancy's eyes widened and she bit her lower lip, grinning. "I guess things happen as they're meant to." She planted a kiss on Jill's cheek.

Jill was relieved that most guests weren't aware of the David situation. By eleven thirty, after everyone had gone home, she went around the house picking up stray glasses, plates, and wadded-up napkins. When the living room and dining room were in order, she finished straightening up the kitchen. Then, feeling adrift, she wandered into the guest room, which still had the aroma of Tom's citrusy aftershave. She sighed, thinking how nice it had been having him there.

She was glad he was taking an interest in Trish. Even if witnessing a blossoming new love brought a twinge of pain, she was still happy for him. He and Trish were good people who deserved each another. Stripping the bedclothes off the mattress, she carried the linens to the laundry room as she considered the events of the evening. David's drunken behavior was so out of character, she had no trouble believing that he was miserable—probably already regretting his actions. Although she sympathized with his desperation, she felt nothing more than that. Even more amazing, the sexual chemistry she once believed immutable had lost its hold over her. Quite simply, she no longer wanted to be with him.

As this astonishing realization took root, she also knew there would always be fondness between them for all the years they had spent together and for the sons they shared. But she couldn't think of anything that could sustain them if they resumed the marriage. Clearly they had no interests in common anymore, and she could no longer carry on a conversation with David without constantly biting her tongue.

She remembered her mother's question, "What reasons would you have for wanting David as your husband?"

Leave it to Mom to always know just what to say, she thought. *Nancy always knows.* Suddenly, a thought struck her, and she understood the answer to her question about why David had cheated. His infidelity had been a symptom of a much bigger issue. Over the years, the interests they'd shared in college had disappeared and they'd grown in separate directions. Without common ground other than their home and their sons, the deeper connection between them had weakened. Although his affair had been a shock, it had helped her see the truth about her relationship with her husband: there no longer was one.

She thought of Tom and their strong friendship and shared creative interests. In many ways, their friendship had taken the place of the closeness and compatibility that should have been present in her marriage. Then she thought of Denny and the easy, uncomplicated way they related to each other, both on and off the job. She was much closer to Denny than to David, even at the earliest stage of getting to know him. Although it was too early to be certain of any long-term potential, Jill recognized that she hoped there was.

Even more telling was the pure, green-eyed jealousy she felt watching Mona flirt with him. It was a clear sign that she cared for Denny. The first thing to do was to tell David of her decision to proceed with the divorce. Then she could reach out to Denny and let him know she was ready to move forward with her life, and with him. She hoped it wasn't too late.

Chapter Twenty-Two

THE PHONE RANG ON JILL'S desk a little after nine o'clock, followed by two short beeps on the intercom and Monica's voice. "It's David on line two."

Jill picked up the phone, her heart pounding. She had been thinking all morning of calling him, but had not yet summoned the necessary courage. No matter how thoroughly she had outlined her thoughts, it surely wouldn't be easy to speak the words. "Hello, there," she said, trying not to sound flustered.

"Are you still speaking to me?"

"Of course, I am. How are you?"

"Sorry for my behavior at the party. I was a little uptight and got carried away with the most available antidote for stress."

Jill sat back in her chair and took a sip of tea. "It wasn't your finest hour, that's for sure, but I'll bet your body punished you enough the next morning."

David groaned. "I lost most of Sunday. It was a good thing Liam took me home. We couldn't really talk much, but I want to take him and Brian out for dinner to apologize."

"That's a wonderful idea, David. It'll mean a lot to them." Jill picked up the phone, stretched out the cord as far as it would go, and nudged the office door shut with her foot.

"The reason I called is because I've cleared my schedule for next weekend to do whatever you want," David said. "Your wish is my command."

"David ...." Jill's heart dropped like a stone. She hadn't been prepared to have this discussion on the phone, but knew it was time to be honest with him. Her plan had been to call and suggest they meet for coffee somewhere.

"I know, I know. I didn't check your schedule. But as I've said, I'll work around whatever you've got going on. If you want to take off somewhere, I'm sure the kids will understand and can make other plans for Sunday dinner." His voice trailed off.

For hours the night before, Jill had played over and over in her mind what she would say to David when the time came. But now that he was suggesting a weekend together, the sick, sharp feeling in her stomach was all the guidance she needed. The time was now. She had to let him know how she felt and what she intended to do. There was no turning back. Her stomach did another sickening flip-flop, a gut reaction she had learned to heed. "I don't want to have this discussion over the phone, David. Could we meet later and talk?"

He was silent for a moment. "If you're planning to end our marriage, what's the point of dragging things out? Just say it." His voice had become clipped and cold.

"I don't think anything I say will come as a surprise. We know things haven't been good between us for a very long time. I've just been a little slow about recognizing that."

"Jill," he interjected with exasperation. "I know things haven't always been easy for you, especially when my job took me away from home so much of the time. But you knew what I wanted in my career, and you wanted that, too."

"I did at the beginning, yes. But it isn't just your career that's been an issue."

"I know that having the affair was wrong and that it changed the way you feel about me. I don't blame you for being hurt and for wanting to get back at me."

"Is that what you think?" Jill rubbed her eyes, suddenly feeling weary. "This isn't about revenge. I believe I've already come a long way toward forgiving you."

"I doubt that," he said. "What else can I do? What do you want me to say?" He blew out a long, ragged breath.

"There's nothing else you can say or do. I want to move forward with the divorce," she said as gently as possible. "This hasn't been an easy decision, but I believe it's for the best."

"How can you say that? How can divorce be in our best interest? Maybe you think it's best for you, but you're not thinking about me!"

Jill rejected the first response that came to mind, choosing to take the high road. "Please listen, David. For me, it's been a long time since we were close. Somewhere along the way—who knows when it started—we became strangers. You think and feel differently than I do about so many things. Our values haven't changed together."

"We don't have to think alike to be married, Jill. You could try to be more interested in what's important to me. And I could make more of an effort to share what's important."

She took a deep breath to avoid saying the next thing that automatically came to mind. He just didn't get it. For her, marriage could not be all about him and his ideas. She wanted a romantic partner who valued her thoughts and ideas, who shared her deepest thoughts of what it meant to be a couple—closeness and compatibility, trust and shared experiences. Instead, she continued in a calm voice, taking time to choose her words carefully, "I've tried all these years, David, but it hasn't brought us closer. Yes, it's true that you were away from home a lot while you built your career, and you should be proud of everything you've accomplished. I am. But all those years of passing each other in the night—whenever you came home and we could steal a little time together—had an unfortunate effect. We lost what we had together, and now I can't seem to get back what I once felt."

"It's because you won't try."

Jill breathed steadily in and out to keep her thoughts firmly grounded. "This isn't about trying or giving up. It's about having an authentic connection. We've spent so little time together that we've ended up on completely separate paths. We're different people now, David, let's face it. Yes, you had an affair, but that wasn't the entire reason our marriage was in trouble. It was just the catalyst that finally brought things to a head and forced us—forced me—to look at reality. I probably knew on some level that we weren't living the way married couples ought to live to be happy together. But I went along pretending, even to myself, that we had a good marriage. Unfortunately, that obviously wasn't true."

"So it's my fault. It always comes back to that."

"David, I'm not saying that. I'm talking about how I think a marriage can be. I can't do this the way I did before. I've made my decision, and although this isn't how I wanted to tell you, I can't let you go on thinking there's still a chance for us."

There was another long silence before he spoke. "I really blew it."

Jill had a strangely detached feeling, as though she were an observer rather than a participant in the moment. "Things happen. People change. We just grew apart. I don't think it's ever just one person who's at fault, and I'm just as sorry for my part in that process."

"Jill, you did nothing wrong. It was my fault, and I'm sorrier than you could ever know."

Now she heard the choking sobs on the other end of the line. "David, I'll always care for you, and I'll always be grateful for the good years we had and the two amazing sons you gave me."

"We're going to be grandparents now. How can I look at you holding that little baby and know what I did?"

"Time will heal this for all of us." She took a deep breath, feeling sad that his apology had come so late—a last-ditch effort to save their marriage when all else failed. She knew this deep down, but there was no rancor. In fact, the truth brought her a welcome feeling of peace. Now she felt his tears mirrored in her own eyes, and her throat tightened in compassion for them both and mourning for the end of their marriage.

"I do love you, Jill."

"I'll always love you, too, David. Let's be good to each other, even if we're no longer living together."

With no more to say except goodbye, she was relieved that the terrible words were finally spoken. Tucking the phone back in its cradle, she picked up her purse and coat and stepped into the hallway. Looking left and right and noticing that there was no one else in the hallway, she shut and locked her office door. "I won't be back today," she said to Monica as she approached her desk. "Would you tell Tom that I'll be in tomorrow?"

Monica looked up, and her eyes clouded over. "I think I can guess what happened. I'm sorry, Jill."

"Thanks. It's okay, but please don't say any more," Jill said. "I don't want to cry again—not here." She coughed to clear the lump lodged in her throat. "Just tell Tom, okay? Tell him I'll talk with him later."

She fled quickly before Monica could say anything else or insist on coming with her. Throwing open the exit door to the stairwell, she ran down the stairs to the parking garage entrance, praying that she wouldn't see anyone she knew. Her heels rang out like hammer strikes on the cement as she hurried to her car. She threw her purse and briefcase into the back, climbed in and slammed the door. Feeling wooden inside, she started the engine with shaking fingers and then laid her head against the steering wheel. She wanted to cry, needed to cry, but couldn't seem to muster any more tears. A strangled feeling rose up in her throat again as she fought to breathe. She thought screaming might be a relief, but decided against it. *Just get out of here. Just breathe; you'll be fine.* Hands gripping the steering wheel, she backed the car out of the parking space and drove out of the parking garage. As she entered the on-ramp to the main highway, she realized she was heading straight for her parents' home.

HAL BRENNEMAN ANSWERED THE DOOR, a look of delight in his crinkled eyes. "What a nice surprise. Nancy, Jill is here!"

Jill stepped inside the foyer and right into her father's arms. "Hi, Dad," she said, her words muffled as she hid her face in his wool sweater. She took a deep breath of the familiar scent of spicy aftershave and cherry pipe tobacco. "Where's Mom?"

"She's in the kitchen. Let's go find her." Hal put his arm around his daughter's shoulder as they walked together.

The smell of freshly baked bread drifted throughout the downstairs from the kitchen, where Nancy was preparing lunch. "What in the world?" Nancy asked, holding out both arms to Jill and drawing her close. "Isn't this a work day?"

Jill burst into tears. Between hiccupping sobs, she updated her parents on what had happened. "I told David I want to go through with the divorce. He took it so hard. I didn't think it could feel worse, but this hurts even more." Jill looked up in anguish. "Does that mean I've made a terrible mistake?"

"I rather think it means you have a heart that's breaking, Jill. It's only natural for you to grieve like this, and you need to cry. You'll feel better." Nancy led Jill to a kitchen chair. "Let me get you a cup of cocoa with marshmallows, just the way you like it. I've got vegetable soup on the stove and bread just out of the oven. You can have some lunch and rest a little."

"Mom, I seriously doubt I can eat anything. I just needed to get away from the office for a while before I exploded."

"Well, we're glad you came here. I'll make you some cinnamon toast, too." Nancy was already reaching into the dish cupboard to retrieve another place setting. "Hal, bring her a new box of tissues—the ones with aloe. Look at her poor nose."

WHEN JILL ARRIVED HOME LATE that afternoon, having been fed, soothed, and reassured by her parents, Denny was there, sitting in his truck in her driveway. Her heart skipped several beats when she saw him. She gave him a quick wave, opened the automatic garage door, and drove inside. She was glad that she had taken her mother's advice and dabbed some coconut oil on her nose to relieve the chapped redness. She quickly checked her makeup in the rearview mirror, fluffed her bangs, and pinched her cheeks to give them a little color. Denny held open the door when she stepped out of the car.

"I've been wondering if everything was okay. It's been almost two days since I've heard from you."

"Everything is fine … now," she said, avoiding his eyes. "Really, I've just had so much going on."

"You haven't answered my last four texts or two voice messages. When I called the office, your assistant said you left suddenly and that I should call you on your cellphone, if it was about a work problem. She usually knows your schedule, so I asked her if you were going to a job site. Then she said you might not be available for a while."

Jill swallowed hard. She was riveted to the spot by those deep, brown eyes and the expressive mouth. She followed the contours of his face for a moment, studying them, memorizing them.

"I'm sorry, Denny. You must think I'm behaving irresponsibly. Are there more issues with Mona? I didn't think your calls or texts were work-related, and I've been dealing with some personal things."

"There are always going to be issues with Mona," he said. "But no, everything is under control with the projects. That's not why I'm here." He jammed his hands inside his jacket pockets. "I was a tad concerned that either you were taking a leave of absence, from what Monica said, or worse, that you were avoiding me."

"No, nothing like that," she said. She wanted to reach out and touch his face, but held back. He looked frustrated and so worried that she felt even worse for ignoring his texts and calls.

"I do want to talk with you, and actually, I'm glad you stopped by." She latched onto his jacket sleeve. "I've missed seeing you."

"All evidence to the contrary," he said, but without a trace of anger. "Never mind. I can see something is troubling you." He moved toward her, reached out and touched her cheek, then ran his thumb lightly across her lips. His touch left a vibration. Her mouth opened involuntarily, but no sound came out.

"Jill?" His eyes narrowed in concern.

"I'm just so …." She paused and took a deep breath to steady herself. "It's been a hard day."

His eyes, trained on hers, were piercing yet patient. "Why don't we go in and sit down, and you can tell me about it. That is, if you want to."

"Of course I want to. You may not agree with what I did, though, or how I handled it. It doesn't necessarily paint me in a good light."

Denny was silent a moment as if trying to think about how to phrase his next words. "In a painting, even the darkest shadow is just another form of light. The dark places in a scene are just as key to understanding what lies before us."

Jill turned to open the door to the kitchen, where she wearily dropped her handbag and briefcase on the table. "This morning, I told David I want to go through with the divorce." Removing her coat, she hung it over a chair and braced herself against it for support. She couldn't read his face.

He raised his eyebrows and bit his lower lip before saying, "I see. How did he take it?"

"He got angry, at first. He tried to convince me that what I was doing wasn't right. A lot of what he said, though, was about him. Then he cried and said he's sorry about what happened. The thing is, Denny, I think he really *is* sorry."

Denny blew out a long breath. "That must've been terrible for you."

"It was worse than I could've imagined, but at the same time, I was relieved that the words were finally spoken. It's over, and

I can honestly say this is what's best for me. But it's true what David said: this may not be what's best for him. I'm taking care of myself now, not doing what I think he wants or needs from me. The truth is, I can't save him."

"This is unfamiliar behavior to you, Jill. But you're the only one you can save."

Jill nodded. "And I really am sorry for not responding to your texts or messages. I couldn't think clearly, and I wasn't in the mood to hear about Mona. Sorry if I let you down."

He shrugged. "We're a team on this project. I didn't even bother going over there today because I thought we should talk first."

"You seem to handle Mona pretty well all by yourself. You don't need me to help you." There, she had said it. Once the words were out of her mouth, however, she regretted uttering something so petty. She had never admired jealous females and she cringed, realizing that's what she was.

"Jill." He took a deep breath, but couldn't hide his lopsided grin. He tossed his jacket onto a kitchen chair. "Do you honestly think there is something going on between Mona and me? Are you completely daft? I don't care for Mona."

"She's very attractive, Denny. You're definitely lined up in her crosshairs."

A quick burst of laughter erupted from his lips. "The visual on that one is truly disturbing. I'll not be caught by the likes of Dr. Mona Gagnon."

Jill remained motionless as Denny leaned in and drew her to him. She met his eyes, and he kissed her gently, lips lingering on hers for a few moments. "It's not Mona I want. You're the one I want. Let me make that clear now."

"Oh." Jill's lungs deflated as if she'd had the wind knocked out of her. She had to take several deep breaths as stars came into view.

Denny said nothing more for a moment, but his eyes never left hers. The house was so still, she could hear the ticking of the grandfather clock in the hallway. They stood that way for a few moments, taking in each other's features.

It was Jill who finally broke the silence. "I think I need to sit down."

Denny shifted from one foot to the other as she sank into a chair. "Maybe we should go have some dinner so we can really talk. You need to eat."

She sighed deeply. "Why is it that everyone thinks I need to be fed today, as if food will fix what's missing in my life? It isn't food I want or need. Denny, would you just take me far away from all of this?" Jill looked up at him beseechingly. "All day long, I've wanted to run somewhere, anywhere. I went to see my parents, but now, I don't know where else to go. The only thing I do know is …"—she moved toward him and took his face in her hands—"you're the only one I want to run away with."

His face registered surprise and then pleasure. "Okay. I guess we can make this up as we go along. Come with me." He kissed her quickly, picked up his jacket, and held out his hand to her.

Jill slung her coat over her shoulders, took her house keys and purse, and followed Denny through the garage to his truck. As he started the motor, she leaned back in the seat. "I meant what I said. Let's just get away from my life."

"You can't ever get that far away. Trust me on that."

"Well, I want to be someone else tonight."

"I'd rather you just be Jill."

He placed one hand protectively over hers and drove without speaking while they traveled out of town and onto a country road. They passed silent fields dusted with frost and bare sienna-colored tree limbs with hair-like twigs that reminded Jill of eyelashes against the dusky-blue sky. They slowed down just once for three deer that stepped out onto the highway from a grove of trees. Denny's hand flew across Jill's middle as he braked to a standstill, veering to the right. The deer stopped to look at them curiously, without fear. Jill smiled at their expressions, feeling the first calming effects of something suspiciously similar to contentment.

"I have an idea. It still involves food, though," Denny said. "Let's go back to my place and I'll cook you dinner—my own brand of comfort food. Don't worry. It isna going to be haggis."

She smiled and took his warm hand, turning it over and running her fingers gently over the palm, tracing his lifeline. "Dinner sounds nice, and by the way, I've never tasted haggis. Maybe I'd like it." The restless, anxious feeling was completely gone now. In this moment, there was no other feeling except joy at being with Denny.

"I doubt it," he said with a grin. "But, anyway, haggis isn't a thirty-minute meal, lass. Someday, I'll make it for you from my maw's recipe."

"And after dinner? What then?"

"Whatever you want. This is your getaway. I'm just along for the adventure."

It was fully dark when they arrived at Denny's home. He unlocked the front door and stepped back to let her enter first. On an end table, a Tiffany lamp shone in its rainbow of cut-glass colors like inviting ribbons of jeweled light. Denny took her coat and hung it in the hall closet.

"This way, love," he said and led her down the long hallway to the kitchen. "Sit down at the island and I'll get you a glass of wine."

"Can I do something to help?"

"Just sit there and be with me. Nothing else is required." He pulled a bottle of white wine from the rack on the kitchen counter and uncorked it, poured a small amount into a glass, and tasted it. Then he poured two glasses of chardonnay and handed one to her. "To better days ahead," he said as they touched glasses.

Jill took a sip of the buttery, fruity wine. "Mm, this is just what I needed."

"I'll make you my version of a classic dish: shrimp scampi over linguini."

"I'd love that." Jill felt as light as a feather as she sipped her wine and watched Denny put water on to boil for pasta. He heated minced garlic in butter and olive oil, sliced fresh lemons, chopped parsley, and defrosted jumbo shrimp for the skillet.

"We need a salad, too," he said. "I've got a nice mixture of fresh greens and some home-grown herbs. The kitchen garden is still producing a few things." He glanced up at her as he began tossing the salad. "Do you need anything else? More wine?"

"I need nothing else at this moment." And she meant it.

When dinner was ready, they sat down together in the dining room. Denny placed a colorful salad in front of Jill and spooned shrimp scampi with garlic-butter sauce over linguine on her plate. He lit candles on the dining room table and sideboard before joining her.

"This smells divine. I had no idea you were such a good cook."

"I like to cook, when I have time." He refilled her wine glass and then his own. "Are you feeling better now?"

"Yes, thank you. This wine is wonderful, by the way. Spending the afternoon with my mom and dad helped, too."

"I'm listening if you want to tell me more."

Jill took a bite of salad as she considered how best to describe the events of the day. "There isn't much to tell, really. David called to say that he was making plans for us to go away this weekend and suggested one of my favorite places. I knew it was time to tell him the truth: that I didn't want to be with him that way and that I still wanted the divorce."

"That must've been rough. You've struggled with what's best for everyone."

"I don't think I really tried to save the marriage after he asked me to." She looked directly at Denny. "Maybe that was wrong of me. After all was said and done, it didn't feel like there was anything to save. But I do feel regret and guilt that this is the avenue I chose—to walk away from him."

"It seems like guilt goes hand in hand with divorce," Denny said. "Any caring person will have mixed feelings about ending a marriage, no matter how long it lasted. You're too hard on yourself. You didn't cause the troubles."

"Ironically, it was his affair that finally helped me see that I don't want to be married to him anymore," Jill continued. "I don't feel about him the way I ought to, and we both deserve better than that. His affair was just the catalyst."

Denny rested his chin on his hands, elbows on the table, in a way that told her she had his full attention. "You're a good woman who deserves to be happy. If you haven't been happy, then perhaps this was meant to be."

Jill paused to consider a new thought. "Maybe that's what happened to David. He just didn't feel about me the way he once had. Maybe that's why he strayed."

"But then he came back," Denny pointed out. "That ought to tell you something. He knew what he was losing."

"He came back for his own needs. That, I know," she said, shaking her head. "I accommodated him, Denny. He liked having me take care of everything so that he could do whatever made him happy. Maybe he missed having someone take care of him. Now he has to take care of himself. But since he's been out of the house, I feel more content, less anxious, more sure of who I am. When he called to tell me his plans for us to be together this weekend, I had to tell him. It's just too little, too late. But I hated telling him over the phone."

The look on Denny's face was pained. "It happens as it should, I suppose." He waited for her to continue.

"The saddest part was that David finally said he was sorry. I believe now he really did want another chance to make things right between us. I think he wanted to go back to the way things were before his affair. But I realized I couldn't go back. Before the affair, I would've done anything for a chance to make a fresh start with him. I would've tried to be a different person, if that's what it took. But knowing that he could have an affair so casually and for so long helped me see that he didn't value me the way I thought he did. I've been making the best of our marriage because that's what married people do. My parents and my friends have had their troubles, but they stayed married. I wanted that, too."

She shook her head, still amazed that she could embrace a new life without David. "I tried to convince myself we had a happy marriage. But I was mostly by myself, and we grew so far apart, I didn't know him anymore. The affair was a huge shock because I thought I was doing everything right—giving him whatever he wanted, whatever made him happy. It's always been that way between us. I was used to being David's girl, and that made me special. I don't know what that means anymore to me or to him. I know for sure, though, that we can't go back."

"Being with him didn't make you special. You were always that, and then some." Denny lifted her hand and kissed it before releasing it. "David is a lucky man to have had you as his wife. He'll always be a lucky man for having those years with you, whether or not he appreciated them. I'm sure he knows that now."

"But was it wrong not to try harder after he asked me to?" she asked plaintively. "I still don't know how I'll move forward without guilt, without feeling that I've failed in my marriage."

"In what way have you failed? It was David who betrayed your vows."

"But he wanted another chance. He was counting on me to give him that, and I've always been the one to hold things together."

"Aye, love," he said, picking up his fork and taking a quick bite. "I understand about holding things together. I did that, too."

"You did? Tell me." She sensed from the expression on Denny's face that what he was about to tell her was still painful for him.

"I haven't shared this with anyone before, but there are

things I've been through that aren't too far from what you're going through with David. I held things together, too, with someone ... until I couldna do it any longer."

Jill waited as Denny paused again, wringing his hands. "For three years, I was involved with an artist friend, Christina. She has a young son. Josh is his name, and I loved him like my own. For a while, I was happy—even tho't I might be in love. But Christina had a problem with the drink. One glass would turn into, well, quite a few more. I think I must have known, on some level, how bad it was getting, but I cared for her and I cared about Josh. Sometimes I stayed the night because I knew he shouldn't be alone with her. Christina tried to hide her problem, but everyone knew. By our second year together, I was staying in the relationship mainly for Josh's sake because I didn't know what would happen to him if I left her. But here's the thing: Christina's problems were her own to solve, and all of my efforts to protect Josh by staying with her weren't really helping him, either." Denny stared into space, remembering.

"What happened? Did something happen to Josh because of her drinking?"

He grimaced. "It was verra bad. The night I told her I didn't see a future for us, she drank too much and the next morning, Josh couldn't wake her. He called me, crying and scared, and I told him to call 911. She ended up in hospital and then went away for rehab. I felt terrible about that, too."

"Like you said, you were taking responsibility for her when she needed to take responsibility for herself."

"Aye, but that thought doesn't set comfortably when you're in the middle of something so difficult with people you care about. Josh went to stay with his dad while Christina was in hospital. The fear of losing Josh made her realize that she had to stop drinking. But as long as I was hanging around thinking I could fix things, she didn't need to consider what she was doing to herself and Josh, or why she drank so much."

"Denny, I understand what you're trying to say, but it's not the same," Jill said sadly. "You weren't married to Christina, and Josh wasn't your own child."

"Jill, any child is your own child if you know they're in need."

Her heart contracted. "That was a beautiful thing to say, Denny. That tells me so much about you."

Jill hadn't fully comprehended the differences between Denny and David before now. She could see that it wasn't in Denny's nature to behave carelessly or selfishly. He would never knowingly act in a way that would cause others pain. He had put Christina's and her child's needs before his own happiness, as she had done for so many years with David. In many ways, she and Denny were kindred spirits, giving of themselves without expectation of anything in return. This was a man who would give love in the same spirit as he received it.

They finished dinner and Denny picked out a jazz CD to play on the stereo system. Then he held out his arms. "Dance with me?"

"It's been years since I've danced. But, yes, I'd love to," she said formally, and entered the circle of his arms.

They moved well together. His hand low on her back, he led her effortlessly around the room. She sighed happily and moved in closer, inhaling the scent of soap and the wool of his sweater. She began to lose track of time, swaying to the music, feeling the softness of his breath on her cheek. How long had it been since she danced this way? As they moved to the sweet sounds of a saxophone and keyboards, she dismissed thoughts of anything but the pleasure of being in his arms. They stopped after two songs to sip their wine. Jill glanced at the clock and saw that it was almost eleven o'clock.

Denny switched off the music. "I'm taking you home now so that you can sleep."

Jill nodded as he went to find her jacket. At this moment, she wanted nothing more than to stay here with him in his arms, to drift off to sleep feeling safe and content, without a care in the world. She recognized by the way he was behaving now, slightly nervous and awkward in his movements, that he felt the same.

"Some night, when things are more settled in your life, I want you to stay," he said. "I'm taking you home now because I don't trust myself."

"I trust you," she said. "I know you're a good man and that you want what's best for me."

"And that's why we're going to wait," Denny said. He helped her on with her jacket and zipped it up, then kissed her on the forehead.

Chapter Twenty-Three

As the chill winds of November blew across the campus quadrangle, Jill shivered and drew her coat more tightly about her. With Thanksgiving approaching, on top of the demands of a particularly busy time at work, she hadn't had much time to prepare for class. From the parking lot, she could see the lights in her classroom windows and a few heads already in place. The career square of the *bagua* was the subject of discussion tonight, and she hoped she could bring some energy to the one who needed help the most: Pam.

Over the past seven weeks, Jill and her students had shared many challenges and insights with one another. They had spent time together socially, and supported Joel through a particularly difficult time while Diana was recovering. She had come to think of each of her students as friends, and she realized how much she would miss them when this class was over.

It had been a long, grueling day, starting with an early meeting with her accountant, followed by a lengthy meeting with the attorney to wrap up the final details of her divorce. The final decree would come sometime after the first of the year.

True to his promise, David had not fought her on anything. In fact, he became surprisingly detached from the entire process, even deciding not to attend a face-to-face meeting to discuss final details of taxes, property, or retirement assets. Once he realized that the divorce was inevitable, a wall had gone up between them. The only communication now was facilitated by their attorneys. Maybe it was easier that way.

Although she was surprised that he did not appear for this important meeting, she also knew that David's decision to detach from the details of the divorce was very much in character. All of the years that she had been married to him, she had been frustrated when he frequently disappeared or showed up conveniently late because he did not want to deal with particular people, issues, or situations. His excuse was always that he worked late or had an important interview with someone important or famous. Most people excused him because they were impressed with his celebrity status. But Jill understood only too well that David used his fame to get out of doing things he didn't want to do. Over the years, he had managed to avoid all the soccer games, missed the twins' piano recitals, left the holiday shopping (even for his own family members) up to her, and avoided most social obligations not related to his career. David's disinterest in the dissolution of their marriage was merely an extension of his indifference to their relationship.

Denny, too, was keeping his distance, although she knew it had more to do with his desire not to overwhelm or take advantage of her during this stressful time. Between her busy schedule and his, they hadn't seen each other in three days, although they spoke by phone at least twice a day and sent texts and emails. She was grateful that he was willing to wait until she was ready to take their relationship to the next level. Although she looked forward to being with him again, she didn't want Denny to become a rebound relationship.

When she told him this, he chuckled. "So I should wait until after you've sown your wild oats and dated every single man within a twenty-five mile radius?"

"I hardly think that will happen," she answered dryly. "All I'm saying is that I'd rather take things slow. I might still be a little raw. I could hurt you without intending to."

"We can take all the time we need to get to know each other," he said. "I'm a verra patient man."

As Jill stood before the class that evening, she noticed the gleam in Chris's eyes, and made a mental note to talk with him on break or after class.

"Tonight, we're talking about our jobs, professions, and our life's work," she began. "But more important, we're talking about work that we actually enjoy and that brings us a secure income and prosperity. Isn't that what we all want?"

"Not everyone can enjoy their work," Kristen said. "What about people who clean up biohazards from crime scenes or pick up rotting, smelly trash?"

"Some people who have those jobs are probably grateful to *have* a job, and maybe they're really good at what they do. Someone has to provide those basic services," Joel pointed out objectively. "I don't have an exciting job, and I don't always like what I do every day, but I know why it matters."

"So what I think I hear you saying, Joel, is that the knowledge of the importance of what you do brings meaning and satisfaction to your work life." Jill smiled encouragement at him. "That's important."

"I've been a paralegal for close to twenty years, and I've never gotten any enjoyment out of helping people sue each other," Pam interjected, shaking her head. "I do a good job, but I don't jump up and down each morning at the thought of what's in store for me."

"So then, perhaps the question is, why do we stay in jobs that don't feel like our true calling?" Jill looked curiously at Pam. "No judgment here, just wondering."

"I can only speak for myself, but my steady paycheck has supported my addiction to romance novels," Pam said. "I've written two of them, but haven't ever taken myself seriously enough to try and get them published. Now I really want to be a romance novelist full time, and I need to take the next step."

"We'll talk about careers this week, and then we'll discuss romance the week after next. Between the two squares, you ought to have a pretty good foundation for achieving your dream."

Jill handed out a list of enhancements for the career area of the *bagua*, which included water, mirrors, glass, anything metal, round objects, black-and-white colors, and symbols of the ideal work desired. The career square was located in the center of the lower three squares, between skills and knowledge and benefactors and travel.

"This is a very important area because, let's face it, our work ought to feed our souls. It's often the primary way we perceive ourselves in the world. If we aren't doing work we love, it's time to figure out what it is that would bring us happiness and then make conscious choices that can bring about the changes we want to see."

Members of the class listened intently as Jill drew the *bagua* on the chalkboard and indicated the career area. "The career square is the entry and departure point of your home," she explained. "It's the last thing you see when you leave for work and the first thing you see when you arrive home. This is not the place to dump clutter. Keep it orderly and clean, and remember to make sure nothing is blocking the doorway—that the door opens and closes easily. If your door sticks, it's really sort of symbolic for being stuck in a dead end job or in work you don't really like. You get the idea. Be deliberate about what you place in this area and where you put it."

"That area of my house is always a mess." Meredith sighed. "The boys drop their muddy shoes and school stuff there every day."

"It can be a challenge to keep an entryway in good order, so you might need to make some special fixes. I understand that it's tough with kids. Just do the best you can. In my experience, the fallback plan is mirrors in that area. How many of you have a mirror in your entryway?"

No one did, except Kristen. She laughed. "The only reason I have one is so I can check my makeup before I go out the door!"

"You say that like it's a bad thing," Jill teased. "That's an excellent reason to have a mirror in this area. You want to look your best before going out into the world every day. But it's more than that. Mirrors are glass, which represents water, a creative element for this area. They also reflect light, which helps keep *chi* moving. Put a round mirror in this area, and you're covered, even if other things aren't perfect."

"Why metal, though?" Trish asked. "You'd think water would rust metal."

"Remember that each element has a creative and destructive ability. In this case, metal and water are creative. Don't worry so much about putting more metal in this area. It's easy to have the metal element because most people have metal doorknobs, which definitely count, and they're round, too."

"What kind of symbols should I put in my career area to enhance my ability to write and sell romance novels?" Pam asked. "Sex toys?"

There was a short burst of laughter. Shelly looked aghast at Pam. Jill rolled her eyes at Pam, but joined in the laughter.

"Think hearts and flowers, Pam. Keep to the high road here. I'll help you with symbols when I do your home consultation. For everyone's general knowledge, you want to put things in this area that represent your ideal career. I'm talking about books, especially if you're still in school and studying for a profession. Display paintbrushes or a painting, if you're an artist. Joni, you might consider a box of chocolates in your entryway. Chris, you've already got a photo of yourself performing on *Stars* in your career area."

"I replaced it with a new photo that was taken professionally." Chris's eyes were twinkling. Jill thought he was about to say something else, but instead he just smiled.

"What if, in order to be successful and do what you love, you have to achieve a certain level of fame, and what if that takes time?" Amy interrupted. "I could sell a yoga DVD if I had an established reputation."

"That's what I worry about, too," Pam chimed in. "It's difficult to find an agent to represent your books unless you already have a name in the romance writing biz."

"All the more reason to make sure your fame and reputation area is in great condition," Jill said. "These squares all work in harmony. But wait, I want to hear what Chris was about to say."

He was beaming. "I have an announcement to make. I just landed a recording contract."

The class erupted into applause and whistles. Joel pumped Chris's hand and pounded him on the back. Pam leapt to her feet and grabbed Chris in a joyful, tearful hug. Even Shelly, who was generally shy and undemonstrative, hugged and kissed him on the cheek.

"That's great! We knew you could do it." Jill was ecstatic. "Tell us how it happened, and don't you dare leave out a single detail."

"I decided to take a chance and use the rest of my savings to record a few songs, including 'First Time for Everything,' " Chris said. "It was the one song I've written and performed that I thought had real commercial potential."

"I love that song!" Jill exclaimed, still unable to contain her pride and excitement.

"I gave a CD with that song plus a few others to my friend, Kat, who I met on *Stars*," Chris explained. "She has one of the best agents in the business, so I asked if she'd give it to him. I figured what the heck. Kat told him all about me and how I was on *Stars* with her. Even though I didn't make it as far as she did, he liked my song. The next thing I knew, I got a call for a meeting, and he said he'd represent me. After that, things happened pretty fast. I just got signed by the Ariel label."

"You deserve this success, Chris," Jill said, eyes shining with pride. "All you needed was a little confidence boost."

"And a little ancient Chinese wisdom," he reminded her.

THE NEXT AFTERNOON, JILL MET with Pam, who lived in a charming bungalow on a quiet side street not far from Denny's place. In fact, she could see the back of his house from Pam's driveway. She had no plans, however, to tell Pam anything about him, since it would open the door to blue-humored teasing in class.

"Welcome to my love nest," Pam said when she opened the front door.

Despite her eccentricity and bawdy sense of humor, Pam was a petite, pretty woman with thick salt-and-pepper gray hair that cascaded over her shoulders in waves. She wore cat's eye glasses with jeweled stems, no makeup, and as usual, loose knit slacks and a jeweled tunic. Pam was fond of Birkenstocks and paired them with colorful hand-knitted socks in cold weather, which only added to her eccentric appearance.

"I've never been to the home of a romance writer," Jill said. "Will I find someone named Fabio in the bedroom?"

Pam snorted. "More than likely, you'll find Sir Puss."

At Jill's look of confusion, Pam motioned with one hand and led her to the romance area of her bungalow, which happened to be the spacious master bedroom. Sure enough, an enormous orange tabby rested luxuriously on a royal blue satin pillow at the foot of the bed. The handsome cat raised his head to study Jill with large green eyes, and hopped down to inspect her, rubbing against her legs in what Jill took to be a gesture of curiosity and affection. But as soon as she reached down to stroke his soft fur, he corrected her with a quick hiss and a swipe of his paw.

"You interrupted his before-dinner nap." Pam shrugged

and shook her finger at the cat. "That's not very gentlemanly. Shame on you!"

Jill checked her ankle for scratches and a torn stocking, but found nothing amiss. "Okay, then, so much for getting to know His Royal Highness." She turned around, surveying the room. "Your romance area is in pretty good shape, Pam. You've already got a burgundy bedspread and curtains. Red is an important color in the romance corner. I like the subdued black-and-white toile wallpaper, too. Normally, I see a lot of pink and coral in women's bedrooms, but red is very effective. You've got end tables on both sides of the bed and two matching candlesticks with red candles—both important symbolically. The only concern I have is that your cat will never allow another man in your life."

She grinned and put an arm around Pam's shoulder. "Let's turn our attention to the career area, shall we?" They walked back to the career square of Pam's house, which included a good-sized foyer with a storage bench, hall table, and walk-in closet. "What's in the closet?" Jill asked, tugging on the doorknob.

"Just seasonal junk: coats, boots, stuff like that," Pam said.

"That's what I thought," Jill said, yanking open the closet door. "Gosh, Pam, do you really need this many coats?" She yanked a rainbow-striped plastic raincoat off a wire hanger. "Somehow I doubt you've worn this in quite a while."

"I've been saving it, just in case."

"In case you decide to time-travel back to the 1970s? Actually, let's keep it and think of it as your amazing Technicolor dream coat. But is there another place to store your vacuum, the ironing board, and your mop and broom? Unless your career ambition is to own a cleaning service, they really don't belong here."

"Okay, okay." Pam laughed good-naturedly. "But you'll approve of what's in the storage bench."

"I will?"

"Voilà!" Pam said, opening the lid to reveal stacks of romance novels.

Jill pulled out several paperbacks and looked over their titles. "Hmm, *Summer Cowgirls, Rapture and Lies, A Nurse's Dilemma*. I can't say I've ever read any of these."

Pam burst out laughing. "I bet you're thinking I'm pretty lowbrow."

"I don't think that at all," Jill said. "I like romance novels. I guess I just haven't read any of these. Are they any good?"

"Eh, they're okay. Like all romances, everyone ends up living happily ever after, and if they do have big problems, they're solved by the end of the book. Not like real life, where people get their hearts broken, lose their homes in a recession, get terminal illnesses, and die alone." The light had suddenly flickered and gone out of Pam's eyes.

"Pam, were you ever married?"

"A long time ago, but that part of my life is over. At least I got a great daughter out of it."

"So you just write about love, but you don't really believe in it anymore?"

Pam's blue eyes widened. "Jill, you're a trip—you and your wide-eyed innocence." She chuckled. "Look at me. Do I look like the kind of woman any man would want? I'm telling you; it doesn't happen for people like me. I had my marriage, and it didn't work out. True love is for other people—younger, prettier people."

Jill's heart contracted with sympathy. "You have such a great personality, Pam. You're really funny, and you have beautiful hair and such a lovely face. Plus, you're a woman of substance. The right man will see you for who you really are."

"I'm not holding my breath."

"You don't have to hold your breath. If you want love, just put forth a positive intention with strong emotion and believe in what you write about: true love with the man of your dreams.

Write about romance as if it was your own real-life story, and I bet those books will sell like hotcakes!"

ON FRIDAY EVENING, DENNY AND Jill got together at his house to cook dinner. It was the perfect night to share a glass or two of wine while sitting on the rug in front of the fireplace or watching a movie. In fact, Denny had picked up two DVDs in case Jill didn't care for what was available on demand through his cable company.

"I got a couple of chick flicks," he announced, handing her *Sleepless in Seattle* and *While You Were Sleeping.*

"Love them both," Jill said as she stirred olive oil into crushed tomatoes and added diced marinated artichokes and thinly sliced scallions for her favorite sauce, which she always served over cheese ravioli. "Why don't you choose the movie, since I selected our menu for tonight?"

"That smells great, by the way," Denny said as he washed and dried the arugula for the salad. "What kind of dressing do you want?" He rummaged through the shelves of his refrigerator door.

"Let's not waste that marinade from the artichoke hearts," she said. "We can use it with some fresh lemon juice."

He raised his eyebrows. "Good idea. I have a nice, peppery zinfandel for us to try, too."

"That will be perfect with the arugula salad and the red sauce." She leaned in for a quick kiss. "This is really fun," she said happily. "I'm not used to having a cooking partner, unless it's Liam." She threw cheese ravioli into a pot of boiling water. "He always enjoyed cooking, even when he was a little boy."

"I bet that went over well with his da." Denny snorted.

"David used to give Liam a difficult time when Finn was outside playing and Liam wanted to be in the kitchen with me. He called him a sissy. At the time, David meant it in good fun. But by the time Liam was about twelve, I began to realize that he might be gay, and I made David stop using that word. Now

I think I should have done more, said more to David to get him to stop."

"Let me guess. David thinks all that time in the kitchen is what caused his son to be gay."

"David is too smart to think something like that," Jill said. "But he was definitely uncomfortable when Liam didn't follow along with the other boys in the neighborhood when it came time to be interested in girls."

"Did David spend much time with the boys when they were growing up? Surely, a parent who is really in touch with a kid just knows."

"David was hardly ever home," Jill said, shaking her head.

"So, when did you find out that Liam was gay?"

"I think I knew when he was in junior high," Jill said, accepting the glass of wine Denny poured for her. "Liam always kept to himself and spent a lot of time in his room. I don't know if he was the butt of jokes at school or not, but we chalked it up to typical middle school behavior, at first. David made a big deal, though, out of what he called Liam's antisocial behavior. David, of course, was always popular in school, and he thought Liam should be, too. In a way, Liam is the twin that David thought was most like him."

"Ah," Denny said. "I'm beginning to see the trouble. David thought that Liam's being gay somehow reflected on his own manhood or his faults as a father. Then, on top of that, Liam looked just like him."

"Exactly right," Jill said. "Finn took girls to dances in junior high, and Missy was his steady girl in high school. David compared Liam to Finn all the time, goading him into acting more like his brother. All it did was cause Liam to retreat more."

"So from the time Liam was a lad, he knew his da didn't approve of him."

"I think that at first, he just wanted Liam to fit in. David does love Liam. He thought he could coach him into being more comfortable with girls. But deep down, David wants him to be someone other than who he is." Jill flinched. "Finn was the first to really know about Liam, but he kept his secret for years."

"Maybe a twin knows instinctively."

"The truth came out after Liam had a terrible bout of depression his freshman year in college at Rutgers. He disappeared from campus for a whole week. I got a call from Rutgers telling me that Liam hadn't been attending classes and that his roommate hadn't seen him in days. I was scared and called David home from a trip. Turns out, Liam hitchhiked to find Finn, who was at the University of Vermont. They spent the weekend together, and Finn encouraged him to go back to school. It was Finn who probably helped Liam the most by telling him that no matter what, he loved him and was proud to be his twin."

"Poor Liam," Denny said, shaking his head. "And then he told you why he left school?"

"He tried to." Jill sighed. "He told me he was unhappy and that he needed my support. I told him that whatever was going on in his life, we loved him and he had our full support. I had guessed, by that time, what was going on. The problem was, he didn't have *our* support, only mine. David was furious, of course, and demanded to know why Liam had done such a stupid thing, leaving school like that, and causing him to have to rush home from an important assignment."

"He inconvenienced his famous father. How inconsiderate of him," Denny said wryly.

Jill took a sip of her wine, recalling the pain on her son's face. "Liam said that he didn't want to disappoint us, but he couldn't hide who he was anymore. David said …"—Jill took in a slow breath—"he said he didn't care who Liam was, as long as he didn't do anything to cause trouble like that ever again. 'Why can't you be more like your brother?' he said to Liam. Then he walked away—just left the kid standing there with his heart and guts hanging out."

"That's awful." Denny put down his wine glass, resting his hands on his crossed arms.

"It never mattered to me that Liam was gay, except for the pain he endured while he was trying to figure out how to be the man he is now. He turned out so well, and it just hurts me so much that he feels less worthy of his father's love than Finn. About a year ago, Liam wanted David to meet Brian, and David refused. Liam and his dad have hardly spoken since—until recently, that is."

"Are things improving between them? You said Liam offered the olive branch by taking his dad home after he got pissed at your party."

Jill smiled slightly at the memory of Liam and Brian taking charge of David. "As bad as things have been between David and Liam, the amazing thing is that it might be what happened—the affair and our divorce—that's paving the way for things to improve between Liam and David," she said. "I guess every cloud really does have a silver lining."

They enjoyed a leisurely dinner and then Denny washed while Jill dried the dishes. "Is there something you'd like to do now?" he asked when she hung up the terrycloth towel. "I mean, we could watch a movie or just listen to some music." He placed his hands on either side of her face and kissed her deeply. Her heart quickened as his hands moved from her face, down her arms, and rested on the sides of her hips.

"Make love to me." The words came so easily to her. She scarcely realized she had said them out loud until his eyes opened wide with surprise.

"Are you sure?"

"Yes, very sure," she answered, wanting nothing more than to feel him against her, as close as humanly possible.

He led her by the hand down the hallway and into his bedroom, which was lit by moonlight through the open drapes. They stood together beside the huge bed, and he kissed her again. Jill had expected to feel nervous, even awkward, as they came together for the first time, but instead felt cherished as he looked at her with longing.

She was conscious of the beauty of the mountain he had painted on the large headboard, a scene that evoked a feeling of being far, far away. All she could see, hear, smell, taste, or feel at this moment was Denny. She entwined her arms around his neck as his hands moved along her body, holding her securely at the hips. He pressed his mouth harder against hers, a kiss that deepened in intensity and that she wanted to go on forever. She felt light headed as his fingers moved beneath her sweater to touch her skin, his feather-light touch exploring her. He lowered his head to kiss the place where her neck and collarbone met. Slowly he began unfastening the buttons on her sweater, taking his time, his mouth never moving far from hers. She stopped breathing for a moment as he removed the sweater from her shoulders and kissed each one, then kissed the swell of her breasts above her white lace bra.

She raised the heavy wool sweater over his head and then began unbuttoning his shirt. She pressed her lips against his chest, feeling the fine, dark hairs as she breathed in his delicious masculine smell. Heat was rising from his chest as she kissed his neck. She sighed as he unzipped and lowered her jeans and dropped them to the floor.

"I've imagined this moment since the first time I laid eyes on you," he said.

She was unable to answer as he kissed her again. Then she stood perfectly still, watching as he removed the rest of his clothing and drew the duvet cover to the bottom of the bed. He pulled her close and unhooked her bra, touching her breasts with his fingertips until he evoked a small sound of startled pleasure.

"Beautiful," he said, and moved against her.

Jill sighed with happiness as he guided her onto the bed, gently laying her on her back. Resting his firm body on top of hers, he continued kissing her. She shifted her legs slightly as an exquisite feeling engulfed her. Now she wrapped her legs around him, feeling his desire for her, the urgency of his movements. She wanted to please him. As her head fell back and her eyes opened wide, she noticed that the mountain peaks above her on the headboard were misty, and knew it was from her own tears.

Afterward, Jill lay there quietly, her face on Denny's chest. She felt the quick, steady beat of his heart and listened to his breath as he stroked her back lightly with his fingertips. They remained that way until she felt certain he must have fallen asleep. She kissed his jaw, ran her fingers over his chest, and knew in that moment that she was in love.

After a little while, he stirred and asked, "Are you cold?"

"A little," she murmured, and he pulled the duvet over them. She shivered in delight at the feeling of warmth that enveloped her as her toes entwined with his. He turned to her, tipped her chin, and kissed her lightly.

"Stay with me, please."

"I will," she answered. She moved closer to him and rested her arm across his chest before they fell asleep.

Chapter Twenty-Four

T HE TOPIC OF CLASS THE following week was the
benefactors—or helpful people—and travel square of the
bagua. This square was located in the lower right-hand corner
of the *bagua,* to the right of the career square. Meredith was the
student most interested in improving this area of her home.
Her goal was to build up her catering business, but she also
wanted to fulfill a lifelong dream of traveling to Italy. In fact, the
benefactors and travel area of the home was the *bagua* square
that Jill was most confident could create immediate change.
Most people were more interested in career, prosperity, love, or
health, but helpful people were essential to all of the squares.

"Tonight we're going to talk about all the helpful people in
our lives: the produce manager who goes out of his way to find
just the right eggplant for your eggplant parmesan, or in my
case, the thoughtful employee at the dry cleaner who called
to remind me that she still had my favorite blue party dress,
which she could have sold by now." Jill grimaced. "It's the shop
owner who gives you a deal on something you really want or
the neighbor who steps in to pick up your child at daycare
when you're running late after work. Some of us have trouble

asking for help because we think we can handle everything ourselves. But we all know that isn't true."

Meredith spoke up. "Jill, you're one of my helpful people. Your referrals have really given a huge boost to my business, and I already know I'll be busy over the holiday season."

"Keep cooking the way you did for my Halloween party, and you'll have more business than you can handle."

Meredith blushed becomingly before saying, "In fact, ever since I first learned there was such a thing as a benefactors and travel area, I've been more conscious of the different ways I'm being helped. My son is always willing to schlep heavy things to and from places where I cater events. My sister has been helping me cook when I need an extra hand, and my other sister helped me get a small business loan to expand."

"Congratulations! We knew you had it in you to take that leap of faith."

With the class offering atta-girls for Meredith, Jill waited for them to quiet down. "Remember that *feng shui* is about identifying what you want—setting forth the intention. For example, you might say, 'I need help finding a new accountant.' That request or thought brings about more thoughts and the activity that eventually produces the desired outcome. And don't forget to express gratitude for the results."

On break that evening, Shelly approached Jill in the hallway. "So, I thought about what you said about enhancing the benefactors and travel area of my house, in addition to creativity and children," she said.

"It's a good idea, because all the areas work together. The *chi* flows throughout the house. Remember that the creativity and children area is just one square away from benefactors and travel." Jill paused. "You might ask for someone, a different medical professional perhaps, who could help you figure out the cause of the infertility."

Shelly's face appeared sullen. "Joe said he's done trying to get me pregnant. He refuses to touch me now. He just says, 'Let it go. It's God's will that we don't have children.' I took matters into my own hands." There was an angry glint in her eyes.

"Has he been tested yet to see if perhaps the problem is something correctable on his end?" Jill asked as tactfully as possible.

"No, he refuses to see a specialist. It really bothers me that every time we're around his family and they want to know how we're coming along with baby-making, he says, 'No, Shelly isn't pregnant yet.' He makes it sound as if he has nothing to do with it! Last night, he said he's tired of trying—not that we ever do it that much, anyway."

Jill tried not to smile and failed. She cleared her throat. "Actually, that's not an unusual reaction to many years of trying to conceive."

"Sometimes I wonder if he's, you know, even interested in sex." Shelly's cheeks colored. "He seems to find it distasteful. Even on our honeymoon, he found reasons to avoid making love."

"Perhaps it's time for couples counseling. Would that help?"

"No." Shelly's voice was flat. "I have a problem, and I'm taking care of it in my own way."

Something about the way her eyes narrowed made Jill wonder what Shelly had in mind. She had given Shelly the card for a counseling center, as well as a brochure on the many faces of abuse, thinking Shelly might understand better what a toll Joe's constant badgering, blame, and put-downs were having on her. She still wondered if that was all that was going on. She hoped that Shelly might decide she was ready to get counseling on her own. It was also possible that she was planning to leave Joe.

When break was over, Jill began the second half of the lecture. "I'm often surprised by how quickly I get help when I need or want something. When I make a request, I try to imagine how I'll feel when my need is fulfilled: relief or excitement, perhaps. Positive emotion really stokes an intent or desire. In this area of the *bagua*, you also want to have a particular location to hold your special requests. I keep a small silver-colored box where I put my requests for help, but I try to keep the number of requests to not more than three. Otherwise, thoughts and intentions can become too scattered."

"Would a gray cash box work?" Joni raised her pen in the air. "I need something I can lock. I don't want anyone else to see my intentions."

"Yes, that's a good point. Metal is an important element in this area of the home, anyway, but if you don't have a silver or gray steel box, it's perfectly fine to wrap a little box in aluminum foil and tuck it away in that area somewhere. Put your specific, most urgent requests into the box and watch how fast the answers come."

She turned on her laptop and showed the class a recent example of a room she designed to enhance the benefactors and travel area. "In this home, the owner loves anything having to do with France. On this wall, we see black-and-white prints of famous French landmarks. He needed a water element, and thankfully I was able to talk him out of a massive water sculpture. He selected a print of Monet water lilies instead. It's important to include symbols of whatever you're trying to enhance in your life. If you want to take a dream trip, you could put a big travel poster on the wall of wherever it is you want to go."

"Shouldn't travel be part of the career area?" Kristen looked puzzled. "Or the prosperity area, since you need money to travel?"

"You and I think the same way, Kristen. I figure that it's good to cover all the bases, so if you want to travel more for your job, it would be helpful to enhance the career area to include a travel symbol, too. And yes, if you need money to travel, by all means include a travel intention in the prosperity corner. Again, remember that each area is enhanced by the strength of every other area. So whatever it is we desire, there is always someone available to help point the way or lend a hand."

As the class ended, Jill called out, "Next week, we'll be focusing on romance. I saved the best for last."

Kristen rolled her eyes. "I'm not sure there are enough helpful people in the world to fix that area of my life."

JILL PARKED HER CAR IN the driveway of Meredith's split-level home in a middle-class neighborhood of Norwalk, not far from where Finn and Missy lived. A FOR SALE sign in front of Meredith's house now had a 'Price Reduced' sticker plastered across the top in bright red. Jill knew that Meredith was becoming increasingly agitated that the house hadn't sold after two months on the market, and that she was anxious to buy a bigger place to accommodate her growing business.

Meredith answered the door wearing a tomato-stained apron. Her long dark curls were contained in a matching hairnet. The house smelled deliciously of onions, garlic, and fresh herbs, and there was a tray of freshly baked Italian cookies on the dining room table. Jill sniffed the air appreciatively, wishing she hadn't skipped lunch as her stomach growled in protest.

"My biggest issue in arranging house showings is that I can't leave at a moment's notice. I work here," Meredith explained. "Realtors aren't happy when they call with a potential client and I have a dish in the oven that I can't leave unattended."

"Since your primary interest in *feng shui* is the benefactors and travel area, I put together a folder of ideas for you," Jill told her, "including some potential solutions for your real estate woes."

"My realtor brought me a statue of Saint Joseph that she planted head down in the front yard," Meredith told Jill as she led her back to the kitchen. "I'm afraid St. Joe is going to have his work cut out for him. Not only can't I leave my house for a showing if I'm preparing for a catering job, I also can't keep the kitchen clean enough—you know, counters cleared and no cooking odors. This is a working kitchen, for heaven's sake!"

"There are some excellent ways to put forth the intention for a real estate sale that are more about envisioning the kind of person who would love your house and want to buy it," Jill said. "Your kitchen is spacious, and you've got top-of-the-line appliances and lots of counter space. It's the kind of kitchen that someone who loves to cook would definitely appreciate."

"That's what I think, too." Meredith went back to the stove, where a pot of red sauce was simmering. "But if no one ever sees the kitchen—"

"I have an idea," Jill interrupted. "Why don't you arrange an open house to specifically highlight the kitchen while providing appetizers for those who come to the showing? You'd need to know how many were expected so you'd have enough food, but if you do it by appointment only, that allows your realtor to market the open house ahead of time to other brokers and agents. The idea is to focus on those clients who are looking for a nicer, more professional kitchen. That way, the people who come for the open house won't mind if you're here because there will be wonderful food in the kitchen especially prepared for them. You could even do short cooking demonstrations. Potential buyers will be entertained, enjoy great food, and have a chance to envision themselves in this space, making their own favorite meals."

"Jill, that's a great idea!" Meredith's eyes lit up. "My realtor had a brokers' open house when the house first went on the market, but she insisted on using her company's own caterer. She also didn't want me here because then the agents' comments wouldn't be honest. If the owner is at home, agents and buyers won't say what they really think."

"You're the client. If you suggest something like a special open house that could attract more potential buyers, even if they're just curious, I can't imagine she wouldn't at least be receptive to the idea. As long as you get some serious buyers, she ought to be thrilled."

Meredith wiped her hands on her apron, and then hung it

on a hook. "Let me show you the benefactors and travel area of this house. It's actually my formal dining room, which doesn't get used much."

"From what you've told me, you actually have three goals you're trying to accomplish," Jill said. "Sell this house, expand your catering business, and travel. Where is it that you most want to go in Italy?"

"I've never seen Tuscany, where my mom is from, or Abruzzo, where some of my dad's family still lives."

"Since it's a dining room, you can easily decorate with an Italian food and wine theme," Jill suggested. "That would take care of the travel aspect and your catering business, too."

"I found a sign, *Food is love,* that I'd like to put above the doorway. But what color would be best on these walls?"

"We want to make metal a primary creative tool in this room," Jill said. That means a wall color that isn't a shade of red, as it is now, since fire melts metal."

Meredith frowned. "I was so hoping not to have to paint the room white to represent metal. It would be so bland. I'd really prefer a little color."

"You might think white would be best, but actually, I believe a soothing gray is the ideal color for this area since it's located between the creativity square, which is white, and the career square, which is black or blue. Any shade of gray would do, but if it were me, I'd use a blue-gray color to also represent water— the other creative element in this square. As for accessories, you've got a gorgeous pewter chandelier, a metal wine rack, and a glass vase of fresh flowers. You could add two pewter candlesticks with white candles to the table, along with that glass vase, and just go with bigger, brighter colored flowers in the vase."

Meredith wrinkled her nose. "That gray paint color still seems kind of bland for my tastes. I picked pomegranate for this room because I like bold colors."

"I agree that you picked a beautiful shade, and it's perfect with your dining room set. I think it's always good, though, when you're trying to sell a house, to keep the colors as neutral as possible so potential buyers can envision their own furniture in the room. Maybe you could spice up the room and enhance your Italian food theme with a few framed posters of Italian country scenes or still life paintings of food and wine. The neutral palette would be a good visual backdrop for the art, too."

"Okay, I like that idea," Meredith said with relief. "Now … if I can just recruit my sons to help me paint the room this weekend, the open house could be held next Sunday. We need to get this house sold before I have to drop the price again."

"Something tells me you'll be out of this house in no time," Jill said. "And with a bigger kitchen in your next house, you'll have no trouble expanding your business and saving enough to take that trip to Italy. Maybe by then, you'll have a new man in your life to go with you. You said it: Food is love."

Denny was cleaning brushes in a mud room off the garage when Jill stopped by. He had his back to her, and he was bent over just enough to give her an appealing view of his jeans-clad bottom. A rather wicked thought suddenly crossed her mind.

Hearing her footsteps, he turned around. "Hey, this is a nice surprise!" He wiped his hands on a towel and gave her a kiss that nearly caused both of them to lose their balance. Jill righted herself by holding tight to his arm.

"I was over at Meredith's house doing a *feng shui* consultation when suddenly my car developed a mind of its own, made a sharp right, and headed over here. I thought maybe I could cook you dinner tonight."

"There's nothing wrong with that idea, except I'm low on provisions." He shrugged. "I've only got eggs, bread, and some strawberry jam."

"We could have breakfast for dinner."

Denny got a gleam in his eye. "I like breakfast in bed." He

scooped her up and carried her to the back door as she shrieked with laughter. "You have to walk from here. I'm still recovering from all the exertion of last night and again this morning."

"Funny, you don't look incapacitated." Jill took his hand and pulled him gently toward the bedroom, where the bed was still a tangle of sheets and blankets. "We could do some warm-up exercises, if that would help." She raised her sweater over her head, unzipped her skirt, and let it fall to the floor, revealing shimmery thigh-high stockings and lacy barely there undergarments.

Denny took in the sight of her. "Are you in the habit of wearing those to work?"

"I am now."

"Sweet Lord," he said, and proved to her that he was a man who could go the distance.

Chapter Twenty-Five

THE LAST *FENG SHUI* CLASS focused on the relationship square of the *bagua*. Jill thought it was important to make it clear that relationships were not just of the romantic persuasion. With Thanksgiving dinner planned at her home later that week, Jill looked forward to having all of her loved ones for dinner, including Denny. She hoped he wouldn't feel too uncomfortable under family scrutiny.

"The relationship corner of the *bagua* isn't just about romance," Jill said as she started class. "But let's face it: romance is obviously a very important reason why people enhance that area of their homes."

She pointed to the relationship square in the upper right hand corner of the *bagua*. "I also overlay my desk at work with an imaginary *bagua*. My rolodex and business card collection is in the relationships corner of my desk—underneath a bag of these." She held up a bag of dark chocolate kisses. Grinning, she passed the bag of dark chocolates to Joel, who took a fistful and passed them to Chris.

"When we talk about the relationship corner, most people

immediately assume it's all about love and romance. But relationships matter in all areas of our lives—family, friends, coworkers, the people you do business with, and so on. Good or bad, every relationship matters. If you're experiencing trouble with someone, you can 'intend' a better relationship through enhancements to this corner. There are important life lessons to learn from every person we know. Of course, if a family member is involved, you could also *feng shui* the family area."

After it made its rounds, Amy handed back the half-empty bag of kisses. "My relationship corner is my master bedroom. I guess that's a good thing, but I don't want to paint it red or pink. I really like the cappuccino color I've already got in there."

Jill popped a chocolate kiss into her mouth and reflected on Amy's comment. "Actually, I don't see a problem with cappuccino as a wall color, since lovers drink coffee together. Perhaps you could arrange two coffee mugs side by side on the end table on the side of the bed you don't sleep on. Anything symbolic of twos can draw a partner."

Amy blushed. "Actually, I'm in pretty good shape in that regard."

The class hooted. Kristen turned to Amy with an exasperated look. "You've been holding out! You'd better tell us all the good stuff while we're on break."

"It's all pretty new. We just met a few weeks ago." Amy deflected a paper clip that Kristen shot at her.

Jill grinned. "Okay, but you still want this new relationship to flourish, so keep up the *feng shui* intentions in that area." She began writing a list of enhancements for the relationship corner on the board: symbols of anything in a pair, sensual music, red or pink colors, champagne and two glasses, and even chocolate kisses. Then she wrote *No cactus plants!*

"Why do you think we need to be careful about cactus plants?" she asked.

"Because it hurts to touch a cactus and love isn't supposed to be about pain." It was Shelly who spoke, but her voice was a monotone, and she didn't smile.

There was silence. The others glanced over in concern, but she didn't meet their eyes as she picked at a bleeding cuticle.

Jill exchanged looks with Pam and Trish before continuing, "Other things to avoid are board games or playing cards in that area because we don't want game-playing in our relationships. Be careful of art that shows solitary figures. Keep the area free of trash and clutter. If you want to leave clothing lying around, make it sexy lingerie—oh, and high heels, girls."

"Woo hoo!" Joel and Chris made lascivious sounds and rude expressions.

"We'd better remember to display our Valentine's Day briefs," Chris said, nudging Joel, who snickered.

"Don't forget the chocolate body paint," Pam quipped.

"Pam, I think you say things like that just to torment me," Jill said with a sigh. "We're descending quickly into the nether region. Come to think of it, we probably should have asked Pam to read from a chapter of one of her novels for this class," Jill said. "But alas, it's our last evening together."

Pam grinned wickedly. "I named the main character of my new novel after you, Jill."

"Oh, great," Jill said. The others laughed. "Before we take a break, I want to make sure to say that the biggest challenges in the relationship corner are window air conditioners or refrigerators, which freeze out relationships in *feng shui*. If you have either of these in the relationship corner, warm things up symbolically by placing photos of people you love—and who love you—with red symbols all over it. I like red hearts, pictures of strawberries—which are heart-shaped—or red roses."

On break, most of the students headed to the snack area for coffee. As she left to join them, Jill noticed Shelly, the epitome of solitary pain, perched on a windowsill outside the classroom, staring out the window. Frost tipped the blades of grass on the campus quadrangle, giving the ground a ghostly glow.

Shelly glanced up when Jill joined her, and then looked out the window again. "It's so ethereal looking out there, like it's not real," she said. "Maybe everything I'm going through isn't real, either. Maybe it's some kind of nightmare."

"Shelly?"

Shelly turned to face Jill, her eyes red-rimmed.

"What's the matter?" Jill was alarmed.

"Over the weekend, I left Joe. Oh, and I'm also pregnant."

"What?" Jill was confused. "Why would you …? Does Joe know?"

"About the baby? Yes, he knows."

"Oh, my." Jill drew in a sharp breath and took Shelly's arm, helping her off the window seat and aiming her down the hall. "How far along are you?"

"Just a few weeks. Joe found a pregnancy test kit in the bathroom closet. He asked me if I was pregnant, and I said yes. Then he slapped me."

"Why would he do such a thing? You're the mother of his child!" Jill remembered her earlier question to Shelly about physical abuse and Shelly's negative response. Had Shelly been truthful? Was she the victim of spousal abuse?

"Jill, it's not his baby. It's his brother's baby."

"Oh, Shelly." Jill's stomach pitched forward.

"Joe's brother, Ron, was making comments about how Joe might be shooting blanks. He told me that if I ever wanted a sure thing, he'd be glad to stand in."

"Oh, Shelly, no, you didn't."

"Jill, I thought it would be safe because his brother wouldn't want the rest of the family to know, since he's married with kids, too, and the baby would have a family resemblance. I thought for sure Joe wouldn't have any way of finding out. Really, no one could know for sure it wasn't Joe's."

"Okay, but how were you planning to tell Joe you were pregnant?"

"Well, I figured it would just happen, eventually. But when he held up the stick, I didn't have a chance to think, so I just said, 'You're going to be a father.' That was when he freaked out. He called me a whore. Jill, he said he was tested, and he's sterile. He never told me that!"

Jill leaned against a painted concrete block wall near the stairwell, a heavy feeling in her chest. "Did you tell him who the father really is?"

"No. I just decided to leave. I went to my parents' house. Like I said, his brother certainly won't admit to what happened, and I don't want more trouble. This baby is still mine, and I don't want anything to do with his brother, Ron, or with Joe anymore. Jill, he never admitted the truth to me. I guess he couldn't stand the thought that he was the reason I couldn't get pregnant. He had to blame me rather than admit to his dad and brothers that it was his problem."

"Wow." Jill shook her head. "Most families would rally around and show sympathy and support. You could've adopted a child!"

"Not with Joe's family," Shelly insisted. "Their manhood is tied up in their ability to keep their wives pregnant and at home, preferably in the kitchen. They gave us a lot of grief, as it is, because I work outside the home. It's all about blaming and pointing fingers, being judgmental—oh, and obviously being hypocritical, too."

"There is plenty of blame to go around on this one." Jill bit her lip. "It isn't going to be that easy, Shelly. You can't just walk away from your husband without repercussions. Trust me on that one."

"Why not? I don't want anything from him or his brother. Joe can keep his perfect house just the way he wants it. As long as I have this baby, *my* baby, I'll be happy."

Jill sighed and brushed a hand down Shelly's silky hair, wanting to comfort her, yet not knowing what more to say. "Whatever happens, I hope you'll call me if there's anything I can do to help," she said and pulled Shelly close for a hug. "Can you get through the rest of class tonight, do you think?"

Shelly nodded. "Getting through class is nothing compared to what I've been through already, or what I'm going to have to go through from now on. Just wait till my parents find out the real reason I moved back home."

THE NEXT MORNING, AS SHE arranged carpet swatches and tile samples on a large work table in her office, her cellphone rang. "Jill Hennessy," she answered, juggling the receiver between ear and shoulder, her arms full of heavy carpet samples.

"Hello, Jill, this is Jessie Webster. I'm a producer with Home and Hearth Television. I'd like to talk with you about an idea we'd like to explore for a new show. We understand you're an expert on *feng shui*."

The armful of samples fell to the floor with a deafening thud. "Oops, sorry about that," Jill said weakly. "I'm so glad you called!"

Monica peeked in to see what all the noise was about as Jill made frantic motions of glee. She motioned with hand signals to shut the door, take a seat, and listen. Then she sat down herself and put the phone on speaker.

"Is this a good time to talk?" Jessie Webster asked. "You could call me back, if you like."

"It's fine, really," Jill said. "That's what I get for answering the phone with my arms full. I'm an interior designer and a *feng shui* consultant. I just taught a class on *feng shui* this past semester."

"I'm not really sure I completely understand what's involved with *feng shui*," Jessie said, "but we're intrigued with the idea of a program where you show people what changes could be made to their homes." Jessie paused. "Sponsors will provide funds or products for you to take care of the homeowners' problems, and then we'll follow up and see whether anything changed for them."

"Well, it's up to the homeowners to decide what they want to fix in their lives, and they do have to have some positive belief that *feng shui* can help." Jill tucked her hair nervously behind her ear. "We might not have answers right away, but we could at least do an update." She was silent for a moment. "I have to ask, how did you hear about me?"

"David Hennessy suggested to our producer that we call you. He said there was no one more qualified than you to be the host of a new show."

Jill was quiet for a few moments, trying to take it all in. "I'm obviously surprised and pleased. It was nice of David to think of me and suggest it to your producer."

Monica's eyes were round as silver dollars as she silently mouthed the words, "What's going on?"

Jill held up her hand. "I'm really glad you called because I've been thinking for some time that it would be a great idea to have a show about *feng shui*."

"Well, now's your big chance to share what you know," Jessie said. "Can we meet next week?"

"That sounds great. I look forward to it." Jill pawed through her desk calendar. "When's a good time for you?"

They decided on the following Wednesday at three o'clock and Jill hung up the phone, a grin spreading from ear to ear. "Oh my gosh, Monica! Home and Hearth Television wants to do a show on *feng shui*."

"How cool is that! You're going to do it, of course."

Jill's stomach lurched, but this time, it felt more like excitement than fear. "Of course I am. It's really fortunate I taught that class this semester because now it's not quite as scary to think about being on television."

"Did David arrange this?"

"Apparently so, but I can hardly believe it. Why would he do that for me? We're in the final stages of a divorce. He's been so angry and distant."

Monica raised her eyebrows. "Jill, you were married to

David for a long time. Maybe he just wants to do something nice for you, to show you he's sorry for what happened. Just tell him thank you."

"You're right. I do want to thank him. This is incredible." Jill picked up the phone. "I'll call him right now."

David's cellphone rang three times before she heard his voicemail message and hung up. She decided it was better to talk, rather than leave a rambling message for such an amazing gesture. It was hard to believe, actually.

She thought about calling Denny, but decided to wait until that evening to share the news with him. They were planning to have dinner and look over color samples for another project. He was barely in the front door and out of his coat before Jill announced, "Today I got an offer from Home and Hearth to do a television show on *feng shui!*"

"That's fantastic!" he said, giving her a hug. "Was this something you approached them about?"

"David made the overture on my behalf," she said, shaking her head. "I still can't quite believe it. How would you like to be my television sidekick, my official color consultant?"

Denny snorted as he headed to the kitchen with a bottle of wine. "Now there's an idea sure to create a buzz in the tabloids. Haven't you already had enough of that kind of publicity?"

"True." She followed him to the kitchen and leaned against the counter. "I just want to share this experience with you."

"You just did, love. I'm happy for you, but this moment belongs to you. You've earned it."

DAVID RETURNED JILL'S SECOND CALL while she and Denny were in the middle of dinner. "Sorry for not calling you back sooner," David said. "I heard your message, but couldn't get a break from the action. What's up?"

"Actually, I wanted to thank you for calling Home and Hearth on my behalf. The producer called yesterday about doing a show about *feng shui*, and we're meeting next week.

David, it was such a wonderful thing for you to do for me. I just wanted to say thank you."

"Actually, I made the call after we had dinner that evening in the city and you mentioned the idea. I wanted to do something special to show my support. I couldn't believe you were actually talking about a television show. It was surprising enough that you were teaching a class. I was proud of you." He paused. "I *am* proud of you."

Jill could hardly believe her ears. "That means the world to me coming from you. I just can't thank you enough."

"Well, I was glad to do it," he said.

"David, before I forget, Finn and Missy want you to join them for dinner this weekend. I think Missy is worried that you'll be alone on Thanksgiving."

"I have plans for Thanksgiving dinner, actually, but thanks. I'm also going away for the weekend," he said quietly. "Sounds like you'll have a house full, anyway."

She knew that he meant Denny. "I'm glad you won't be alone," she said sincerely. "And thank you again."

"You're welcome," David repeated. "Well, I need to run. Take care of yourself." He hung up.

Jill turned to Denny, shaking her head. "I'm just now beginning to understand that what happened in August was actually a blessing in disguise. I wish it hadn't happened the way it did, but I'm happy to be where I am now. I can't believe I'm saying that."

Chapter Twenty-Six

THANKSGIVING MORNING ARRIVED WITH A dusting of crystalline snow that reminded Jill of superfine sugar shaken over the grass, trees, and rooftops of the houses on Briar Lane. After feeding Denny a quick breakfast of coffee and toast, she bade him goodbye, but only after making him promise to return by five o'clock. Jill took a luxurious bath while she watched the Macy's Thanksgiving Day parade on a small television in the bathroom. Then she got busy cooking.

She was glad that Denny didn't seem nervous about meeting her parents. "It's important for a man to meet a woman's mother so he knows what his beloved will look like as an older woman," he proclaimed as he leaned back against the kitchen counter, a grin on his face.

"My mother is perfectly beautiful," Jill said, slapping him lightly with a dish towel.

"Well, I'd be surprised if your maw had whiskers sprouting from her chin or missing teeth," he said, dodging as Jill flicked the towel at him again, laughing.

She gave him a mock-stern look. "When my parents get here, you'd better straighten up and fly right. If my mother and dad don't approve, I'll have to send you packing."

Finn, Missy, Liam, and Brian had already made it clear they thought Denny should come up for official inspection at Thanksgiving dinner. Her mother had agreed that it was time for Denny to meet all the other major players in Jill's life. Even her father seemed anxious to meet the man who had been such an agent of change in his only daughter's life from devastating grief to happiness. It was clear to everyone that Denny had played a significant role in Jill's emotional recovery following David's betrayal.

Overall, Thanksgiving promised to be an interesting holiday right through the weekend, with an official invitation from Joni for an "Evening of Chocolate" the Saturday after at her home. Jill and Denny planned to go together, as did Liam and Brian. Jill hoped that Joni's plan to reunite her family would meet with success and that the party would be as fun and festive as Joni dreamed it could be.

Jill hummed as she diced potatoes into cold salted water, prepared the traditional herb stuffing, and made a decadent sweet potato casserole with the twins' favorite crunchy pecan topping. Of course, there also would be the traditional green bean casserole, homemade yeasty rolls, and an enormous turkey. After cleaning pots and pans for the second time, she arranged a white linen tablecloth over the dining room table and set each guest's place with new white china—a gift to herself. For several weeks, she had felt sadness at the thought of using the wedding china she and David had received so many years ago. It hadn't taken more than a few words of encouragement from Nancy for Jill to decide that the china she had admired for so long was the ideal way to ensure that this year's Thanksgiving would be celebrated for what it was—a new start on holiday traditions.

Nancy and Hal arrived at three thirty bearing Nancy's traditional mince, pumpkin, and apple pies. She also brought roasted chestnuts and a gigantic tray of assorted holiday cookies. This signaled the official start of the holiday season for Jill. From the time Jill was a toddler, Nancy had been a generous baker, providing elaborate cookie trays for family, neighbors, and friends.

"It smells great in here," Hal observed as he turned on the television to watch sports, snatching a handful of mixed nuts from a dish on the coffee table.

"Hi, Dad," she said, hugging him as he crunched in her ear. "I'll put you in charge of making sure everyone has drinks."

Nancy went straight to work basting the turkey again and punching down the bread dough that rested in a huge, oiled bowl next to the stove. Missy, whose pregnancy was beginning to show under her bulky sweater, walked through the kitchen on her way to the extra refrigerator in the garage. Her pretty porcelain face beamed radiant good health these days. Missy reported feeling much better as the pregnancy progressed and claimed to have more energy than ever. She tucked a huge mixed greens salad into the refrigerator and grabbed a bottle of water.

Finn kissed his mother on the cheek. "Happy Thanksgiving, Momma," he said.

Jill placed her hands on the sides of his freshly shaved face and gave him a peck on the lips. "Same to you, baby. I'm so happy to have all my favorite people under one roof today."

Liam and Brian arrived at four o'clock bearing a calorie-dense dried-corn casserole that was a favorite in Brian's family. Liam produced an assortment of dilly beans, marinated olives, artichoke hearts, hearts of palm, and roasted red peppers. Wine was poured, craft beers uncapped, and the celebration officially began with Brian perched in his usual spot at the piano, playing holiday classics. By the time Denny arrived with wine and a bouquet of flowers for Jill, she knew this would be a holiday to remember.

"Hi," he said, giving her a chaste kiss as she greeted him at the front door. He glanced in her father's direction. "To be continued," he offered in a stage whisper.

There was no mention of David throughout the evening. Jill had decided not to share her news about the *feng shui* television program, not wanting to invoke David's name during this first holiday without him. She sensed that the boys were holding something back about their father, but was determined not to ask what it was. Not today—not with the joy she experienced being with those she loved. As they gathered around the table, Hal offered the blessing while family members and Denny held hands. Eyes closed, basking in the fragrant smells and a new, welcome lightness of being, Jill knew there was nothing she could imagine wanting beyond this moment.

"Amen," she said and opened her eyes to meet those of the man she loved.

"Was it rough on you tonight?" Jill asked as she and Denny lay cuddled up together under the flannel sheets, the drapes parted to let in the moonlit sky. She rested her hand on his chest.

"It wasn't so bad, though I did catch your da watching me out of the corner of his eye. I guess fathers always feel protective of their daughters. And, after all, I am corrupting your morals."

A low, throaty laugh escaped her lips. "You certainly are."

"So, did I pass muster?" he asked softly. "I mean, will I be welcome back again at family dinners?"

"Just try and stay away," she said, kissing him. "My mother thinks your Scottish accent is adorable."

"Aye, there is that about me, at least."

Jill laughed again. "The one I worried about most was Finn. He's had a harder time than Liam with the divorce."

"That's because Finn is so much like you," Denny said. "I mean, it's obvious that everything he does in his life, he does for love."

"Why, what a nice thing to say," she said, squeezing him. "And now he understands that even the kind of perfect love he and Missy share takes effort to keep it magical and alive."

Later, as a light snow began to fall outside the bedroom window, she placed her head on the curve of his shoulder, traced her fingertips over the soft skin, and sighed with contentment. They lay together for several minutes before Denny began to croon a soft melody in Gaelic. Jill listened to the words, not understanding the lyrics, but recognized it as a Scottish lovers' lullaby.

On Saturday evening, Liam and Brian picked up Jill and Denny for the half-hour drive to Joni's house. Joni had called earlier in the day to tell her that the entire Weintraub family would be there that evening. "I'm so nervous," she said. "I hope my mother behaves herself tonight. She can be quite a diva."

"I'm sure everything will be fine. We're excited about being included, Joni. Thank you for inviting Liam and Brian—oh, and Denny, my friend."

"The more, the merrier. Jill, I'm glad you wanted to be here. Your presence will make things so much easier for me."

Jill hung up the phone, certain that all would be well. That evening, she donned a midnight blue dress with a taffeta skirt and an off-the-shoulder neckline. She dusted her neck and décolletage with a subtle, pearlescent powder and applied soft, rosy lipstick. When Denny arrived at seven o'clock, looking even more handsome than usual, Jill's heart swelled with pride. In his best gray suit with a silk navy tie, he looked gorgeous, and she told him so. She reached up on tiptoes to kiss him and realized that even wearing her favorite three-inch black pumps, Denny was still taller by nearly a head.

With Liam at the wheel, they piled into the car for the short drive to Joni's home. Along the way, Jill told Liam and Brian about the offer from Home and Hearth. "I could hardly believe my ears," she said. "I had an idea for a show like that a few months ago, but never actually thought it could happen. Obviously, it was your dad who made that overture for me."

Liam glanced over at Brian sitting in the front passenger

seat. "We knew about that, Mom. We had dinner with Dad last Monday night. He's real proud of you." Liam, a man of few words, was even more cryptic tonight. For once, Brian said nothing.

"Where did you guys go for dinner?" Now Jill was on high alert, listening intently as Liam and Brian exchanged another uncomfortable glance.

"We went to his apartment."

"Your dad cooked?" Jill laughed out loud. "That's a shock."

"His girlfriend cooked, Mom. Her name is Andrea."

"Oh." Jill swallowed hard, remembering the appearance of the apartment David had been subletting, the distinctly feminine décor, and the casual way David had explained that he was subletting from a friend while she was out of the country. Denny took her left hand in both of his, but said nothing.

"I'm not sure they were together when he moved into her apartment, Jill," Brian said in his most polite tone of voice. "It might just have been a relationship of convenience. You know, they could have just drifted together as a couple after she let him stay there, after you told him you wanted the divorce." He cleared his throat.

Jill had an out-of-body sensation as Denny wrapped his arm around her shoulder and drew her closer.

"I went there to see your dad while Andrea was working out of the country," she said, embarrassed by the strangled sound of her own voice. "It did seem strange, at the time, that she would allow him to live there, even if they were colleagues."

Liam remained silent, his hands clenched on the steering wheel. After a few moments, he relaxed and glanced in the rearview mirror. "She isn't as pretty as you are, Mom. In fact, wouldn't you agree, Bri, that Andrea is sort of hard looking? All those years of reporting in hot climates, I guess."

"I thought so," Brian said in a solemn tone.

An undercurrent of warm laughter filled the car. Denny's chuckle allowed Jill to take a deep breath as they turned into the

Silversmiths' driveway. Later, she would have time to process this new information about David and Andrea. She hoped it was true that they had come together as a couple after Jill told him she wanted a divorce. If they had been close friends before, this was a plausible scenario. But given what she now knew about David, she doubted it had been that innocent. For now, she decided to let it go and enjoy herself at the party.

"Are you okay?" Denny tucked her cold hand into his coat pocket.

"I'm fine," she said, smiling at him. "Let's just enjoy ourselves tonight. I think I already knew why David was in that apartment. And now I know for sure that I made the right decision."

Joni greeted them at the front door, the low sounds of conversation in the background. Behind her was her husband, Pete, who took their coats. The elegant home displayed gorgeous Hanukkah heirlooms, a holiday so important for families and tradition.

"I'm glad to meet you, Jill," Pete said as they shook hands. "Joni talks about you all the time."

Joni hugged Jill and whispered, "So far, so good. No fireworks yet."

Jill introduced Brian, Liam, and Denny to Joni and Pete before being ushered by Joni down the long hallway into the family room. A sumptuous buffet of chocolate ganache and rainbow fruit tarts, chocolate cookies, fudge-dipped cupcakes, cocoa-dusted truffles, chocolate-covered pretzels, fresh fruits, and Joni's chocolate candies were arranged near the entrance.

But it was the imposing black grand piano that stood center stage, commanding the guests' attention. Polished to perfection, it gleamed in the bright lights of the overhead crystal chandelier. Joni had thoughtfully arranged seating in circular groups around the perimeter of the room to encourage conversation. It took a full minute for Jill to register the other faces in the room; she was so enthralled at Joni's enhancements to the room. With Brian oblivious to anything except the grand piano, Liam gave up trying to talk to him.

"There it is." Brian's eyes were focused only on the piano as he moved forward.

"Mother?" Joni motioned with a small hand wave and smile to Paget Weintraub. "I have someone I think you'll want to meet."

"I've already met this young man," the older woman said as she watched Brian circle the piano. "He's a fine composer and pianist, you know." Paget's heavily lidded eyes rimmed with black mascara gave her a dramatic air. As she rose in regal fashion to meet Brian, she unfolded her long, slender, and surprisingly girlish legs, outlined discreetly beneath her elegant deep-green, pleated tea-length skirt.

Brian moved forward to take her hand. "Ms. Weintraub, it's wonderful to see you this evening, and such a privilege to view this incredible instrument. I've never seen anything like it."

"Yes, it is quite a beauty." Paget's voice, sultry from long years of affectation, sounded almost comical to Jill's ears. "Daddy gave it to me when I was eighteen, upon the occasion of my first recital."

Liam watched in fascination as Brian took the proffered bejeweled hand with care. "Watch this," he said under his breath to Jill and Denny. "Brian has been practicing all week. I hope to hell he doesn't decide to curtsy, too."

Brian's manners were as genuine as they were elegant. "It would be the highlight of the evening, not to mention the most exciting moment of my entire musical career, if you'd play us something. I'll be so disappointed if you don't."

Paget blinked, cat-like, as she considered the request. "Oh, it's been so long, and I haven't prepared anything appropriate."

"Please, Mother." Joni took a step toward her. "Play *Greensleeves,* just like you always did for PapPap. He loved the way you played that song. Do you remember?" Joni's eyes glowed with tears that threatened to spill over, as she awaited her mother's response.

Jill took a deep breath. Depending on how Paget felt about her father's memory, this was a risky request. If she refused, part of Joni's vision for the evening would remain unfulfilled.

"Very well, but surely you know that I haven't played on a concert stage in years. The result may be quite alarming."

Even so, Paget flexed her long, slender fingers, the joints enlarged with arthritis. She appeared engrossed in her task. Brian and the others stood nearby as she took a seat on the piano bench, arranged the flowing skirt around her, and ran through several arpeggios.

Paget frowned. "Joni, has it been tuned recently?"

"I had it tuned yesterday, Mother. I hope it's to your liking."

"Good girl." Paget paused for effect and then looked up, eyes wide in surprise, to find family members gathered around her, expectantly waiting. Taking a deep breath, she closed her eyes and began working her magic on the keys. The first notes were breathtakingly simple and delicate before the chords gained strength and complexity. As the melody ebbed and flowed under Paget's gifted hands, Jill glanced up at the ceiling, certain that the chandelier was swaying with the music. No one spoke as Paget played. All eyes focused on her as she performed for her amazed family. As the last notes of the song echoed in the room, she bowed her head.

There was utter silence for a moment before Joni said, "I have never heard you play that song more beautifully, Mother."

Applause rang out as Paget's family members rushed forward to embrace her. A beatific smile lit up her face. Joni was sobbing openly now.

"I'd say the evening is a success," Jill murmured to Denny.

He touched the small of her back, causing her to lean in to hear him. "Will Paget want her piano back now, do you think?" He took a refined sip of his tea.

"Actually, I'm betting that she'll want to enjoy it right where it sits, in her daughter's home."

Joni's face was radiant as tears of joy ran down her cheeks.

Her husband handed her his handkerchief then wrapped his arms around her and whispered something in her ear that made her smile. They embraced.

Joni turned her attention back across the room to Jill. Clutching Pete's handkerchief, she raised it to her lips and mouthed the words, "Thank you."

Chapter Twenty-Seven

⚜

O^N THE TUESDAY AFTER THANKSGIVING, Jill drove to the
house that Kristen had purchased just months earlier
and was still in the process of redecorating. It was located just
three blocks from the house where Jill had grown up. In fact,
her parents still lived in the older neighborhood of gracious
federal-style stone, frame, and red-brick homes with mature
trees. Wrap-around porches hearkened back to an earlier, less
hectic era, when people relaxed in rocking chairs and drank
iced tea or enjoyed their dessert and coffee with neighbors. Jill
remembered all the evenings Nancy had served dinner on the
porch—meals that often lasted hours as neighbors stopped by
for cups of tea or glasses of wine.

Kristen, a corporate attorney, lived in a red-brick house
with black-and-white shutters and a three-season front porch.
As she rang the doorbell, Jill heard yipping barks. Kristen
answered the door with an adorable West Highland Terrier
wriggling frantically in her arms. Westies were Jill's favorite
dogs.

"Please come in. This is Tucker," Kristen said, introducing
the dog, who sniffed Jill's fingers and then licked them.

"He's so cute," Jill said, ruffling the soft white fur, unable to resist smiling back at the black shoe-button eyes and the doggy grin. "What a lover," she said and kissed him on the top of his furry head.

"He is so spoiled. He knows he's the only man in my life," Kristen said in a flat, pleasant tone.

"Well, these conditions are fleeting," Jill said cheerfully. "It's super easy to attract a man. The more difficult part is attracting one you actually want."

"True." Kristen rolled her eyes.

Jill glanced about the foyer and into the living room, which was Kristen's benefactor and travel area. Everything there was in good order, with a painting of a windmill and tulips in the Netherlands. She noticed with a satisfied smile that Kristen had a silver jewelry box on the coffee table—no doubt where she kept her intentions.

"I'm not sure the kind of man I want even exists." Kristen blew out a frustrated breath. "Three years ago my engagement to a guy I met at a bar association event went south. After he broke off our engagement, I went on a couple of online dating sites and even tried the whole speed-dating thing. Jill, I understand that a relationship requires compromise. But I don't want to compromise who I am just to have a man in my life."

"You shouldn't have to. Why do you think that's been the pattern so far?"

"I guess I don't expect much anymore." Kristen stroked her upper lip with a delicate rose-colored fingernail. "I don't seem to be what most men want. It's particularly difficult being an attorney, although I imagine it would be tough for any independent woman. As soon as I say I'm a lawyer, I get some pretty interesting reactions. Apparently some men think that makes me a ball-buster, when in reality, I have a nine-to-five desk job. I've never even argued a case in a courtroom, except in law school."

"I remember you said one time that some men seem to want a sugar momma." Jill looked thoughtful. "Nowadays, women make as much or even more than men. It wasn't like that when I was your age."

"I've met several like that," Kristen said. "My fiancé and I had a really great, very equitable relationship, I thought. He understood what I did professionally, and we made almost the same amount of money. I didn't have to dumb down for him, and we contributed equally to the home we shared."

"So what happened?"

"He just 'fell out of love,' he said." Kristen's brown eyes were dull now. "He said he couldn't go through with the wedding knowing that he didn't love me the way I deserved to be loved. Two weeks later, I saw him with another woman. An elementary school teacher."

"I know what it's like to have someone you love betray your trust." Jill perched on the edge of a wing chair, not wanting to rush Kristen as she talked.

"I know you do. That's why it's easy to tell you about this. I was too embarrassed to tell anyone, even my family, what really happened. I just said that he and I wanted different things in life."

"But that was true. You did want different things, and you deserve to have them. You *can* have them, Kristen. Let's take a look at your relationship area." Jill took Kristen's arm as they walked to the rear right corner of the house, the kitchen area.

"I painted the walls tomato red, and I even put a nightlight over by the coffee maker with a red bulb. I've got a red strawberry candle in the middle of the table." Kristen looked perturbed by the failure of her *feng shui* fixes.

Jill turned to look at Kristen, who was stroking Tucker's fur. "The refrigerator isn't good to have in this area because you want things to be red-hot," Jill said. "I know lots of people, though, who have refrigerators in their romance corners. Fix that issue by decorating it with photo magnets of people you love, along with red hearts."

Kristen chuckled. "Wow, so a refrigerator is the whole issue. That would explain why I've had such a hard time attracting warm, loving men."

Jill smiled. "Go ahead and blame it on the refrigerator, if you like. You're going to take care of that problem and start fresh. I believe there are lots of soul mates out there for us, depending on where we are in our lives and what we want. Do you know what you want in a man?"

"I think so, but my mom says I'm too picky."

"I agree we can be too picky. It's good to make a list of all the qualities you want in a romantic partner. Then pick out your top ten qualities. If you get those, you can live without perfection in a man. None of us is perfect. Would you be happy with seventy-five percent of what you want?"

Kristen laughed. "I see what you mean. The most important quality I want is for a man to accept who I really am, not who he wants me to be."

"I think that if you're happy with yourself, then some lucky man will find you irresistible. Now let's look at your relationship corner upstairs and then at your bedroom."

They went upstairs, and Jill went into a guest room that was in the relationship corner on the second floor. The room was painted white with a pink tint, and there was a pink-and-white rosebud coverlet on the bed, lacy white pillows, and a plush rose-colored throw on a rocking chair. The fact that no one slept in the guest room meant that it was important to *feng shui* Kristen's bedroom for romance. Seeing nothing in the guest room that needed fixing, she moved on to the master bedroom—a large airy room with a southwest exposure. The walls were painted a cool green, and Kristen's queen-size bed was covered in a colorful quilt. A braided rug in neutral colors covered the hardwood floor.

"I'd like to see some symbols of relationships in this room. After all, the bedroom is a pretty important place in a relationship." Jill winked. "What about twin rose-colored candles in ceramic or metal candleholders?"

"I have some glass candleholders. Will that be okay?"

"Glass represents water and will put out the flames of love. Just place the candles together on the bedside table. The other side of the bed—where a partner would sleep."

Kristen sat at the foot of the bed. "Do you think I should paint this room pink, too?"

"I wouldn't go that far. If I've got my bearings, this room is in the prosperity corner of the house. Is that right?"

Kristen nodded. "What about soft lavender?"

"If you like, that would be fine. But actually, this airy green paint, the warm wood furniture, and the accessory colors you've chosen are perfect for the prosperity corner. Even though this isn't the relationship corner, remember that prosperity is about more than just money. It's about the number and quality of the relationships in our lives, too. We want to prosper in the amount of love in our lives."

"I get it," Kristen, said, her eyes shining now.

Jill's eyes took in the perimeter of the room. "It'd be great to have photos that show two of something. That would symbolize a relationship."

"I have a photo of two swans with their necks intertwined to create a heart." Kristen hurried to the walk-in closet, where Jill could hear tissue paper rustling. "Here it is."

"That's nice. With those swans, the two candles, and the two bedside tables, I think the stage is set."

"I think I told you that I didn't have a very good experience with online dating sites." Kristen rolled her eyes. "I'm not sure I'm ready to go that route again."

"Was it that bad?"

"Not all bad. I did meet a couple of nice men, but they wanted someone different, I guess. You have to be really careful because not all of the people you meet are honest—or even single. I'm sure it's not just men who do this, but one guy I dated a few times was actually still married, not even separated. Another guy was a swinger."

"You mean—?"

"Yes. I mean that he wanted to invite another couple to 'join us sometime.' We hadn't gotten that far in the relationship yet, so it was lucky I found out about him early on."

"Gah!" Jill exclaimed. "Different strokes for different folks, I guess. But I can't imagine someone actually bringing that up so early in the dating process. He must have been pretty intent on finding someone who shared his preferences." She raised her eyebrows. "You're lucky you found out before you risked your health with someone like that. Wow, you really have been through the wringer."

"I want a relationship, but the truth is that I'm afraid of dating."

"I wonder if you'd be more likely to find the ideal man if you met him while doing something else that you really enjoy, by happenstance."

"That's true. I met my fiancé through the bar association. We were all about our work and not a lot else."

"I mean fun things. What other activities do you enjoy? Do you paint, sing? Can you cook?"

"I like to sing!" Kristen's eyes lit up. "I've thought about trying out for the community choir."

"That sounds like a great place to start—after you finish enhancing your kitchen and this bedroom. Just make sure you believe that while you're enjoying yourself in the choir and waiting for Mr. Right, he's looking for you, too."

During a casual lunch with Tom the next day, Jill had her own very un-businesslike agenda. "So, how are things going with Trish?" she asked as she daintily bit into her sandwich, averting her eyes from Tom's and trying to act nonchalant. In reality, she was dying to know how their relationship was progressing. Tom wasn't much for talking about his feelings, but she sensed a new lightness of being about him these days. The plot had thickened last evening when Jill and Trish walked to their cars after class. Trish informed her that she was "head over heels" and hoped Tom felt the same.

Tom paused and took a large gulp of his iced tea. He stiffened slightly at the question, but then his eyes softened. "After Janice died, I had at least a thousand memories that hit me like punches to the gut of all the things I appreciated about her but hadn't bothered to tell her—mostly small stuff like the way she waited until I took my first bite of something so she could see whether I liked it before she tried it herself."

"Maybe she was trying to make sure she wasn't poisoning you. Janice hated cooking," Jill said with a chortle. "She was my friend, so I can say that."

"Okay, so that wasn't such a good example." Tom grinned. "It's tough to explain all the ways she put me first. On some level, I recognized it, of course, but I don't think I appreciated her as I should have, and I certainly didn't tell her enough how much I loved her. I thought I was ready to jump in to love again with both feet, but I don't want to make the same mistake with Trish. She deserves to know how much she's loved."

Loved. He said loved. Jill blinked several times in delight. "Trish is a grownup, Tom. She has experienced heartbreak and difficult times just like you have, but I think rather than hardening her heart, they've added to her strength and patience. She had a great life with her husband, she thought, and then lost it all quite suddenly like you did when Janice died. She can appreciate what it means to be cared for by someone stable and grounded like you. From what I can tell, she's always been a giver, too. But you're right: she deserves to get as much as she gives. Just do your best to show her how you feel."

"The way Janice died …." He flinched at the memory. "She handed me coffee, and I took a sip and handed the cup back to her before I flew out the door. I think I kissed her goodbye. I'm pretty sure I did, but I'm recalling that it was one of those perfunctory kisses, one that you do without thinking much about it. She died just a few hours later. I wish I had thanked her for being such a good wife, really taken the time to sit down and enjoy my coffee with her that morning. I'm not sure I could stand to lose another woman I loved."

Tom rolled his straw wrapper between his thumb and forefinger until it was the size of a dried pea. Then he grabbed Jill's wrapper and started to do the same with it. Jill watched him and knew that he would get through this, but that he needed encouragement and patience. Trish could do that. She was the ideal woman for Tom.

"Given your recent health issues, Trish could worry about losing you enough to walk away as well, but I know that's not the case. Don't shut down your heart, honey. The doctor fixed it all brand new." She took his hand. "Trish is healthy, and you're healthier now, too. I'm sure you'll have many good years together."

Tom catapulted the paper peas one at a time across the table. "Jill, I wanted to talk with you about something very serious. It's not about Trish."

Jill had a sudden churning in her stomach. Did Tom already know about Denny? If so, what was the best way to respond? "What's up?" she asked, averting her eyes.

"I've decided to move to San Diego to be closer to Meghan and her husband. With Meghan pregnant now and with her busy career, I'd like to know my grandchild and help my daughter. I know I've told you before that I've always wanted to live in California, but I was never ready to pull the trigger until recently."

"Tom!" Jill's eyes flew open, and she clutched the table with both hands. "Can't you just spend a few weeks or a month there, now and then, and still continue as managing partner here? You could go back and forth. You can't just abandon us all … Trish … me."

"First of all, yes, I could go back and forth, and I will for a while. I'll transition slowly until I know that everything is under control under the new managing partner. But then I want to be in California permanently. I think it was the heart attack that convinced me not to put what I want on hold."

"But what about Trish?" Jill wailed.

"Trish is definitely included in my plans, if she wants to be. We haven't been seeing each other very long, just a few weeks, but I know how I feel about her right now, and I think she feels the same. We've talked a little bit about future plans, and she thinks she'd enjoy the change of scenery. She can get away from all the not-great memories here and make new ones with me. She doesn't have to worry about selling a house, so she can join me whenever she's ready. I hope that will be soon, but I can be patient, if she's not quite ready yet."

"Oh." Jill was silent, absorbing the news. "Of course, you ought to have what you want in life. I guess I've never thought about you not being here, though. I'm trying not to be selfish, but to tell you the truth, what I really want to do right now is have a tantrum." She smiled wanly.

"Please don't do that." Tom grinned. "I should also explain something. Although you're a full partner and the one with the most history at the company other than me, I think we need a managing partner with architectural experience and an MBA to take over the top spot. I'm thinking of Charlie Johnson." He peered at her cautiously, gauging her response with his calm, steady eyes.

"I don't have a problem with that, Tom." Jill met his gaze directly. "I've always been content to do my design work without having to worry so much about the business end of things."

Tom breathed a sigh of relief. "I'm glad you're not upset. Besides, didn't you say you wanted to keep teaching the *feng shui* class? And now, you'll have the television show, too. This way, you'll have time to do that."

Jill smiled. "I do enjoy teaching, and I'm really excited about the television show. What a surprise, huh? When I look back at the day you suggested I teach that class, I feel like you were talking to a whole different person. But yes, I also want time to spend with my family, especially now that Missy is pregnant."

"Trish said last night she thinks you might have a new man in your life. 'She's got that glow,' was the way she put it. Is it true?"

"I do." Jill blushed clear to the roots of her hair. "I haven't told you yet because I was worried you might have a problem with it. But I've always intended to tell you, eventually. I'm seeing Denny MacBride."

Tom chuckled, his eyes twinkling with mischief. "Did you think I couldn't figure that out? I sign the checks, remember? MacBride's the only painting contractor you've used the past two billing cycles. I thought at first that you were just impressed with his painting skills. But then, while I was at your house, I thought I recognized definite 'mooning behavior,' and I knew there was something else going on."

" 'Mooning behavior'? I have never mooned in my life."

Tom gave a hearty laugh. Jill kicked him under the table. Then she held up a warning finger. "I mean it. If you tell anyone else at the company about Denny, I'll tell Trish about your affinity for late-night chick flicks."

"She already knows."

Chapter Twenty-Eight

DENNY SHOWED UP PROMPTLY AT the stroke of seven o'clock that evening for dinner as Jill tossed a Caesar salad.

"I smell garlic," he said hopefully, grabbing her about the waist and kissing her until she had to step away to take a breath. He held her hand up to his nose and inhaled her fingers as though they were a Cuban cigar. "Aye, garlic is a fine perfume."

"As long as we're both eating it," Jill replied. She peeked inside the oven, saw that the parchment paper surrounding the tilapia filets was browning, and removed the pan.

"I brought a nice sauvignon blanc," he said as he opened and shut drawers in search of a corkscrew. "I thought you might enjoy it, for a change."

Jill produced a corkscrew. "You have impeccable taste in wine," she said as she arranged tilapia filets on each plate with a generous helping of salad. Then she placed crusty French bread in a basket with a small serving dish of herbed butter.

"How are things at work?" Denny asked. "I'd imagine the place is still spinning with the big news."

"Tom's announcement that he's moving to California has

been hard on our partners and staff. Then, of course, there are the financial and legal issues of selling off his share of the business to the rest of us." She sighed. "We've always had a plan in place for partners who want to leave, but I'm still a little off-balance from the news. This is Tom we're talking about."

"The heart attack did it, eh?"

"Well, yes—that and a grandchild due in the spring. But I think it's also about meeting Trish and wanting to move forward with his life. He says he doesn't want to wait any longer to do the things he's always wanted to do."

"That must've been hard for you to hear. Did you have any idea that he was plannin' to do this before he told you?"

"He's talked about California off and on for a long time. I guess I've been in denial again, but I thought he was happy here now that he was involved with Trish. His absence won't affect the way I do my work, but the whole environment at the company will change. Tom wasn't just the managing partner. He founded the company and set the tone for the creative environment. I can't even remember a time when he and I haven't worked together."

"It might be time to think about what comes next in your life—professionally, I mean. You'll have your design work plus the television show. Can you do both?" Denny took a bite of tilapia. "This is really good." He dug into the Caesar salad with relish.

Jill was quiet. "I don't know. I'll just have to try it and see. Gosh, it's hard to think about even more life changes."

"Not all changes have to be hard, Jill. I think back to the way I came to America. I wouldn't have thought of doing it on my own. Sometimes we get pushed into changes, or they happen unexpectedly, and we either embrace or fear them."

Jill looked intently at him. "Do you have any fears?"

Denny looked serious. "Sure, I do. I wonder if my maw is going to die anytime soon and will I see her before that happens? Every time I stand in front of the easel to paint, I fear that nothing will come. I fear growing old alone."

His plaintive look touched her. Jill recognized that he sought reassurance. Taking a sip of wine before responding, she said, "I've never really been alone until recently. Alone time can be energizing, I've learned, but it's still nicer to have someone special in my life."

"I feel the same. I'd like to do more traveling, but not by myself. Perhaps we might consider a trip to Scotland so you can see where I come from."

"I'd love that. I've never been to Scotland, but I've thought about going there for years."

"It's beautiful. I think you'd enjoy it. We can visit my family and then drive around and see other parts of the country, if you like."

"I do want to see where you grew up," Jill said. "You know so much more about me than I know about you. I want to meet the people who most influenced who you are now."

Denny laughed. "Well, sometimes even the people and situations we don't remember with such fondness contribute to who we become. But yes, my family had a lot to do with who I am now. My family was verra close, like yours is, and they'll all want to meet you. Meeting my brothers and sisters will tell you a lot about how we were raised. They're all great people. I think you'll get on well with my maw too, and that she'll like you."

"I hope so," Jill said quickly. "What if she doesn't?"

"Don't worry, love. Maw wasn't keen on my fiancée, Cara, and wasn't a bit upset that I broke things off with her. You see, Cara was difficult and demanding, quick to show temper. You, on the other hand, are a lamb. You've similar personalities and you're both easygoing and devoted to those you love." Denny grinned suddenly. "And speaking of difficult and demanding, I forgot to tell you that Miss Mona is thinking of another color change."

"Good grief! I'll call her first thing." Jill clucked her tongue.

"You've been very patient with her, considering all the changes she's wanted. It must get tiresome dodging her passes, too."

Denny's grin grew broader. "Aye, it's a burden."

"I don't understand that kind of desperate behavior to find love," Jill said, shaking her head. She told Denny about visiting Kristen at her home. "Kristen is such a wonderful person and such a beautiful woman—a much better catch than Mona. Yet she's had such a hard time meeting a man. She was telling me about all the experiences she's had with Internet dating sites. Have you ever done that?"

"I tried it a few times. It wasn't bad at all. I'm not suggesting you try it, though!" He glanced up in mock alarm.

Jill smiled sweetly. "I'm not even tempted. But speaking of temptation, I've got dessert planned in the other room."

"Should I make a fire?"

Jill took his hand and drew him to his feet. "I wasn't thinking about building a fire, although that's a nice idea, too. I thought we'd warm up another way. Rubbing two sticks together isn't the only way to start a fire, you know."

"Does your mother know how you talk?"

Wine glasses in hand, they made their way upstairs to Jill's master suite, where she lit the lamps on either side of the four-poster bed. "In *feng shui*, this is the relationship corner of the house. I'm intending to enhance our relationship tonight, starting right now."

She smiled and started to take off Denny's sweater. He finished the job while she started in on the buttons of his shirt. She inhaled Denny's warm, masculine smell, so familiar and dear to her now. He buried his face in her neck, peppering warm kisses there from her jaw to her shoulder. Wordlessly, he raised the silk sweater over her head, tossed it aside, and unbuttoned her jeans. Then she unhooked her bra and let it drop, standing very still as Denny placed his hands on her breasts and kissed her more deeply. Lifting her into his arms, he laid her gently on the bed and quickly finished undressing.

"I think of you all day long," he said as he covered her with his body.

Charmed as much by his tone as the words he spoke, Jill wrapped her arms around his neck. They kissed with unrestrained longing, the result of a long day of shared thoughts. Jill ran her fingers along both sides of his back until he shivered, and she felt the gooseflesh under her fingertips. She loved exploring all the sensitive places on his body, the way his skin was surprisingly soft and smooth, the way his chest hairs tickled her nose as she kissed him there. Most of all, she loved feeling him move within her in ways that seemed unfamiliar, as though they were reinventing the act of lovemaking.

Love is always new. In her mind, she thought she heard the music and lyrics to Chris's song. Now it was Denny's voice she heard murmuring as he lowered himself against her chest, laying his cheek next to hers.

"I love you, Jill. I do."

As THE FIRST OF DECEMBER arrived, Tom continued his careful transition out of the business he had founded. Charlie Johnson, the fellow senior partner Tom had recommended as his successor, was tapped to manage the business. Jill thought Charlie was a wonderful architect, and he believed in *feng shui* principles as strongly as Tom did. She felt comfortable that nothing about her position would change. Tom had already begun transitioning out of his responsibilities and planned to be in the office just three days a week prior to moving to California the following month.

"It won't be the same without you here. Who will I go to lunch with every Monday?" Jill frowned and tucked her arm through Tom's, allowing his body to serve as a windbreaker against the chill wind as they left the office for lunch.

"I'm sure Charlie Johnson eats lunch. You two need to talk regularly, anyway, just like we do."

"It won't be the same. Charlie and I don't have the same

history. I've known you my entire adult life!"

"It'll be weird for me, too, not seeing you all the time. But I hope you'll come to see me as often as you can get to California. Bring Denny along."

Tom's step had lightened considerably since announcing his pending retirement, and he was already clearing his house in preparation for putting it on the market. Jill had done a pre-market staging, but without any enthusiasm. Even so, she knew the house would sell and that Tom was likely to get multiple offers.

"Maybe I'd better ask you to *feng shui* my house for a quick sale," he said. "Or is the staging you already did the same thing?"

"It's definitely not the same thing, but I'm not sure you should trust me at this point. My intentions might not be completely focused on helping the house sell."

In response, Tom put his arm around her shoulders and kissed the top of her head. "You've never been one to embrace change easily."

Chapter Twenty-Nine

Jill held her umbrella high above her head, dodging other pedestrians on the crowded sidewalks of Manhattan. It was May, a time when balmy, overcast skies and a warm drizzle left reflective puddles of colorful neon from retail signs along the streets of the city. She had just finished meeting with the producer and staff at Home and Hearth, including her new personal assistant, Melanie. It had been necessary to take a short leave of absence from her job at the architectural and design firm as taping of the first season's episodes of *Finding Feng Shui* got underway. The pace of production was surprising to Jill, who'd already helped two homeowners solve *feng shui* challenges in their homes.

A couple in their mid-forties in Rhode Island was experiencing difficulty in adopting a five-year-old girl from China. Time and again, paperwork challenges kept them from bringing home the child they had come to love through correspondence and photographs. Generous funding from sponsors had allowed the renovation of their home that would most help them—creativity and children, as well as the family areas. Within weeks, they were able to schedule a trip to bring their new daughter home.

A widower who'd lost his job just three months after his wife died was concerned about being unemployed and possibly losing his home. Jill enhanced the career, helpful people and travel, and prosperity areas of his home. Within two weeks, he found another job with a company that was a competitor of his former employer.

Jill had selected Joel and Diana Foster for an episode on the health square of the *bagua*. Although Diana's cancer was still in remission, Jill knew it was important to continually strengthen good health intentions. This week, a more extensive remodeling of the Fosters' health and family areas was underway. After viewing initial footage, Jill knew it would be a powerful segment.

For the romance episode, she had thought about asking Kristen to be on the show and had emailed her to ask if she was interested in being featured. Jill hadn't spoken with her in several months, although Kristen had sent congratulations upon hearing about the new television show.

She dialed Kristen's number. "Kristen, hey, it's Jill! I haven't talked with you in a while and wondered how things are going." She went on to ask whether Kristen was interested in participating in an episode about the relationship square of the *bagua*.

"I would be, except I've met someone," Kristen said, sounding jubilant.

"You did? Tell me!" Jill was thrilled at the news.

"About two months ago, I needed some electrical work done on my house. I called a company listed in the yellow pages, and the owner came right over. His name is Tim. Turns out, he's one of the bass-baritones in that chorus I joined just after you did my home consultation. Tim sits right behind me, but we'd never actually spoken before. One thing led to another, and we started dating. He's really, really nice, Jill. He's not like anyone I've ever dated."

"I'm happy for you," Jill said, smiling as she listened to Kristen talk about her new friend.

"Jill, I can't thank you enough," Kristen said. "Your class changed my life in so many ways. You're doing a real public service taking your class to the next level. I can't wait to see you on TV when the show airs! Are you already feeling like a big star?"

"To tell you the truth, it's all a little surreal," Jill admitted. "I don't think it's sunk in yet."

"I'm not the only one you helped in a big way," Kristen continued. "You've probably already heard Chris's newest song on the radio."

"I did! I tried to call him, but he's on tour now, I was told."

"I ran into Shelly at the mall last week," Kristen said. "She is hugely pregnant and was buying a few things for the baby. She left that awful husband of hers, you know, and then moved out of her parents' house into her own apartment. I think she's happier than I've ever seen her. She said if it hadn't been for your class, she wouldn't have realized that you have to take action to help yourself."

"Ugh. Actually, I take no credit for the action Shelly took," Jill said quickly, "especially how she chose to get pregnant. But sometimes life takes weird twists and turns that may start out looking terrible and tragic, but end up being a blessing. Who knows?"

"I also saw Pam recently," Kristen continued. "She came to see me about a part-time paralegal job at my firm. She wants to spend less time working and more time writing romance novels. She'll transition into full-time writing at some point, after she retires."

"Good for her!" Jill said. "It took a lot of courage to make that decision. Has anyone heard from Amy?"

"Amy said her yoga and meditation classes are going well, and she wishes you'd join, as soon as your schedule permits. I go on Wednesday evenings, and it's been really fun. Maybe you could take the same class."

"Oh, gosh, I've barely got time to eat these days," Jill said. "But I did promise her I'd join her class, at some point, so I will."

That month a promotional announcement for *Finding Feng Shui* aired—one that involved a camera crew following Jill around for several days. Although at first she had been uncomfortable with the constant attention, the availability of a makeover and wardrobe consultation turned out to be an enjoyable part of the process. Nevertheless, she was astonished one evening, following a commercial break for fabric softener, to see herself on her forty-two inch screen as part of the show's first advertisement.

She'd been relaxing with a cup of tea in her living room, watching an episode of a landscaping design show, when she heard the announcer's voice mention *feng shui*. She did a double-take, her mouth hanging open in amazed delight. "Love, wealth, good health, and happiness can be yours if you follow the ancient Chinese art of *feng shui*. Let *feng shui* and interior design expert Jill Hennessy solve your personal challenges and make your dreams come true. Watch the premiere episode of *Finding Feng Shui*, premiering June second on Home and Hearth, the network you love to come home to."

Jill froze in front of the television screen, hardly able to believe her eyes as an image of herself surrounded by Chinese symbols appeared in living color. It didn't take long for excited family members, friends, and co-workers to begin calling and texting.

Her mother and father were first. "Congratulations, Jill! Dad and I are just beside ourselves with pride. He says you'll be more famous than me, and that I'll have to take a back seat from now on."

Jill laughed. "I seriously doubt that. Actually, Mom, it might be nice if you'd appear on the show occasionally with your helpful hints—a little mother/daughter time. What do you think?"

"That's very sweet of you, dear, but no thanks." Nancy's voice was adamant. "I'm perfectly happy writing my little column and remaining anonymous at the grocery store. One television star in the family is enough."

Denny's reaction was predictable. He was painting a new landscape when she showed up at his front door.

"Don't sputter, love," he said mildly as she started to explain why she was there. He smiled as Jill described the commercial. "I'm glad you're happy. I'm verra verra proud of you."

"It was so weird to hear my name that way and see my face on television, Denny."

"Well," he said, "I just hope I don't read in the tabloids that you're having an affair with a co-star and having his baby."

"That really would be newsworthy," Jill said dryly. "The most exciting thing you're likely to read about me is that I've taken up crocheting."

"Speaking of babies, any word yet?"

"Well, the due date was yesterday, and Finn said earlier this week that he thought the baby was planning to try out as a kicker for the Jets. But then the little guy quieted down, and Missy's having a lot of trouble sleeping, so I expect news any minute now."

THE NEXT DAY AFTER WORK, Jill stood in the produce section of Shoprite, her ear resting on a cantaloupe. She sniffed the sweet aroma and rapped it lightly before putting it in her cart.

"Hey, there." Someone touched her coat sleeve. It was Meredith, and she was beaming.

"Meredith!" Jill was delighted to see her former student and grabbed her for a big hug.

She already knew from an email months earlier that Meredith's house had sold and that there had even been a bidding war. Meredith shared that she had gotten two thousand dollars more than her original asking price *before* the price was lowered. Thirty prospective buyers turned up at Meredith's open house to participate in a cooking demonstration and food-tasting. Offers started coming in immediately, and the house sold the next day.

"So, all is well?" Jill hugged her. "What's new?"

"Gosh, I hardly know where to begin," Meredith said, running her hand through her dark curls. "The boys and I love the new house. Business is booming, and right now I'm buying travel-size toiletries for my trip to Italy. My sister and I are leaving the day after tomorrow."

"Wow! I hope you have a great time." Jill beamed from ear to ear at Meredith's good fortune. "I'm so happy for you. And it's wonderful to hear about your business, too. Now you're really on your way."

"Thanks to you," Meredith said, holding tightly to Jill's hand. "The *feng shui* class and your suggestion about the open house made it all possible."

"You're the one who made it possible, Meredith—your talents and your intentions. I just pointed out a few ancient Chinese secrets."

Three days later, on Sunday, as Jill stirred marinara sauce for eggplant parmesan, it occurred to her how much her life had changed in less than a year. Who could have guessed it would all be for the better? From shock over David's affair to the pain of divorce after twenty-five years of marriage, to new love with Denny, the joyful anticipation of a new grandchild, and the excitement of her own television show. She hadn't expected that she'd survive, much less thrive, and end up happier than ever before.

Denny was engrossed in watching World Cup soccer playoffs when Brian appeared in the kitchen, carrying a wood bowl full of salad. "Hi, Mom," Brian said, kissing her on the cheek.

She looked at him for a moment before pressing her cheek to his. "I love it when you call me that."

Liam wrapped his arms around his mother from behind. "I brought a special bottle of wine, something I know you'll like."

She glanced at the bottle and laughed out loud. It was a Chinese Riesling. "I didn't know the Chinese grew Riesling grapes!"

"In honor of *feng shui*," Liam said. "We're celebrating your new celebrity status."

As they stood together around the kitchen island, sipping wine, the phone rang. Liam answered and his eyes popped. "Really?" He put his hand over the speaker, his eyes round as half dollars. "It's Finn," he said. "Missy's in labor. They're not coming over for dinner. They're heading straight for the hospital."

Jill placed her hands over her heart. "Do they want us to be there?"

Liam shook his head. "Finn says they'll call us when the baby is born. Missy says she'd rather we wait at home since it might take a while."

"Keep us posted," he told his brother before hanging up.

"Well, now I'm too excited to eat," Jill said, mindlessly grabbing handfuls of snack mix and pretzels. She reached for a thick slice of garlic bread, dipped it in olive oil, and took a huge bite. "How can anyone have an appetite at a time like this? We might not have time to eat, anyway."

The men exchanged amused glances. "Keep your fingers away from her mouth and nobody will get hurt," Liam said to Brian and Denny as he carefully removed the snacks out of Jill's reach. "We're just teasing you, Mom."

Jill flashed him a dark look and began layering roasted eggplant slices, sauce, and cheeses into a pan, her fingers moving at a rapid pace. "Very funny. I need to stay busy. I'll just keep cooking. I probably should have made another pan to freeze for them when they come home from the hospital."

Denny grinned at Liam and Brian. "On such an important occasion, I think it's important to keep up our strength. We need to eat enough to keep us going." He smiled sweetly at Jill. "Don't babies take a long time to be born?"

Brian leaned against a countertop. "The man has a point. It won't help Missy if we pass out from hunger."

Jill rolled her eyes. "Okay, so you all think I need to chill out. Fine, but pour me another glass of wine then."

Denny handed her a glass of merlot. "It doesn't help to be sober, either, from what I've heard."

As they sat down to eat dinner, Brian's face suddenly lit up. "Hey, did I tell you that Paget Weintraub asked me to compose a song for her?"

Jill clapped her hands in glee. "Wow, you really did make an impression on her. That's wonderful, Brian! What kind of song does she want?"

"She said she'd like a signature piece—something she can perform and record. I think she actually wants to be back on the stage again. Right now, I'm leaning more toward classical."

"I was surprised that after so many years of not playing at all, she could perform so beautifully," Denny said. "Her playing was flawless, almost as if she'd practiced beforehand."

Brian chewed his upper lip. "I'll bet that she never really stopped playing. I think she'd been playing all along."

"Why would she deny playing the piano?" Denny asked, opening another bottle of wine. "Why make such a fuss?"

Jill shook her head as the realization came to her. "Because she was nursing a grudge and wanted to make Joni think she was the reason the world was denied the talents of the great Paget Weintraub. The piano was in Joni's house—the house Paget thought should have been hers." She started setting the table. "I don't understand how families can behave that way toward one another."

"Every family has its problems," Denny pointed out quietly. "Even families that get along famously most of the time can still knock heads over big or little things."

Jill knew that this comment held deep meaning for each of them. There was silence all around. Finally, Liam let out a long breath. "Dad sure seems to be a lot less quick to judge these days. At least he isn't ignoring Brian anymore."

Brian shrugged. "Jill, did you hear that he just bought a house in Greenwich? It's on the water."

"I didn't hear that, but it makes sense. He's always loved the sea." She wondered whether he and Andrea were going to share this new house. On the one hand, she knew David had as much right as she did to pursue happiness. On the other hand, it still bothered her that David likely had underplayed his real relationship with Andrea when he moved into her apartment.

"He broke things off with Andrea," Liam told her, as if reading her mind. "He says he wants time to himself for a while."

"Time alone for him would be good," Jill said. "Let's hope that in the process, he finds whatever insights he's looking for."

"It does seem that there are important things he's figuring out about himself." Brian looked thoughtful. "Maybe it will affect how he views others, too. You know, people in glass houses and all that."

"Well, however it happened, I'm glad things are better between you and your dad," Jill said to Liam and held up her wineglass. "To healing old hurts and to new beginnings ... starting with this new baby." She grinned. "Goodness! I hope we hear something soon."

THE CALL FROM FINN DIDN'T come until eight o'clock the next morning. "He's here!" he announced in a voice hoarse from lack of sleep.

Jill bobbled her cellphone, nearly dropping it in her haste to answer. She had been awake for over two hours, drinking coffee and pacing the house. "Tell me all about him! Is he okay?" she asked. "Is Missy okay? What's the baby's name?"

Missy and Finn had elected not to announce their choice of a name until after the baby boy was born, claiming they wanted to see how the name fit the baby.

"The baby is fine and Missy is fine, too. She's sleeping now. It sure was a long night, but she came through it great. Shaun Connor is seven pounds, two ounces and nineteen-and-a-half inches long. He's perfect." Finn said. "All the parts are there. Actually, he looks like an infant version of Dad, only without as much dark hair."

"Shaun Connor Hennessy," Jill said, taking a deep breath. "That's beautiful, Finn." She dabbed at the tears welling up. "And there are certainly worse things than bearing a resemblance to your father," she added with a laugh. "How could he not be a handsome boy, though, with you and Missy for parents?"

When she and Denny entered Missy's hospital room early that afternoon, Jill was glad to see Missy looking rested and radiant, cuddling her new son. Finn was dozing in the easy chair next to her bed, still unshaven, his clothing rumpled.

"Would you like to hold him?" Missy whispered to Jill.

"I'd love to." Jill extended her arms and carefully accepted the swaddled baby from Missy. Shaun Connor's eyes were closed tight, his mouth pursed as if in deep thought.

"I had no idea how this would feel. It's not even possible to describe," she said, her heart expanding in love for the baby as she kissed the top of his head through the knitted cap. The sweet newborn smell of him filled her nose. "There should be a perfume called New Baby," she said, tears streaming down her cheeks. She put her cheek against his forehead. "I can't believe this."

Denny put his arm around Jill's shoulder. "Congratulations," he said and looked down on the newborn face with awe.

As she watched Finn change the baby's diaper a few minutes later, Jill was conscious of movement just behind her and turned to see David in the doorway, looking tentative. "David, come and meet your new grandson," she said quietly, holding out her hand to welcome him.

The drawn look on David's face disappeared as he peered

over Finn's shoulder at the baby, now freshly changed and swaddled. His eyes widened as he saw his first grandson. "He's beautiful," he said in a voice shaky with emotion.

"Here, Dad," Finn said.

David gingerly accepted the baby, holding him tightly to his chest. There were no words spoken for a moment as he stared in wonder. "I'd forgotten how small they are," he said finally. "Welcome to the world, little man," he whispered and touched his lips to the baby's forehead. He glanced up to meet Jill's eyes. "Can you believe this?" He looked close to tears.

Denny cleared his throat and excused himself. "I'll be back," he said to Jill. "I need a cup of tea."

Jill smiled her thanks at him. "Don't go too far."

After a half hour, David excused himself to get back to the television studio. Jill followed him into the hallway. "Hey, I heard you have a new home in Greenwich. The boys told me. It sounds great."

"Well, it won't have your design touch, or maybe it will. I ought to have you look at it and tell me what kind of furniture to buy."

"I'd be glad to. Would you like a *feng shui* consultation?" she teased.

"I'll get back to you on that." He offered a tired smile. "It was time for me to get out of the city. There's too much noise in my head. I've decided to write a book, and I can use the quiet time."

"What's the subject?"

"It's a retrospective piece about changing times and how we as Americans respond to them." He chewed on the side of his mouth. "Not that I have all the answers."

"I'm sure you'll do a great job." She smiled at him gently.

There was a moment of silence as David's eyes met hers. "Are you happy, Jill?" The question was meant sincerely; she could tell from the expression in his eyes.

She smiled gently. "I am, David, and I hope you will be, too."

"I'm getting there." He moved closer, and Jill walked into his embrace. They stood like that for a few moments before stepping away from each other.

"Take care of yourself, David."

"You, too." He flashed the familiar one hundred-watt smile and walked away.

THE AIR CANADA FLIGHT ATTENDANT handed Jill and Denny dinner menus as they sat together in first class, drinking mimosas. The massive jet was turning now, heading over the Atlantic Ocean on its way to Aberdeen Airport.

"Are you sure your mother is ready to meet me?" Jill sipped her mimosa. "What did you tell her about the two of us?"

"That I was bringing the girl I intend to marry, that's all." Denny bared his teeth in an exaggerated grin.

"You did not!" Jill smacked his knee playfully.

"I did. I said I wanted her to meet the woman of my dreams." Denny reached for Jill's hand and folded his fingers over hers. "I hope that's okay, because it's true. I do love you, Jill, and I want us to be married someday."

Jill's cheeks turned rosy as she met Denny's clear, trusting eyes. In them she saw reflected all her hopes and dreams, with none of the usual fears. "Well, then, as they say in Scotland, let the *banns* begin."

"They don't actually say it like that, Jill. But is it a good idea? Do ye think we'd be happy as a married couple?"

"I do," she said and linked her arm through his.

Feng Shui Bagua

Elements, Creative Colors and Shapes

PROSPERITY	FAME/REPUTATION	LOVE/RELATIONSHIPS
wood, water purple, green, red, gold	fire red triangles, points	fire pink, white, red
FAMILY	HEALTH	CREATIVITY/CHILDREN
wood green rectangular	earth, fire yellow, earthy colors, red obelisk, points, peaks	metal white round, circles
KNOWLEDGE/SKILLS	CAREER	BENEFACTORS/TRAVEL
earth blue, black, green	water, metal black, white, blue round, free-forms	metal gray, white, black

majors in English and philosophy. She is also a published poet and a professional artist. She makes her home in the Chicago area.

For more information, go to:
www.robinstrachanauthor.com.